PRAISE FOR PETER S. BEAGLE

"For over forty years, Peter S. Beagle has been the gold standard of fantasy, one of the most elegant and genuine writers of fantastic fiction out there. His stories are jewels. In Japan they declare their finest, most irreplaceable artists national treasures, and if there was any justice in the world Peter S. Beagle would be declared a treasure and be left alone to get on with making magic."
—Neil Gaiman, author of *Sandman* and *American Gods*

"Peter S. Beagle has both opulence of imagination and mastery of style."
—*New York Times Book Review*

"One of my favorite writers."
—Madeleine L'Engle, author of *A Wrinkle in Time* & *A Swiftly Tilting Planet*

"Peter S. Beagle illuminates with his own particular magic.... For years a loving readership has consulted him as an expert on those hearts' reasons that reason does not know."
—Ursula L. Le Guin, author of *A Wizard of Earthsea* & *The Left Hand of Darkness*

"...the only contemporary to remind one of Tolkien..."
—*Booklist*

"Peter S. Beagle is (in no particular order) a wonderful writer, a fine human being, and a bandit prince out to steal readers' hearts."
—Tad Williams, author of *The Dragonbone Chair* & *Tailchaser's Song*

"It's a fully rounded region, this other world of Peter Beagle's imagination... an originality that is wholly his own."
—*Kirkus*

"Peter S. Beagle is the magician we all apprenticed ourselves to. Before all the endless series and shared-world novels, Beagle was there to show us the amazing possibilities waiting in the worlds of fantasy, and he is still one of the masters by which the rest of the field is measured."
—Lisa Goldstein, author of *The Red Magician*

"Our best modern fabulist in the tradition of Hawthorne and Twain."
—Jack Cady, author of *The Night They Buried Road Dog*

PRAISE FOR *WE NEVER TALK ABOUT MY BROTHER*

"Hugo and Nebula Award-winner Beagle showcases his narrative breadth in this eclectic new collection with nine powerful fantasy tales and a short set of poems based on the famous Unicorn Tapestries.... Impressively diverse themes, styles and subject matter make this collection addictive."
—*Publishers Weekly*, starred review

"Beagle's true strength in the last few years lies with his short fiction, an area in which he's been both prolific and brilliant. His latest collection, from Tachyon Publications, showcases the best of his recent output."
—Amazon.com, Omnivoracious Book Blog

"Rooted in rich, thoughtful prose...each tale is a beautifully crafted gem, cut and polished to perfection..."
—*Library Journal*

"Pure poetry. Beagle is an American bard."
—io9

"...Peter S. Beagle [has] rejoined the main flow of literature with a vengeance...his work is marvelous."
—*Green Man Review*

"A perfect little assemblage of oddities, a handful of extremely well-realized sketches with unusual, unpredictable endings...instantly addictive."
—*The Onion*

PRAISE FOR *THE LINE BETWEEN*

"At his best, Peter S. Beagle outshines the moon, the sun, the stars, the entire galaxy."
—*Seattle Times*

"Ever since *Last Unicorn*, one of the most beloved fantasies ever written, fantasy critics and readers have treasured [Beagle's] work, all the more so because he isn't prolific. For all their variety—'Four Fables,' a children's story for all ages, a Sherlock Holmes pastiche, an old tar's tall tale, a sequel to one novel (*Last Unicorn*) and a prequel to another (*The Innkeeper's Song*, 1993), and the germ of a prospective witch novel—all eleven stories in this book are lucid and refreshing as spring water, full of amusement, humanity, and wisdom."
—*Booklist*, starred review

"Delicate shadings and subtle prose."
—*Publishers Weekly*

"A cornucopia of delights; mark this as a major contender for Collection of the Year."
—*Locus*

"Everything Beagle writes is a pleasure to read."
—*Denver Post*

Cover design by Ann Monn
Interior by Elizabeth Story

Tachyon Publications
1459 18th Street #139
San Francisco CA 94110

smart science fiction & fantasy
www.tachyonpublications.com

Series Editor: Jacob Weisman
Editor: Jill Roberts

Printed in the United States of America by Worzalla
9 8 7 6 5 4 3 2 1

Peter S. Beagle

SLEIGHT OF HAND

tachyon publications | san francisco

OTHER WORKS BY PETER S. BEAGLE

For news and information about Peter S. Beagle and his creations, please visit www.peterbeagle.com or www.conlanpress.com. To receive Peter's free email newsletter, *The Raven,* sign up at either site.

NOVELS

A Fine and Private Place, 1960
The Last Unicorn, 1968
The Folk of the Air, 1986 (Mythopoeic Fantasy Award)
The Innkeeper's Song, 1993 (Locus Award)
The Unicorn Sonata, 1996
Tamsin, 1999 (Mythopoeic Fantasy Award)

COLLECTIONS

The Fantasy Worlds of Peter S. Beagle, 1978
The Magician of Karakosk, 1997 (originally published in the United States as *Giant Bones*)
The Rhinoceros Who Quoted Nietzsche and Other Odd Acquaintances, 1997
The Line Between, 2006
We Never Talk About My Brother, 2009
The 52/50 Project, 2009—2010

CHAPBOOKS

Lila the Werewolf, 1974
Your Friendly Neighborhood Magician: Songs and Early Poems, 2006
Strange Roads, 2008

LIMITED EDITION HARDCOVERS

The Last Unicorn: The Lost Version, 2007
Mirror Kingdoms: The Best of Peter S. Beagle, 2010
Return, 2010
A Beagle Double, 2011

NONFICTION

I See By My Outfit: Cross-Country by Scooter, an Adventure, 1965
The California Feeling, 1969
American Denim, 1975
The Lady and Her Tiger, 1976 (with Pat Derby)
The Garden of Earthly Delights, 1982
In the Presence of Elephants, 1995

PRODUCED SCREENPLAYS AND TELEPLAYS

The Dove, 1974
The Greatest Thing That Almost Happened, 1977
J.R.R. Tolkien's The Lord of the Rings, 1978 (animated)
The Last Unicorn, 1982 (animated)
"Sarek," 1990 (*Star Trek: The Next Generation*)
A Whale of a Tale, 1992 (animated; pilot for TV series of *The Little Mermaid*)

THEATER

The Fountain, 1957 (musical book & lyrics; college production)
The Last Unicorn, 1988 (dance/theater adaptation, script & incidental lyrics)
The Midnight Angel, 1993 (opera libretto, adaptation of "Come Lady Death")

RECORDINGS

Phil Sigunick & Peter Beagle Acoustic: The Lost '62 Tape, 2007

This book is for Jenella DuRousseau

TABLE OF CONTENTS

The Rock in the Park

In 2008, The Green Man Review, a delightful online magazine of fantasy, music, folklore, and much indescribable else, asked me to create and record four seasonally-themed podcasts. I wound up writing five, all of them revisiting the world of my Bronx 1950s childhood, taking my three oldest friends and myself from the age of eleven or so to the summer we all turned fifteen, with inevitable separation and the great world beyond Gunhill Road looming ahead.

This story was the autumn entry in the series, and I'll swear to my grave that it really did happen just like this, back when Phil Sigunick and I were thirteen. Some things you can't make up.

❁

Van Cortlandt Park begins a few blocks up Gunhill Road: past the then-vacant lot where us neighborhood kids fought pitched battles over the boundaries of our parents' Victory Gardens; past Montefiore Hospital, which dominates the entire local skyline now; past Jerome Avenue, where the IRT trains still rattle overhead, and wicked-looking old ladies used to sit out in front of the kosher butcher shops, savagely plucking chickens. It's the fourth-largest park in New York City, and on its fringes there are things like golf courses, tennis courts, baseball diamonds, bike and horse trails, a cross-country track and an ice-skating rink—even a cricket pitch. That's since my time, the cricket pitch.

But the heart of Van Cortlandt Park is a deep old oak forest. Inside it you can't hear the traffic from any direction—the great trees simply swallow the sound—and the place doesn't seem to be in anybody's flight path to JFK or LaGuardia. There are all sorts of animals there, especially black squirrels, which I've never seen anywhere else; and possums and rabbits and raccoons. I saw a coyote once, too. Jake can call it a dog all he likes. I know better.

It's most beautiful in fall, that forest, which I admit only grudgingly now. Mists and mellow fruitfulness aren't all that comforting when bloody school's starting again, and no one's ever going to compare the leaf-changing season in the Bronx to the shamelessly flamboyant dazzle of October New Hampshire or Vermont, where the trees seem to turn overnight to glass, refracting the sunlight in colors that actually hurt your eyes and confound your mind. Yet the oak forest of Van Cortlandt Park invariably, reliably caught fire every year with the sudden *whoosh* of a building going up, and it's still what I remember when someone says the word *autumn*, or quotes Keats.

It was all of Sherwood to me and my friends, that forest.

Phil and I had a rock in Van Cortlandt that belonged to us; we'd claimed it as soon as we were big enough to climb it easily, which was around fourth grade. It was just about the size and color of an African elephant, and it had a narrow channel in its top that fit a skinny young body perfectly. Whichever one of us got up there first had dibs: the loser had to sit beside. It was part of our private mythology that we had worn that groove into the rock ourselves over the years, but of course that wasn't true. It was just another way of saying *get your own rock, this is ours.* There are whole countries that aren't as territorial as adolescent boys.

We'd go to our Rock after school, or on weekends—always in the afternoons, by which time the sun would have warmed the stone surface to a comfortable temperature—and we'd lie on our backs and look up through the leaves and talk about painters Phil had just discovered, writers I was in love with that week, and girls neither of us quite knew how to approach. We never fixated on the same neighborhood vamp, which was a good thing, because Phil was much more aggressive and experienced than I. Both of us were highly romantic by nature, but I was already a *princesse lointaine* fantasist, while Phil had come early to the understanding that girls were human beings like us. I couldn't see how that could possibly be true, and we argued about it a good deal.

One thing we never spoke of, though, was our shared awareness that the oak forest was magic. Not that we ever expected to see fairies dancing in a ring there, or to spy from our warm, safe perch anything like a unicorn, a wizard or a leprechaun. We knew better than *that*: as a couple of New Yorkers, born and bred, cynicism was part of our bone marrow. Yet even so, in our private hearts we always expected something wild and extraordinary from our Rock and our forest. And one hot afternoon in late September, when we were thirteen, they delivered.

That afternoon, I had been complaining about the criminal unfairness of scheduling a subway World Series, between the Yankees and the Dodgers, during school hours, except for the weekend, when there would be no chance of squeezing into little Ebbets Field. Phil, no baseball fan, dozed in the sun, grunting a response when absolutely required ("Love to do a portrait of Casey Stengel; *there's* a face!"). I was spitballing ways to sneak a portable radio and earpiece into class, so I could follow the first game, when we heard the hoofbeats. In itself, that wasn't unusual—there was a riding stable on the western edge of the Park—but there was a curious hesitancy and wariness about the sound that had us both sitting up on our Rock, and me saying excitedly, "Deer!"

These days, white-tail deer dropping by to raid your vegetable garden are as common in the North Bronx as rabbits and squirrels. Back then, back when I knew Felix Salten's *Bambi* books by heart, they were still an event. But Phil shook his head firmly. "Horse. You don't hear deer."

True enough: like cats, deer are just *there,* where they weren't a moment before. And now that it was closer it didn't sound like a deer to my city ears— nor quite like a horse, either. We waited, staring toward a grove of smaller trees, young sycamores, where something neither of us could quite make out was moving slowly down the slope. Phil repeated, "Horse—look at the legs," and lay back again. I was just about to do the same when the creature's head came into view.

It didn't register at first; it couldn't have done. In that first moment what I saw—what I allowed myself to see—was a small boy riding a dark-bay horse not much bigger than a colt. Then, somewhere around the time that I heard myself whisper "Jesus *Christ,*" I realized that neither the boy nor the horse was *that* small, and that the boy wasn't actually riding. The two of them were *joined,* at the horse's shoulders and just below the boy's waist. In the Bronx, in Van Cortlandt Park, in the twentieth century—in our little lives—a centaur.

They must operate largely on sight, as we do, because the boy only became aware of us just after we spotted him. He halted instantly, his expression a mix of open-mouthed curiosity and real terror—then whirled and was gone, out of sight between the great trees. His hoofbeats were still fading on the dead leaves while we stared at each other.

Phil said flatly, "Just leave me out of your hallucinations, okay? You got weird hallucinations."

"This from a person who still thinks Linda Darnell's hot stuff? You know what we saw."

"I never. I wasn't even here."

"Okay. Me neither. I got to get home." I slid down off the Rock, picking up my new schoolbook bag left at its base. Less than a month, and already my looseleaf notebook looked as though I'd been teething on it.

Phil followed. "Hell, no, it was your figment, you can't just leave it on a doorstep and trust to the kindness of strangers." We'd seen the Marlon Brando *Streetcar Named Desire* a year earlier, and were still bellowing "STELLA!!!" at odd moments in the echoing halls of Junior High School 80. "You saw it, you saw it, I'm gonna tell—Petey saw a centaur—*nyaahh, nyaahh,* Petey saw a centaur!" I swung the book bag at him and chased him all the way out of the Park.

On the phone that evening—we were theoretically doing our biology homework together—he asked, "So what do the Greek myths tell you about centaurs?"

"Main thing, they can't hold their liquor, and they're mean drunks. You don't ever want to give a centaur that first beer."

"I'll remember. What else?"

"Well, the Greeks have two different stories about where they came from, but I can't keep them straight, so forget it. In the legends they're aggressive, always starting fights—there was a big battle with the Lapiths, who were some way their cousins, except human, don't ask, and I think most of the centaurs were killed, I'm not sure. But some of them were really good, really noble, like Cheiron. Cheiron was the best of the lot, he was a healer and an astrologer and a teacher—he was the tutor of people like Odysseus, Achilles, Hercules, Jason, Theseus, all those guys." I paused, still thumbing through the worn Modern Library Bulfinch my father had given me for my tenth birthday. "That's all I know."

"Mmmff. Book say anything about centaurs turning up in the Bronx? I'll settle for the Western Hemisphere."

"No. But there was a shark in the East River, a couple of years back, you remember? Cops went out in a boat and shot at it."

"Not the same thing." Phil sighed. "I still think it's your fault, somehow. What really pisses me off, I didn't have so much as a box of Crayolas to draw the thing with. Probably never get another chance."

But he did: not the next day, when, of course, we cut P.E. and hurried back to the Park, but the day after that, which was depressingly chilly, past pretending that it was still Indian Summer. We didn't talk much: I was busy scanning for centaurs (I'd brought my Baby Brownie Special camera and a pair of binoculars), and Phil, mumbling inaudibly to himself, kept rummaging through his sketch pads and colored pencils, pastels, gouaches, charcoals and crayons. I made small jokes about his equipment almost crowding me off the Rock, and he glared at me in a way that made me uneasy about that "almost."

I don't remember how long we waited, but it must have been close to two hours. The sun was slanting down, the Rock's surface temperature was actually turning out-and-out cold, and Phil and I were well past conversation when the centaurs came. There were three of them: the young one we had first seen, and the two who were clearly his parents, to judge by the way they stood together on the slope below the sycamore grove. They made no attempt to conceal themselves, but looked directly at us, as we stared back at them. After a long moment, they started down the slope together.

Phil was shaking with excitement, but even so he was already sketching as they came toward us. I was afraid to raise my camera, for fear of frightening the centaurs away. They had a melancholy dignity about them, even the child, that I didn't have words for then: I recall it now as an air of royal exile, of knowing where they belonged, and knowing, equally, that they could never return there. The male—no, the *man*—had a short, thick black beard, a dark, strong-boned face, and eyes of a strange color, like honey. The woman…

Remember, all three of them were naked to the waist, and Phil and I were thirteen years old. For myself, I'd seen nude models in my uncles' studios since childhood, but this woman, this *centauride* (I looked the word up when I got home that night), was more beautiful than anyone I knew. It wasn't just a matter of round bare breasts: it was the heartbreaking grace of her neck, the joyous purity of the line of her shoulders, the delicacy of her collarbones. Phil had stopped sketching, which tells you more than I can about what we saw.

The boy had freckles. Not big ones, just a light golden dusting. His hair was the same color, with a kind of reddish undercoloring, like his mother's hair. He looked about ten or eleven.

The man said, "Strangers, of your kindness, might either of you be Jersey Turnpike?"

He had a deep, calm voice, with absolutely no horsiness in it—nothing of a neigh or a whinny, or anything like that. Maybe a slight sort of funny gurgle in the back of the throat, but hardly noticeable—you'd really have to be listening for it. When Phil and I just gaped, the woman said, "We have never come this way south before. We are lost."

Her voice was low, too, but it had a singing cadence to it, a warm offbeat lilt that entranced and seduced both of us even beyond her innocent nudity. I managed to say, "South…you want to go south…um, you mean south like down south? Like *south* south?"

"Like Florida?" Phil asked. "Mexico?"

The man lifted his head sharply. "Mexico, yes, that was the name, I always forget. It is where we go, all of us, every year, when the birds go. *Mexico.*"

"But we set out too late," the woman explained in her soft, singing voice. "Our son was ill, and we traveled eastward to seek out a healer, and by the time we were ready to start, all the others were gone—"

"And Father took the wrong road," the boy broke in, his tone less accusatory than excited. "We have had such adventures—"

His mother quelled him with a glance. Embarrassment didn't sit easily on the man's powerful face, but he flushed and nodded. "More than one. I do not know this country, and we are used to traveling in company. Now I am afraid that we are completely lost, except for that one name someone gave me—Jersey Turnpike. Can Jersey Turnpike lead us to Mexico?"

We looked at each other. Phil said, "Jersey Turnpike isn't a person, it's a road, a highway. You can go south that way, but not to Mexico—you're way off course for Mexico. I'm sorry."

The boy mumbled, "I *knew* it," but not in a triumphant, wise-ass sort of way; if anything, he appeared suddenly very weary of adventures. The man looked utterly stricken. He bowed his head, and the color seemed to fade visibly from his bright chestnut coat. The woman's manner, on the other hand, hardly altered with Phil's news, except that she moved closer to her husband and pressed her light-gray flank against his, in a gesture of silent trust and confidence.

"You're too far east," I said. "You have to cut down through Texas." They stared uncomprehendingly. I said, "Texas—I *think* you'd go by way of Pennsylvania, Tennessee, maybe Georgia..." I stopped, because I couldn't bear the growing fatigue and bewilderment in their three faces, nor in the way their shining bodies sagged a little more with each state name. I told them, "What you need is a map. We could bring you one tomorrow, easy."

But their expressions did not change. The man said, "We cannot read."

"Not now," the woman said wistfully. "There was a time when our folk were taught the Greek in colthood, every one, and some learned the Roman as well, when it became necessary. But that was in another world that is no more...and learning unused fades with long years. Now only a few of our elders know letters enough to read such things as maps in your tongue—the rest of us journey by old memory and starlight. Like the birds."

Her own eyes were different from her husband's honey-colored eyes: more like dark water, with deep-green wonder turning and glinting far down. Phil never could get them right, and he tried for a long time.

He said quietly now, "I could draw you a picture."

I can't say exactly how the centaurs reacted, or how they looked at him. I was too busy gawking at him myself. Phil said, "Of your route, your road. I could draw you something that'll get you to Mexico."

The man started to speak, but Phil anticipated him. "Not a map. I said a *picture*. No words." I remember that he was sitting cross-legged on the Rock, like our idea of a swami or a yogi; and I remember him leaning intensely forward, toward the centaurs, so that he seemed almost to be joined to the Rock, growing out of it, as they were joined to their horse bodies. He was already drawing invisible pictures with his right forefinger on the palm of his left hand, but I don't think he knew it.

I opened *my* mouth then, but he cut me off too. "It'll take me all day tomorrow, and most likely all night too. You'll be okay till the day after tomorrow?"

The woman said to Phil, "You can do this?"

He grinned at her with what seemed to me outrageous confidence. "I'm an artist. Artists are always drawing people's journeys."

I said, "You could wait right here, if you like. We hardly ever see anybody but us in this part of the park. I mean, if it would suit you," for it occurred to me that I had no idea what they ate, or indeed how they survived in the twentieth century. "I guess we could bring you food."

The man's teeth showed white and large in his black beard. "The forage here is most excellent, even this late in the year."

"There are lots of acorns," the boy said eagerly. "I love acorns."

His mother turned her dark gaze to me. "Can you also make such pictures?"

"Never," I said. "But I could maybe write you a poem." I wrote a lot of poems for girls when I was thirteen. She seemed pleased.

Phil was gathering his equipment and scrambling off the Rock, imperiously beckoning me to follow. "Quit fooling around, Beagle. We got work to do." Standing among them, the size and sheer presence of all three centaurs was, if not intimidating, definitely daunting. Even the boy looked down at us, and we barely came up to the shoulders of his parents' horse-bodies. I've always enjoyed the smell of horses—in those days, they were among the very few animals I wasn't allergic to—but centaurs in groups smell like thunder, like an approaching storm, and it left me dizzy and a bit disoriented. Phil repeated briskly, "Day after tomorrow, right here."

We were halfway up the slope when he snapped his fingers, said, "Ah, *shit!*", dropped his equipment and went running back toward the centaurs. I waited, watching as he moved swiftly between the three of them; but I couldn't, for the life of me, make out what he was doing. He came back almost as quickly, and I noticed then that he was tucking something into his shirt pocket. When I asked what it was, he told me it was nothing I needed to trouble my pretty little head about. You couldn't do anything with him in those tempers, so I left it alone.

He didn't say much else on the walk home, and I managed to keep my curiosity in check until we were parting at my apartment building. Then I burst out with it: "Okay, you're going to draw them a picture that's going to get a family of migrating centaurs all the way to Mexico. This, excuse me, I want to hear." His being on the hook meant, as always, *us* being on the hook, so I felt entitled to my snottiness.

"I can do it. It's been done." His jaw was tight, and his face had the ferocious pallor that I associated entirely with street fights, usually with fat Stewie Hauser and Miltie Mellinger, who never tired of baiting him. "Back in the Middle Ages, I read about it—Roger Bacon did it, somebody like that. But you have to get me some maps, as many as you can. A *ton* of maps, a *shitload* of maps, covering every piece of ground between here—right here, your house—and the Texas border. You got that? *Maps.* Also, you should stop by Bernardo's and see can you borrow that candle of his mother's. He says she got it from a *bruja*, back in San Juan, what could it hurt?"

"But if they can't read maps—"

"Beagle, I have been extraordinarily lenient about that two bucks—"

"Maps. Right. Maps. You think they came down from Canada? Summer up north, winter in Mexico? I bet that's what they do."

"*Maps*, Beagle."

The next day was Saturday, and he actually called me around seven in the morning, demanding that I get my lazy ass on the road and start finding some maps for him. I said certain useful things that I had picked up from Angel Salazar, my Berlitz in such affairs, and was at the gas station up the block by 7:30. By 10:00, I'd hit every other station I could reach on my bike, copped my parents' big Rand McNally road atlas, and triumphantly dumped them all—Bernardo's mother's witch-candle included—on Phil's bed, demanding, "*Now* what, fearless leader?"

"Now you take Dusty for her morning walk." He had his favorite easel set up, and was rummaging through his paper supplies. "Then you go away and write your poem, and you come back when it's time to take Dusty for her evening walk. Then you go away again. All well within your capacities."

Dusty was his aged cocker spaniel, and the nearest thing I had to the longed-for dog of my own. I went home after tending to her, and sat down at the desk in my bedroom to write the poem I'd promised to the centaur mother. I still remember the first lines:

> *If I were a hawk,*
> *I would write you letters—*
> *featherheaded jokes,*
> *scribbled on the air.*

> *If I were a dog*
> *I would do your shopping.*
> *If I were a cat*
> *I would brush your hair.*
> *If I were a bear,*
> *I would build your fires,*
> *bringing in the wood,*
> *breaking logs in two.*
> *If I were a camel*
> *I'd take out the garbage.*
> *If I were a fox*
> *I would talk to you...*

There was more and sillier, but never mind. I was very romantic at thirteen, on very short notice, and I had never seen beauty like hers.

Okay, a little bit extra, because I do like the way it ended:

> *If I were a tiger,*
> *I would dance for you.*
> *If I were a mouse,*
> *I would dance for you.*
> *If I were a whale,*
> *I would dance for you...*

When I came back in the evening to walk Dusty again, Phil was working in his bedroom with the door closed, and an unattended dinner plate cooling on the sill. His parents were more or less inured to his habits by now, but it fretted at them constantly, just as my unsociability worried my mother, who would literally bribe Phil and Jake to get me out of the house. I reassured them, as I always did, that he was working on a really demanding, really challenging project, then grabbed up dog and leash and was gone. It was dark when I brought her back, but Phil's door was still shut.

As it was the next morning, and remained until mid-afternoon, when he called me to say, "Done. Get over here."

He sounded awful.

He looked worse. His eyes were smudgy red pits in a face so white that his own small freckles stood out, and he moved like an old man, as though no part of his body could be trusted not to hurt. He said, "Let's go."

"You're kidding. You wouldn't make it to Lapin's." That was the candy-and-newspaper store across the street. "Take a nap, for God's sake, we'll go when you wake up."

"Now." When he cleared his throat, it sounded exactly like my father's car trying to start on a cold morning.

He was holding a metal tube that I recognized as a tennis-ball can. I reached for it, but he snatched it away. "You'll see it when *they* see it." Just then, he didn't look like anyone I'd ever known.

So we trudged to Van Cortlandt Park, which seemed to take the rest of the afternoon, as slowly as Phil was walking. He had clearly been sitting in more or less the same position for hours and hours on end, and the cramps weren't turning loose without a fight. Now and then he paused to shake his arms and legs violently, and by the time we reached the Park, he was moving a little less stiffly. But he still hardly spoke, and he clung to that tennis-ball can as though it were a cherished trophy, or a life raft.

The centaurs were waiting at the Rock. The boy, a little way up the forest slope from his parents, saw us first, and called out, "They're here!" as he galloped to meet us. But he turned shy midway, as children will, and ran back to the others as we approached. I remember that the man had his arms folded across his chest, and that there were a couple of dew-damp patches on the *centauride*'s coat, the weather having turned cloudy. They said nothing.

Phil said, "I brought it. What I promised. Here, I'll show you."

They moved close, plainly careful not to crowd him with their bodies, as he opened the air-tight can and took out a roll of light, flexible drawing paper. He handed the free end to the man, saying, "See? There you are, all three of you. And there's your road to Mexico."

Craning my neck, I could see a perfectly rendered watercolor of the oak forest, so detailed that I saw not only our Rock with its long groove along the top surface, but also such things as the bird's nest in the upper branches of the tallest sycamore and its family of occupants. I couldn't tell what sort of birds they were, but I knew past doubt that Phil knew. The centaurs in the painting, on the other hand, were not done in any detail beyond the generic, except for relative size, the boy being obviously smaller than the other two. They might have been pieces in a board game.

The man said slowly, not trying to conceal his puzzlement, "This is very pretty, I can see that it is pretty. But it is not our road."

"No, you don't understand," Phil answered him. "Look, take both ends, so." He handed the whole roll to the centaur. "Now...hold it up so you can watch it, and walk straight ahead. Just walk."

The man moved slowly forward, his eyes fixed on the image of the very place where he stood. He had not gone more than a few paces when he cried out, "But it moves! It moves!"

His wife and son—and I—pressed close now, and never mind who stepped on whose feet. The watercolor had changed, though not by much; only a few paces' worth. Now it showed a distinctly marked path in front of the centaur's feet: the path we ourselves took, coming and going in the oak forest. He said again, this time in a near-whisper, *"It moves..."*

"And we too," the woman said. "The little figures—as we move, so do they."

"Not always." Phil's voice was sounding distinctly fuller and stronger. "Go left now, walk off the path—see what happens."

The man did as directed—but the figures remained motionless in the watercolor, reproving him with their stillness. When he returned to the path and stepped along it, they moved with him again, sliding like the magnet-based toys we had then. I noticed for the first time that each one's painted tail had a long, coarse hair embedded in the pigment: chestnut, gray, dark-bay.

Almost speechless, the man turned to Phil, holding up the roll to stare at it. "And all our journey is in this picture, truly? And all we need do is follow these...poppets of ourselves?"

Phil nodded. "Just pay attention, and they won't let you go wrong. I fixed it so they'll guide you all the way to Nogales, Texas—that's right on the Mexican border. You'll know the way from there." He looked up with weary seriousness at the proud, bearded face above him. "It's a very long way—almost two thousand miles. I'm sorry."

"We have made longer journeys, and with no such guide." The man was still moving forward and back, watching in fascination as the little images mimicked his pacing. "Nothing to compare," he murmured, "not in all my life..." He halted and faced Phil again. "One with the wisdom to create this for us is also wise enough to know that there is no point in even trying to show our gratitude properly. Thank you."

Phil reached up to take the proffered hand. "Just go carefully, that's all. Stay off the main roads—the way I drew it, you shouldn't ever have to set foot on a highway. And don't ever let that picture out of your sight. Definitely a one-shot deal."

He climbed up onto the Rock and instantly fell asleep. The man seemed to doze on his feet, as horses do, while the boy embarked on one last roundup of every last acorn in the area. For myself, I spent the time saying my poem over and over to the *centauride,* until she had it perfectly memorized, and could repeat it back to me, line for line. "Now I will never forget it," she told me. "The last time anyone wrote a poem for me, it was in the Greek, the oldest Greek that none speak today." She recited it to me, and while I understood not one word, I would know it if I heard it again.

Phil was still asleep when the centaurs left at twilight. I did try to wake him to bid them farewell, but he only blinked and mumbled, and was gone again. I watched them out of sight among the oaks: the man in the lead, intently following the little moving images on Phil's painting; the boy trotting close behind, exuberant with adventure, for good or ill. The woman turned once to look back at us, and then went on.

I don't remember how I finally got Phil on his feet and home; only that it was late, and that both sets of parents were mad at us. The next day was school, and after that I had a doctor's appointment, and Phil had flute lessons, and what with one family thing or another, we had almost no time together until close to the end of the week. We didn't go to the Rock—the weather had turned too grim even for us—rather we sat shivering on the front stoop of my apartment building, like winter birds on a telephone line, and didn't say much of anything. I asked if Phil thought they'd make it all the way to Mexico, and he shrugged and answered, "We'll never know." After a moment, he added, "All *I* know, I got a roomful of stupid maps, and my whole body hurts. Never again, boy. You and your damn hallucinations."

I said, "I didn't know you could do stuff like that. Like what you made for them."

He turned to stare intently into my face. "You saw those hairs in those little figures? I saw you seeing them." I nodded. "Well, each was from one of their tails—Mom, Pop or the Kid. And I plucked a few more hairs, wove those into my brushes. That was the magic part: centaurs may have a lousy sense of direction, but they're still magic. Wouldn't have worked for a minute without that." I stared, and he sighed. "I keep telling you, the artist isn't the magic. The artist is the *sight*, the artist is someone who knows magic when he sees it. The magic doesn't care whether it's seen or not—that's the artist's business. My business."

I tried earnestly, stumblingly, to absorb what he was telling me. "So all that—I mean, the painting moving and guiding them, and all…"

Phil gave me that crooked, deceptively candid grin he's had since we were five years old. "I'm a good artist. I'm really good. But I ain't *that* good."

We sat in silence for a while, while the leaves blew and tumbled past us, and a few sharp, tiny raindrops stung our faces. By and by Phil spoke again, quietly enough that I had to lean closer to hear him. "But we were magic too, in our way. You rounding up every single map between here and Yonkers, and me…" He hunched over, arms folded on his knees, the way he still does without realizing it. "Me at that damn easel, brush in one hand, gas-station map in the other, trying to make art out of the New Jersey Turnpike. Trying to make all those highways and freeways and Interstates and Tennessee and Georgia come alive for a family of mythological, nonexistent…hour after goddam miserable, backbreaking, cockamamie hour, and that San Juan candle dropping wax everywhere…"

His voice trailed off into the familiar disgusted mumble. "I don't *know* how I did it, Beagle. Don't ask me. All I knew for sure was, you can't let centaurs wander around lost in the Bronx—you can't, it's all wrong—and there I was."

"It'll get them to Mexico," I said. "I know it will."

"Yeah, well." The grin became a slow, rueful smile, less usual. "The weird thing, it's made me…I don't know *better*, but just *different*, some way. I'm never going to have to do anything like that again, thank God—and I bet I couldn't. But there's other stuff, things I never thought about trying before, and now it's all I'm doing in my head, right now—my head's full of stuff I have to do, even if I can't ever get it right. Even *though*." The smile faded, and he shrugged and looked away. "That's them. They did that."

I turned my coat collar up around my face. I said, "I read a story about a boy who draws cats so well that they come to life and fight off demons for him."

"Japanese," Phil said. "Good story. Listen, don't tell anybody, not even Jake and Marty. It gets out, they'll want me to do all kinds of stuff, all the time. And magic's not an all-the-time thing, you're not ever *entitled* to magic—not ever, no matter how good you are. Best you can do—all you can do—is make sure you're ready when it happens. If."

His voice had grown somber again, his eyes distant, focusing on nothing that I could recognize. Then he brightened abruptly, saying, "Still got the brushes, anyway. There's that. Whatever comes next, there's the brushes."

SLEIGHT OF HAND

This story was crafted out of childhood memories, a chance encounter with a preposterous ad in an even more preposterous location, and the raw, constant terror I felt when my closest cousin was about to go into surgery for a brain aneurysm. At the time I was too paralyzed by fear for her to do anything but call her husband twice a day for news of her condition. Afterward, when she came out of the operation in fine shape, and I could think again, I found myself writing what follows.

*

She had no idea where she was going. When she needed to sleep she stopped at the first motel; when the Buick's gas gauge dropped into the red zone she filled the tank, and sometimes bought a sandwich or orange juice at the attached convenience store. Now and then during one of these stops she spoke with someone who was neither a desk clerk nor a gas-station attendant, but she forgot all such conversations within minutes, as she forgot everything but the words of the young policeman who had come to her door on a pleasant Wednesday afternoon, weeks and worlds ago. Nothing had moved in her since that point except the memory of his shakily sympathetic voice, telling her that her husband and daughter were dead: ashes in a smoking, twisted, unrecognizable ruin, because, six blocks from their home, a drowsy adolescent had mistaken his accelerator for his brake pedal.

There had been a funeral—she was present, but not there—and more police, and some lawyer; and Alan's sister managing it all, as always, and for once she was truly grateful to the interfering bitch. But that was all far away too, both the gratitude and the old detestation, made nothing by the momentary droop of a boy's eyelids. The nothing got her snugly through the days after the funeral, dealing with each of the endless phone calls, sitting down to answer every condolence card and e-mail, informing Social Security and CREF of Alan's death, going with three of his graduate students to clean out his office, and attending the memorial on campus, which was very tasteful and genuinely moving, or so the nothing was told. She was glad to hear it.

The nothing served her well until the day Alan's daughter by his first marriage came to collect a few of his possessions as keepsakes. She was a perfectly nice girl, who had always been properly courteous in an interloper's presence, and her sympathy was undoubtedly as real as good manners could make it; but when she had gone, bearing a single brown paper grocery bag of photographs and books, the nothing stepped aside for the meltdown.

Her brother-in-law calmed her, spoke rationally, soothed her out of genuine kindness and concern. But that same night, speaking to no one, empty and methodical, she had watched herself pack a small suitcase and carry it out to Alan's big old Buick in the garage, then go back into the house to leave her cell phone and charger on Alan's desk, along with a four-word note for her sister-in-law that read *Out for a drive.* After that she had backed the Buick into the street and headed away without another look at the house where she used to live, once upon a time.

The only reason she went north was that the first freeway on-ramp she came to pointed her in that direction. After that she did not drive straight through, because there was no *through* to aim for. With no destination but away, without any conscious plan except to keep moving, she left and returned to the flat ribbon of the interstate at random intervals, sometimes wandering side roads and backroads for hours, detouring to nowhere. Aimless, mindless, not even much aware of pain—that too having become part of the nothing— she slogged onward. She fell asleep quickly when she stopped, but never for long, and was usually on her way in darkness, often with the moon still high. Now and then she whistled thinly between her teeth.

The weather was warm, though there was still snow in some of the higher passes she traversed. Although she had started near the coast, that was several states ago: now only the mountains were constant. The Buick fled lightly over them, gulping fuel with abandon but cornering like a deer, very nearly operating and guiding itself. This was necessary, since only a part of her was behind the wheel; the rest was away with Alan, watching their daughter building a sandcastle, prowling a bookshop with him, reaching for his hand on a strange street, knowing without turning her head that it would be there. At times she was so busy talking to him that she was slow to switch on the headlights, even long after sunset. But the car took care of her, as she knew it would. It was Alan's car, after all.

From time to time the Buick would show a disposition to wander toward the right shoulder of the road, or drift left into the oncoming lane, and she would observe the tendency with vague, detached interest. Once she asked aloud, "Is this what you want? I'm leaving it to you—are you taking me to Alan?" But somehow, whether under her guidance or its own, the old car always righted itself, and they went on together.

The latest road began to descend, and then to flatten out into farm and orchard country, passing the occasional township, most of them overgrown crossroads. She had driven for much of the previous night, and all of today, and knew with one distant part of herself that it would soon be necessary to stop. In early twilight, less than an hour later, she came to the next town. There was a river winding through it, gray and silver in the dusk, with bridges.

Parking and registering at the first motel with a VACANCY sign, she walked three blocks to the closest restaurant, which, from the street, looked like a bar with a 1950s-style diner attached. Inside, however, it proved larger than she had expected, with slightly less than half of the booths and tables occupied. Directly to the left of the PLEASE WAIT TO BE SERVED sign hung a poster showing a photograph of a lean, hawk-nosed man in late middle age, with white hair and thick eyebrows, wearing evening dress: tailcoat, black bowtie, top hat. He was smiling slightly and fanning a deck of playing cards between long, neat fingers. There was no name under the picture; the caption read only DINNER MAGIC. She looked at it until the young waitress came to show her to her booth.

After ordering her meal—the first she had actually sat down to since leaving home—she asked the waitress about Dinner Magic. Her own voice sounded strange in her ears, and language itself came hard and hesitantly. The girl shrugged. "He's not fulltime—just comes in now and then, does a couple of nights and gone again. Started a couple of weeks ago. Haven't exchanged two words with him. Other than my boss, I don't know anybody who has."

Turning away toward the kitchen, she added over her shoulder, "He's good, though. Stay for the show, if you can."

In fact, the Dinner Magic performance began before most of the current customers had finished eating. There was no stage, no musical flourish or formal introduction: the man in evening dress simply walked out from the kitchen onto the floor, bowed briefly to the diners, then tossed a gauzy multicolored scarf into the air. He seized it again as it fluttered down, then held it up in front of himself, hiding him from silk hat to patent-leather shoes...

...and vanished, leaving his audience too stunned to respond. The applause began a moment later, when he strolled in through the restaurant's front door.

Facing the audience once more, the magician spoke for the first time. His voice was deep and clear, with a certain engaging roughness in the lower range. "Ladies, gentlemen, Dinner Magic means exactly what it sounds like. You are not required to pay attention to me for a moment, you are free to concentrate on your coffee and pie—which is excellent, by the way, especially the lemon meringue—or on your companion, which I recommend even more than the meringue. Think of me, if you will, as the old man next door who stays up all night practicing his silly magic tricks. Because that, under this low-rent monkey suit, is exactly what I am. Now then."

He was tall, and older than the photograph had suggested—how old, she could not tell, but there were lines on his cheeks and under his angled eyes that must have been removed from the picture; the sort of thing she had seen Alan do on the computer. From her booth, she watched, chin on her fist, never taking her eyes from the man as he ran through a succession of tricks that bordered on the miraculous even as his associated patter never transcended a lounge act. Without elephants or tigers, without a spangled, long-legged assistant, he worked the room. Using his slim black wand like a fishing rod he reeled laughing diners out of their seats. Holding it lightly between his fingertips, like a conductor's baton or a single knitting needle, he caused the napkins at every table to lift off in a whispering storm of thin cotton, whirl wildly around the room, and then settle docilely back where they belonged. He identified several members of his audience by name, address, profession, marital status, and, as an afterthought, by driver's license state and number. She was never one of these; indeed, the magician seemed to be consciously avoiding eye contact with her altogether. Nevertheless, she was more intrigued—more *awakened*—than she had meant to let herself be, and she ordered a second cup of coffee and sat quite still where she was.

Finishing at last with an offhanded gesture, a bit like an old-fashioned jump shot, which set all the silverware on all the tables chiming applause, the magician walked off without bowing, as abruptly as he had entered. The waitress brought her check, but she remained in her booth even after the busboy cleared away her dishes. Many of the other diners lingered as she did, chattering and marveling and calling for encores. But the man did not return.

The street was dark, and the restaurant no more than a quarter full, when she finally recollected both herself and her journey, and stepped out into the warm, humid night. For a moment she could not call to mind where she had parked her car; then she remembered the motel and started in that direction. She felt strangely refreshed, and was seriously considering the prospect of giving up her room and beginning to drive again. But after walking several blocks she decided that she must have somehow gone in the wrong direction, for there was no motel sign in sight, nor any landmark casually noted on her way to the restaurant. She turned and turned again, making tentative casts this way and that, even starting back the way she had come, but nothing looked at all familiar.

Puzzlement had given way to unease when she saw the magician ahead of her, under a corner streetlamp. There was no mistaking him, despite his having changed from evening clothes into ordinary dress. His leanness gave him the air of a shadow, rather than a man: a shadow with lined cheeks and long bright eyes. As she approached, he spoke her name. He said, "I have been waiting for you." He spoke more slowly than he had when performing, with a tinge of an accent that she had not noticed.

Anxiety fled on the instant, replaced by a curious stillness, as when Alan's car began to drift peacefully toward the guardrail or the shoulder and the trees. She said, "How do you know me? How did you know all about those other people?"

"I know nearly everything about nearly everyone. That's the curse of my position. But you I know better than most."

She stared at him. "I don't know you."

"Nevertheless, we have met before," the magician said. "Twice, actually, which I confess is somewhat unusual. The second time was long ago. You were quite small."

"That's ridiculous." She was surprised by the faint touch of scorn in her voice, barely there yet still sharp. "That doesn't make any sense."

"I suppose not. Since I know how the trick's done, and you don't, I'm afraid I have you at a disadvantage." He put one long finger to his lips and pursed them, considering, before he started again. "Let's try it as a riddle. I am not entirely what I appear, being old as time, vast as space, and endless as the future. My nature is known to all, but typically misunderstood. And I meet everyone and everything alive at least once. Indeed, the encounter is entirely unavoidable. Who am I?"

She felt a sudden twist in the nothing, and knew it for anger. "Show's over. I'm not eating dinner anymore."

The magician smiled and shook his head very slightly. "You are lost, yes?"

"My motel's lost, I'm not. I must have taken a wrong turn."

"I know the way," the magician said. "I will guide you."

Gracefully and courteously, he offered his arm, but she took a step backward. His smile widened as he let the arm fall to his side. "Come," he said, and turned without looking to see whether she followed. She caught up quickly, not touching the hand he left open, within easy reach.

"You say we've met before. Where?" she asked.

"The second time was in New York City. Central Park," the magician said. "There was a birthday party for your cousin Matthew."

She stopped walking. "Okay. I don't know who you are, or how you knew I grew up in New York City and have a cousin named Matthew. But you just blew it, Sherlock. When we were kids I *hated* stupid, nasty Matthew, and I absolutely never went to any of his birthday parties. My parents tried to make me, once, but I put up such a fuss they backed down. So you're wrong."

The magician reached out abruptly, and she felt a swift, cool whisper in her hair. He held up a small silver figure of a horse and asked with mock severity, "What are you doing, keeping a horse up in there? You shouldn't have a horse if you don't have a stable for it."

She froze for an instant, wide-eyed and open-mouthed, and then clutched at the silver horse as greedily as any child. "That's *mine!* Where did you get it?"

"I gave it to you." The magician's voice sounded as impossibly distant as her childhood, long gone on another coast.

And then came his command: "*Remember.*"

At first she had enjoyed herself. Matthew was fat and awful as usual, but his birthday had been an excuse to bring together branches of the family that rarely saw one another, traveling in to Central Park from places as whispered and exotic as Rockaway and Philadelphia. She was excited to see her *whole* family, not just her parents and her very small baby brother, and Matthew's mother and father, but also uncles and aunts and cousins, and some very old relatives she had never met before in her life. They all gathered together in one corner of the Sheep Meadow, where they spread out picnic blankets, coverlets, beach towels, anything you could sit down on, and they brought out all kinds of old-country dishes: *piroshki, pelmeni, flanken, kasha, rugelach, kugel mit mandlen,* milk bottles full of *borscht* and *schav*—and hot dogs and hamburgers too, and baked beans and deviled eggs, and birthday cake and candy and cream soda. It was a hot blue day, full of food.

But a four-year-old girl can only eat and drink so much...and besides, after a while the uncles all began to fall asleep on the grass, one by one, much too full to pay attention to her...and all the aunts were sitting together telling stories that didn't make any sense...and Matthew was fussing about having a "stummyache," which she felt he certainly deserved. And her parents weren't worth talking to, since whenever she tried they were busy with her infant brother or the other adults, and not really listening. So after a time she grew bored. Stuffed, but bored.

She decided that she would go and see the zoo.

She knew that Central Park had a zoo because she had been taken there once before. It was a long way from the picnic, but even so, every now and then she could hear the lions roaring, along with the distant sounds of busses and taxis and city traffic that drifted to her ears. She was sure that it would be easy to find her way if she listened for the lions.

But they eluded her, the lions and the zoo alike. Not that she was lost, no, not for a minute. She walked along enjoying herself, smiling in the sunlight, and petting all the dogs that came bouncing up to her. If their owners asked where her parents were, she pointed firmly in the direction she was going and said "right up there," then moved on, laughing, before they had time to think about it. At every branching of the path she would stop and listen, taking whatever turn sounded like it led toward the lions. She didn't seem to be getting any closer, though, which eventually grew frustrating. It was still an adventure, still more exciting than the birthday picnic, but now it was beginning to annoy her as well.

Then she came around a bend in the path, and saw a man sitting by himself on a little bench. To her eyes he was a *very* old man, almost as old as her great-uncle Wilhelm—you could tell that by his white hair, and the deep lines around his closed eyes, and the long red blanket that his legs stretched out in front of him. She had seen other old men sitting like that. His hands were shoved deep into his coat pockets, and his face lifted to the angle of the afternoon sun.

She thought he was asleep, so she started on past him, walking quietly, so as not to wake him. But without opening his eyes or changing his position, he said in a soft, deep voice, "An exceptional afternoon to you, young miss."

Exceptional was a new word to her, and she loved new words. She turned around and replied, trying to sound as grown up as she could, "I'm very exceptional, thank you."

"And glad I am to hear it," the old man said. "Where are you off to, if I may ask?"

"I'm going to see the lions," she told him. "And the draffs. Draffs are excellent animals."

"So they are," the old man agreed. His eyes, when he opened them, were the bluest she had ever seen, so young and bright that they made the rest of him look even older. He said, "I used to ride a draff, you know, in Africa. Whenever I went shopping."

She stared at him. "You can't ride a draff. There's no place to *sit*."

"I rode way up on the neck, on a little sort of platform." The old man hadn't beckoned to her, or shifted to make room for her on the bench, but she found herself moving closer all the same. He said, "It was like being in the crow's-nest on the mast of a ship, where the lookout sits. The draff would be swaying and flowing under me like the sea, and the sky would be swaying too, and I'd hang onto the draff's neck with one hand, and wave to all the people down below with the other. It was really quite nice."

He sighed, and smiled and shook his head. "But I had to give it up, because there's no place to put your groceries on a draff. All your bags and boxes just slide right down the neck, and then the draff steps on them. Draffs have very big feet, you know."

By that time she was standing right in front of him, staring into his lined old face. He had a big, proud nose, and his eyebrows over it were all tangly. To her they looked mad at each other. He said, "After that, I did all my shopping on a rhinoceros. One thing about a rhinoceros"—and for the first time he smiled at her—"when you come into a store, people are always remarkably nice. And you can sling all your packages around the rhino's horn and carry them home that way. *Much* handier than a draff, let me tell you."

He reached up while he was talking and took an egg out of her right ear. She didn't feel it happen—just the quick brush of his long fingers, and there was the egg in his hand. She grabbed for her other ear, to see if there might be an egg in there too, but he was already taking a quarter out of that one. He seemed just as surprised as she was, saying, "My goodness, now you'll be able to buy some toast to have with your egg. Extraordinary ears you have—my word, yes." And all the time he was carrying on about the egg, he was finding all kinds of other things in her ears: seashells and more coins, a couple of marbles (which upset him—"You should *never* put marbles in your ears, young lady!"), a tangerine, and even a flower, although it looked pretty mooshed-up, which he said was from being in her ear all that time.

She sat down beside him without knowing she was sitting down. "How do you *do* that?" she asked him. "Can *I* do that? Show me!"

"With ears like those, everything is possible," the old man answered. "Try it for yourself," and he guided her hand to a beautiful cowrie shell tucked just behind her left ear. Then he said, "I wonder…I just wonder…" And he ruffled her hair quickly and showed her a palm full of tiny silver stars. Not like the shining foil ones her preschool teacher gave out for good behavior, but glittering, sharp-pointed metal stars, as bright as anything in the sky.

"It seems your hair is talented, too. *That's* exceptional."

"More, please!" she begged him.

The old man looked at her curiously. He was still smiling, but his eyes seemed sad now, which confused her.

"I haven't given you anything that wasn't already yours," he said. "Much as I would otherwise. But *this* is a gift. From me to you. Here." He waved one hand over his open palm, and when it passed she saw a small silver figure of a horse.

She looked at it. It was more beautiful, she thought, than anything she had ever seen.

"I can keep it? Really?"

"Oh yes," he said. "I hope you will keep it always."

He put the exquisite figure in her cupped hands, and closed her fingers gently over it. She felt the curlicues of the mane, blowing in a frozen wind, against her fingertips.

"Put it in your pocket, for safekeeping, and look at it tonight before you go to bed." As she did what he told her, he said "Now I must ask where your parents are."

She said nothing, suddenly aware how much time had passed since she had left the picnic.

"They will be looking everywhere for you," the old man said. "In fact, I think I can hear them calling you now." He cupped his hands to his mouth and called in a silly, quavering voice, "Elfrieda! *Elfrieda!* Where are you, Elfrieda?"

This made her giggle so much that it took her a while to tell him, "*That's* not my name." He laughed too, but he went on calling, "*Elfrieda! Elfrieda!*" until the silly voice became so sad and worried that she stood up and said, "Maybe I ought to go back and tell them I'm all right." The air was starting to grow a little chilly, and she was starting to be not quite sure that she knew the way back.

"Oh, I wouldn't do that," the old man advised her. "If I were you, I'd stay right here, and when they come along you could say to them, 'Why don't you sit down and rest your weary bones?' That's what *I'd* do."

The idea of saying something like that to grownups set her off giggling again, and she could hardly wait for her family to come find her. She sat down by the old man and talked with him, in the ordinary way, about school and friends and uncles, and all the ways her cousin Matthew made her mad, and about going shopping on rhinoceroses. He told her that it was always hard to find parking space for a rhino, and that they really didn't like shopping, but they would do it if they liked you. So after that they talked about how you get a rhinoceros to like you, until her father came for her on the motorcycle.

"I lost it back in college." She caressed the little object, holding it against her cheek. "I looked and looked, but I couldn't find it anywhere." She looked at him with a mix of wonder and suspicion. She fell silent then, frowning, touching her mouth. "Central Park...there was a zoo in Central Park."

The magician nodded. "There still is."

"Lions. Did they have lions?" She gave him no time to answer the question. "I do remember the lions. I heard them roaring." She spoke slowly, seeming to be addressing the silver horse more than him. "I wanted to see the lions."

"Yes," the magician said. "You were on your way there when we met."

"I remember now," she said. "How could I have forgotten?" She was speaking more rapidly as the memory took shape. "You were sitting with me on the bench, and then Daddy...Daddy came on a motorcycle. I mean, no, the *policeman* was on the motorcycle, and Daddy was in the...the sidecar thing. I remember. He was so furious with me that I was glad the policeman was there."

The magician chuckled softly. "He was angry until he saw that you were safe and unharmed. Then he was so thankful that he offered me money."

"Did he? I didn't notice." Her face felt suddenly hot with embarrassment. "I'm sorry, I didn't know he wanted to give you money. You must have felt so insulted."

"Nonsense," the magician said briskly. "He loved you, and he offered what he had. Both of us dealt in the same currency, after all."

She paused, looking around them. "This isn't the right street either. I don't see the motel."

He patted her shoulder lightly. "You will, I assure you."

"I'm not certain I want to."

"Really?" His voice seemed to surround her in the night. "And why would that be? You have a journey to continue."

The bitterness rose so fast in her throat that it almost made her throw up. "If you know my name, if you know about my family, if you know things *I'd* forgotten about, then you already know why. Alan's dead, and Talley—my Mouse, oh God, *my little Mouse*—and so am I, do you understand? I'm dead too, and I'm just driving around and around until I rot." She started to double over, coughing and gagging on the rage. "I wish I were dead with them, that's what I wish!" She would have been desperately happy to vomit, but all she could make come out were words.

Strong old hands were steadying her shoulders, and she was able, in a little time, to raise her head and look into the magician's face, where she saw neither anger nor pity. She said very quietly, "No, I'll tell you what I really wish. I wish *I* had died in that crash, and that Alan and Talley were still alive. I'd make that deal like a shot, you think I wouldn't?"

The magician said gently, "It was not your fault."

"Yes it was. It's my fault that they were in my car. I asked Alan to take it in for an oil change, and Mouse...Talley wanted to go with him. She loved it, being just herself and Daddy—oh, she used to order him around so, pretending she was me." For a moment she came near losing control again, but the magician held on, and so did she. "If I hadn't asked him to do that for me, if I hadn't been so selfish and lazy and sure I had more important things to do, then it would have been me that died in that crash, and they'd have lived. They *would* have lived." She reached up and gripped the magician's wrists, as hard as she could, holding his eyes even more intently. "You see?"

The magician nodded without answering, and they stood linked together in shadow for that moment. Then he took his hands from her shoulders and said, "So, then, you have offered to trade your life for the lives of your husband and daughter. Do you still hold to that bargain?"

She stared at him. She said, "That stupid riddle. You really *meant* that. What *are* you? Are you Death?"

"Not at all. But there are things I can do, with your consent."

"My consent." She stood back, straightening to her full height. "Alan and Talley...nobody needed *their* consent—or mine, either. I meant every word."

"Think," the magician said urgently. "I need you to know what you have asked, and the extent of what you think you mean." He raised his left hand, palm up, tapping on it with his right forefinger. "Be very careful, little girl in the park. There *are* lions."

"I know what I wished." She could feel the sidewalk coiling under her feet.

"Then know this. I can neither take life nor can I restore it, but I *can* grant your wish, exactly as it was made. You have only to say—and to be utterly certain in your soul that it *is* your true desire." He chuckled suddenly, startlingly; to her ear it sounded almost like a growl. "My, I cannot recall the last time I used that word, *soul*."

She bit her lip and wrapped her arms around herself, though the night continued warm. "What can you promise me?"

"A different reality—the exact one you prayed for just now. Do you understand me?"

"No," she said; and then, very slowly, "You mean, like running a movie backward? Back to...back to *before*?"

The old man shook his head. "No. Reality never runs backward; each thing is, and will be, as it always was. Choice is an uncommon commodity, and treasured by those few who actually have it. But there *is* magic, and magic can shuffle some possibilities like playing cards, done right. Such craft as I control will grant your wish, precisely as you spoke it. Take the horse I have returned to you back to the place where the accident happened. The *exact* place. Hold it in your hand, or carry it on your person, and take a single step. One single step. If your commitment is firm, if your choice is truly and finally made, then things as they always were will *still* be as they always were—only now, the way they always were will be forever different. Your husband and your daughter will live, because they never drove that day, and they never died. *You* did. Do you understand now?"

"Yes," she whispered. "Oh, yes, *yes*, I do understand. Please, do it, I accept, it's the only wish I have. Please, *yes*."

The magician took her hands between his own. "You are certain? You know what it will mean?"

"I can't live without them," she answered simply. "I told you. But...how—"

"Death, for all His other sterling qualities, is not terribly bright. Efficient and punctual, but not bright." The magician gave her the slightest of bows. "And I am very good with tricks. You might even say exceptional."

"Can't you just send me there, right this minute—transport me, or e-mail me or something, never mind the stupid driving. Couldn't you do that? I mean, if you can do—you know—*this*?"

He shook his head. "Even the simplest of tricks must be prepared...and this one is not simple. Drive, and I will meet you at the appointed time and place."

"Well, then." She put her hands on his arms, looking up at him as though at the sun through green leaves. "Since there are no words in the world for me to thank you with, I'm just going to go on back home. My family's waiting."

Yet she delayed, and so did he, as though both of them were foreigners fumbling through a language never truly comprehended: a language of memory and intimacy. The magician said, "You don't know why I am doing this." It was not a question.

"No. I don't." Her hesitant smile was a storm of anxious doubt. "Old times' sake?"

The magician shook his head. "It doesn't really matter. Go now."

The motel sign was as bright as the moon across the street, and she could see her car in the half-empty parking lot. She turned and walked away, without looking back, started the Buick and drove out of the lot. There was nothing else to collect. Let them wonder in the morning at her unruffled bed, and the dry towels never taken down from the bathroom rack.

The magician was plain in her rear-view mirror, looking after her, but she did not wave, or turn her head.

Free of detours, the road back seemed notably shorter than the way she had come, though she took it distinctly more slowly. The reason, to her mind, was that before she had been so completely without plans, without thought, without any destination, without any baggage but grief. Now, feeling almost pregnant with joy, swollen with eager visions—*they will live, they will, my Mouse will be a living person, not anyone's memory*—she felt a self that she had never considered or acknowledged conducting the old car, as surely as her foot on the accelerator and her hands on the wheel. A full day passed, more, and somehow she did not grow tired, which she decided must be something the magician had done, so she did not question it. Instead she sang nursery songs as she drove, and the sea chanteys and Gilbert and Sullivan that Alan had always loved. *No, not loved. Loves! Loves now, loves now, and will go on loving, because I'm on my way. Alan, Talley, I'm on my way.*

For the last few hundred miles she abandoned the interstate and drove the coast road home, retracing the path she and Alan had taken at the beginning of their honeymoon. The ocean was constant on her right, the massed redwoods and hemlocks on her left, and the night air smelled both of salt and pinesap. There were deer in the brush, and scurrying foxes, and even a porcupine, shuffling and clicking across the road. Once she saw a mountain lion, or thought she had: a long-tailed shadow in a shadow, watching her shadow race past. *Darlings, on my way!*

It was near dawn when she reached the first suburbs of the city where she had gone to college, married, and settled without any control—or the desire for control—over very much of it. The city lay still as jewels before her, except when the infrequent police siren or fire-engine clamor set dogs barking in every quarter. She parked the Buick in her driveway, startled for a moment at her house's air of abandonment and desolation. *What did you expect, disappearing the way you did, and no way to contact you?* She did not try the door, but stood there for a little, listening absurdly for any sound of Alan or Talley moving in the house. Then she walked away as calmly as she had from the magician.

Six blocks, six blocks. She found the intersection where the crash had occurred. Standing on the corner angle of the sidewalk, she could see the exact smudge on the asphalt where her life had ended, and this shadowy leftover had begun. Across the way the light grew beyond the little community park, a glow as transparent as seawater. She drank it in, savoring the slow-rising smells of warming stone and suburban commuter breakfasts. *Never again... never again,* she thought. Up and down the street, cars were backing out of garages, and she found herself watching them with a strange new greed, thinking, *Alan and Mouse will see them come home again, see the geese settle in on the fake lake for the night. Not me, never again.*

The street was thickening with traffic, early as it was. She watched a bus go by, and then the same school van that always went first to the farthest developments, before circling back to pick up Talley and others who lived closer to school. *He's not here yet,* she thought, fingering the silver horse in her pocket. *I could take today. One day—one day only, just to taste it all, to go to all the places we were together, to carry that with me when I step across that pitiful splotch—tomorrow? My darlings will have all the other days, all their lives...couldn't I have just the one? I'd be right back here at dawn, all packed to leave—surely they wouldn't mind, if they knew? Just the one.*

· Behind her, the magician said, "As much as you have grieved for them, so they will mourn you. You say your life ended here; they will say the same, for a time."

Without turning, she said, "You can't talk me out of this."

A dry chuckle. "Oh, I've suspected that from the beginning."

She did turn then, and saw him standing next to her: unchanged, but for a curious dusk, bordering on tenderness, in the old, old eyes. His face was neither pitying nor unkind, nor triumphant in its foreknowledge, but urgently attentive in the way of a blind person. "There she was, that child in Central Park, stumping along, so fierce, so determined, going off all alone to find the lions. There was I, half-asleep in the sun on my park bench..."

"I don't understand," she said. "Please. Before I go, tell me who you are."

"You know who I am."

"I don't!"

"You did. You will."

She did not answer him. In silence, they both turned their heads to follow a young black man walking on the other side of the street. He was carrying an infant—a boy, she thought—high in his arms, his round dark face brilliant with pride, as though no one had ever had a baby before. The man and child were laughing together: the baby's laughter a shrill gurgle, the father's almost a song. Another bus hid them for a moment, and when it passed they had turned a corner and disappeared.

The magician said, "Yet despite your certainty you were thinking, unless I am mistaken, of delaying your bargain's fulfillment."

"One day," she said softly. "Only to say goodbye. To remind myself of them and everything we had, before giving it all up. Would that...would it be possible? Or would it break the...the spell? The charm?"

The magician regarded her without replying immediately, and she found that she was holding her breath.

"It's neither of those. It's just a trick, and not one that can wait long on your convenience." His expression was inflexible.

"Oh," she said. "Well. It would have been nice, but there—can't have everything. Thank you, and goodbye again."

She waited until the sparse morning traffic was completely clear. Then deliberately, and without hesitation, she stepped forward into the street. She was about to move further when she heard the magician's voice behind her. "Sunset. That is the best I can do."

She wheeled, her face a child's face, alight with holiday. "*Thank* you! I'll be back in time, I promise! Oh, *thank* you!"

Before she could turn again the magician continued, in a different voice, "I have one request." His face was unchanged, but the voice was that of a much younger man, almost a boy. "I have no right to ask, no claim on you— but I would feel privileged to spend these hours in your company." He might have been a shy Victorian, awkwardly inviting a girl to tea.

She stared back at him, her face for once as unreadable as his. It was a long moment before she finally nodded and beckoned to him, saying, "Come on, then—there's so little time. Come on!"

In fact, whether or not it was due to his presence, there was time enough. She reclaimed the Buick and drove them first up into the hills, to watch the rest of dawn play itself out over the city as she told him stories of her life there. Then they joined an early-morning crowd of parents and preschoolers in the local community playground. She introduced the magician to her too-solicitous friends as a visiting uncle from Alan's side of the family, and tried to maintain some illusion of the muted grief she knew they expected of her; an illusion that very nearly shattered with laughter when the magician took a ride with some children on a miniature train, his knees almost up to his ears. After that she brought them back down to the bald flatlands near the freeway, to the food bank where she had worked twice a week, and where she was greeted with cranky affection by old black Baptist women who hugged her and warned her that she needn't be coming round so soon, but if she was up to it, well, tomorrow was likely to be a particularly heavy day, and Lord knows they could use the extra hand. The magician saw the flash of guilt and sorrow in her eyes, but no one else did. She promised not to be late.

Time enough. They parked the car and took a ferry across the bay to the island where she had met Alan when they were both dragged along on a camping trip, and where she and Alan and Talley had picnicked often after Talley was born. Here she found herself chattering to the magician compulsively, telling him how Alan had cured their daughter of her terror of water by coaxing her to swim sitting up on his back, pretending she was riding a dolphin. "She's become a wonderful swimmer now, Mouse has, you should see her. I mean, I guess you *will* see her—anyway you *could* see her. I won't, but if you wanted to..." Her voice drifted away, and the magician touched her hand without replying.

"We have to watch the clock," she said. "I wouldn't want to miss my death." It was meant as a joke, but the magician did not laugh.

Time enough. Her vigilance had them back at the house well before sunset, after a stop at her family's favorite ice cream shop for cones: coffee for herself—"Double scoop, what the hell?"—and strawberry, after much deliberation, for the magician. They were still nibbling them when they reached the front door.

"God, I'll miss coffee," she said, almost dreamily; then laughed. "Well, I guess I won't, will I? I mean, I won't know if I miss it or not, after all." She glanced critically up at the magician beside her. "You've never eaten an ice-cream cone before, have you?"

The magician shook his head solemnly. She took his cone from him and licked carefully around the edges, until the remaining ice-cream was more or less even; then handed it back to him, along with her own napkin. "We should finish before we go in. Come on." She devoted herself to devouring the entire cone, crunching it up with a voracity matching the sun's descent.

When she was done she used her key to open the door, and stepped inside. She was halfway down the front hall, almost to the living room, when she realized the magician had not followed.

"Hey," she called to him. "Aren't you coming?"

"I thank you for the day, but this moment should be yours alone. I will wait outside. You needn't hurry," he said, glancing at the sky. "But don't dawdle, either."

With that he closed the door, leaving her to the house and her memories.

Half an hour later, six blocks away, she stood slightly behind him on the sidewalk and studied the middle of the intersection. He did not offer his hand, but she lifted it in both of hers anyway. "You are very kind."

He shook his head ruefully. "Less than you imagine. Far less than I wish."

"Don't give me that." Her tone was dismissive, but moderated with a chuckle. "You were waiting for me. You said so. I would have bumped into you wherever I drove, wouldn't I? If I'd gone south to Mexico, or gotten on a plane to Honolulu or Europe, sooner or later, when I was ready to listen to what you had to say, when I was ready to make this deal, I'd have walked into a restaurant with a sign for Dinner Magic. Right?"

"Not quite. You could only have gone the way you went, and I could only have met you there. Each thing is, and will be, as it always was. I told you that."

"I don't care. I'm still grateful. I'm still saying thanks."

The magician said softly, "Stay."

She shook her head. "You know I can't."

"This trick...this misdirection...I can't promise you what it will buy. Your husband and daughter will live, but for how long cannot be known by anyone. They might be killed tomorrow by another stupid, sleepy driver—a virus, a plane crash, a madman with a gun. What you are giving up for them could be utterly useless, utterly pointless, by next sunrise. Stay—do not waste this moment of your own choice, your own power. *Stay.*"

He reached out for her, but she stepped away, backing into the street so suddenly that a driver honked angrily at her as he sped by. She said, "Everything you say is absolutely true, and none of it matters. If all I could give them was one single extra second, I would."

The old man's face grew gentle. "Ah. You are indeed as I remembered. Very well, then. I had to offer you a choice. You have chosen love, and I have no complaint, nor would it matter if I did. In this moment you are the magician, not I."

"All right, then. Let's do this."

The huge red sun was dancing on tiptoe on a green horizon, but she waited until the magician nodded before she started toward the intersection. Traffic had grown so heavy that there was no way for her to reach the stain that was Alan and Talley's fading memorial. The magician raised his free hand, as though waving to her, and the entire lane opened up, cars and drivers frozen in place, leaving her free passage to where she needed to be. Over her shoulder she said, "Thank you," and stepped forward.

The little girl shook her head and looked around herself. She was confused by what she saw, and if anyone in the park other than the old man had been watching, they would have wondered at the oddly adult way that she stood still and regarded her surroundings.

"Hello," the magician said to her.

"This...isn't what I expected."

"No. The audience sees a woman cut in half, while the two women folded carefully within separate sections of the magic box experience it quite differently. You're in the trick now, so of course things are different than you expected. It's hardly magic if you can guess in advance how it's done."

She looked at her small hands in amazement, then down the short length of her arms and legs. "I *really* don't understand. You said I would die."

"And so you will, on the given day and at the given time, when you think about asking your husband to take care of your oil change for you and then decide—in a flickering instant, quite without knowing why—that you should do this simple errand yourself, instead." He looked enormously sad as he spoke. "And you will die now, in a different way, because that one deeply buried flicker is the only hint of memory you may keep. You won't remember this day, or the gifts I will give you, or me. The trick won't work, otherwise. Death may not be bright, but he's not stupid, either—all the cards have to go back in the deck, or he *will* notice. But if you and I, between us, subtly mark one of the cards...that should slip by. Just."

He stopped speaking; and for a little it seemed to the woman in the girl, staring into the finality of his face as though into a dark wood, that he might never again utter a word. Then he sighed deeply. "I told you I wasn't kind."

She reached up to touch his cheek, her eyes shining. "No one could possibly be kinder. You've not only granted my wish, you're telling me I'll get to see them again. That I'll meet Alan again, and fall in love again, and hold my little Mouse in my arms, exactly as before. That *is* what you are saying, isn't it?"

He held both his hands wide, elegant fingers cupped to catch the sun. "You are that child in Central Park, off to see the lions. And I am an old man, half-asleep on a bench...from this point on the world proceeds just as it ever was, and only one thing, quite a bit ahead of today and really not worth talking about, will be any different. Please look in your pocket, child."

She reached into the front of her denim coverall, then, and smiled when she felt her four-year-old hand close around the silver horse. She took it out, and held it up to him as if she were offering a piece of candy.

"I don't know who you are, but I know what you are. You're something good."

"Nonsense," he said, but she could see he looked pleased. "And now..." The magician placed his vast, lined hands around hers, squeezed once, gently, and said "*Forget.*" When he took his hands away the silver horse was gone.

The little girl stood on the green grass, looking up at the old man with the closed eyes. He spoke to her. "Where are you off to, if I may ask?"

"I'm going to see the lions," she told him. "And the draffs. Draffs are excellent animals."

"So they are," the old man agreed, tilting his head down to look at her. His eyes, when he opened them, were the bluest she had ever seen.

THE CHILDREN OF THE SHARK GOD

Ellen Datlow and Terri Windling are remarkable editors with an enviable track record of success in fantasy publishing. This story was written for an original anthology of theirs called The Beastly Bride, which collected tales drawn from the many different legends of humans who marry—knowingly or in ignorance—dragons, were-bears, were-lions, Celtic selchies, or other shape-shifters. All the contributing writers got to claim unique cultures, starting out, and I decided on the South Seas.

This is, without question, my homage to Robert Louis Stevenson, since I've always thought of Stevenson as one of my major storytelling ancestors (especially the Samoan Stevenson of "The Bottle Imp" and "The Beach of Falesá"). I was quite consciously imitating his later folkloric style in "The Children of the Shark God," and I have absolutely no qualms about saying so. Homage is neither mimicry nor parody, but a way of saying thank you.

❈

Once there was a village on an island that belonged to the Shark God. Every man in the village was a fisherman, and the women cooked their catch and mended their nets and sails, and painted their little boats. And because that island was sacred to him, the Shark God saw to it that there were always fish to be caught, and seals as well, in the waters beyond the coral reef, and protected the village from the great gray typhoons that came every year to flood other lagoons and blow down the trees and the huts of other islands. Therefore the children of the village grew fat and strong, and the women were beautiful and strong, and the fishermen were strong and high-hearted even when they were old.

In return for his benevolence the Shark God asked little from his people: only tribute of a single goat at the turn of each year. To the accompaniment of music and prayers, and with a wreath of plaited fresh flowers around its neck, it would be tethered in the lagoon at moonrise. Morning would find it gone, flower petals floating on the water, and the Shark God never seen—never in *that* form, anyway.

Now the Shark God could alter his shape as he pleased, like any god, but he never showed himself on land more than once in a generation. When he did, he was most often known to appear as a handsome young man, light-footed and charming. Only one woman ever recognized the divinity hiding behind the human mask. Her name was Mirali, and this tale is what is known about her, and about her children.

Mirali's parents were already aging when she was born, and had long since given up the hope of ever having a child—indeed, her name meant "the long-desired one." Her father had been crippled when the mast of his boat snapped during a storm and crushed his leg, falling on him, and if it had not been for their daughter the old couple's lives would have been hard indeed. Mirali could not go out with the fishing fleet herself, of course—as she greatly wished to do, having loved the sea from her earliest memory—but she did every kind of work for any number of island families, whether cleaning houses, marketing, minding young children, or even assisting the midwife when a birthing was difficult or there were simply too many babies coming at the same time. She was equally known as a seamstress, and also as a cook for special feasts; nor was there anyone who could mend a pandanus-leaf thatching as quickly as she, though this is generally man's work. No drop of rain ever penetrated any pandanus roof that came under Mirali's hands.

Nor did she complain of her labors, for she was very proud of being able to care for her mother and father as a son would have done. Because of this, she was much admired and respected in the village, and young men came courting just as though she were a great beauty. Which she was not, being small and somewhat square-made, with straight brows—considered unlucky by most—and hips that gave no promise of a large family. But she had kind eyes, deep-set under those regrettable brows, and hair as black and thick as that of any woman on the island. Many, indeed, envied her; but of that Mirali knew nothing. She had no time for envy herself, nor for young men, either.

Now it happened that Mirali was often chosen by the village priest to sweep out the temple of the Shark God. This was not only a grand honor for a child barely turned seventeen but a serious responsibility as well, for sharks are cleanly in their habits, and to leave his spiritual dwelling disorderly would surely be to dishonor and anger the god himself. So Mirali was particularly attentive when she cleaned after the worshippers, making certain that no prayer whistle or burned stick of incense was left behind. And in this manner did the Shark God become aware of Mirali.

But he did not actually see her until a day came when, for a wonder, all her work was done, all her tasks out of the way until tomorrow, when they would begin all over again. At such times, rare as they were, Mirali would always wander down to the water, borrow a dugout or an outrigger canoe, and simply let herself drift in the lagoon—or even beyond the reef—reading the clouds for coming weather, or the sea for migrating shoals of fish, or her own young mind for dreams. And if she should chance to see a black or gray or brown dorsal fin cutting the water nearby, she was never frightened, but would drowsily hail the great fish in fellowship, and ask it to convey her most respectful good wishes to the Shark God. For in that time children knew what was expected of them, by parents and gods alike.

She was actually asleep in an uncle's outrigger when the Shark God himself came to Mirali—as a mako, of course, since that is the most beautiful and graceful of all sharks. At the first sight of her, he instantly desired to shed his fishy form and climb into the boat to wake and caress her. But he knew that such behavior would terrify her as no shark could; and so, most reluctantly, he swam three times around her boat, which is magic, and then he sounded and disappeared.

When Mirali woke, it was with equal reluctance, for she had dreamed of a young man who longed for her, and who followed at a respectful distance, just at the edge of her dream, not daring to speak to her. She beached the dugout with a sigh, and went home to make dinner for her parents. But that night, and every night thereafter, the same dream came to her, again and again, until she was almost frantic with curiosity to know what it meant.

No priest or wisewoman could offer her any useful counsel, although most suspected that an immortal was concerned in the matter in some way. Some advised praying in a certain way at the temple; others directed her to brew tea out of this or that herb or tree bark to assure herself of a deep, untroubled sleep. But Mirali was not at all sure that she wanted to rid herself of that dream and that shy youth; she only wanted to understand them.

Then one afternoon she heard a man singing in the market, and when she turned to see she knew him immediately as the young man who always followed her in her dream. She went to him, marching straight across the marketplace and facing him boldly to demand, "Who are you? By what right do you come to me as you do?"

The young man smiled at her. He had black eyes, smooth dark-brown skin—with perhaps a touch of blue in it, when he stood in shadow—and fine white teeth, which seemed to Mirali to be just a trifle curved in at the tips. He said gently, "You interrupted my song."

Mirali started to respond, "So? You interrupt my sleep, night on night"— but she never finished saying what she meant to say, because in that moment she knew the Shark God. She bowed her head and bent her right knee, in the respectful manner of the island folk, and she whispered, "*Jalak...jalak,*" which means *Lord.*

The young man took her hand and raised her up. "What my own people call me, you could not pronounce," he said to Mirali. "But to you I am no *jalak,* but your own faithful *olohe,*" which is the common word for *servant.* "You must only call me by that name, and no other. Say it now."

Mirali was so frightened, first to be in the presence of the Shark God, and then to be asked to call him her servant, that she had to try the word several times before she could make it come clearly out of her mouth. The Shark God said, "Now, if you wish it, we will go down to the sea and be married. But I promise that I will bear no malice, no vengefulness, against your village or this island if you do not care to marry me. Have no fear, then, but tell me your true desire, Mirali."

The market folk were going about their own business, buying and selling, and more chatting than either. Only a few of them looked toward Mirali where she stood talking with the handsome singer; fewer seemed to take any interest in what the two might be saying to each other. Mirali took heart from this and said, more firmly, "I do wish to marry you, dear *jalak*—I mean, my *olohe*—but how can I live with you under the sea? I do not think I would even be able to hold my breath through the wedding, unless it was a very short ceremony."

Then the Shark God laughed aloud, which he had truly never done in all his long life, and the sound was so full and so joyous that flowers fell from the trees and, unbidden, wove themselves into Mirali's hair, and into a wreath around her neck. The waves of the sea echoed his laughter, and the Shark God lifted Mirali in his arms and raced down to the shore, where sharks and dolphins, tuna and black marlin and barracuda, and whole schools of shimmering wrasse and clownfish and angelfish that swim as one had crowded into the lagoon together, until the water itself turned golden as the morning and green as sunset. The great deepwater octopus, whom no one ever sees except the sperm whale, came also; and it has been said—by people who were not present, nor even born then—that there were mermaids and merrows as well, and even the terrible Paikea, vast as an island, the Master of All Sea Monsters, though he prudently stayed far outside the reef. And all these were there for the wedding of Mirali and the Shark God.

The Shark God lifted Mirali high above his head—she was startled, but no longer frightened—and he spoke out, first in the language of Mirali's people, so that she would understand, and then in the tongue known by everything that swims in every sea and every river. "This is Mirali, whom I take now to wife, and whom you will love and protect from this day forth, and honor as you do me, and as you will honor our children, and their children, always." And the sound that came up from the waters in answer is not a sound that can be told.

In time, when the lagoon was at last empty again, and when husband and wife had sworn and proved their love in the shadows of the mangroves, she said to him, very quietly, "Beloved, my own *olohe,* now that we are wed, shall I ever see you again? For I may be only an ignorant island woman, but I know what too often comes of marriages between gods and mortals. Your children will have been born—I can feel this already—by the time you come again for your tribute. I will nurse them, and bring them up to respect their lineage, as is right...but meanwhile you will swim far away, and perhaps father others, and forget us, as is also your right. You are a god, and gods do not raise families. I am not such a fool that I do not know this."

But the Shark God put his finger under Mirali's chin, lifting her face to his and saying, "My wife, I could no more forget that you *are* my wife than forget what I am. Understand that we may not live together on your island, as others do, for my life is in the sea, and of the sea, and this form that you hold in your arms is but a shadow, little more than a dream, compared to my true self. Yet I will come to you every year, without fail, when my tribute is due—every year, here, where we lie together. Remember, Mirali."

Then he closed his eyes, which were black, as all sharks' eyes are, and fell asleep in her arms, and there is no woman who can say what Mirali felt, lying there under the mangroves with her own eyes wide in the moonlight.

When morning came, she walked back to her parents' house alone.

In time it became plain that Mirali was with child, but no one challenged or mocked her to her face, for she was much loved in the village, and her family greatly esteemed. Yet even so it was considered a misfortune by most, and a disgrace by some, as is not the case on certain other islands. If the talk was not public, it was night talk, talk around the cooking fire, talk at the stream over the slapping of wash on stone. Mirali was perfectly aware of this.

She carried herself well and proudly, and it was agreed, even by those who murmured ill of her, that she looked more beautiful every day, even as her belly swelled out like the fishermen's sails. But she shocked the midwife, who was concerned for her narrow hips, and for the chance of twins, by insisting on going off by herself to give birth. Her mother and father were likewise troubled; and the old priest himself took a hand, arguing powerfully that the birth should take place in the very temple of the Shark God. Such a thing had never been allowed, or even considered, but the old priest had his own suspicions about Mirali's unknown lover.

Mirali smiled and nodded respectfully to anyone who had anything to say about the matter, as was always her way. But on the night when her time came she went to the lagoon where she had been wed, as she knew that she must; and in the gentle breath of its shallows her children were born without undue difficulty. For they were indeed twins, a boy and a girl.

Mirali named the boy Keawe, after her father, and the girl Kokinja, which means *born in moonlight*. And as she looked fondly upon the two tiny, noisy, hungry creatures she and the Shark God had made together, she remembered his last words to her and smiled.

Keawe and Kokinja grew up the pets of their family, being not only beautiful but strong and quick and naturally kindly. This was a remarkable thing, considering the barely veiled scorn with which most of the other village children viewed them, taking their cue from the remarks passed between their parents. On the other hand, while there was notice taken of the very slight bluish tinge to Keawe's skin, and the fact that Kokinja's perfect teeth curved just the least bit inward, nothing was ever said concerning these particular traits.

They both swam before they could walk properly; and the creatures of the sea guarded them closely, as they had sworn. More than once little Keawe, who at two and three years regarded the waves and tides as his own servants, was brought safely back to shore clinging to the tail of a dolphin, the flipper of a seal, or even the dorsal fin of a reef shark. Kokinja had an octopus as her favorite playmate, and would fall as trustingly asleep wrapped in its eight arms as in those of her mother. And Mirali herself learned to put her faith in the wildest sea as completely as did her children. That was the gift of her husband.

Her greatest joy lay in seeing them grow into his image (though she always thought that Keawe resembled her father more than his own), and come to their full strength and beauty in a kind of innocence that kept them free of any vanity. Being twins, they understood each other in a wordless way that even Mirali could not share. This pleased her, for she thought, watching them playing silently together, *they will still have one another when I am gone.*

The Shark God saw the children when he came every year for his tribute, but only while they were asleep. In human form he would stand silently between their floor mats, studying them out of his black, expressionless eyes for a long time, before he finally turned away. Once he said quietly to Mirali, "It is good that I see them no more often than this. A good thing." Another time she heard him murmur to himself, "*Simpler for sharks...*"

As for Mirali herself, the love of the Shark God warded off the cruelty of the passing years, so that she continued to appear little older than her own children. They teased her about this, saying that she embarrassed them, but they were proud, and likewise aware that their mother remained attractive to the men of the village. A number of those came shyly courting, but all were turned away with such civility that they hardly knew they had been rejected; and certainly not by a married woman who saw her husband only once in a twelvemonth.

When Keawe and Kokinja were little younger than she had been when she heard a youth singing in the marketplace, she called them from the lagoon, where they spent most of their playtime, and told them simply, "Your father is the Shark God himself. It is time you knew this."

In all the years that she had imagined this moment, she had guessed—so she thought—every possible reaction that her children might have to these words. Wonder...awe...pride...fear (there are many tales of gods eating their children)...even laughing disbelief—she was long prepared for each of these. But it had never occurred to her that both Keawe and Kokinja might be immediately furious at their father for—as they saw it—abandoning his family and graciously condescending to spare a glance over them while passing through the lagoon to gobble his annual goat. Keawe shouted into the wind, "I would rather the lowest palm-wine drunkard on the island had sired us than this...this *god* who cannot be bothered with his wife and children but once a year. Yes, I would prefer that by far!"

"That one day has always lighted my way to the next," his mother said quietly. She turned to Kokinja. "And as for you, child—"

But Kokinja interrupted her, saying firmly, "The Shark God may have a daughter, but I have no more father today than I had yesterday. But if I *am* the Shark God's daughter, then I will set out tomorrow and swim the sea until I find him. And when I find him, I will ask questions—oh, indeed, I will ask him questions. And he *will* answer me." She tossed her black hair, which was the image of Mirali's hair, as her eyes were those of her father's people. Mirali's own eyes filled with tears as she looked at her nearly grown daughter, remembering a small girl stamping one tiny foot and shouting, "Yes, I will! Yes, I will!" *Oh, there is this much truth in what they say,* she thought to her husband. *You have truly no idea what you have sired.*

In the morning, as she had sworn, Kokinja kissed Mirali and Keawe farewell and set forth into the sea to find the Shark God. Her brother, *being her brother,* was astonished to realize that she meant to keep her vow, and actually begged her to reconsider, when he was not ordering her to do so. But Mirali knew that Kokinja was as much at home in the deep as anything with gills and a tail; and she further knew that no harm would come to Kokinja from any sea creature, because of their promise on her own wedding day. So she said nothing to her daughter, except to remind her, "If any creature can tell you exactly where the Shark God will be at any given moment, it will be the great Paikea, who came to our wedding. Go well, then, and keep warm."

Kokinja had swum out many a time beyond the curving coral reef that had created the lagoon a thousand or more years before, and she had no more fear of the open sea than of the stream where she had drawn water all her life. But this time, when she paused among the little scarlet-and-black fish that swarmed about a gap in the reef, and turned to see her brother Keawe waving after her, then a hand seemed to close on her heart, and she could not see anything clearly for a while. All the same, the moment her vision cleared, she waved once to Keawe and plunged on past the reef out to sea. The next time she looked back, both reef and island were long lost to her sight.

Now it must be understood that Kokinja did not swim as humans do, being who she was. From her first day splashing in the shallows of the lagoon, she had truly swum like a fish, or perhaps a dolphin. Swimming in this manner she outsped sailfish, marlin, tunny and tuna alike; even had the barracuda not been bound by his oath to the Shark God, he could never have come within snapping distance of the Shark God's daughter. Only the seagull and the great white wandering albatross, borne on the wind, kept even with the small figure far below, utterly alone between horizon and horizon, racing on and on under the darkening sky.

The favor of the waters applied to Kokinja in other ways. The fish themselves always seemed to know when she grew hungry, for then schools of salmon or mackerel would materialize out of the depths to accompany her, and she would express proper gratitude and devour one or another as she swam, as a shark would do. When she tired, she either curled up in a slow-rocking swell and slept, like a seal, or clung to the first sea turtle she encountered and drowsed peacefully on its shell—the leatherbacks were the most comfortable—while it courteously paddled along on the surface, so that she could breathe. Should she arrive at an island, she would haul out on the beach—again, like a seal—and sleep fully for a day; then bathe as she might, and be on her way once more.

Only a storm could overtake her, and those did frighten her at first, striking from the east or the north to tear fiercely at the sea. Not being a fish herself, she could not stay below the vast waves that played with her, Shark God's daughter or no, tossing her back and forth as an orca will toss its prey, then suddenly dropping out from under her, so that she floundered in their hollows, choking and gasping desperately, aware as she so rarely was of her own human weakness and fragility. But she was determined that she would not die without letting her father know what she thought of him; and by and by she learned to laugh at the lightning overhead, even when it struck the water on every side of her, as though *something* knew she was near and alone. She would laugh, and she would call out, not caring that her voice was lost in wind and thunder, "Missed me again—so sorry, you missed me again!" For if she was the Shark God's daughter, who could swim the sea, she was Mirali's stubborn little girl too.

Keawe, Mirali's son, was of a different nature than his sister. While he shared her anger at the Shark God's neglect, he simply decided to go on living as though he had no father, which was, after all, what he had always believed. And while he feared for Kokinja in the deep sea, and sometimes yearned to follow her, he was even more concerned about their mother. Like most grown children, he believed, despite the evidence of his eyes, that Mirali would dwindle away, starve, pine and die should both he and Kokinja be gone. Therefore he stayed at home and apprenticed himself to Uhila, the master builder of outrigger canoes, telling his mother that he would build the finest boat ever made, and in it he would one day bring Kokinja home. Mirali smiled gently and said nothing.

Uhila was known as a hard, impatient master, but Keawe studied well and swiftly learned everything the old man could teach him, which was not merely about the choosing of woods, nor about the weaving of all manner of sails and ropes, nor about the designing of different boats for different uses; nor how to warp the bamboo float, the *ama,* just so, and bind the long spars, the *iaka,* so that the connection to the hull would hold even in the worst storms. Uhila taught him, more importantly, the understanding of wood, and of water, and of the ancient relationship between them: half alliance, half war. At the end of Keawe's apprenticeship, gruff Uhila blessed him and gave him his own set of tools, which he had never done before in the memory of even the oldest villagers.

But he said also to the boy, "You do not love the boats as I do, for their own sake, for the joy of the making. I could tell that the first day you came to me. You are bound by a purpose—you need a certain boat, and in order to achieve it you needed to achieve every other boat. Tell me, have I spoken truly?"

Then Keawe bowed his head and answered, "I never meant to deceive you, wise Uhila. But my sister is far away, gone farther than an ordinary sailing canoe could find her, and it was on me to build the one boat that could bring her back. For that I needed all your knowledge, and all your wisdom. Forgive me if I have done wrong."

But Uhila looked out at the lagoon, where a new sailing canoe, more beautiful and splendid than any other in the harbor danced like a butterfly at anchor, and he said, "It is too big for any one person to paddle, too big to sail. What will you do for a crew?"

"He will have a crew," a calm voice answered. Both men turned to see Mirali smiling at them. She said to Keawe, "You will not want anyone else. You know that."

And Keawe did know, which was why he had never considered setting out with a crew at all. So he said only, "There is a comfortable seat near the bow for you, and you will be our lookout as you paddle. But I must sit in the rear and take charge of the tiller and the sails."

"For now," replied Mirali gravely, and she winked just a little at Uhila, who was deeply shocked by the notion of a woman steering any boat at all, let alone winking at him.

So Keawe and his mother went searching for Kokinja, and thus—though neither of them spoke of it—for the Shark God. They were, as they had been from Keawe's birth, pleasant company for one another: Keawe often sang the songs Mirali had taught him and his sister as children, and she herself would in turn tell old tales from older times, when all the gods were young, and all was possible. At other times, with a following sea and the handsome yellow sail up, they gave the canoe its head and sat in perfectly companionable silence, thinking thoughts that neither of them ever asked about. When they were hungry, Keawe plunged into the sea and returned swiftly with as much fish as they could eat; when it rained, although they had brought more water than food with them, still they caught the rain in the sail, since one can never have too much fresh water at sea. They slept by turns, warmly, guiding themselves by the stars and the turning of the earth, in the manner of birds, though their only real concern was to keep on straight toward the sunset, as Kokinja had done.

At times, watching his mother regard a couple of flying fish barely missing the sail, or turn her head to laugh at the dolphins accompanying the boat, with her still-black hair blowing across her cheek, Keawe would think, *god or no god, my father was a fool.* But unlike Kokinja, he thought it in pity more than anger. And if a shark should escort them for a little, cruising lazily along with the boat, he would joke with it in his mind—*Are you my aunt? Are you my cousin?*—for he had always had more humor than his sister. Once, when a great blue mako traveled with them for a full day, dawn to dark, now and then circling or sounding, but always near, rolling one black eye back to study them, he whispered, "Father? Is it you?" But it was only once, and the mako vanished at sunset anyway.

On her journey Kokinja met no one who could—or would—tell her where the Shark God might be found. She asked every shark she came upon, sensibly enough; but sharks are a close-mouthed lot, and not one hammerhead, not one whitetip, not one mako or tiger or reef shark ever offered her so much as a hint as to her father's whereabouts. Manta rays and sawfishes were more forthcoming; but mantas, while beautiful, are extremely stupid, and taking a sawfish's advice is always risky: ugly as they know themselves to be, they will say anything to appear wise. As for cod, they travel in great schools and shoals, and think as one, so that to ask a single cod a question is to receive an answer—right or wrong—from a thousand, ten thousand, a hundred thousand. Kokinja found this unnerving.

So she swam on, day after day: a little weary, a little lonely, a good deal older, but as determined as ever not to turn back without confronting the Shark God and demanding the truth of him. *Who are you, that my mother should have accepted you under such terms as you offered? How could you yourself have endured to see her—to see us, your children—only once in every year? Is that a god's idea of love?*

One night, the water having turned warm and silkily calm, she was drifting in a half-dream of her own lagoon when she woke with a soft bump against what she at first thought an island. It loomed darkly over her, hiding the moon and half the stars, yet she saw no trees, even in silhouette, nor did she hear any birds or smell any sort of vegetation. What she did smell awakened her completely and set her scrambling backward into deeper water, like a frightened crab. It was a fish smell, in part, cold and clear and salty, but there was something of the reptilian about it: equally cold, but dry as well, for all that it emanated from an island—or *not* an island?—sitting in the middle of the sea. It was not a smell she knew, and yet somehow she felt that she should.

Kokinja went on backing into moonlight, which calmed her, and had just begun to swim cautiously around the island when it moved. Eyes as big and yellow-white as lighthouse lamps turned slowly to keep her in view, while an enormous, seemingly formless body lost any resemblance to an island, heaving itself over to reveal limbs ending in grotesquely huge claws. Centered between the foremost of them were two moon-white pincers, big enough, clearly, to twist the skull off a sperm whale. The sound it uttered was too low for Kokinja to catch, but she felt it plainly in the sea.

She knew what it was then, and could only hope that her voice would reach whatever the creature used for ears. She said, "Great Paikea, I am Kokinja. I am very small, and I mean no one any harm. Please, can you tell me where I may find my father, the Shark God?"

The lighthouse eyes truly terrified her then, swooping toward her from different directions, with no head or face behind them. She realized that they were on long whiplike stalks, and that Paikea's diamond-shaped head was sheltered under a scarlet carapace studded with scores of small, sharp spines. Kokinja was too frightened to move, which was as well, for Paikea spoke to her in the water, saying against her skin, "Be still, child, that I may see you more clearly, and not bite you in two by mistake. It has happened so." Then Kokinja, who had already swum half an ocean, thought that she might never again move from where she was.

She waited a long time for the great creature to speak again, but was not at all prepared for Paikea's words when they did come. "I could direct you to your father—I could even take you to him—but I will not. You are not ready."

When Kokinja could at last find words to respond, she demanded, "Not *ready*? Who are *you* to say that I am not ready to see my own father?" Mirali and Keawe would have known her best then: she was Kokinja, and anything she feared she challenged.

"What your father has to say to you, you are not yet prepared to hear," came the voice in the sea. "Stay with me a little, Shark God's daughter. I am not what your father is, but I may perhaps be a better teacher for you." When Kokinja hesitated, and clearly seemed about to refuse, Paikea continued, "Child, you have nowhere else to go but home—and I think you are not ready for that, either. Climb on my back now, and come with me." Even for Kokinja, that was an order.

Paikea took her—once she had managed the arduous and tiring journey from claw to leg to mountainside shoulder to a deep, hard hollow in the carapace that might have been made for a frightened rider—to an island (a real one this time, though well smaller than her own) bright with birds and flowers and wild fruit. When the birds' cries and chatter ceased for a moment, she could hear the softer swirl of running water farther inland, and the occasional thump of a falling coconut from one of the palms that dotted the beach. It was a lonely island, being completely uninhabited, but very beautiful.

There Paikea left her to swim ashore, saying only, "Rest," and nothing more. She did as she was bidden, sleeping under bamboo trees, waking to eat and drink, and sleeping again, dreaming always of her mother and brother at home. Each dream seemed more real than the one before, bringing Mirali and Keawe closer to her, until she wept in her sleep, struggling to keep from waking. Yet when Paikea came again, after three days, she demanded audaciously, "What wisdom do you think you have for me that I would not hear if it came from my father? I have no fear of anything he may say to me."

"You have very little fear at all, or you would not be here," Paikea answered her. "You feared me when we first met, I think—but two nights' good sleep, and you are plainly past *that*." Kokinja thought she discerned something like a chuckle in the wavelets lapping against her feet where she sat, but she could not be sure. Paikea said, "But courage and attention are not the same thing. Listening is not the same as hearing. You may be sure I am correct in this, because I know everything."

It was said in such a matter-of-fact manner that Kokinja had to battle back the impulse to laugh. She said, with all the innocence she could muster, "I thought it was my father who was supposed to know everything."

"Oh, no," Paikea replied quite seriously. "The only thing the Shark God has ever known is how to be the Shark God. It is the one thing he is supposed to be—not a teacher, not a wise master, and certainly not a father or a husband. But they *will* take human form, the gods will, and that is where the trouble begins, because they none of them know how to be human—how can they, tell me that?" The eye-stalks abruptly plunged closer, as though Paikea were truly waiting for an enlightening answer. "I have always been grateful for my ugliness; for the fact that there is no way for me to disguise it, no temptation to hide in a more comely shape and pretend to believe that I am what I pretend. Because I am certain I would do just that, if I could. It is lonely sometimes, knowing everything."

Again Kokinja felt the need to laugh; but this time it was somehow easier not to, because Paikea was obviously anxious for her to understand his words. But she fought off sympathy as well, and confronted Paikea defiantly, saying, "You really think that we should never have been born, don't you, my brother and I?"

Paikea appeared to be neither surprised nor offended by her bold words. "Child, what I know is important—what I *think* is not important at all. It is the same way with the Shark God." Kokinja opened her mouth to respond hotly, but the great crab-monster moved slightly closer to shore, and she closed it again. Paikea said, "He is fully aware that he should never have taken a human wife, created a human family in the human world. And he knows also, as he was never meant to know, that when your mother dies—as she will—when you and your brother in time die, his heart will break. No god is supposed to know such a thing; they are simply not equipped to deal with it. Do you understand me, brave and foolish girl?"

Kokinja was not sure whether she understood, and less sure of whether she even wanted to understand. She said slowly, "So he thinks that he should never see us, to preserve his poor heart from injury and grief? Perhaps he thinks it will be for our own good? Parents always say that, don't they, when they really mean for their own convenience. Isn't that what they say, wise Paikea?"

"I never knew my parents," Paikea answered thoughtfully.

"And *I* have never known *him*," snapped Kokinja. "Once a year he comes to lie with his wife, to snap up his goat, to look at his children as we sleep. But what is that to a wife who longs for her husband, to children aching for a real father? God or no god, the very least he could have done would have been to tell us himself what he was, and not leave us to imagine him, telling ourselves stories about why he left our beautiful mother...why he didn't want to be with us..." She realized, to her horror, that she was very close to tears, and gulped them back as she had done with laughter. "I will never forgive him," she said. "Never."

"Then why have you swum the sea to find him?" asked Paikea. It snapped its horrid pale claws as a human will snap his fingers, waiting for her answer with real interest.

"To *tell* him that I will never forgive him," Kokinja answered. "So there is something even Paikea did not know." She felt triumphant, and stopped wanting to cry.

"You are still not ready," said Paikea, and was abruptly gone, slipping beneath the waves without a ripple, as though its vast body had never been there. It did not return for another three days, during which Kokinja explored the island, sampling every fruit that grew there, fishing as she had done at sea when she desired a change of diet, sleeping when she chose, and continuing to nurse her sullen anger at her father.

Finally, she sat on the beach with her feet in the water, and she called out, "Great Paikea, of your kindness, come to me, I have a riddle to ask you." None of the sea creatures among whom she had been raised could ever resist a riddle, and she did not see why it should be any different even for the Master of All Sea Monsters.

Presently she heard the mighty creature's voice saying, "You yourself are as much a riddle to me as any you may ask." Paikea surfaced close enough to shore that Kokinja felt she could have reached out and touched its head. It said, "Here I am, Shark God's daughter."

"This is my riddle," Kokinja said. "If you cannot answer it, you who know everything, will you take me to my father?"

"A most human question," Paikea replied, "since the riddle has nothing to do with the reward. Ask, then."

Kokinja took a long breath. "Why would any god ever choose to sire sons and daughters with a mortal woman? Half-divine, yet we die—half-supreme, yet we are vulnerable, breakable—half-perfect, still we are forever crippled by our human hearts. What cruelty could compel an immortal to desire such unnatural children?"

Paikea considered. It closed its huge, glowing eyes on their stalks; it waved its claws this way and that; it even rumbled thoughtfully to itself, as a man might when pondering serious matters. Finally Paikea's eyes opened, and there was a curious amusement in them as it regarded Kokinja. She did not notice this, being young.

"Well riddled," Paikea said. "For I know the answer, but have not the right to tell you. So I cannot." The great claws snapped shut on the last word, with a grinding clash that hinted to Kokinja how fearsome an enemy Paikea could be.

"Then you will keep your word?" Kokinja asked eagerly. "You *will* take me where my father is?"

"I always keep my word," answered Paikea, and sank from sight. Kokinja never saw him again.

But that evening, as the red sun was melting into the green horizon, and the birds and fish that feed at night were setting about their business, a young man came walking out of the water toward Kokinja. She knew him immediately, and her first instinct was to embrace him. Then her heart surged fiercely within her, and she leaped to her feet, challenging him. "So! At last you have found the courage to face your own daughter. Look well, sea-king, for I have no fear of you, and no worship." She started to add, "Nor any love, either," but that last caught in her throat, just as had happened to her mother Mirali when she scolded a singing boy for invading her dreams.

The Shark God spoke the words for her. "You have no reason in the world to love me." His voice was deep and quiet, and woke strange echoes in her memory of such a voice overheard in candlelight in the sweet, safe place between sleep and waking. "Except, perhaps, that I have loved your mother from the moment I first saw her. That will have to serve as my defense, and my apology as well. I have no other."

"And a pitiful enough defense it is," Kokinja jeered. "I asked Paikea why a god should ever choose to father a child with a mortal, and he would not answer me. Will you?" The Shark God did not reply at once, and Kokinja stormed on. "My mother never once complained of your neglect, but I am not my mother. I am grateful for my half-heritage only in that it enabled me to seek you out, hide as you would. For the rest, I spit on my ancestry, my birthright, and all else that connects me to you. I just came to tell you that."

Having said this, she began to weep, which infuriated her even more, so that she actually clenched her fists and pounded the Shark God's shoulders while he stood still, making no response. Shamed as she was, she ceased both activities soon enough, and stood silently facing her father with her head high and her wet eyes defiant. For his part, the Shark God studied her out of his own unreadable black eyes, moving neither to caress nor to punish her, but only—as it seemed to Kokinja—to understand the whole of what she was. And to do her justice, she stared straight back, trying to do the same.

When the Shark God spoke at last, Mirali herself might not have known his voice, for the weariness and grief in it. He said, "Believe as you will, but until your mother came into my life, I had no smallest desire for children, neither with beings like myself, nor with any mortal, however beautiful she might be. We do find humans dangerously appealing, all of us, as is well-known—perhaps precisely because of their short lives and the delicacy of their construction—and many a deity, unable to resist such haunting vulnerability, has scattered half-divine descendants all over your world. Not I; there was nothing I could imagine more contemptible than deliberately to create such a child, one who would share fully in neither inheritance, and live to curse me for it, as you have done." Kokinja flushed and looked down, but offered no contrition for anything she had said. The Shark God said mildly, "As well you made no apology. Your mother has never once lied to me, nor should you."

"Why should I ever apologize to you?" Kokinja flared up again. "If you had no wish for children, what are my brother and I doing here?" Tears threatened again, but she bit them savagely back. "You are a god—you could always have kept us from being born! *Why are we here?*"

To her horror, her legs gave way under her then, and she sank to her knees, still not weeping, but finding herself shamefully weak with rage and confusion. Yet when she looked up, the Shark God was kneeling beside her, for all the world like a playmate helping her to build a sand castle. It was she who stared at him without expression now, while he regarded her with the terrifying pity that belongs to the gods alone. Kokinja could not bear it for more than a moment; but every time she turned her face away, her father gently turned her toward him once more. He said, "Daughter of mine, do you know how old I am?"

Kokinja shook her head silently. The Shark God said, "I cannot tell you in years, because there were no such things at my beginning. Time was very new then, and Those who were already here had not yet decided whether this was...*suitable*, can you understand me, dear one?" The last two words, heard for the first time in her life, caused Kokinja to shiver like a small animal in the rain. Her father did not appear to notice.

"I had no parents, and no childhood, such as you and your brother have had—I simply *was*, and always had been, beyond all memory, even my own. All true enough, to my knowledge—and then a leaky outrigger canoe bearing a sleeping brown girl drifted across my endless life, and I, who can never change...I changed. Do you hear what I am telling you, daughter of that girl, daughter who hates me?"

The Shark God's voice was soft and uncertain. "I told your mother that it was good that I saw her and you and Keawe only once in a year—that if I allowed myself that wonder even a day more often I might lose myself in you, and never be able to find myself again, nor ever wish to. Was that cowardly of me, Kokinja? Perhaps so, quite likely unforgivably so." It was he who looked away now, rising and turning to face the darkening scarlet sea. He said, after a time, "But one day—one day that *will* come—when you find yourself loving as helplessly, and as certainly wrongly, as I, loving against all you know, against all you are...remember me then."

To this Kokinja made no response; but by and by she rose herself and stood silently beside her father, watching the first stars waken, one with each heartbeat of hers. She could not have said when she at last took his hand.

"I cannot stay," she said. "It is a long way home, and seems longer now."

The Shark God touched her hair lightly. "You will go back more swiftly than you arrived, I promise you that. But if you could remain with me a little time..." He left the words unfinished.

"A little time," Kokinja agreed. "But in return..." She hesitated, and her father did not press her, but only waited for her to continue. She said presently, "I know that my mother never wished to see you in your true form, and for herself she was undoubtedly right. But I...I am not my mother." She had no courage to say more than that.

The Shark God did not reply for some while, and when he did his tone was deep and somber. "Even if I granted it, even if you could bear it, you could never see all of what I am. Human eyes cannot"—he struggled for the exact word—"they do not *bend* in the right way. It was meant as a kindness, I think, just as was the human gift of forgetfulness. You have no idea how the gods envy you that, the forgetting."

"Even so," Kokinja insisted. "Even so, I would not be afraid. If you do not know *that* by now..."

"Well, we will see," answered the Shark God, exactly as all human parents have replied to importunate children at one time or another. And with that, even Kokinja knew to content herself.

In the morning, she plunged into the waves to seek her breakfast, as did her father on the other side of the island. She never knew where he slept—or if he slept at all—but he returned in time to see her emerging from the water with a fish in her mouth and another in her hand. She tore them both to pieces, like any shark, and finished the meal before noticing him. Abashed, she said earnestly, "When I am at home, I cook my food as my mother taught me—but in the sea..."

"Your mother always cooks dinner for me," the Shark God answered quietly. "We wait until you two are asleep, or away, and then she will come down to the water and call. It has been so from the first."

"Then she *has* seen you—"

"No. I take my tribute afterward, when I leave her, and she never follows then." The Shark God smiled and sighed at the same time, studying his daughter's puzzled face. He said, "What is between us is hard to explain, even to you. Especially to you."

The Shark God lifted his head to taste the morning air, which was cool and cloudless over water so still that Kokinja could hear a dolphin breathing too far away for her to see. He frowned slightly, saying, "Storm. Not now, but in three days' time. It will be hard."

Kokinja did not show her alarm. She said grimly, "I came here through storms. I survived those."

"Child," her father said, and it was the first time he had called her that, "you will be with me." But his eyes were troubled, and his voice strangely distant. For the rest of that day, while Kokinja roamed the island, dozed in the sun, and swam for no reason but pleasure, he hardly spoke, but continued watching the horizon, long after both sunset and moonset. When she woke the next morning, he was still pacing the shore, though she could see no change at all in the sky, but only in his face. Now and then he would strike a balled fist against his thigh and whisper to himself through tight pale lips. Kokinja, walking beside him and sharing his silence, could not help noticing how human he seemed in those moments—how mortal, and how mortally afraid. But she could not imagine the reason for it, not until she woke on the following day and felt the sand cold under her.

Since her arrival on the little island, the weather had been so clement that the sand she slept on remained perfectly warm through the night. Now its chill woke her well before dawn, and even in the darkness she could see the mist on the horizon, and the lightning beyond the mist. The sun, orange as the harvest moon, was never more than a sliver between the mounting thunderheads all day. The wind was from the northeast, and there was ice in it.

Kokinja stood alone on the shore, watching the first rain marching toward her across the waves. She had no longer any fear of storms, and was preparing to wait out the tempest in the water, rather than take refuge under the trees. But the Shark God came to her then and led her away to a small cave, where they sat together, listening to the rising wind. When she was hungry, he fished for her, saying, "They seek shelter too, like anyone else in such conditions— but they will come for me." When she became downhearted, he hummed nursery songs that she recalled Mirali singing to her and Keawe very long ago, far away on the other side of any storm. He even sang her oldest favorite, which began:

> When a raindrop leaves the sky,
> it turns and turns to say good-bye.
> "Good-bye, dear clouds, so far away,
> I'll come again another day...."

"Keawe never really liked that one," she said softly. "It made him sad. How do you know all our songs?"

"I listened," the Shark God said, and nothing more.

"I wish...I *wish*..." Kokinja's voice was almost lost in the pounding of the rain. She thought she heard her father answer, "I, too," but in that moment he was on his feet, striding out of the cave into the storm, as heedless of the weather as though it were flowers sluicing down his body, summer-morning breezes greeting his face. Kokinja hurried to keep up with him. The wind snatched the breath from her lungs, and knocked her down more than once, but she matched his pace to the shore, even so. It seemed to her that the tranquil island had come malevolently alive with the rain; that the vines slapping at her shoulders and entangling her ankles had not been there yesterday, nor had the harsh branches that caught at her hair. All the same, when he turned at the water's edge, she was beside him.

"*Mirali.*" He said the one word, and pointed out into the flying, whipping spindrift and the solid mass of sea-wrack being driven toward land by the howling grayness beyond. Kokinja strained her eyes and finally made out the tiny flicker that was not water, the broken chip of wood sometimes bobbing helplessly on its side, sometimes hurled forward or sideways from one comber crest to another. Staring through the rain, shaking with cold and fear, it took her a moment to realize that her father was gone. Taller than the wavetops, taller than any ship's masts, taller than the wind, she saw the deep blue dorsal and tail fins, so distant from each other, gliding toward the wreck, on which she could see no hint of life. Then she plunged into the sea—shockingly, almost alarmingly warm, by comparison with the air—and followed the Shark God.

It was the first and only glimpse she ever had of the thing her father was. As he had warned her, she never saw him fully: both her eyesight and the sea itself seemed too small to contain him. Her mind could take in a magnificent and terrible fish; her soul knew that that was the least part of what she was seeing; her body knew that it could bear no more than that smallest vision. The mark of his passage was a ripple of beaten silver across the wild water, and although the storm seethed and roared to left and right of her, she swam in his wake as effortlessly as he made the way for her. And whether he actually uttered it or not, she heard his fearful cry in her head, over and over—"*Mirali! Mirali!*"

The mast was in two pieces, the sail a yellow rag, the rudder split and the tiller broken off altogether. The Shark God regained the human form so swiftly that Kokinja was never entirely sure that she had truly seen what she knew she had seen, and the two of them righted the sailing canoe together. Keawe lay in the bottom of the boat, barely conscious, unable to speak, only to point over the side. There was no sign of Mirali.

"Stay with him," her father ordered Kokinja, and he sounded as a shark would have done, vanishing instantly into the darkness below the ruined keel. Kokinja crouched by Keawe, lifting his head to her lap and noticing a deep gash on his forehead and another on his cheekbone. "Tiller," he whispered. "Snapped...flew straight at me..." His right hand was clenched around some small object; when Kokinja pried it gently open—for he seemed unable to release it himself—she recognized a favorite bangle of their mother's. Keawe began to cry.

"Couldn't hold her...*couldn't hold*..." Kokinja could not hear a word, for the wind, but she read his eyes and she held him to her breast and rocked him, hardly noticing that she was weeping herself.

The Shark God was a long time finding his wife, but he brought her up in his arms at last, her eyes closed and her face as quiet as always. He placed her gently in the canoe with her children, brought the boat safely to shore, and bore Mirali's body to the cave where he had taken Kokinja for shelter. And while the storm still lashed the island, and his son and daughter sang the proper songs, he dug out a grave and buried her there, with no marker at her head, there being no need. "I will know," he said, "and you will know. And so will Paikea, who knows everything."

Then he mourned.

Kokinja ministered to her brother as she could, and they slept for a long time. When they woke, with the storm passed over and all the sky and sea looking like the first morning of the world, they walked the shore to study the sailing canoe that had been all Keawe's pride. After considering it from all sides, he said at last, "I can make it seaworthy again. Well enough to get us home, at least."

"Father can help," Kokinja said, realizing as she spoke that she had never said the word in that manner before. Keawe shook his head, looking away.

"I can do it myself," he said sharply. "I built it myself."

They did not see the Shark God for three days. When he finally emerged from Mirali's cave—as her children had already begun to call it—he called them to him, saying, "I will see you home, as soon as you will. But I will not come there again."

Keawe, already busy about his boat, looked up but said nothing. Kokinja asked, "Why? You have always been faithfully worshipped there—and it was our mother's home all her life."

The Shark God was slow to answer. "From the harbor to her house, from the market to the beach where the nets are mended, to my own temple, there is no place that does not speak to me of Mirali. Forgive me—I have not the strength to deal with those memories, and I never will."

Kokinja did not reply; but Keawe turned from his boat to face his father openly for the first time since his rescue from the storm. He said, clearly and strongly, "And so, once again, you make a liar out of our mother. As I knew you would."

Kokinja gasped audibly, and the Shark God took a step toward his son without speaking. Keawe said, "She defended you so fiercely, so proudly, when I told her that you were always a coward, god or no god. You abandoned a woman who loved you, a family that belonged to you—and now you will do the same with the island that depends on you for protection and loyalty, that has never failed you, done you no disservice, but only been foolish enough to keep its old bargain with you, and expect you to do the same. And this in our mother's name, because you lack the courage to confront the little handful of memories you two shared. You shame her!"

He never flinched from his father's advance, but stood his ground even when the Shark God loomed above him like a storm in mortal shape, his eyes no longer unreadable but alive with fury. For a moment Kokinja saw human and shark as one, flowing in and out of each other, blurring and bleeding together and separating again, in and out, until she became dazed with it and had to close her eyes. She only opened them again when she heard the Shark God's quiet, toneless voice, "We made fine children, my Mirali and I. It is my loss that I never knew them. My loss alone."

Without speaking further he turned toward the harbor, looking as young as he had on the day Mirali challenged him in the marketplace, but moving now almost like an old human man. He had gone some little way when Keawe spoke again, saying simply, "Not only yours."

The Shark God turned back to look long at his children once again. Keawe did not move, but Kokinja reached out her arms, whispering, "Come back." And the Shark God nodded, and went on to the sea.

THE BEST WORST MONSTER

I like monsters. My children liked monsters (they often asked for monster stories at bedtime). I also like dogs, and poets—one day I'll set that poem of Beppo the Beggar's to music—and of course I was raised on mad scientists at Saturday matinees. So here they are, the lot of them, an all-star assemblage recalled for one last farewell performance, as though I were still leaning against a bunk bed in a room cluttered with picture books and stuffed animals...

✻

From the tips of his twisted, spiky horns all the way down to his jagged claws, the monster was without any doubt the biggest, ugliest, most horrible creature ever made. Since his master had put him together out of spare parts lying around the house, some bits of him were power tools and old television sets, while other bits were made of plastic and wood and stone. His fiery eyes were streaked red and yellow, like the autumn moon, and even his ears and his hair had claws.

"There!" his master said proudly. "Aren't you a fine fellow?"

"Am I?" the monster asked. He had just seen himself in a mirror, and wasn't sure.

"You certainly are," said his master. Then he sent the monster off to stamp the post office flat, because the mailman never delivered any nice letters. This was a real pleasure for the monster, with all the mail flying in every direction, and boxed packages crunching like toast under his feet. It was even better the next day, when his master ordered him to use his great claws to pull the town's dance pavilion to pieces, just because no girl ever asked his master to dance with her. That was as much fun as a birthday party. He tore down the strings of bright colored lights, and chased the musicians away, and jumped up and down on the bandstand until all that remained was a lot of tiny splinters and a few small shreds of sheet music. The monster was sorry when there was nothing left to smash, because he would have loved to do it all over again.

That night though, while his master slept, the monster sat outside in the cold, clear air and noticed something that troubled him. He could see quite as well at night as in day, so it was easy for him to look down the rocky slope of his master's home and study the town curled up in the valley below. He could count every leaf and tile, every window and chimney. And he could see the small dark gaps where the post office and dance pavilion had stood. They were like two hollow eyes in a mask, staring back at him.

The monster didn't know much, being only two days old, but he knew that he didn't like how he was feeling. He wondered if there was something wrong with him.

Monsters are afraid of wondering, so when morning came he went to his master and said, "Something is happening to me. I don't know what it is, but it frightens me. Maybe you ought to order me to build something today—just for the change, just until this feeling goes away. I'm sure it will go away."

His master was horrified, and very angry too. "I can't *believe* this!" he screamed at the monster. "Are you growing a soul in that unspeakable patchwork body of yours? Well I'll take care of *that,* and right now!"

Whereupon he sprayed the monster from horns to claws to antenna-tipped tail with a nasty-smelling mixture called "SoulAway," which he had invented himself for just such occasions. After that he opened up the monster's intake valves and poured in gallons of another potion called "SoulBegone." Then he fed the monster an enormous pill that didn't have a name, and which stuck in the monster's throat. He had to climb up on a tall ladder and pound the monster on his back until it went down.

"There!" he said, "*That* should do it. A soul's no trouble to get rid of, if you catch it early."

"I still feel all funny," the monster mumbled.

But his master told him not to be a fool, and ordered him to go out and pull up the train tracks, because the whistle of the train was half a note sharp. "And while you're at it, smash up the bakery—I practically broke a tooth on a walnut in a cupcake yesterday. Go!"

From that morning on, no matter how hard the monster tried to please his master, things kept going wrong. Sometimes he actually found himself being kind, in a monsterish sort of way—like not trampling a home all the way flat, or making a lot of noise before he arrived, so people would have time to run away. Once he even ran away himself, to keep from being sent to squash a whole school where his master was never asked to come speak at graduation. But he couldn't stay away, because he got lonely. And that worried him even more, because he knew that wicked, soulless monsters were never *ever* supposed to feel lonely.

Then one evening, while the monster was watching the stars and wishing he were someone else, his master called for him. After giving him an extra-large dose of "SoulAway," his master smiled and ordered him to go into town and find a poet named Beppo the Beggar. When he found him, the monster was supposed to step on him, just as though he were a bakery or a post office.

"Why?"

"Because he made up a song about me, and I don't like it. Go and get him. Not his house, mind. *Him*."

So the monster trudged unhappily away to trample a poet.

He found Beppo the Beggar lying on the riverbank with his hands behind his head, watching the sky and making up a poem. Beppo's little dog, who was called Pumpernickel, was fast asleep by his side, covered by Beppo's ragged old coat.

Beppo's poem began like this:

> *"We fish together every night,*
> *My Uncle Moon and I.*
> *We bait our hooks with dreams,*
> *And throw them in the sky..."*

He looked over at Pumpernickel to see what his best friend thought of the poem so far, but the dog did not even open his eyes. Beppo sighed and chuckled. He tucked the coat closer around his pet, and continued:

> *"My Uncle Moon, he catches stars,*
> *All burning white and blue.*
> *But I keep angling for your heart—*

No other fish will do..."

It was only then that he looked up and saw the monster's foot poised high over him, hiding the night sky and all the stars.

Beppo did not leap up, screaming and begging for his life. Instead he turned to Pumpernickel and shook him gently awake, telling him, "Run away now, little one. Take care of yourself, and remember me."

The monster stood on one foot, not moving, not saying a word.

Pumpernickel got to his feet, looked at Beppo with his head tilted to one side, and then trotted off into the darkness. Beppo the Beggar lay down again, smiling cheerfully up at that huge foot ready to squash him like a bug. He asked politely, "Would you mind very much letting me finish my poem? I *think* there's only one more verse."

The monster nodded. Beppo closed his eyes and considered, tracing words in the air with his right forefinger. After a moment he went on:

> *"But if I caught you on my line,*
> *Or in my net below,*
> *No matter you're my one desire,*
> *I'd always let you go."*

He looked straight at the monster again, and said, "Not great for a last poem, but then I'm not exactly a great poet." He spread his arms out wide, beckoning the foot down. "It's a great riverbank, anyway," he said, and he laughed.

The monster's foot came down...

...not on Beppo the Beggar, but very slowly and gently on the ground next to him.

Neither of them said a word. But after a moment the monster turned and started back the way he had come, along the road and up the stony hill to his master's house. He stamped along as noisily as he could, and for the first time in his life he sang, making up his own music, louder and louder and louder, like a marching song:

> *"I don't know if I have a soul,*
> *I don't know if I WANT a soul—*

But whatever Beppo the Beggar has,
I want one of those!"

He was a really terrible singer.

His master heard him coming from a long way off, and he knew exactly what all that racket meant. He stayed just long enough to grab up some monster-making tools and his one good suit, and then he ran out the back door of his house before his monster even got there. And whatever became of him, nobody knows...

But everybody in town can tell you what became of his monster.

That very day the monster set about rebuilding everything he had ever smashed to pieces. When he was done with that, he built a house in town for himself, a very big house, with a back garden and a birdbath. After a time people began to ask him to come to dinner: he always went, and was careful not to eat too much or stay too long. He even learned to dance in the new pavilion...in a monsterish sort of way.

From time to time, though, he still felt lonely. On those nights he would sit on the hilltop where his master's house lay abandoned, and ask himself questions with no answers. "Do I have a soul? Do I only *think* I have a soul? Does it matter?"

And then—after waiting just the right amount of time, because that's what friends do—Beppo the Beggar would call up to him with a cheery hello. And Beppo's little dog, Pumpernickel, would jump up on his huge lap to lick his frightful face. And the monster would smile, with his fangs and his forked tongue and his puzzled, happy heart, and he'd pick Beppo and Pumpernickel up and carry them back down into town on his shoulders, singing dreadfully all the way.

WHAT TUNE THE ENCHANTRESS PLAYS

It's no secret that my greatest pleasure—and so my greatest strength—in writing fiction is to create character, most often through dialog and speech patterns. Structure and pacing, on the other hand, often force me through repeated time-consuming drafts, until I finally understand what a story is really about, and how it wants to be told and has to be told. It's never the story's fault; it's always right there, and I just can't see it. "What Tune the Enchantress Plays" is set in what I've come to call my Innkeeper's World, already the home of ten other stories and a novel; only it takes place in a corner of that world that I didn't know at all, and had to discover as I went on. But that, of course, is the scary, wonderful part of doing what storytellers do.

✻

Ah, *there* you are. I was beginning to wonder.

No, no. Come in, do—it's your lair, after all. Tidy, too, for a demon. I'd do something about those bones, myself, and whatever *that* is, over in the corner, that smelly wet thing. But each to his taste, I say; you probably wouldn't think much of my notions of décor, either. Gods know, my mother doesn't.

Ah-ah-*ah*, no bolting—don't embarrass us both on such a pleasant evening. Sit down, and let's chat a little, you and I, like the old friends we practically are. Well, we might as well be, don't you think, as long as it's taken me to track you here. You're very good, you know. *Sit.*

Now.

You're good, as I said, but as shortsighted with it as all your kind. Whatever possessed you to come to Kalagira, when you could have been happily ravaging Coraic, or the fat, juicy villages around Chun? Didn't you know about Kalagira?

Forgive me—that was most rude, and foolish as well. Why expect a demon to be aware of one small southern province, tucked away beyond the Pass of Soshali, when so few humans are? Let me enlighten you, then. Kalagira is a country of *majkes:* witches like my grandmother, sorceresses like my mother...and the occasional enchantress, like me. There are certain differences worth note, but we will come to that. There is time.

There is time, until moonset.

At moonset I will sing to you, as I sang you here—oh, yes, that was my song you followed, with its whispers of blood and rapine, its bait of helpless victims, so close. At moonset I will sing another song, and you will go wherever it is that such as you go, when ended in this world.

Meanwhile, we will talk, because it amuses me, because it passes the time, and for one other reason. I shall tell you of my first encounter with a creature like you. Perhaps it will amuse you in your turn.

Well, it was not quite like you, really, that first demon of mine. If *demon* is what it truly was—it was larger, and rather more...majestic, excuse me, and definitely more powerful—but I run ahead of myself. Bide, Breya Drom, bide. The moon is still high.

Well, then.

Not all Kalagira women are witches or sorceresses—far from it—but there has been no male with such power born here in the entire history of the province, as far back as the old tales tell us, or the chronicles go. What is known, and known well, is that if the men of Kalagira cannot themselves work magic, still they are its *carriers,* if you understand me. A Kalagira *maj* who marries a local man will invariably find the knack—as we call it—making itself felt in all of her girl children; while one who weds Outside will see it come to an end in her own line, never to reappear. For that reason, Kalagira magic stays in Kalagira. In the oldest and most powerful families, it may have run true for five, six, seven generations, or even more. This can lead to old rivalries at times, old grudges.

Do you have males and females, your kind? I've never been certain. Well out of it, if you don't, but it's the sort of thing I wonder about in the early mornings, when I'm trying not to wake.

Do you have parents? Do you have children?

No?

Then attend, please, for these details matter. My mother's name is Willalou.

In her time she was the most powerful sorceress in Kalagira, though today she spends her time gardening and translating the later poems of Lenji. My father is Dunreath, the potter. They live together in the house he built for my mother. She was powerful enough to have brought it into being with a chant and a gesture—a single scribing in the air—but he would never allow it, and she was wise enough to leave such matters entirely to him. You may not know this, being a demon, but it is not easy, in Kalagira or anywhere else, for a proud, skilled man to be with a woman like my mother. But they loved each other, always, and they have lived well together.

One evening, when I was perhaps five years old, my father brought home a small boy.

He brought him home under his arm, squirming and snarling like a trapped *shukri*. I remember as though it were yesterday: the fire smoking, and the smell of wet wool; the rain—little more than a mist—sighing against the windows, and my mother rising from her loom, saying, "Dunreath?" And me, asking loudly—quite loudly, I fear—"What is *that*? Papa, what is *that*?"

"It's not a *that*, dear," my father answered wearily. "It's a he—a very dirty he—but I can't tell you his name, because he won't say." He looked at my mother and raised his bushy eyebrows slightly. I loved his eyebrows.

"His name is Lathro," my mother said. "Lathro Baraquil." The boy's eyes widened, but his mouth remained almost invisible, so tightly was it shut. "He lives with his Aunt Yunieska and her son Pashak, and he needs a bath. He needs two baths." My father put the boy down; my mother held out her hand, and he went with her, mutely still, but obediently. My mother had that effect on people.

I heard them talking that night, and was surprised when my father asked, "How did you know he was Yunieska's boy?" Didn't he realize that Mother was magic, and knew everything?

"He's her nephew," my mother answered. "I've seen him in the street now and then, filthier even than this sometimes. That woman has no business with a child, none."

"Cleans up well enough," my father said. "I had no idea he's got freckles."

My mother laughed softly. "He's very brave, too. He *looked* at me when I put him in the tub—Dunreath, I don't think he's ever had a bath in his life, not an all-over one. He must have thought I was going to drown him, but he gave me that *look,* and then he stepped into the tub like a prince. There's definitely somebody under all that dirt."

"I wasn't planning on keeping him," my father said quickly. "I just thought maybe you could clean him up a little, find him something to eat, and shoo him off home. I'll clean the tub."

My mother did not answer for a time, and then not directly. She said only, "I'm going to speak to Yunieska the next time I see her." The way she said *speak* made me giggle, but it made me shiver a little as well.

That was how Lathro came.

He stayed two days, that first time, hardly saying a word he didn't have to, but behaving with a kind of silent grace and courtesy that must have been natural to him; he certainly couldn't have learned it from his aunt and his cousin. On the third day he got into a fight with my older brother Jadrilja, and disappeared for very nearly a month, which is difficult in a small village like ours.

But then he came back.

I found him myself this time, standing in front of our house, balanced on one bare foot and scratching it with the toes of the other. He looked at me, looked away, and mumbled the first words he ever addressed directly to me, "I come for a wash."

Jadrilja was more than ready to pick up his debate with Lathro where our father had halted it, but that didn't happen for a good day and a half; and by that time I had noticed that Lathro Baraquil's brown eyes stood forth with a rich warmth disconcerting in that fierce little face. My own eyes are green, like my mother's; my father's are almost black, like those of all the men in his family. I had never seen eyes like Lathro Baraquil's eyes. I still haven't.

So it began, long and long before either of us was aware that anything was beginning. It was much like inviting a wary, untrusting feral animal first into the yard, then a little way up onto the veranda; then into the house, if only by leaving the door ajar for the creature to choose as it will. First Lathro came, as he said, only for a bath, and once in a great while for my mother to trim his thatch of thick brown hair. Then he began to arrive, more and more, at dinnertime, for my mother to stuff him like a Thieves' Day piglet. She was not a particularly good cook, no more than I—magic never provided a proper meal for anyone—but Lathro never complained.

And in time he began to come for me.

I knew it, accepted it, and gave it no further thought beyond our pleasure in being together. We wandered, raced, climbed trees, told each other stories; squabbled on many occasions, made up quickly, and often fell asleep on a hillside or under a tree, piled together as warmly and innocently as puppies. And when Lathro fought with one or another of my brothers—he simply could not keep from it—they had me to deal with as well. Utterly disloyal, but there you are.

Was I aware that one of us was heir to power such as the other could never possibly know, merely by virtue of being born the right sex? I suppose I must have been, but I cannot recall it making the least bit of difference or discord between us. It might well have done so, as the years passed, if I had paid the heed I should have to my mother's grimly patient attempts to instruct me in shapeshifting, in spirit-summoning, thaumaturgy, rhymes and songs of lore, and all the other arts I was condemned to master. But surely even a demon can see that I was fatally happy as I was. I had my mother for any magic I needed, my father for those moments when I was sad for no reason that I could put a name to...and for all the rest I had Lathro Baraquil.

We must have seemed a strange pair to many, even as children. I was considered beautiful from my earliest youth, while for his part Lathro grew up plain—beautifully, beguilingly plain—and stubby with it, being no taller than I, ever. His best features, to the outside eye, would have been that tumbly brown hair that I loved to comb (useless as the effort was), and those brown eyes, kind for all the wide wildness they held.

He grew up strong as well, much stronger than could be imagined at sight. At fifteen he was working at Jarg's smithy, handling such tasks as holding the back of a haywagon up for as long a time as it took Jarg to replace a wheel or improvise an axle. I recall seeing him turn with his bare hands a frozen bolt that old Jarg couldn't budge with a sledgehammer and a bucket of grease. Lathro hurt his right hand badly doing that once, and I healed it on the spot in a way my mother had taught me when I happened to be actually paying attention. I was proud of myself then.

If my parents thought us too close in those days, I never knew about it. My belief is that they still saw us as children, and Lathro as family, or the very next thing to it. At all events, they made no objection to the hours we spent together, and the only time my mother ever became annoyed with us was the day when I saw five of the village boys harassing a blind madman, snatching away his crutch so that he fell, and then breaking it over his shoulders. I ran to tell Lathro, who came down on them like a storm out of the Northern Barrens. Two or three of them went limping around on crutches themselves for some while.

Unhappily, these very ones happened to be the sons of the wealthiest merchants in our village. Their fathers descended on Jarg, insisting that Lathro be discharged immediately; and from his Aunt Yunieska they demanded he be given swift and merciless punishment. I can still see their puffy, bearded faces, red as vultures' pates, and hear their voices splitting with fury, and the spittle flying. As I can still feel Lathro's firm, gentle hand in mine as we looked on.

My mother put a stop to it all, as I knew she would the moment I saw her approaching. The merchants fell silent before her gaze, and I realized—for the first time, really—that they were dreadfully afraid of her.

She said to the merchants, "If I had seen what your sons were at, I can assure you, there would not be one of them who got away from there on less than four legs. Quite possibly six." I had never heard her voice sound like that. She said, "Count yourselves fortunate, and go away. Now."

They went away, and my mother turned on me before I could cheer her triumph. "Child, what on earth possessed you to place Lathro in such jeopardy, doing your work for you? You know who you are—you could have run those boys into the next shire with three words I taught you long ago. You are a stupid, stupid girl, and I am ashamed of you."

I hung my head. I muttered, "I am ashamed too, Mother. But I was afraid. I did not think. I ask your forgiveness."

"Breya is *not* stupid," Lathro said. "She is *not*."

As angry as my mother was, that took more courage than attacking those five fools. My mother ignored him, seemingly, but her voice softened. She said, "My daughter, after me you are already the most powerful woman in Kalagira, whether you know it or not, and there will come a time when you will be far more powerful than I. Others can afford not to think; you never can, or you will do great damage. Do you understand what I am saying to you, Breya Drom? And why I say it?"

I nodded. I whispered, "Yes."

My mother turned to Lathro, and she actually smiled slightly. "Boy," she said, "inhumanly dirty and hungry small boy, you cannot conquer all the cruelty in the world by yourself. Not even you." She patted his cheek then, and turned away. Over her shoulder, she added, "But there's no harm in trying. I'll say that for you."

Was it with that last light glance that she understood what was between us, Lathro and me? I will never know, and she will certainly never tell me. Not even now.

What I do know, for always, is that on that very same day, Lathro Baraquil kissed me for the first time.

It was a clumsy kiss, as unruly as his hair, and it stumbled blindly over my face for what felt like a lifetime before it found my mouth. I was just as awkward: the two of us like blind newborn kittens, scrambling through a forest of fur toward the nipple—toward life. It was so sweet that I wept as though my heart were breaking, and poor Lathro was terrified, thinking that he had somehow hurt me or frightened me. But I reassured him.

And where to from there? What did we whisper, what did we promise each other? What gift did we exchange to seal our troth? And again, what did my mother know before we did? No business of any demon's.

When the time finally came to speak I never told my mother, "Lathro Baraquil has my heart." I was much too clever for that, well knowing that she could have crumbled the notion like stale bread with a few gently scornful words, and blown the fragments away with a look or a gesture. What I said was, "Lathro is my heart," which was the truth.

But Willalou my mother was more clever than I by far. She embraced me immediately—not the least moment of hesitation, mind—and cried out, "My dear, my Breya, I am so happy for you—*so* happy!" Thus she caused me to lower my guard, to ease my anxiety regarding her reaction to my news; and, indeed, *almost* to miss her wistful little sideways murmur, "But a bit sad for myself..."

I didn't miss it, nor was I meant to. With a suddenly lurching heart, I demanded, "Sad? Why should you be sad?"

My mother smiled valiantly. "I'm sorry, darling. Do forgive an old woman her self-indulgence." She sighed deeply, perfectly. "It's terrible of me, but I have to say it, forgive me. It's the children, you see."

I wasn't prepared. I was ready for a lot of things that she might say, but not that. I said indignantly, "Children? And why should there not be children?"

Oh, Mother. Clever, clever Mother. No sorcery of any sort: not even that thing she did with the fingers of her left hand, out of sight by her side, to change someone's mind. No, she merely let her eyes fill slowly, and stepped back, still with her hands tight on my arms, and she whispered, "My dear, my dear, didn't he tell you?"

This time it was no lurch, but a freezing drop, as though through a gallows trapdoor. "Tell me *what?*"

"He didn't tell you he was from Outside? He really didn't tell you? He was very little when they came here, Yunieska and Pashak. From Chun, I think, although it's hard to remember...maybe I mean Oun, I'm not sure. But anyway."

I said, "I don't care." She didn't hear me. I couldn't hear myself.

She drew me close now, saying, "Darling, darling, you mustn't blame the boy. Think how frightened he must have been at the thought of telling you that if you married him you could never have children of...our sort. I certainly don't blame him, and you *mustn't.*"

"I don't," I said, louder this time. "Oh, I don't." Then I ran away. I could feel her looking after me—one always can with *our sort*—but she did not call, and I did not look back.

Lathro was not at the smithy—I could tell that from a good distance by the silence of the forge. I hurried on by, and found him mucking out Dree Shandriladze's livery stable, as I had thought he would be. No one ever accused my Lathro of not knowing the meaning of real work.

He looked up as I entered the stable, and I could have wept without shame for the pure joy and welcome in his eyes. The next moment, I did weep, for he raised a hand in warning, saying, "Wait, Moon Fox—" such was always his pet name for me—"wait only a moment, while I make this midden-heap fit for your feet." Then, after laying down every board and bit of sacking he could find, he strode to me anyway, scooped me high in his arms, and carried me over to the nest of straw bales he had made for us when he began working there. We held each other, and I breathed his breath and burrowed my way under his arm, and asked, "When did you know?"

He had no idea what I meant. Lathro never lied, not to anyone. I told him the truth of his Outside birth, and of his coming to Kalagira as an infant, and he took it in as flesh parts before the candor of an arrow: I even heard the soft gasp as it went home. Then I made him make love with me, there, for the very first time, with half a dozen coach horses looking on, because it was all I knew to do to comfort him.

In time, when we could at last distinguish the beating of his heart from my own, he said, "Breya. You have to leave me."

I stared at him. There was no answer in me. He said, "You come from a great line of *majkes,* and you will grow to be the greatest of all that line, as your mother said. Am I to be the cause of that line ending with you? I love you better than that, Breya Drom."

"And I love you better than my grandchildren," I answered him. "What have they ever done for me?" I meant to make him laugh, but clearly failed. I went on, "I am not responsible to my *line,* Lathro. I am responsible for my *life*—our life together. For the rest of it, I could be as happy here, right here with you, as anywhere else in the world. I would never ask for more than this—cleaning stables, rubbing down horses, currying them, loving in their good smell. This is happiness for me, Lathro, don't you understand?"

He quieted me with a finger across my lips. "Beloved, this is contentment, nothing more. I haven't your education, but I know the difference. I am no one, son of nothing, and always will be. But magic is part of what you are— you could no more abandon it than step out of that beautiful tea-colored skin you wear so well. And with no daughters to pass it on to, and they to theirs—"

"What if I married someone else, but only had sons? The magic would end then just as surely."

"But at least they would be Kalagira men, such children, able to pass the knack to their own daughters if fate so willed. Ours could not."

"It wouldn't matter!" I tried to hush him with kisses, but he put me aside. "Yes, it would, Breya. Yes, you would live in joy with me anywhere—a stable, a woodcutter's shack, a swineherd's one-room hovel—I know that, how could I not know that? And you would never think for a moment of envying the life of another person on this earth, or of using power to make us more than we already were together." He kissed my fingers then, slowly, one by one. He said, "But children...grandchildren...great-grandchildren...all without magic, never to have it, none of them—look at me, Breya, and tell me you would not ever regret your choice. No, straight at me, there's my girl. Tell me now."

Unlike Lathro, I am a very good liar. Daughter of Willalou, how should I not be? What is all magic but lying, a grandly ruthless reshaping of reality to our purposes? I lied you here, did I not, singing to you of slaughter, luring you with your own hunger? But I could not lie to Lathro in that moment. I wanted him to be wrong, with all my heart...but I was not certain, so I lowered my eyes and turned away.

"There's my girl," he said again, and there was more love and understanding in his voice than I could bear. I took my leave of him as soon as I could, and he did not try to keep me, though I wanted him to. Love as we might, I was a long time forgiving him for knowing me.

We did not see each other for some while after that. My doing.

Nor did I have much to do with my mother and father. I stayed in my own quarters, speaking to no one, eating hardly at all, creating small, spiteful enchantments that shame me today, for their pettiness as much as their malice; and generally *sulking*—I can find no kinder word for my behavior, and I have tried. Something was so, and its so-ness stood between me and my heart's desire; and though I willed it not to be so, it was more powerful than my will.

I did much of my sulking in one shuttered storeroom, perhaps because of its particular air of dank misery, perhaps merely because my parents always knew where I was, and what I was doing, and could come and find me there doing it, if they really wanted to. Only they had better not try.

Dunreath chanced on me when he came into the storeroom looking for the ingredients to a glaze he had not used in years. He might well have missed me, huddled silent in a corner as I was; but, blundering in the darkness, he stumbled over me, letting out a yelp of startlement. He is a big, absent-minded sort of man, my father, happiest at his wheel and kiln; but he does know about love, and at a glance he had my measure.

"Child," he said, awkward as a troll at a tea party. "Child, Breya, don't, please. Don't cry, Breya." And he patted my hair with his rough potter's hand.

I wasn't crying then, for a wonder, but that clumsy touch opened the sluicegates in earnest. I fell on his chest, wailing loudly and wildly enough to deafen the dead. My father held me, whispering whatever lame comfort he could, stroking my neck and shoulders as though I were clay to be petted and kneaded into life.

"Girl, don't weep so," he begged me. "Don't weep, I can't bear it. I like the boy myself, always did, and if you want him so much, you should have him, that's the way *I* look at it. To hell with our line, we've known magic long enough. Your mother would have married *me* if I'd been born Outside, everybody knows that. What bloody difference, hey?"

Is there giving in marriage among demons? If that is so, then maybe— just maybe—you understand something about my father's loyalty. If I knew anything about Willalou, it's that she would never have married a man who was not from Kalagira. My mother loved Dunreath more than anyone, but she loved her heritage more, for good or ill. And Dunreath knew it, but loved her enough not to say so. There is more magic in this world than magicians dream.

"I wish men could be *majkes*," I told him when I finally stopped crying. "I *do,* I wish I could give Lathro my knack. He'd be so good—he'd know the right way to use the power, and I don't, and I don't *care* that I don't. Mother's determined to make me into a great enchantress, but it's not what I want. Doesn't what *I* want matter to *anybody?* Can't I ever be ordinary and happy, like a man?"

"No, love," my father answered me. "No, you can't be—and if you could be, you wouldn't like it." He went back to holding me then, and I went back to weeping. At some point he said, "Breya, you're a hawk, born to soar, born for the heights. You were never meant for the barnyard."

And I remember wailing, "I'm not a bird—I'm human, I'm *me!*" and running away to find Lathro, with my heart wild in my throat and my eyes blind with loneliness and dread.

By instinct, I looked for him neither in the smithy nor the stable, but at the moribund *dika* tree that had been our meeting place since we were children. It was dying then, and it is still stubbornly dying now; but our pet superstition was that our presence—and, in time, our love—was all that kept it putting out the occasional blossom or pale sprig of leaves. It is where I would have gone.

But he was not there, under the tree. He had vanished completely, from the village and from my days, leaving not a trace of his passage.

There are certain obvious advantages to being a *maj* of any sort. One is the ability to track down almost anyone you really set out to find. But nothing that I tried worked. And even Willalou, when I went to her, finally threw up her hands and said, "Daughter, wherever he may be, he has passed beyond my reach. Which is a worry by itself, as much as his being gone."

"Yes," I said. "How thoughtless of him." If my words sound harsh and unfilial...well, remember that I was trying not to shatter into very small fragments. I said, "I will find him, Mother."

My mother said, "You will not."

I stared at her. Dunreath had spoiled me shamelessly, with no slightest regard to its effect on my future character; and while Willalou was sterner, I had known all my life that her *no* truly meant *not now, don't bother me, try me again in a day or two*. But in this moment her lips were thinner, her eyes harder, than I had ever seen them. Protest dried up in my own mouth, and I actually backed away from her.

She said, "Wherever that boy has run off to is no fit place for you. Not as you are, gifted beyond my imagining, and vulnerable as a newborn. You have disregarded my instruction all your life, shirked every lesson you could manage to avoid, studied nothing you found boring—and where are you now? Not only would you be useless in any peril when I am not by to rescue you, but you are utterly powerless to aid the one you claim to love. Tell me I am wrong, my daughter. I want to hear you tell me I am wrong."

She had never spoken so to me in my life. There was nothing for me to say; and if there had been, I would have known better than to say it. I waited in silence, staring down at the intricacies of my sandal straps, until she finally ran out of rage and breath more or less together. She said, "So. Now, at bloody last, we begin."

And so, indeed, it began: that insanely intensive course of training in everything that should have been woven into my bones and brain before ever I had need of them. My mother was absolutely pitiless, driving me without rest for either of us, constantly humiliating me to tears, whether over the nursery-simple rhymes that can confer invisibility, locate water in a desert, or heal a fatal wound; or when I, for the hundredth time, tangled up one of her fiendishly complicated invocations with another that was almost identical. She drilled me endlessly in the doggerel chants, phrases, and rituals of a dozen languages, all seemingly unrelated, that could, even so, be fitted together in a remarkable number of different ways to produce strikingly varied results. We battled through the night many a time, I and this terrible woman with my mother's face: me with my mind turning to watery curds, and she haranguing me without cease, barking, "I taught you that when you were seven years old—or I thought I had—you should know it in your sleep. Where is your head?" To this day, I still hate that contemptuous question with no answer. "Where is your head?" over and over. *"Where is your head?"*

Fortunately I learn quickly, when I learn at all; fortunately also, I have an ear for music. This is crucial for an enchantress, as it is not for a witch or a sorceress, since so much of our power lies in song. My mother has a perfectly good voice, but much preferred to recite her spells in a decidedly flat, plain manner—always while *moving*, letting her body sing the magic. But if I could not sing, I might as well be a witch in a cave, growling my incantations over a greasy, smoky fire. (Meaning no disrespect to Grandmother, who was actually a cheerful, sociable soul, like most witches.) As it was, Willalou sang me hoarse, day on day, night on night. "No, do it *again*—can't you hear where you lose the rhythm? *Where is your head?*"

Five endless months. Nearly six. I am grateful beyond words that the memory blurs. It was coming on autumn when my mother finally announced, with no preamble, "Well, I've done what I could. You're still the poorest excuse for a proper enchantress I've ever seen, but at least I'm not quite so feared that you'll put a spell on yourself, or call something you don't want when you're trying to summon Lathro." She paused for a moment, and then added quietly, her voice that of the mother I knew for the first time in forever, "Which, by the way, would *not* do. Do not ever try to bring that boy of yours to you by magic, despite all temptation. Do you understand me, Breya?"

Her eyes were dark with urgency, as I have only rarely seen them. I said, "I understand your meaning, mother. But not your reason. Why not?"

My mother hesitated again, longer this time. She said finally, her voice uncharacteristically muffled, almost mumbling, "Because it will alert the Being he has gone to seek. And may have found by now."

I gaped at her. She went on, increasingly defensive, "He came to me the very day before he ran off. He wanted me to know—though he swore me not to tell you—that he was away in search of a creature he had heard tell of, powerful enough to change fate and make *maj* of an ordinary man." She paused a third time. "Even a man of Kalagira. He thought such a change might help him carry magic for you, even Outside born, and would not listen when I warned him of the terrible price the Being would claim."

There is a difference between being truly speechless and not having the air to make the sound come out. I felt as though I had been struck in the stomach, having had no warning and no chance to brace myself. I said stupidly, "A creature."

"A Being," my mother said. "It was old when your grandmother was not yet born, and its power is not of this world. I believe, if it so chose—"

"A *maj*." My voice was rising slowly, like floodwaters. "You think Lathro has gone to this—thing—to be magicked into the knack, so that he and I might perhaps have..." My mother nodded, looking guiltier by the minute. I whispered, "And you tell me this *now?*"

"It would have done no good before. You would have hared off straight after him, and you no more suited for such a quest than a—a *chicken!*"

"All this time," I said. I was cold with fury, shaking uncontrollably. "All these days wasted going over and over this stupid spell, that baby rhyme, the Three Theories—"

"—which you should have *learned* as a baby—"

"And all the time, Lathro going further and further away, *disappearing...*" I couldn't speak anymore; it was language disappearing now. I turned and walked out of the house. My mother said nothing, and did not follow.

I left the next morning on Belgarth, the warhorse my father had accepted in payment for a great floral vase, so huge as to require three handles, that he had created for a lord's wedding. Belgarth was getting on by then, and grown fat with inactivity; but I had learned to ride on his king's couch of a back, and we were fond of each other. Besides, he always smelled wonderful, like a dew-damp hayfield warming in the morning sun, and his chestnut hide set off my coloring to perfection. And yes, *majkes* do indeed think about such things, like anyone else.

Dunreath made no objection to my taking his horse, but he looked so wretched that it hurt my heart, and I would have turned back then, if I could have. When he held me, I whispered, "I'm sorry," which I could not say to Willalou, even when she held my stirrup while I mounted, and we bade each other farewell. Nor did she ask forgiveness for what she had said and done, but only stood at Belgarth's head, tall and beautiful and dry-eyed, looking straight at me. She said, "I have no counsel for you, and only one suggestion. Accept it or not, as you choose."

I waited, not speaking. My mother said, "All I know of this Being that you and Lathro seek, is that it is in some way bound to running water. Look for it near rivers, brooks, the smallest streams, search where running water is used by men—in mills, in tanneries, canals, weirs. And if you go north, towards Chun—remember, Lathro may have been born there—seek out a river town called Mulleary, and a woman named Dragine. We were acquainted long ago. If anyone in the land knows where this Being can be found, it will be Dragine." The way she held my gaze with her own was as near to an embrace as makes no matter. "Goodbye, then, my daughter," and she stood aside to let Belgarth pass.

I did not look back as I rode away.

I had never been beyond the borders of Kalagira, nor even close to them. I had never been away from home for longer than three days. Yet here I was, journeying alone into what, for me, was wilderness: the country roads winding more or less towards Chun, so ill-kept and overgrown that half a dozen bandits could be crouched within arm's-reach and you not know— and beyond those, the bare hills surrounding Fors na' Shachim and the Queen's black castle. Belgarth wasn't much concerned with scenery—he's all for tiltyards, short, lumbering charges with murderous clashes at the end of them—and he wasn't happy with stony little roads overhung with brambly vines. Yet he strode on gallantly all the same, a warhorse ever, war or no. There would have been little forage for him, in the normal way; but I made certain to bring rich grass to birth unseasonably, wherever we made camp, and water pooling out of stones. And yes, it *was* my mother who finally hammered that smallest charm into me—and yes, I *should* have learned it at the same time I learned to dress myself.

It seemed the most practical thing—grudge it as I might—to follow Willalou's suggestion and seek out the Dragine woman. I had no notion of what a Being—and did that signify demon, lamia, *yaroth,* or some other monster?—powerful enough to turn a mortal man into a *maj* might look or be like, and if there was someone who did I had many questions to ask. I heeded my mother's hint about running water as well, and set out to trace the course of everything flowing south of Fors na' Shachim. Of course it was a completely absurd notion—was that a laugh? Does your kind actually make a sound to express amusement?—but I was frightened for my man, and certain that nothing was beyond one as much in love as I.

Yes, that *is* a laugh-sound, isn't it? But as dark and distorted as you are.

Often I let Belgarth choose our road—why not, since all horses, left to themselves, will go toward the smell of water, and all paths were the same to me so long as they headed eventually toward Chun? Meanwhile I practiced my spells, like any novice, as we covered the country foot by plodding foot: singing to mark earth and stone and the air itself, to keep us from wandering in circles or unwittingly doubling back on our trail.

As for what I would do when I at last saw Lathro Baraquil's face, I had forced myself, days and miles back, to banish such imaginings altogether. I might—or might not, even after Willalou's improvised disciplines—be a match for the Being I sought; but even if I were, that was no guarantee Lathro would choose to return home with me when I found him. What if he had not yet found the Being, but insisted on continuing the search? Or what if he had already become a *maj* and considered himself far too grand now for a scab-kneed childhood playmate? Too many unknown factors; nothing to do but trudge on, singing.

We kept almost entirely to the mountains: since so many of the streams and rivers of this region spring up there, it did seem to improve the odds at least somewhat. But we might as well have been seeking roses in the Northern Barrens, for I encountered no smallest trace of Lathro, nor of the Being I was hunting so steadfastly. I learned not a thing from the rare traveler, and nothing at all in any of the few villages in which I stabled Belgarth and passed the night. Yet I could not rid myself of the *awareness* of both of them, the conviction that they were somewhere nearby, whatever my training, my observations, or my inborn senses told me to the contrary. The heart is not the infallible guide it claims to be, but it does get a few things right now and then.

The nights were turning seriously chilly, and Belgarth was even showing early suggestions of a winter coat, when we followed a swift, restless little river into a town called, not Mulleary, but Mul*deary*, rather larger than any we had come across in some while. I asked if a woman named Dragine lived there, and was told that she was visiting in a distant village, but would return in two days' time. Belgarth and I spent those days doing little else but eating and sleeping. I had been running for nearly two months on nothing but vague memories of rest, real meals, and a proper bed; and for all that happened in Muldeary, I will remember it as the town in which I *slept*. And took baths.

Dragine arrived at dawn of the second day, walking briskly out of a dust storm that drifted away when she told it to. She was a tiny creature with a face like a spiderweb and hair so black you could hardly see it, if you understand me. I caught up with her crossing Beggars' Square, where the homeless of Muldeary are fed every morning, and began to introduce myself, but she kept striding on without even looking at me until I said, "I am Willalou's daughter. Willalou of Kalagira."

Dragine stopped in her tracks then, and I saw her eyes for the first time. I had expected them to be as black as her hair, but they were a tawny brownish-yellow, or yellowish-brown. She peered at me—I suppose I should say 'up at me,' small as she was, but somehow it felt as though our eyes were on a level—and she said, "I know your mother." Her voice sounded like sand blowing against the sides of an empty house.

"Yes," I said. "She told me not to leave Muldeary until I had seen you." She started to turn away, and I grabbed at flattery to hold her attention, adding "She speaks well of you."

Dragine said, "You are a liar," but she said it indifferently, as though she were already tired of me. "I never could abide your mother, and she never had anything but contempt for me. Why are you still bothering me?"

"Because my mother told me you had knowledge to fit my need." Dragine did not reply, but she did not walk away, either, or turn her strange eyes from mine. We stood there together in Beggars' Square, and I told her about Lathro Baraquil.

Her expression never changed, nor did her tone. She looked me up and down for a time, then shrugged very slightly and said, "Come to my house tonight. Ten minutes to midnight, no sooner." She never mentioned where her house could be found, nor did I think then to ask her for directions.

Whatever she actually might be—witch, sorceress like my mother, or even a true enchantress—in her presence I had trouble thinking at all.

I took Belgarth out for a fast trot, bordering on a canter, and spent the rest of the day searching for someone willing to tell me where Dragine lived. It was an interesting experience: none of them recoiled in obvious terror at the idea of revealing her location, and yet somehow I came away from none of them with an exact address. In the end I had to employ a finding spell, which is so childishly simple that it always gives me a headache. But I was there precisely at the appointed time, and I came on foot, to show respect, though it meant a long walk.

It was an ordinary house she lived in, neither a mansion nor a hovel: it might well have been the home of an honest and energetic farmwife, one who spent great amounts of time scrubbing and polishing worn kitchen flagstones that would never come quite clean. I remember that it smelled of old fires, and that the river ran near enough that I could see its banks from the front yard, and hear its rambling chatter as I stood on the threshold.

Lathro Baraquil opened the door to me.

Do your folk have hearts? Do they serve another purpose, as ours do, besides hurrying the impatient blood along through your veins, if you even *have* veins? Mine stopped—just for an instant, but completely—and then it surged to the size of Belgarth, so that my chest could not nearly contain it, and with a cry the Queen must have heard in Fors na' Shachim I threw myself into Lathro's arms. I think we mortals must each be allowed one moment like that in our lives. I don't believe we are constructed to withstand two.

For the sake of accuracy, however, I must admit that I threw myself against Lathro's arms, not into them. He made no effort to embrace me, but only stood still, looking not into my eyes but over my shoulder, his own eyes empty as eggshells of feeling. He did not know me at all; and what stood in his place, in his clothes—I had made him that shirt; *made* it, not conjured it—I could never possibly know.

He did not recoil, nor thrust me away. He stood still, staring over my shoulder at the night, with every treasured bump and bone and angle of him turned foreign, after years of being as much my own as his. I babbled his name, but it had no more effect than the sound of the stream. Nothing in him knew me.

Beyond him Dragine waited, her face as unreadable as ever, but her eyes glowing like the eyes of a hunting *shukri*. She said, "He has been here for some while, waiting for the Being to be called. I myself, however, have been waiting for you."

I pushed past Lathro to confront her, demanding, "What have you done to him? Tell me now, or I will kill you where you stand!" Eighteen and gently bred up, can you imagine me saying such a thing to anyone? I have not even said it to you, although the moon is on its way to setting.

In her voice of blowing sand, Dragine answered me, "That would be wrong and foolish of you, since it was not I who set this spell upon him."

I could not respond. I simply stared. Dragine said, "It happens with humans. They often desire something so greatly, for so long, that with the proper push they cannot remember why they craved it in the first place. So it is with your man—he was in this state when he found his way here. Only if he came from where you did, I suspect there was little *finding* on his path. He has been here quite some time." She paused, watching me take that in, and then went on, "In the end, it is your doing, even more than his."

"*My* doing?" The absurdity of the claim outraged me, but it frightened me as well. "How can it have been my doing?"

Dragine pointed at Lathro, standing completely motionless, not even blinking. "When you told him that you two could never marry, because of his being an Outsider, what did you *think* he would do? You say you have known him since childhood—what did you *think*?"

I could hear my mother's "*Where is your head?*" under my own whispered reply. "I never told him that. I would never have..."

"No? Well, someone did." Dragine's yellow teeth bared their tips in a smile of mean delight. "And that same someone directed him straight here, to me. What do you think of that, Breya Drom, daughter of Willalou?"

There was a taste of copper in my mouth, and a distant braying in my ears. I said, "My mother set Lathro searching for you? I don't believe it." But I did, I did, even before Dragine answered me.

"I would never dream of lying to you—I am enjoying the truth far too much, little witch-girl." She was beginning to laugh, like a sandstorm gathering strength.

Strangely, the contempt in the word *witch-girl* cleared my head, leaving me more coldly, stubbornly rational than I had been since I left home. I said, as haughtily as I was able, "I am no witch, but an enchantress, as you well know, and the daughter of one who could crumble you and a dozen like you into her soup." The laughter grew until I could actually feel the sand against my skin, like tiny blades. Beside me, Lathro showed no reaction at all, his entire attention focused on nothing I could see or imagine. His eyes had not met mine squarely since he had opened Dragine's door to me. I said again, "Tell me why you hate my mother so. Because she doesn't know, I'm sure."

"You think not?" Dragine's laughter did not return; rather, she looked at me with something almost like pity. "She told you nothing she did not *have* to tell you, did she then? Nothing?"

I had no answer for her. With no further word, she turned and led me— and silent, obedient Lathro too—through the house to a curious place I'd not noticed from outside: neither a room nor a yard nor a veranda, but a plain high-walled space open in part to the sky. The walls were white and bare. There were no chairs, or even cushions, to sit on; the only distinguishing feature of the area was a small pool, ringed round with large stones, carefully arranged. There was no moon that night, but the stars were reflected thickly in the pool, darting like bright fish, as the current from some hidden inlet stirred the surface. I could see my shadow in it, but not my face.

Dragine squatted on her heels, and gestured to me to do the same. She did not look at Lathro, who stood by, hands folded in front of him, staring away at nothing. She said, "I was born in Kalagira. I grew up with your mother. Did she tell you *that*, at least?" I shook my head. "Well, so it was. And as you and this one here—" she jerked a gaunt finger at Lathro—"have been to each other, so was I with your father. Dunreath the potter." When she spoke his name she closed her eyes, barely for longer than a blink, but I saw.

"Were you promised?" I could not imagine her young with Dunreath— the bitter spider-lines gone, the tawny eyes innocently yearning—but my folk take handfasting seriously, and I had to know.

Dragine looked at me for a long, cold time before she replied. "Breathe easy, witch-girl, your father never deceived me. We were close to promising— he even spoke of it, a time or two—but I was shy still. I was shy..." Her voice had grown soft when she spoke of Dunreath, almost wistful; but it turned to blowing sand again with her next words. "Then came your mother."

Oh, perhaps you can see it; perhaps you can take my word for my young father's first sight of a maiden Willalou. Dragine must have seen the vision in my face, for she said, "Aye, there was never a day when I could match her for beauty. Nor for power, either...not then."

The last two words were uttered in a near-animal growl, and I could hardly catch them, but I did. I said, "And now?"

Dragine smiled fully for the first time, granting me, as though by a flash of lightning, an instant's glimpse of the girl who had had every reason to believe that Dunreath belonged to her, with her. She said, "I was not born a *maj*, or to a gifted line. There has never been so much as the feeblest barnyard witch in my family, search as far back as you will. How should my potter not have been drawn to such a face, such a gift, as Willalou's? No, I blame him not at all, your father."

"But my mother must take the blame for everything," I said, "every misfortune that has befallen you since you lost Dunreath to her. Even before then, am I wrong?"

"I blame her for being exactly what she is, no more: for knowing that what is not hers is hers to take. Do you feel that unjust, witch-girl? Too bad. I also honor her for making me what I am." The smile thinned, curling into the newest of new moons. "The Being your foolish man seeks draws no line between one sex and another. It responds simply to desire. To need."

"Such as yours," I said, and she nodded. I said, "But it could not bring my father back to you. He loved my mother on sight, loves her still. Nothing could have changed that."

"The Being gave me a greater gift." Dragine's voice was surprisingly gentle, almost dreamy. "Shall I show you?"

She raised both arms, crossed them at the wrists, pointed at me with both pairs of middle and index fingers, and spoke a rhyme that Willalou had drummed into my head so hard, so often, that I knew to drop flat on my belly as two gouts of fire, shaped like dragon heads, leaped from Dragine's fingertips and shot past me, hissing like full-sized wyrms. Ordinarily such sendings burst within seconds, harmless as Thieves' Day crackers; but these doubled on their sizzling trails and came racing for me again. There were eyes in those tiny fire-faces, and they saw me.

But I know a rhyme worth two of that, and I sang it, rising to a crouch—

sang it back at Dragine, not at the dragon-heads, and they promptly popped like milkweed seedpods, and were gone.

I stood up slowly, glancing sideways at Lathro as I did so. He had not moved, nor did he appear to have noticed what had taken place. I said loudly to Dragine, "*That* was what your Being taught you? *That* was worth a slice of your soul? You ought to ask for your payment back."

Dragine was breathing hard: deep animal inhalations—such as you breathe now, in the darkness, waiting for the moon to be gone. She said, "The Being has no interest in souls. What it took in payment for my new power was my ability to love, for which I had no more use in any case, nor ever would. I have no complaints. See now!"

And with those last words—and a few others—she Shifted, and on the instant it was a great *sheknath* who stood in her place: hindquarters higher than the mighty bowed forelegs, jaws and chest and shoulders still muddy from digging out its most recent meal. It rose on its hind legs and roared at me, but I sang my mother's favorite old lullaby, and it dropped down and promptly went to sleep. Dragine was some little while regaining her true shape, and she was not pleased when she finally managed it.

"I will not fight with you," she declared. "I did not summon you for that, but to watch you lose your man to a fantasy, as I lost mine. It lasts longer than destruction, grief does. As you will learn."

Whereupon she made a sign before Lathro's face. The eager life came back into his brown eyes to break my heart, but he never looked at me, only asking Dragine, "Is it time? Has the Being come at last?"

"Soon, boy," she answered him soothingly. "Very soon now." Her eyes were full of triumph as she looked back at me, saying, "You see how it is? He has no care for you, nor for anything but his desire. The memory of Willalou's daughter has vanished, making you a ghost to him, and any dream of your future together just that, a dream, long slipped away with the morning. Nor will being made a *maj*—oh, yes, the Being will certainly grant his wish—bring him home to you, no more than I will ever have your father back. So here we both are, abandoned forever by our loves—" and this time the smile was as joyously murderous as a rock-*targ*'s skull-baring grin, just before it strikes for the throat or the contents of your stomach—"and all of it, *all*, due to the devices of the clever, wicked woman from whose wickedness you spring. Do you understand me at last, witch-girl?"

"No," I said. "I will not. I will not understand you." Rather than listen further to her, or to myself, I turned desperately to Lathro, saying, "Love, love, here I am, your Moon-Fox, your Breya. Can't you see me, don't you know me at all?" I even shook him a little, grasping his shoulders, to no avail.

His eyes were warm and alive, as I have said, but I was not in them. Whoever he saw standing before him, shrilling like a locust, it was not I. He spoke for the first time, saying, with some wonder in his voice, "You are so pretty. I never imagined the Being would be pretty."

I choked on my own sudden tears, and Dragine laughed in purest delight, sounding almost like a happy child. "Nay, she's no Being, boy, she can give you nothing you need, my word on it. Come, we'll call now, you and I."

She moved to the edge of the pool, spread her hands over the star-fish shimmering in its depths, and spoke to them too rapidly for me to catch more than a few of the words. They were in a tongue I had heard my mother speak: it is very old, and there are some bad stories about its origins. Lathro joined in the calling, briefly and stumblingly, as Dragine's voice rose to a kind of shrill croon, not loud, but *high,* high enough that it disappeared at the end, like a lark or a falcon climbing out of sight. I wanted to cover my ears, but I didn't. A moment later I very nearly covered my eyes, because the surface of the pool gradually began to swirl counterclockwise, right to left, gaining speed until the sound of its spinning echoed Dragine's uncanny wail. It no longer looked like water: first it was black stone—then starlit spiraling diamond—and finally it was jeweled smoke, sparkling pale-blue smoke, whirling slowly into shape, like clay on my father's wheel. A figure began to rise out of the little pool.

It was man-shaped, but not a man. I never did determine what it was, or even what it chose to resemble, so sinuously and playfully did it sport from form to smoky near-form. At one moment it might have been a sort of hornless goat, dancing on its hind legs; but step closer to the pool, or consider it from another angle—or simply *wait*—and it seemed an enormous head, with black wriggly-wet things like eels where its teeth should have been, and that head was dancing too. Or let a small pewter cloud hide a star or two, and behold then a dead tree, its skeletal boughs aswarm with glittering, watchful stone eyes; or again you might suddenly be staring at a great almost-butterfly, burning as it whirled, yet never consumed, though its blaze dazzled even Dragine's eyes. She turned from it to stare at me, and though she said nothing, yet I heard her in my mind, her silent laughter echoing within me.

"She arranged it all, witch-girl. She set your man all afire to get rid of him... then set you to find him, after training you up to face the Being who comes when I call, as she well knows. A Being who has more power than she ever dreamed of having, for all her hopes, all her craving..."

When the Being spoke out of its flaming, shifting whirlwind, it addressed itself directly to me. Through all its constant transformations its voice remained the same: a deep, deep buzzing that I heard along my spine and in my cheekbones more than in my ears. "There will be no confrontation between us, Breya Drom, because there is no reason for such a thing. You have already lost any battle there could be."

"Have I, then?" Compared to that voice, I sounded to myself like a little girl refusing to go to bed. But I was profoundly weary, and deeply frightened, and more stubbornly angry than either. I said, "Whatever battles my mother had in mind, she will have to find someone else to fight them. All I came for was Lathro Baraquil."

"And all *he* came for, he has already found." The Being extended what was momentarily a hand toward Lathro, and he *hungered* toward it—that is the best word I can find—reaching out with his whole self, but I pushed his hand away before they could meet.

"We are going home," I said. "Lathro and I."

The Being chuckled. It had slowed its spinning—a dizzying effect by itself—and was regarding me out of a single eye in the flat face of a creature a bit like a furry fish. It buzzed. "Tell *him* that, girl." Lathro looked as though he were about to jump into the pool: not to gain any gift from the Being, but to join with it, to become part of it, as he had been part of me so long ago. The Being said to him, "Ask and have, Lathro Baraquil."

Behind me Dragine laughed once, a single bark, bruising my ears. "Yes! Ask and have, boy. Ask and have!"

And suddenly it was all too much for me—too much and too little at the same time. All of it, all: Lathro's dream of carrying magic...Willalou's shameless machinations...Dragine's vengefulness...my own idiot journey in pursuit of my useless fantasies...the Being's benign disregard...even being called *witch-girl* one time too many. Suddenly I wanted no further part of it, even if it cost me my one love. "Do what you will," I said aloud, though none seemed to hear me. "Do what you please, I'm done." And I turned my back on the lot of them, and I walked away.

Nor did I turn again, not until I heard the Being's insect-whirr once more, "Ask and have of me, Lathro Baraquil," and Lathro's voice, that I had first heard mumbling *I come for a wash,* saying now, loudly and boldly, "Then I ask for the full powers and abilities of a true *maj,* and I ask further—"

But by then I was singing.

I have no memory of making that decision, or of choosing the charm I sang. It has only happened so for me once or twice, since. What I do remember is that Lathro went mute on the instant, and that Dragine whirled, wrinkled lips drawn back, furiously chanting a counterspell that I warded off easily with a gesture. That made me overconfident—I was young, after all—and I was not prepared when the Being struck at me with...with what? A spell, was it? A cantrip of some sort? A hex, even? Did the Being know any of those words, did it think in those terms? No matter: my brain was too occupied with careening from one side of the universe to the other, and I could not find my legs and arms. There was a howling in my head.

I stood up—somebody did, anyway—and saw that the Being had flowed into the form of something that might have set out to be a clawfooted, stinking *churfa,* and changed its mind halfway along, for the worse. It said, "Give over, Breya Drom. Go your way and leave me to mine, and your man to the way he has chosen. What he pays to walk it may not be what Dragine paid—but in any case, he is lost to you. Give over, child. Go home."

I might have done just that, had Dragine not squalled at that moment, "And tell your mother we are quits when you get there." Her face was as savagely satisfied as though she had been making love all night long.

Lathro was silent still, but not staring worshipfully at the Being now. He was looking directly toward me, and it seemed to me that there was at least *something* like recognition in his face—something surfacing that was near to being my Lathro. I dared not think any further than that.

Not that there was time for it, since I had no illusions that the Being's words meant truce; they certainly didn't to me. Lathro was coming home with me, whether he wanted to or not—his desires had just become completely irrelevant. Dragine aimed a second spell at me: a spiteful thing that would likely have cost me a few years in beetle shape, had she managed it, but I batted it back at her like a featherball, such as children play with, and kept my attention focused on the Being. Willalou may indeed have decoyed me to its den and its acolyte to destroy it; my only concern now was to keep it from destroying me. Nothing in my body was working properly, except my blood, and that was up and raging. I took a deep breath, began walking directly towards the Being, and I sang as I went.

Not until I began that song had I truly known I was an enchantress, for all my proud disdain. Do you understand me, huddling there, as far from me as the walls of your lair will let you, with your red eyes counting the minutes until the moon is gone? It was one of the many things I had never bothered to learn, you see. I knew who my mother was, for good or ill, and that my power descended from her, and from my mothers before her. I knew that Willalou was a sorceress, and that a sorceress thinks about magic—with great care, in most cases. But an enchantress *is* magic, *is* what she does: an enchantress dwells in a place, not without thought, but beyond it, somewhere on some other side. And I hadn't known that, for all my mother's harping on how much greater than herself I was born to be. Some things cannot be known, only experienced.

With that song, with those charmed notes leaping up out of me like children—for all I knew at the time, the only children I was ever likely to have—I came of age.

The Being had reverted to the whirling cone of pale-blue smoke that I had first seen rising out of the pool. I felt its enormous blasts of heat and energy hammering at me, and I know most of them connected somewhere, but it did not seem to matter, it seemed to be happening very far off, to someone else. The song I sang was our family's ancient war chant: few beyond the family have ever heard it, and nobody sings it but us. I knew the Being could not have heard it before.

The song built up momentum, like a sling whirled round and round the head until you at last let go. When I did, with the last stanza, the recoil—there is no other word—lifted me and hurled me across that open space, helpless as a new-hatched canary in a cloudburst. It slammed me first into a white wall, then tumbled me straight into Dragine's pool. I seem to remember the water tasting somehow burned, but I could be wrong. I was drowning at the time.

It was a shallow little pool, but you can drown just as easily in inches as in fathoms, and I wasn't even conscious enough to lift my head out of the water. Lathro it was who picked me up, and then put me down carefully and dried my wet clothes as best he could. He whispered *"Moon Fox...Moon Fox,"* over and over as he did so.

The Being itself was out of the pool, stumbling near me—almost over me, as I sat up—on absurdly pink pigeon feet far too small for the hulking, unwieldy form it appeared to have been trapped in by my song. I cannot adequately describe that shape: it had something of flesh to it, but more was quite simply wooden, or almost wooden...and there was, about the face, if that is what it was, a sort of...No. No. All I know is that it was dying, and blind, and that I felt sorry for it, for the Being, whatever it had so nearly cost Lathro and me. And when it managed to buzz out, *"I have had my price, all the same..."* before it toppled and crashed down, there were tears in my eyes. I did not understand what it had told me, not then.

Lathro took my hand without speaking. I said, "Well, there goes your chance at magic. Perhaps you'll forgive me one day."

Dragine was on her knees beside the fallen Being. After a moment she reached out slowly to touch the blind face, that face that I cannot portray any more than I could the look in her eyes. Lathro took my own face between his hands, as of old, this time so gently and timorously that I could barely feel it. He said, "The question is whether you can forgive me. I only wanted to be a proper match for you, Breya."

I stopped him, and not gently. "And just exactly what have you been to me since we were five years old? Can you honestly imagine me partnered with anyone else in the entire world? Anyone?"

"No. No, I never could, you know that. But then our children—"

"Bugger the children!" I picked that word up from Dunreath when I was quite small, and he was having a bad day with his pots and jugs. "If my line's knack comes to an end with me—well, so it does. Too many *majkes* in the family, anyway, and not enough blacksmiths." Bruised and hurting everywhere, I was yet holding him so hard that I was having as much trouble breathing as he was. I said, "Home. We are going home now."

Strangely—or perhaps not—Dragine showed me no rancor for having caused the end of the Being; indeed, she showed nothing at all, but only crouched on her heels by the great dead thing, still touching it now and again. Once, when she looked up and saw me staring, as I could not help doing, she said in her desert voice, "It was my friend. Go away."

So we took the road home to Kalagira, the two of us astride Belgarth, who carries double easily, though he complains vigorously in the mornings. It took us a long time, but we didn't mind. There's little to tell of that passage, except for a moment I do like to remember, when I suggested proudly to Lathro that he had but to say the word and I could surely make our journey a great deal easier for everyone involved, and perhaps even eliminate it altogether. What's the good of being an enchantress, after all, if you can't show off for your beloved once in a while?

But Lathro refused. He said—and I have it still in my head, word for firm word—"Breya Drom, through my foolishness we have already missed too much of our time together in this world, and risked all. I will not lose another minute of you, another second, for good or ill, ever again."

When we reached my home, I asked Lathro to stable Belgarth for me, and he nodded understandingly. "You'll want some time alone with your mother. Of course." I watched him walk away with the old horse, and felt my heart floating after him. Then I left my shoes at the door, and went in.

She was practicing on her *kiit* in her workroom; I could hear the music as I came along the corridor. Her hands are not quite big enough for the full-sized instrument she insists on using, but she plays well all the same—I loved to have her play me to sleep when I was small.

She spoke to me before I had even reached her workroom. "Welcome, daughter. Welcome, my pride." No one catches Willalou unaware: and what I now was she would have sensed two villages away.

She put down the *kiit* and came swiftly to enfold me, but I held her off with a raised hand. How strange that did feel, evading my mother's embrace for the first time in my life. I could hear the comforting old sound of Dunreath's wheel going, deep in his own studio, and was desperately glad that he was not present. I said, "We talk."

She stood straight now, as always, and looked into my eyes and shrugged slightly. She said, "I did what was necessary. No more, and no less."

"I think not," I said. "I think bloody not."

"The Being is dead. There will be no others, and so no witches or sorceresses who should never have been *majkes,* not ever. Dragine had no power in her before her desperate bargain, and she is broken now, no danger to anyone. You did these things, not I, and it is a little late for qualms and regrets. As though you had any need of them."

I had to fight off the appeal of her smile, exactly as I had had to deal with Dragine's spells, except that this was much harder, and took much more of me. I said, "You manipulated everything. *Everything.* You goaded Lathro into running off to make himself worthy of me, thinking that would be the end of him—and then you put me through that whole charade of *training—*"

"Charade?" My mother spat the word out, genuinely furious; no elegant playacting here. "I saved your life, ungrateful idiot! You would be dead now—or worse, much worse—if I had not forced you to become what you were supposed to be, what I had come to despair of your ever bothering to be. I made you an enchantress, my daughter, which was more than your inheritance or your own nature could have done, and what matter if I used all the world to do it. Will you give me the lie, then?"

Rage can often make plain, homely people beautiful, or almost so. It does not have the same effect on beautiful ones like my mother. I said, "It was poor Dragine, and the Being itself, who made me an enchantress. You made me a tool." I fell silent for a moment, because my own anger suddenly had me by the throat, and I could barely breathe with it. "And I could have stood that—I could have endured it all and still trusted you, and loved you—but for the look of my Lathro when he opened Dragine's door and did not know me."

My mother had the grace not to speak. My mother has a great deal of grace.

"You ensorcelled my love," I said. "You *dared,*" and how I got that word out, I will never know. "Lathro was under your spell from the moment he left this house and set off to find the Being, as you had charged him, bidding him forget me. But you had not counted on the strength of his love; he was throwing off the charm before ever I defeated the Being." I actually smiled at her then, so proud I was of Lathro. "You should have known better, Mother."

There was no surrender in Willalou, no smallest yielding; I would never have expected any. "When I was training you, I knew that it might one day come to this—that if you survived the trials for which I was preparing you,

you would return with mastery enough to punish me for deceiving you. Do it, then. I did what I did, and unlike you I regret none of it. Do as you choose, Breya. Don't dally, girl, *do* it."

I think she may very well have expected death, but I could not do that to Dunreath. So I did something else instead.

She never lowered her eyes from mine as I sang three words that stripped her power from her, leaving her as mortal as my father, as vulnerable to the world as Lathro's first kiss had made me feel. She took a single long breath— then went back to her chair, picked up the *kiit,* and began to play again.

We have not spoken since.

And, yes, if it could possibly interest a demon, I regret that. But it was to be expected, for the Being's last words were spoken truly. I did pay a price that night in Muldeary: I lost my mother. At need an enchantress can deceive anyone or anything but herself, but no spell in my throat could ever hide the truth of Willalou from me, no matter how much I may sometimes wish it.

So here I sit now, in your lair, watching the moon over your spine-crested shoulder, and feeling the quickening inside me. Not even Lathro knows yet, but I am with child. Actually, I think I am with children, for I can already sense the doubleness, though it is too soon for them to be much more than two breaths. Daughters, I hope, though *majkes* they will not be, neither of them. They are Lathro's children. That is magic enough.

The moon is down and gone, and it has come time for me to sing you to your end—or, for all I know, your beginning—in some demon afterworld. It seems a pity, after having spent this night telling you things I have never spoken of to another human, but there it is. You can only be what you are, with that nasty fixation of yours on other people's livers and hearts...and I can only be myself. It has cost me what it has cost me, but I am an enchantress, which is different from a witch or a sorceress, and I have more lives to guard than just the two I carry. You do understand? I would truly prefer to think so.

Goodbye, demon. Goodbye.

LA LUNE T'ATTEND

I've always had a soft spot for shape-shifters in general, and the loup-garou legend in particular, yet my only two werewolf stories—"Lila the Werewolf" and this one—are more than forty years apart in age. A good deal has changed in that time. It's worth mentioning that "Lila," written on simple impulse in 1967, originally couldn't find any other publisher than an obscure UC Santa Cruz literary magazine; while "La Lune T'Attend" was specifically commissioned for an anthology of urban werewolf tales from a major publishing house, and hit bookstores in a world where such creatures have become a pop culture staple.

I've never yet been to Louisiana, but I've known many Creoles and Cajuns over time, listened to a lot of family stories, and read and studied and questioned all I could into vodun, Santería, and other rich and flourishing transplants from West African soil. (Arceneaux's prayers to the Yoruba god Damballa, by the way, were originally notated during late-night conversations that took place very long ago.) That said, "La Lune T'Attend" isn't a cultural treatise or an academic dissertation of any sort. It's a family story.

✺

Even once a month, Arceneaux hated driving his daughter Noelle's car. There was no way to be comfortable: he was a big old man, and the stick-shift hatchback cramped his legs and elbows, playing Baptist hell with the bad knee. Garrigue was dozing peacefully beside him in the passenger seat, as he had done for the whole journey; but then, Garrigue always adapted more easily than he to changes in his circumstances. *All these years up north in the city, Damballa, and I still don't fit nowhere, never did.*

Paved road giving way to gravel, pinging off the car's undercarriage...then to a dirt track and the shaky wooden bridge across the stream; then to little more than untamed underbrush, springing back as he plowed through to the log cabin. *Got to check them shutters—meant to do it last time. Damn raccoons been back. I can smell it.*

Garrigue didn't wake, even with all the jouncing and rattling, until Arceneaux cut the engine. Then his eyes came open immediately, and he turned his head and smiled like a sleepy baby. He was a few months the elder, but he had always looked distinctly younger, in spite of being white, which more often shows the wear. He said, "I was dreaming, me."

Arceneaux grunted. "Same damn dream, I ain't want to hear about it."

"No, wasn't that one. Was you and me really gone fishing, just like folks. You and me in the shade, couple of trotlines out, couple of Dixie beers, nice dream. A *real* dream."

Arceneaux got out of the car and stood stretching himself, trying to forestall a back spasm. Garrigue joined him, still describing his dream in detail. Arceneaux had been taciturn almost from birth, while Garrigue, it was said in Joyelle Parish, bounced out of his mother chattering like a squirrel. Regarding the friendship—unusual, in those days, between a black Creole and a *blanc*—Arceneaux's father had growled to Garrigue's, "Mine cain't talk, *l't'en* cain't shut up. Might do."

And the closeness had lasted for very nearly seventy years (they quarreled mildly at times over the exact number), through schooling, work, marriages, family struggles, and even their final, grudging relocation. They had briefly considered sharing a place after Garrigue moved up north, but then agreed that each was too old and cranky, too stubbornly set in his ways, to risk the relationship over the window being open or shut at night. They met once a week, sometimes at Arceneaux's apartment, but more usually at the home of Garrigue's son Claude, where Garrigue lived; and they both fell asleep, each on his own side of the great park that divided the city, listening to the music of Clifton Chenier, Dennis McGee and Amede Ardoin.

Garrigue glanced up at the darkening overcast sky. "Cut it close again, moon coming on so fast these nights. I keep telling you, Jean-Marc—"

Arceneaux was already limping away from the rear of the car, having opened the trunk and taken out most of the grocery bags. Still scolding him, Garrigue took the rest and followed, leaving one hand free to open the cabin door for Arceneaux and then switch on the single bare light in the room. It was right above the entrance, and the shadows, as though startled themselves to be suddenly awakened, danced briefly over the room when Garrigue stepped inside, swung the door to, and double-locked it behind them.

Arceneaux tipped the bags he carried, and let a dozen bloody steaks and roasts fall to the floor.

The single room was small but tidy, even homely, with two Indian-patterned rag rugs, two cane-bottomed rockers, and a card table with two folding chairs drawn up around it. There was a fireplace, and a refrigerator in one corner, but no beds or cots. The two windows were double-barred on the inside, and the shutters closing them were not wooden, but steel.

Another grocery bag held a bottle of Calvados, which Arceneaux set on the table, next to the two glasses, deck of cards and cribbage board waiting there. In a curiously military fashion, they padlocked and dropbolted the door, carefully checked the security of the windows, and even blocked the fireplace with a heavy steel screen. Then, finally, they sat down at the table, and Arceneaux opened the Calvados and said, "Cut."

Garrigue cut. Arceneaux dealt. Garrigue said, "My littlest grandbaby, Manette, she going to First Communion a week Saturday. You be there?" Arceneaux nodded wordlessly, jabbing pegs into the cribbage board. Garrigue started to say "She so excited, she been asking me, did I ever do First Communion, what did it feel like and all..." but then his words dissolved into a hoarse growl as he slipped from the chair. Garrigue was almost always the first, neither understood why.

Werewolves—*loups-garoux* in Louisiana—are notably bigger than ordinary wolves, running to larger skulls with bolder, more marked bones, deeper-set eyes, broader chests, and paws, front and rear, whose dewclaw serves very nearly as an opposable thumb. Even so, for a small, chattery white man Garrigue stood up as a huge wolf, black from nose to tail-tip, with eyes unchanged from his normal snow-gray, shocking in their humanity. He was at the food before Arceneaux's front feet hit the floor, and there was the customary snarling between them as they snapped up the meat within minutes. The table went over, cards and brandy and all, and both of them hurled themselves at walls and barred windows until the entire cabin shook with their frenzied fury. The wolf that was Arceneaux stood on its hind legs and tried to reach the window latches with uncannily dextrous paws, while the wolf that was Garrigue broke a front claw tearing at the door. They never howled.

First madness spent, they circled the room restlessly, their eyes glowing as dogs' and wolves' eyes do not glow. In time they settled into a light, reluctant sleep—Garrigue under a chair, Arceneaux in the ruins of the rug he had torn to pieces. Even in sleep they whined softly and eagerly, lips constantly twitching back from the fangs they never quite covered.

Towards dawn, with the moon gray and small, looking almost triangular because of the moisture in the air, something brought Arceneaux to the barred window nearest the door, rearing once again with his paws on the sill. There was nothing to see through the closed metal shutters, but the deep, nearly inaudible sound that constantly pulsed through his body in this form grew louder as he stared, threatening to break its banks and swell into a full-throated howl. Once again he clawed at the bars, but Garrigue had screwed down the bolts holding them in place too tightly even for a *loup-garou*'s deftness, and Arceneaux's snarl bared his fangs to the black gums. Garrigue joined him, puzzled but curious, and the two of them stood side by side, panting rapidly, ears flattened against their skulls. And still there was no hint of movement anywhere outside.

Then the howl came, surging up from somewhere very near, soaring over the trees like some skeletal ancient bird, almost visible in its dreadful ardency. The werewolves went mad, howling their own possessed challenges, even snapping furiously at each other. Arceneaux sprang at the barred windows until they shivered. He was crouching to leap again when he heard the familiar whimper behind him, and simultaneously felt the brief but overwhelming pain, unlike any other, of distorted molecules regaining their natural shape. Coming back always took longer, and hurt worse.

As always afterward, he collapsed to the floor and lay there, quickly human enough to curse the weakness that always overtook a returning *loup-garou*, old or young, He heard Garrigue gasping, "*Duplessis...Duplessis...*" but could not yet respond. A face began to form in his mind: dark, clever, handsome in a way that meant no good to anyone who responded to it.... Still unable to speak, Arceneaux shook his head against the worn, stained floorboards. He had better reason than most to know why that sound, that cold wail of triumph, could not have been uttered by Alexandre Duplessis of Pointe Coupee Parish.

They climbed slowly to their feet, two stiff-jointed old men, looking around them at the usual wreckage of the cabin. Over the years that they had been renting it together, Garrigue and Arceneaux had made it proof, as best they could, against the rage of what would be trapped there every month. Even so, the rugs were in shreds, the refrigerator was on its side, there were deep claw-marks on the log walls to match the ones already there, and they would definitely need a new card table. Arceneaux pointed at the overturned Calvados bottle and said, "Shame, that. Wish I'd got the cap back on."

"Yeah, yeah." Garrigue shivered violently—common for most after the return. He said, "Jean-Marc, it was Duplessis, you know and I know. Duplessis *back*."

"Not in this world." Arceneaux's voice was bleak and slow. "Maybe in some other world he back, but ain't in this one." He turned from the window to face Garrigue. "I killed Duplessis, man. Ain't none of us come back from what I done, Duplessis or nobody. You was there, Rene Garrigue! You saw how I done!"

Garrigue was hugging himself to stop the shivering, closing his eyes against the seeing. Abruptly he said in a strangely quiet tone, "He outside right now. He *there*, Jean-Marc."

"Naw, man," Arceneaux said. "Naw, Rene. He gone, Rene, my word. You got my word on it." But Garrigue was lunging past him to fumble with the locks and throw the door wide. The freezing dawn air rushed in over the body spilled across the path, so near the door that Garrigue almost tripped over it. It was a woman—a vagrant, clearly, wearing what looked like five or six coats, sweaters and undergarments. Her throat had been ripped out, and what remained of her intestines were draped neatly over a tree branch. Even in the cold, there were already flies.

Arceneaux breathed the name of his god, his *loa,* Damballa Wedo, the serpent. Garrigue whispered, "Women. Always the women, always the belly. Duplessis."

"He carry her here." Arceneaux was calming himself, as well as Garrigue. "Killed her somewhere back there, maybe in the city, carry her here, leave her like a business card. You right, Rene. Can't *be,* but you right."

"Business card." Garrigue's voice was still tranquil, almost dreamy. "He know this place, Jean-Marc. If he know this place, he know everything. *Everything.*"

"Hush you, man, hush now, mind me." Arceneaux might have been talking to a child wakened out of a nightmare. "Shovel out back, under the crabapple, saw it last time. We got to take her off and bury her, first thing. You go get me that shovel, Rene."

Garrigue stared at him. Arceneaux said it again, more gently. "Go on, Rene. Find me that shovel, *compe'*."

Alone, he felt every hair on his own body standing up; his big dark hands were trembling so that he could not even cover the woman's face or close her eyes. *Alexandre Duplessis, c'est vraiment li, vraiment, vraiment;* but the knowledge frightened the old man far less than the terrible lure of the crumpled thing at his feet, torn open and emptied out, gutted and drained and abandoned, the reek of her terror dominating the hot, musky scent of the beast that had hunted her down in the hours before dawn. *The fear, Damballa, the fear—you once get that smell in you head, you throat, you gut, you never get it out. Better than the meat, the blood even, you smell the fear.* He was shaking badly now, and he knew that he needed to get out of there with Garrigue before he hurled himself upon the pitiful remains, to roll and wallow in them like the beast he was. *Hold me, Damballa. Hide me, hold me.*

Garrigue returned with the rusty shovel and together they carried the dead woman deeper into the woods. Then he stood by, rubbing his mouth compulsively as he watched Arceneaux hack at the hard earth. In the same small voice as before, he said, "I scare, me, Ti-Jean," calling Arceneaux by his childhood nickname. "What we do to him."

"What he did to us." Arceneaux's own voice was cold and steady. "What he did to *ma Sophie*."

As he had known it would, the mention of Arceneaux's sister immediately brought Garrigue back from wherever terror and guilt together had taken him. "I ain't forgot Sophie." His gray eyes had closed down like the steel shutters whose color they matched. "I ain't forgot nothing."

"I know, man," Arceneaux said gently. He finished his work, patted the new grave as flat as he could make it—*one good rain, two, grass cover it all*—and said, "We come back before next moon, clean up a little. Right now, we going home." Garrigue nodded eagerly.

In the car, approaching the freeway, Garrigue could not keep from talking about Sophie Arceneaux, as he had not done in a very long while. "So pretty, that girl, that sister of yours. So pretty, so kind, who wouldn't want to marry such a fine woman like her?" Then he hurriedly added, "Of course, my Elizabeth, Elizabeth was a fine woman too, I don't say a word against Elizabeth. But Sophie...*la Sophie*..." He fell silent for a time, and then said in a different voice, "I ain't blame Duplessis for wanting her. Can't do that, Jean-Marc."

"She didn't want him," Arceneaux said. There was no expression at all in his voice now. "Didn't want nothing to do with him, no mind what he gave her, where he took her, never mind what he promised. So he killed her." After a pause, he went on, "You know how he killed her."

Garrigue folded his hands in his lap and looked at them.

So low he could barely be heard, he answered, "In the wolf...in the wolf shape. Hadn't seen it, I wouldn't have believed."

"Ripped her throat out," Arceneaux said. "*Ma colombe, ma pauv' p'ti,* she never had no chance—no more than him with her." He looked off down the freeway, seeing, not a thousand cars nor a distant city skyline, but his entire Louisiana family, wolves all, demanding that as oldest male he take immediate vengeance on Duplessis. For once—and it was a rare enough occurrence—he found himself in complete agreement with his blood kin and their ancient notions of honor and retribution. In company with Garrigue, one of Sophie's more tongue-tied admirers, he had set off on the track of his sister's murderer.

"Duplessis kill *ma Sophie,* she never done nothing but good for anyone. Well, I done what I done, and I ain't sorry for it." His voice rose as he grew angry all over again, more than he usually allowed himself these days. He said, "Ain't a bit sorry."

Garrigue shivered, remembering the hunt. Even with an entire werewolf clan sworn to avenge Sophie Arceneaux, Duplessis had made no attempt to hide himself, or to flee the region, so great was his city man's contempt for thick-witted backwoods bumpkins. Arceneaux had run him to earth in a single day, and it had been almost too easy for Garrigue to lure him into a moonshiner's riverside shebeen: empty for the occasion and abandoned forever after, haunted by the stories of what was done there to Alexandre Duplessis.

It had taken them all night, and Garrigue was a different man in the morning.

After the first scream, Garrigue had never heard the others; he could not have done otherwise and held onto his sanity. Sometimes it seemed to him that he had indeed gone mad that night, and that all the rest of his life—the flight north, the jobs, the marriage, the beloved children and grandchildren, the home—had never been anything but a lunatic's hopeless dream of forgetfulness. More than forty years later he still shuddered and moaned in his sleep, and at times still whimpered himself awake. *All the blood, all the shit...the...the...*sound *when Ti-Jean took that old cleaver thing...and that man wouldn't die, wouldn't die... wasn't nothing* left *of him but open mouth, awful open mouth, and he wouldn't* die....

"Don't make *no* sense," Arceneaux said beside him. "Days burying...four, five county lines—"

"Five," Garrigue whispered. "Evangeline. Joyelle. St. Landry. Acadia. Rapides. Too close together, I *told* you...."

Arceneaux shook his head. "Conjure. Conjure in it somewhere, got to be. Guillory, maybe, he evil enough...old Fontenot, over in St. Landry. Got to be conjure."

They drove the rest of the way in near silence, Arceneaux biting down hard on his own lower lip, Garrigue taking refuge in memories of his wife Elizabeth, and of Arceneaux's long-gone Pauline. Both women, non-Creoles, raised and encountered in the city, believed neither in werewolves nor in conjure men; neither one had ever known the truth about their husbands. *Loups-garoux* run in families: Arceneaux and Garrigue, marrying out of their clans, out of their deep back-country world, had both produced children who would go through their lives completely unaware of that part of their ancestry. The choice had been a deliberate one, and Garrigue, for his part, had never regretted it. He doubted very much that Arceneaux had either, but it was always hard to tell with Arceneaux.

Pulling to the curb in front of the frame house where Garrigue lived with Claude and his family, Arceneaux cut the engine, and they sat looking at each other. Garrigue said finally, "Forgot to fish. Grandbabies always wanting to know did we catch anything."

"Tell them fish wasn't biting today. We done that before."

Garrigue smiled for the first time. "Claude, he think we don't do no fishing, we goes up there to drink, get away from family, get a little wild. Say he might just come with us one time." Arceneaux grunted without replying. Garrigue said, "I keeps ducking and dodging, you know? Ducking and dodging." His voice was growing shaky again, but he never took his eyes from Arceneaux's eyes. He said, "What we going to do, Ti-Jean?"

"Get you some sleep," Arceneaux said. "Get you a good breakfast, tell Claude you likely be late. We go find Duplessis tomorrow, you and me."

Garrigue looked, for a moment, more puzzled than frightened. "Why we bothering that? He know right where we live, where the chirrens lives—"

Arceneaux cut him off harshly. "We find him fast, maybe we throw him just that little bit off-balance, could help sometime." He patted Garrigue's shoulder lightly. "We use what we got, Rene, and all we got is us. You go on now—my knee biting on me a little bit."

In fact—as Garrigue understood from the fact that Arceneaux mentioned it at all—the bad knee was hurting him a good deal; he could only pray that it wouldn't have locked up on him by morning. He brought the car back to Noelle, who took one look at his gait and insisted on driving him home, lecturing him all the way about his need for immediate surgery. She was his oldest child, his companion from her birth, and the only one who would ever have challenged him, as she did now.

"Dadda, whatever you and *Compe'* Rene are up to, I *will* find it out—you know I always do. Simpler tell me now, *oui?*"

"Ain't up to one thing," Arceneaux grumbled. "Ain't up to nothing, you turning such a suspicious woman. You *mamere,* she just exactly the same way."

"Because you're such a bad liar," his daughter replied tenderly. She caressed the back of his neck with a warm, work-hardened hand. "*Ma'dear* and me, we used to laugh so, nights you'd be slipping out to drink, play cards with *Compe'* Rene and your old zydeco friends. Make some crazy little-boy story—*whoo,* out the door, gone till morning, come home looking like someone dragged you through a keyhole backwards. Lord, didn't we *laugh!*"

There had been a few moments through the years when pure loneliness had made him seriously consider turning around on her and telling her to sit herself down and listen to a story. This moment was one of them; but he only muttered something he forgot as soon as he'd said it, and nothing more until she dropped him off at his apartment building. Then she kissed his cheek and told him, "Come by for dinner tomorrow. Antoine will be home early, for a change, and Patrice just *got* to show his *gam'pair* something he drew in school."

"Day after," Arceneaux said. "Busy tomorrow." He could feel her eyes following him as he limped through the lobby doors.

The knee was still painful the next morning, but it remained functionally flexible. He could manage. He caught the crosstown bus to meet Garrigue in front of Claude's house, and they set forth together to search for a single man in a large city. Their only advantage lay in possessing, even in human form, a wolf's sense of smell; that, and a bleak awareness that their quarry shared the very same gift, and undoubtedly already knew where they lived, and—far more frightening—whom they loved. *We ain't suppose to care, Damballa. Bon Dieu made the loup-garou, he ain't mean us to care about nothing. The kill only. The blood only...the fear only. Maybe Bon Dieu mad at us, me and Rene, disobeying him like we done. Too late now.*

Garrigue had always been the better tracker, since their childhood, so Arceneaux simply stayed just behind his left shoulder and went where he led. Picking up the werewolf scent at the start was a grimly easy matter: knowing Duplessis as they did, neither was surprised to cross his trail not far from the house where Garrigue's younger son Fernand lived with his own wife and children. Garrigue caught his breath audibly then, but said no word. He plunged along, drawn by the strange, unmistakable aroma as it circled, doubled back on itself, veered off in this direction or that, then inevitably returned to patrolling the streets most dear to two weary old men. Frightened and enraged, stubborn and haunted and lame, they followed. Arceneaux never took his eyes from Garrigue, which was good, because Garrigue was not using his eyes at all, and would have walked into traffic a dozen times over, if not for Arceneaux. People yelled at him.

They found Duplessis in the park, the great Park that essentially divided the two worlds of the city. He wore a long red-leather coat over a gray suit of the Edwardian cut he always favored—*just like the one we tear off him that night, Damballa, just like that suit*—and he was standing under a young willow tree, leaning on a dainty, foppish walking stick, smiling slightly as he watched children playing in a sandbox. When Arceneaux and Garrigue came up with him, one on each side, he did not speak to them immediately, but stood looking calmly from one face to the other, as his smile broadened. He was as handsome as ever, velvet-dark and whip-lean, unscarred in any way that they could see; and he appeared no older than he had on the night they had spent whittling him down to screaming blood, screaming shit, *Damballa*....

Duplessis said softly, "My friends."

Arceneaux did not answer him. Garrigue said inanely, "You looking well, *Compe'* Alexandre."

"Ah, I have my friends to thank for that." Duplessis spoke, not in Creole, but in the Parisian French he had always affected. "There's this to say for hell and death—they do keep a person in trim." He patted Garrigue's arm, an old remembered habit of his. "Yes, I am quite well, *Compe'* Rene. There were some bad times, as you know, but these days I feel as young and vigorous as...oh, say, as any of your grandchildren." And he named them then, clearly tasting them, as though to eat the name was to have eaten the child. "Sandrine... Honore...your adorable little Manette...." He named them all, grinning at Garrigue around the names.

Arceneaux said, "Sophie."

Duplessis did not turn his head, but stopped speaking.

Arceneaux said it again. "Sophie, you son of a bitch—*pere de personne, fils de cent mille.* Sophie."

When Duplessis did turn, he was not smiling, nor was there any bombast or mockery in his voice. He said, "I think you will agree with me, Jean-Marc, that being slashed slowly to pieces alive pays for all. Like it or not, I own your poor dear Sophie just as much as you do now. I'd call that fair and square, wouldn't you?"

Arceneaux hit him then. Duplessis hadn't been expecting the blow, and he went over on his back, shattering the fragile walking stick beneath him. The children in the sandbox looked up with some interest, but the passersby only walked faster.

Duplessis got up slowly, running his tongue-tip over a bloody upper lip. He said, "Well, I guess I don't learn much, do I? That's exactly how one of you—or was it both?—knocked me unconscious in that filthy little place by the river. And when I came to...." He shrugged lightly and actually winked at Arceneaux. He said softly, "But you haven't got any rope with you this time, have you Jean-Marc? And none of your little—ah—sculptor's tools?" He tasted his bloody mouth again. "A grandfather should be more careful, I'd think."

The contemptuous lilt in the last words momentarily cost Garrigue his sanity. Only Arceneaux's swift reaction and strong clutch kept him from knocking Duplessis down a second time. His voice half-muffled against Arceneaux's chest, Garrigue heard himself raging, "You touch my chirren, you—you touch the *doorknob* on my grandbabies' house—I cut you up all over again, cut you like Friday morning's bacon, you hear me?" And he heard Duplessis laughing.

Then the laughter stopped, almost with a machine's mechanical *click,* and Duplessis said, "No. You hear *me* now." Garrigue shook himself free of Arceneaux's preventive embrace, nodded a silent promise, and turned to see Duplessis facing them both, his mouth still bleeding, and his eyes as freezingly distant as his voice. He said, "I am Alexandre Duplessis. You sent me to hell, you tortured me as no devils could have done—no devils would have conceived of what you did. But in so doing, you have set me free, you have lost all power over me. I will do what I choose to you and yours, and there will be nothing you can do about it, nothing you can threaten me with. Would you like to hear what I choose to do?"

He told them.

He went into detail.

"It will take me some little while, obviously. That suits me—I want it to take a while. I want to watch you go mad as I strip away everything you love and cannot protect, just as you stripped away my fingers, my face, my organs, piece by piece by piece." The voice never grew any louder, but remained slow and thoughtful, even genial. The soulful eyes—still a curious reddish-brown— seemed to have withdrawn deep under the telltale single brow and contracted to the size of cranberries. Arceneaux could feel their heat on his skin.

"This is where I live at present," Duplessis said, and told them his address. He said, "I would be delighted if you should follow me there, and anywhere else—it would make things much more amusing. I would even invite you to hunt with me, but you were always too cowardly for that, and by the looks of you I can see you've not changed. Wolves—God's own *wolves* caging themselves come the moon, not even surviving on dogs and cats, mice and squirrels and rabbits, as you did in Joyelle Parish. *Lamisere a deux...Misere et Compagnie*—no wonder you have both grown so old, it's almost pitiful. Now *I*"—a light inward flick of his two hands invited the comparison—"I dine only on the diet that *le Bon Dieu* meant for me, and it will keep me hunting when you two are long-buried with the humans you love so much." He clucked his tongue, mimicking a distressed old woman, and repeated, "Pitiful. Truly pitiful. *A très—très—tot*...my friends."

He bowed gracefully to them then, and turned to stroll away through the trees. Arceneaux said, "Conjure." Duplessis turned slowly again at the word, waiting. Arceneaux said, "You ain't come back all by yourself, we took care. You got brought back—take a conjure man to do that. Which one—Guillory? I got to figure Guillory."

Duplessis smiled, a little smugly, and shook his head. "I'd never trust Guillory out of my sight—let alone after my death. No, Fontenot was the only sensible choice. Entirely mad, but that's always a plus in a conjure man, isn't it? And he hated you with all his wicked old heart, Jean-Marc, as I'm sure you know. What on earth did you *do* to that man—rape his black pig? Only thing in the world he loved, that pig."

"Stopped him feeding a lil boy to it," Arceneaux grunted. "What he do for you, and what it cost you? Fontenot, he come high."

"They all come high. But you can bargain with Fontenot. Remember, Jean-Marc?" Duplessis held out his hands, palms down. The two little fingers were missing, and Arceneaux shivered with sudden memory of that moment when he'd wondered who had already taken them, and why, even as he had prepared to cut into the bound man's flesh....

Duplessis laughed harshly, repeating, "My insurance policy, you could say. Really, you should have thought a bit about those, old friend. There's mighty conjuring to be done with the fingers of a *loup-garou*. It was definitely worth Fontenot's while to witch me home, time-consuming as it turned out to be. I'm sure he never regretted our covenant for a moment."

Something in his use of the past tense raised Arceneaux's own single brow, his daughters' onetime plaything. Duplessis caught the look and grinned with the flash of genuine mischief that had charmed even Arceneaux long ago, *though not ma Sophie, never—she* knew. "Well, let's be honest, you couldn't have a man with that kind of power and knowledge running around loose—not a bad, bad man like Hipolyte Fontenot. I was merely doing my duty as a citizen. *Au 'voir* again, *mon ami. Mon assassin.*"

Watching him walk away, Arceneaux was praying so hard for counsel and comfort to Damballa Wedo, and to Damballa's gentle wife, the rainbow Ayida, that he started when Garrigue said beside him, "Let's go, come *on*. We don't let that man out of our sight, here on in."

Arceneaux did not look at him. "No point in it. He *want* us to follow him—he want us going crazy, no sleep, no time to think straight, just wondering *when....* I ain't go play it his way, me, unh-uh."

"You know another way? You got a better idea?" Garrigue was very nearly crying with impatience and anxiety, all but dancing on his toes, straining to follow Alexandre Duplessis. Arceneaux put his hands on the white man's arms, trying to take the trembling into himself.

"I don't know it's a better idea. I just know he still think we nothing but a couple back-country fools, like he always did, and we got to keep him thinking that thing—*got* to. Because we gone kill him, Rene, you hearing me? We done it before—this time we gone kill him *right,* so he stay dead. Yeah, there's only two of us, but there's only one of him, and he ain't God, man, he just one damn old *loup-garou* in a fancy suit, talking fancy French. You hear what I'm saying to you?"

Garrigue did not answer. Arceneaux shook him slightly. "Right now, we going on home, both of us. He ain't go do nothing tonight, he want us to spend it thinking on all that shit he just laid on us. Home, Rene."

Still no response. Arceneaux looked into Garrigue's eyes, and could not find Garrigue there, but only frozen, helpless terror. "Listen, Rene, I tell you something my daddy use to say. Daddy, he say to me always, '*Di moin qui vous lamein, ma di cous qui vous ye.*' You tell me who you love, I tell you who you are." Garrigue began returning slowly to his own eyes, looking back at him: expressionless, but present. Arceneaux said, "You think just maybe we know who we are, *Compe'* Rene?"

Garrigue smiled a little, shakily. "Duplessis...Duplessis, he don't love nobody. Never did."

"So Duplessis ain't nobody. Duplessis don't exist. You gone be scared of somebody don't exist?" Arceneaux slapped his old friend's shoulder, hard. "Home now. Ti-Jean say." They did go to their homes then, and they slept well, or at least they told each other so in the morning. Arceneaux judged that Garrigue might actually have slept through the night; for himself, he came and went, turning over a new half-dream of putting an end to Alexandre Duplessis each time he turned in his bed. Much of the waking time he spent simply calling into darkness inside himself, calling on his *loa*, as he had been taught to do when young, crying out, *Damballa Wedo, great serpent, you got to help us, this on you.... Bon Dieu can't be no use here, ain't his country, he don't speak the patois.... Got to be you, Damballa....* When he did sleep, he dreamed of his dead wife, Pauline, and asked her for help too, as he had always done.

A revitalized Garrigue was most concerned the next morning with the problem of destroying a werewolf who had already survived being sliced into pieces, themselves buried in five different counties. "We never going to get another chance like that, not in this city. City, you got to *explain* why you do somebody in—and you definitely better not say it's cause he turn into a wolf some nights. Be way simpler if we could just shoot him next full moon, tell them we hunters. Bring him home strap right across the hood, hey Ti-Jean?" He chuckled, thinking about it.

"Except we be changing too," Arceneaux pointed out. "We all prisoners of the moon, one way another."

Garrigue nodded. "Yeah, you'd think that'd make us—I don't know—hold together some way, look out for each other. But it don't happen, do it? I mean, here I am, and I'm thinking, I ever do get the chance, I'd kill him wolf to wolf, just like he done Sophie. I would, I just don't give a damn no more."

"Come to that, it come to that. Last night I been trying to work out how we could pour some cement, make him part of a bridge, an underpass—you know, way the Mafia do. Couldn't figure it."

Garrigue said, "You right about one thing, anyway. We can't be waiting on the moon, cause he sure as hell won't be. Next full moon gone be short one *loup-garou* for certain."

"Maybe two," Arceneaux said quietly. "Maybe three, even. Man ain't going quietly no second time."

"Be worth it." Garrigue put out his hand and Arceneaux took it, roughness meeting familiar lifelong roughness. Garrigue said, "Just so it ain't the little ones. Just so he don't ever get past us to the little ones." Arceneaux nodded, but did not answer him.

For the next few days they pointedly paid no attention to Duplessis's presence in the city—though they caught his scent in both neighborhoods, as he plainly made himself familiar with family routines—but spent the time with their children and grandchildren, delighting the latter and relieving the men of babysitting duties. Garrigue, having only sons, got away without suspicions; but neither Noelle nor Arceneaux's daughter-in-law Athalie were entirely deceived. As Athalie put it, "Women, we are so used to men's stupid lies, we're out of practice for a good one, Papajean," which was her one-word nickname for him. "I *know* you're lying, some way, but this one's really good."

On Saturday Arceneaux, along with most of his own family, accompanied Garrigue's family to the Church of Saints Philip and James for Manette Garrigue's First Communion. The day was unseasonably warm, the group returning for the party large, and at first no one but Arceneaux and Garrigue took any notice of the handsome, well-dressed man walking inconspicuously between them. Alexandre Duplessis said thoughtfully, "What a charming little girl. You must be very proud, Rene."

Garrigue had been coached half the night, or he would have gone for Duplessis's throat on the instant. Instead he answered, mildly enough, "I'm real proud of her, you got that right. You lay a hand on her, all Fontenot's *gris-gris* be for nothing next time."

Duplessis seemed not to have heard him. "Should she be the first—not Jean-Marc's Patrice or Zelime? It's so hard to decide—"

The strong old arms that blocked Garrigue away also neatly framed Duplessis's throat. Arceneaux said quietly, "You never going to make it to next moon, *Compe'* Alexandre. You know that, don't you?"

Duplessis looked calmly back at him, the red-brown eyes implacable far beyond human understanding. He said, "*Compe'* Jean-Marc, I died at your hands forty and more years ago, and by the time you got through with me I was very, very old. You cannot kill such a man twice, not so it matters." He smiled at Arceneaux. "Besides, the moon is perhaps not everything, even for a *loup-garou*. I'd give that a little thought, if I were you." His canine teeth glittered wetly in the late-autumn sunlight as he turned and walked away.

After a while Noelle dropped back to take her father's arm. She rubbed her cheek lightly against Arceneaux's shoulder and said, "Your knee all right? You're looking tired."

"Been a long morning." Arceneaux hugged her arm under his own. "Don't you worry about the old man."

"I do, though. Gotten so I worry about you a whole lot. Antoine does too." She looked up at him, and he thought, *Her mama's eyes, her mama's mouth, but my complexion—thank God that's all she got from me....* She said, "How about you spend the night, hey? I make gumbo, you play with the grandbabies, talk sports with Antoine. Sound fair?"

It sounded more than fair; it sounded such a respite from the futile plans and dreaded memories with which he and Garrigue had been living that he could have wept. "I'm gone need take care some business first. Nothing big, just a few bits of business. Then I come back, stay the night." She prompted him with a silent, quizzical tilt of her head, and he added, "Promise." It was an old ritual between them, dating from her childhood: he rarely used the word at all, but once he did he could be absolutely relied on to keep it. His grandchildren had all caught onto this somewhat earlier than she had.

He slipped away from the party group without even signaling to Garrigue: a deliberately suspicious maneuver that had the waiting Duplessis behind him before he had gone more than a block from the house. It was difficult to pretend not to notice that he was being followed—this being one of the wolf senses that finds an echo in the human body—but Arceneaux was good at it, and took a certain pleasure in leading Duplessis all over the area, as the latter had done to him and Garrigue. But the motive was not primarily spite. He was actually bound for a certain neighborhood *botanica* run by an old Cuban couple who had befriended him years before, when he first came to the city. They were kind and brown, and spoke almost no English, and he had always suspected that they knew exactly what he was, had known others like him in Cuba, and simply didn't care.

He spent some forty-five minutes in the crowded little shop, and left with his arms full of brightly colored packages. Most amounted to herbal and homeopathic remedies of one sort and another; a very few were gifts for Damballa Wedo, whose needs are very simple; and one—the only one with an aroma that would have alerted any *loup-garou* in the world—was a largish packet of wolfbane.

Still sensing Duplessis on his track, he walked back to Noelle's house, asked to borrow her car briefly, claiming to have heard an ominous sound from the transmission, and took off northeast, in the direction of the old cabin where he and Garrigue imprisoned themselves one night in every month. The car was as cramped as ever, and the drive as tedious, but he managed it as efficiently as he could. Arriving alone, for the first time ever, he spent some while tidying the cabin, and the yet-raw grave in the woods as well; then carefully measured out all the wolfbane in a circle around the little building, and headed straight back to the city. He bent all his senses, wolf and human alike, to discovering whether or not Duplessis had trailed him the entire way, but the results were inconclusive.

"Way I been figuring it over," he said to Garrigue the next day, drinking bitter chicory coffee at the only Creole restaurant whose cook understood the importance of a proper *roux*, "we lured him into that blind pig back on the river, all them years ago, and he just know he way too smart for us to get him like that no second time. So we gone do just exactly what we done before, cause we ain't but pure-D country, and that the onliest trick we know." His sigh turned to a weary grunt as he shook his head. "Which ain't no lie, far as I'm concerned. But we go on paying him no mind, we keep sneaking up there, no moon, no need...he smell the wolfbane, he keep on following us, we got to be planning *something*.... All I'm hoping, *Compe'* Rene, I'm counting on a fool staying a fool. The smart ones, they do sometimes."

Garrigue rubbed the back of his neck and folded his arms. "So what you saying, same thing, except with the cabin? Man, *I* wouldn't fall for that, and you *know* I'm a fool."

"Yeah, but see, see, we know we fools—we used to it, we live with it like everybody, do the best we can. But Duplessis...." He smiled, although it felt as though he were lifting a great cold weight with his mouth. "Duplessis *scary*. Duplessis got knowledge you and me couldn't even spell, never mind understand. He just as smart as he think he is, and we just about what we were back when we never seen a city man before, we so proud to be running with a city man." He rubbed the bad knee, remembering Sophie's warnings, not at all comforted by the thought that no one else in the clan had seen through the laughter, the effortless charm, the *newness* of the young *loup-garou* who came so persistently courting her. He said, "There's things Duplessis never going to understand."

He missed Garrigue's question, because it was mumbled in so low a tone. He said, "Say what?"

Garrigue asked, "It going to be like that time?" Arceneaux did not answer. Garrigue said, "Cause I don't think I can do that again, Ti-Jean. I don't think I can watch, even." His face and voice were embarrassed, but there was no mistaking the set of his eyes, not after seventy years.

"I don't know, me." Arceneaux himself had never once been pursued by dreams of what they had done to Alexandre Duplessis in Sophie's name; but in forty years he had gently shaken Garrigue out of them more than once, and held him afterward. "We get him there—just you, me and him, like before—I know then. All I can tell you now, Rene."

Garrigue made no reply, and they separated shortly afterward. Arceneaux went home, iced his knee, turned on his radio (he had a television set, but rarely watched it), and learned of the discovery of a second homeless woman, eviscerated and partly devoured, her head almost severed from her body by the violence of the attack. The corpse had been found under the Viaduct, barely two blocks from Arceneaux's apartment, and the police announced that they were taking seriously the disappearance of the woman Arceneaux had buried. Arceneaux sat staring at the radio long after it had switched to broadcasting a college football game.

He called Garrigue, got a busy signal, and waited until his friend called him back a moment later. When he picked up the phone, he said simply, "I know."

Garrigue was fighting hysteria; Arceneaux could feel it before he spoke the first word. "Can't be, Ti-Jean. Not full moon. Can't *be*."

"Well," Arceneaux said. "Gone have to ask old Duplessis what else he sold that Fontenot." He had not expected Garrigue to laugh, and was not surprised. He said, "Don't be panicking, you hear me, Rene? Not now. Ain't the time."

"Don't know what else to do." But Garrigue's voice was slightly steadier. "If he really be changing any damn time he like—"

"Got to be rules. *Le Bon Dieu*, he wouldn't let there not be rules—"

"Then we got to tell them, you hear *me*? They got to know what out there, what we dealing with—what coming *after* them—"

"And what we are? What they come from, what they part of? You think your little Manette, my Patrice, you think they ready for that?"

"Not the grandbabies, when I ever said the grandbabies? I'm talking the chirren—yours, mine, they husbands, wives, all them. They old enough, they got a right to know." There was a pause on the other end, and then Garrigue said flatly, "You don't tell them, I will. I swear."

It was Arceneaux's turn to be silent, listening to Garrigue's anxious breathing on the phone. He said finally, "Noelle. Noelle got a head on her. We tell her, no one else."

"She got a husband, too. What about him?"

"Noelle," Arceneaux said firmly. "Antoine ain't got no werewolf for a daddy."

"Okay." Garrigue drew the two syllables out with obvious dubiousness. "Noelle." The voice quavered again, sounding old for the first time in Arceneaux's memory. "Ti-Jean, he could be anywhere right now, we wouldn't know. Could be *at* them, be tearing them apart, like that woman—"

Arceneaux stopped him like a traffic cop, literally—and absurdly—with a hand held up. "No, he couldn't. Think about it, Rene. Back in Louzianne— back *then*—what we do after that big a kill? What *anybody* do?"

"Go off...go off somewhere, go to sleep." Garrigue said it grudgingly, but he said it.

"How long for? How long you ever sleep, you and that full belly?"

"A day, anyway. Slept out two whole days, one time. And old Albert Vaugine...." Garrigue was chuckling a bit, in spite of himself. He said, "Okay, so we maybe got a couple of days—*maybe*. What then?"

"Then we get ourselves on up to the cabin. You and me and him." Arceneaux hung up.

It had long been the centerpiece of Arceneaux's private understanding of the world that nothing was ever as good as you expected it to be, or as bad. His confession of her ancestry to Noelle fell into the latter category. He had expected her reaction to be one of horrified revulsion, followed by absolute denial and tearful outrage. Instead, after withdrawing into silent thought for a time, and then saying slow, mysterious things like, "So *that's* why I can never do anything with my hair," she told him, "You do know there's no way in the world you're going without me?"

His response never got much beyond, "The hell you preach, girl!" Noelle set her right forefinger somewhere between his Adam's apple and his collarbones, and said, "Dadda, this is my fight too. As long as that man's running around loose"—the irony of her using the words that Alexandre Duplessis had used to justify his murder of the conjure man Fontenot was not lost on Arceneaux—"my children aren't safe. You know the way I get about the children."

".This won't be no PTA meeting. You don't know."

"I know you and Uncle Rene, you may both be werewolves, but you're *old* werewolves, and you're not exactly in the best shape. Oh, you're going to need me, cause right now the both of you couldn't tackle Patrice, never mind Zelime." He was in no state to tackle her, either; he made do with a mental reservation: *Look away for even five minutes and we're out of here, me and Rene. You got to know how to handle daughters, that's all. Specially the pushy ones.*

But on the second day, it didn't matter, because it was Noelle who was gone. And Patrice with her. And her car.

After Antoine had called the police, and the house had begun to fill with terrified family, but before the reporters had arrived, and before Zelime had stopped crying for her mother and little brother, Arceneaux borrowed his son Celestin's car. It was quite a bit like renting it, not because Celestin charged him anything, but because answering all his questions about why the loan was necessary almost amounted to filling out a form. Arceneaux finally roared at him, in a voice Celestin had not heard since his childhood, "Cause I'm your father, me, and I just about to snatch you balder than you already are, you don't hand me them keys." He was on the road five minutes later.

He did not stop to pick up Garrigue. His explanation to himself was that there wasn't time, that every minute was too precious to be taken up with a detour; but even as he made it, he knew better. The truth lay in his pity for Garrigue's endless nightmares, for his lonesome question, "It gone be like that time?" and for his own sense that this was finally between him and the man whom he had carved to obscene fragments alive. *I let him do it all back to me, he lets them two go. Please, Damballa, you hear? Please.*

But he was never certain—and less now than ever before—whether Damballa heard prayers addressed to him in English. So for the entire length of the drive, which seemed to take the rest of his life, he chanted, over and over, a prayer-song that little Ti-Jean Arceneaux, who spoke another language, had learned young, never forgotten, and, until this moment, never needed.

> *"Baba yehge, amiwa saba yehge,*
> *De Damballa e a miwa,*
> *Danou sewa yehge o, djevo de.*
> *De Damballa Wedo, Bade miwa...."*

Rather than bursting into the cabin like the avenging angel he had planned to be, he hardly had the strength or the energy to open the car door, once he arrived. The afternoon was cold, and he could smell snow an hour or two away; he noticed a few flakes on the roof of Noelle's car. There was flickering light in the cabin, and smoke curling from the chimney, which he and Garrigue mistrusted enough that they almost never lighted a fire. He moved closer, noticing two sets of footprints leading to the door, *Yeah, she'd have been carrying Patrice, boy'd have been too scared to walk.* The vision of his terrified four-year-old grandson made him grind his teeth, and Duplessis promptly called from within, "No need to bite the door down, Jean-Marc. Half a minute, I'll be right there."

Waiting, Arceneaux moved to the side of the house and ripped down the single power line. The electric light went out inside, and he heard Duplessis laugh. Standing on the doorstep as Arceneaux walked back, he said, "I thought you might do that, so I built a handsome fire for us all—even lit a few candles. But if you imagine that's going to preclude the use of power tools, I feel I should remind you that they all run on batteries these days. Nice *big* batteries. Come in, Jean-Marc, I bid you welcome."

It was not the shock of seeing Noelle tied in a chair that almost caused Arceneaux to lose what control he had and charge the smiling man standing beside her. It was the sight of Patrice, unbound on her lap, lighting up at the sight of him to call *"Gam'pair!"* He had been crying, but his face made it clear that everything would be all right now. Duplessis said pleasantly, "I wouldn't give it a second thought, old friend. I'm sure you know why."

"Fontenot," Arceneaux said. "Never knowed the old man had *that* much power."

"Oh, it cost me an arm and a leg...so to speak." Duplessis laughed softly.

"Another reason he had to go. I mean, suppose everyone could change whenever he chose, things might become a bit...chaotic, don't you agree? But it certainly does come in handy, those nights when you're suddenly peckish, just like that, and everything's closed."

Noelle's eyes were terrified, but her voice was surprisingly steady. She said, "He broke in in the night, I don't know how. I couldn't fight him, because he had Patrice, and he said if I screamed...."

"Yeah, honey," Arceneaux said. "Yeah, baby."

"He made me drive him up here. Poor Patrice was so frightened."

Patrice nodded proudly. "I was *scared, Gam'pair.*"

"He tried to rape me," Noelle said evenly. "He couldn't."

Duplessis looked only mildly abashed. "Everything costs. And it did seem appropriate—you and little Rene working so hard to entice me up here. I thought I'd just take you up on it a bit early."

Arceneaux took a step, then another; not toward Duplessis, but toward Noelle in the chair. Duplessis said, "I really wouldn't, Jean-Marc."

Noelle said, "Dadda, get *out* of here! It's you he wants!"

Arceneaux said, "He got me. He ain't getting you."

Duplessis nodded. "I'll let them go, you have my word. But they have to watch first. That's fair. Her and the little one, watching and remembering...you know, that might even make up for what you did to me." His smile brightened even more. "Then we'll be quits at last, just think, after all the years. I might even leave some of the others alive—lagniappe, don't you know, our greatest Louzianne tradition. As your folks say down in the swamp, lagniappe *c'est bitin qui bon*—lagniappe is lawful treasure."

Arceneaux ignored him. To Patrice he said, "Boy, you get off your mama's lap now, I got to get those ropes off her. Then we all go get some ice cream, you like that?"

Patrice scrambled down eagerly. Noelle said, "Dadda, *no.* Take Patrice and get *out*—" just as Duplessis's voice sharpened and tightened, good cheer gone. "Jean-Marc, I'm warning you—"

The ropes were tight for stiff old fingers, and Noelle's struggling against them didn't help. Behind him, Arceneaux heard Patrice scream in terror. A moment later, looking past him, Noelle went absolutely rigid, her mouth open but no smallest sound emerging. He turned himself then, knowing better than they what he would see.

Petrifying as the sight of a werewolf obviously is, it is the transformation itself that is the smothering fabric of nightmare. On the average, it lasts no more than ten or fifteen seconds: but to the observing eyes and mind the process is endless, going on and on and on in everlasting slow-motion, as the grinning mouth twists and lengthens into a fanged snarl, while the body convulses, falls forward, catches itself on long gray legs that were arms a lifetime ago, and the eyes lengthen, literally reseat themselves in the head at a new angle, and take on the beautiful insane glow that particularly distinguishes the *loup-garou.* Alexandre Duplessis—cotton-white, except for the dark-shaded neck-ruff and the jagged black slash across the chest— uttered a shattering half-human roar and sprang straight at Arceneaux.

Whether it was caused by the adrenaline of terror or of rage he couldn't guess, but suddenly the ropes fell loose from the chair and his fingers, and Noelle, in one motion, swept up the wailing Patrice and was through the door before the wolf that had been Duplessis even reached her father. The bad knee predictably locked up, and Arceneaux went down, with the wolf Duplessis on him, worrying at his throat. He warded the wide-stretched jaws off with his forearm, bringing the good knee up into the *loup-garou's* belly, the huge white-and-black body that had become all his sky and all his night. Duplessis threw back his head and bayed in triumph.

Arceneaux made a last desperate attempt to heave Duplessis away and get to his feet. But he was near to suffocation from the weight on his chest—*Saba yehge, amiwa saba yehge, de Damballa e a miwa*—and then the werewolf's jaws were past his guard, the great fangs sank into his shoulder, and he heard himself scream in pain—*Danou sewa yehge o, djevo de, Damballa come to us, they are hurting us, Damballa come quickly...*

...and heard the scream become a howl of fury in the same moment, as he lunged upward, his changing jaws closing on Duplessis's head, taking out an eye with the first snap. Wolf to wolf—the greatest sin of all—they rose on their hind legs, locked together, fangs clashing, each streaked and blotched with the other's blood. Arceneaux had lost not only who he was, but *what*— he had no grandchildren now, no children either, no lifelong down-home friend, no memories of affection...there had never been anything else but this murderous twin, and no joy but in hurting it, killing it, tearing it back once again to shreds, where it belonged. He had never been so happy in his life.

In the wolf form, *loups-garoux* do not mate; lovemaking is a gift for ordinary animals, ordinary humans. Yet this terrible, transcendent *meshing* was like nothing Arceneaux had ever known, even as he was aware that his left front leg was broken and one side of his throat laid open. Duplessis was down now...or was that some other wolf bleeding and panting under him, breath ragged, weakened claws finding no purchase in his fur? It made no difference. There was nothing but battle now, nothing but hunger for someone's blood.

Most of the lighted candles had been knocked over—some by Noelle's flight to the door, some during the battle. The rag rugs that he and Garrigue had devastated and not yet replaced were catching fire, and spreading the flames to dry furniture and loose paper and kindling. Arceneaux watched the fire with a curious detachment, as intense, in its way, as the ecstasy with which he had he had closed his wolf jaws on Duplessis's wolf flesh. He was aware, with the same disinterest, that he was bleeding badly from a dozen wounds; still, he was on his feet, and Duplessis was sprawled before him, alive but barely breathing, lacking the strength and will to regain the human shape. Arceneaux was in the same condition, which was a pity, for he would have liked to give his thanks to Damballa in words. He considered the helpless Duplessis for a moment longer, as the fire began to find its own tongue, and then he pushed the door open with his head and limped outside.

Noelle cried out at first as he stumbled toward her; but then she knew him, as she would always have known him, and knelt down before him, hugging his torn neck—Duplessis had come very near the throat—and getting blood all over the pajamas in which she had been kidnapped. She had no words either, except for *Dadda*, but she got plenty of mileage out of that one, even so.

The cabin was just reaching full blaze, and Patrice had worked up the courage to let the strange big dog lick his face, when the police car came barreling up the overgrown little path, very nearly losing an axle to the pothole Garrigue had been warning them about for the last couple of miles. Antoine was with them too, and Garrigue's son Claude, and a police paramedic as well. There was a good deal of embracing among one group, and an equal amount of headscratching, chinrubbing and cell-phone calling by the other.

And Jean-Marc Arceneaux—"Ti-Jean" to a very few old friends—nuzzled his grandson one last time, and then turned and walked back into the blazing cabin and threw himself over the body of the wolf Alexandre Duplessis. Noelle's cry of grief was still echoing when the roof came down.

When Garrigue could talk—when anyone could talk, after the fire engine came—he told Noelle, "The ashes. He done it because of the ashes."

Noelle shook her head weakly. "I don't understand."

Garrigue said, "Duplessis come back once, maybe do it again, even from ashes. But not all mixed up together with old Ti-Jean, no, not with their jaws locked on each other in the other world and the *loa* watching. Not even a really good conjure man out of Sabine, Vernon Parish, pull off that trick. You follow me?"

"No," she said. "No, Rene. I don't, I'm trying."

Garrigue was admirably patient, exhausted as he was. "He just making sure you, the grandbabies, the rest of us, we never going to be bothered by *Compe'* Alexandre no more." His gray eyes were shining with prideful tears. "He thought on things like that, Ti-Jean did. Knew him all my life, that man. All my life."

Patrice slept between her and Antoine that night: the police psychologist who had examined him said that just because he was showing no sign of trauma didn't mean that he might not be affected in some fashion that wouldn't manifest itself for years. For his part, Patrice had talked about the incident in the surprisingly matter-of-fact way of a four-year-old for the rest of the day; but after dinner he spent the evening playing one of Zelime's mysterious games that seemed, as far as adults could tell, to have no rules whatsoever. It was only when he scrambled into bed beside his mother that he asked seriously, "That man? Not coming back?"

Noelle hugged him. "No, sweetheart. Not coming back. Not ever. You scared him away."

"*Gam'pair* come back." It was not a question.

You're not supposed to lie to children about anything. Bad, bad, bad. Noelle said, "He had to go away, Patrice. He had to make sure that man wouldn't come here again."

Patrice nodded solemnly. He wrapped his arms around himself and said, "I hold *Gam'pair* right here. *Gam'pair* not going anywhere," and went to sleep.

Up the Down Beanstalk:
A Wife Remembers

—SPECIAL TO THE CUMULONIMBUS WEEKLY CHRONICLE,
AS RECOUNTED BY MRS. EUNICE GIANT, 72 FAIRWEATHER LANE,
EAST-OF-THE-BEAN, SUSSEX OVERHEAD—

The first draft of this story was written by hand on a yellow legal pad, while I curled up in an armchair in a hotel lobby in Houston, Texas. After some polishing drafts on the computer, it appeared in Troll's Eye View, *a collection of fairy tales seen from the angle of their classic villains. I'd first asked if I could reimagine Rumplestiltskin, but I made my request too late, and someone beat me to it. Even so, I had a great time being Mrs. Eunice Giant, and I'm quite proud of her. She's a woman who definitely has her priorities in order. Not to mention her kitchen.*

✳

He seemed like such a nice boy.

And he *was* a nice boy, really, for all the vexation he caused. They always are, I've never eaten a bad one yet. Oh, there's some don't care for the crunchiness, I know that, and there's others who complain about that sort of salty aftertaste. But you clean the palate with a couple of firkins of ale, and where's the harm, that's what I say. No, I like boys just fine. Always have.

The funny thing is that poor old Harvey didn't like them, not really. Oh, he'd eat one now and then, if we were having dinner at someone's house—I mean, you have to be polite, don't you? But for himself, no...you could keep that man perfectly happy with a couple of cows, a couple of horses smothered in sheep, the way my mother used to do them, he loved that. Which wasn't exactly what you might call labor-saving, because, after all, cows and horses don't come running to you, do they? I mean, you have to go out and *get* them, and then you have to carry them all the way home. Not like people—you see what I'm getting at?

It's funny, the way most of them think that boy—Jack, his name was, I keep getting their names mixed up—most of them think that Jack was the first to climb up here. Truth of it is, you can't hardly keep them away. See a beanstalk, they've just *got* to climb it. It's their nature, I suppose, like kittens with a curtain. Practically all over the place they are, some seasons, what else can you do but eat them? I used to tell Harvey, I don't know how many times I warned him to get that beanstalk trimmed back, so it wouldn't be *quite* so noticeable. But you know how men are, they just put things off and put them off, and then they tell you you're nagging. I think now, if I'd only nagged him a bit more, who knows? Ah, well, mustn't complain.

They tell some story down there, a whole business of magic beans, and trading the family cow to a crafty peddler, something like that. Now *there's* nonsense for you. What happened, the cow was wandering loose—whose fault was *that,* I'd like to know?—and Harvey brought her home, so I could have breakfast in bed. Of course that boy naturally followed her tracks right straight to the beanstalk, and maybe he saw her back legs or something vanishing into the sky, that could be. Anyway, he went right up after her and pops into my kitchen, because of the way Harvey trained that beanstalk to grow. I call that clever of him, don't you?

Now, what I always do, I scatter things like rosemary, thyme, salt and pepper, a *bit* of basil, all around that hole in the floor—that way, they're already seasoned, you can just whisk them right onto the grill. But this Jack—my goodness, he was so *quick!* I had to chase him all around the kitchen with a broom, if you'll believe it, before I finally got him backed into a corner. And then—now I *know* you won't believe *this*—the dear boy looks up at me, just as calm as you please, with his little hands on his hips, and he says, "Where's my cow, you thieving giant? I want my cow back!" Cheeky? I ask you!

"I ate your cow on a breakfast tray," I says, "and a tough old thing she was, too. And we'll be having you for lunch, as an appetizer, so behave yourself!" None of that grinding his bones to make my bread, by the by—I mean, who'd ever want to make bread like that, all gritty and nasty?

Anyway. That Jack, he says right back to me, bold as brass, "What about that hen of yours? The one that lays the golden eggs? I'd consider that fair exchange for my cow."

"Golden eggs?" I says. "Golden eggs? Whoever put that in your quaint little head?" The things they believe about us down there! I says, "What would Harvey and I ever want with an egg we couldn't scramble? Now hop up on that grill, and don't be fussing at me so!" Because I was already starting to get one of my heads, you know how I am. It's their voices, I think, that must be it. So *shrill*, they just go right through my temples, but do they care? You've got a hope.

"Well, then, what about that harp?" Jack demands—still just as cheeky as he can be. "I know all about that singing harp, and it'll talk to you too, and tell you the future. Hand it over, and I'll be gone, and we'll say no more about it."

Now you can't help admiring impudence like that, can you? I know *I* can't.

But. "No harp, no hen," I says, "and if you aggravate me any more than you already have, I'm going to be really vexed with you. I've never known an appetizer to cause so much trouble." I'm sorry, sometimes you just have to be firm with them.

Now all this while, mind you, I'd been moving closer, step by the tiniest step I could manage, me not being exactly built to sneak up on things. But he was too sharp for that; he zinged and darted around the kitchen like a fly. I hate it when they do that. They never taste nearly as good when they've been overexerting themselves. And if by chance you step on them, or you lose your temper and swat them...well, you can just forget it, you know that as well as I do. There is just *no* salvaging a squashed human.

I'd have called for Harvey to help me, but I knew where he was—off with his great boon companion Claude, helping him to fix his septic tank or drain a field, something like that. I have, personally, never been able to stand Claude. He's loud, and he's extremely vulgar, and he's *never* clean, not what you could call clean, and I always thought him a terrible influence on Harvey. But there, try to say *that* to a man, and see what it gets you. The more I expressed my opinion of Claude, the closer friends they became. I should have known better than to say a single word, but honesty's my weakness, always has been. Anyway, I didn't waste any time looking around for Harvey. As much as he and Claude drank when they got together, he'd not have been much use anyway.

But that Jack! I was closing in on him, narrowing down his escape routes—there's a trick to it, I'll show you—but I couldn't ever quite get my hands on him. And *he* couldn't get past me to the hole in the floor, either, so there we were, both just dancing round and round, you might say, and it would have been funny, except that I was starting to get really hungry. It's a blood sugar thing, I think.

"For goodness sake, we can't keep this up forever," I said to him. I was puffing a bit, I don't deny it, but he was losing speed too by then. "Why can't we just sit down for a moment, and get our breaths, and talk like people?"

"Because you're not people, ma'am," says he, not giving an inch. "You're a monster and you'll crunch me up if I take my eyes off you for a solitary minute. Deny it if you can, monster lady."

"I'm not either a monster!" says I, straight back in his face. I mean, that really hurt my feelings, him saying that, as I'm sure you'd have been hurt the same. "I'm big, yes, and I've got dietary needs like you or anyone else. But that certainly does *not* make me any monster."

"Yes, it does, ma'am," Jack says—flat, like that. He still wouldn't let me come any nearer, and he obviously wasn't about to trust me even one pennyworth. So I did the only thing I could do—I just sat down myself, whether he sat or no. Oh, I stayed close enough to that hole so that I could block him with my leg if I missed with a grab. Just in case he really thought we were all as stupid as the stories say.

And by and by...well, I won't say he actually *sat,* but he did sort of crouch down on his heels—eigh, dear, what it is to have young legs—and we did chat, in a bit of a way. I asked after his mother, I remember, and about his brothers and sisters—they have them in absolute *litters,* you know—and did he climb lots of things, or was it just beanstalks? Making conversation, that's all.

And he was actually answering my questions, most of them, and even asking one or two of his own, in his cheeky way—would you believe it, he wondered where we ever got underpants in our size—when who should come lumbering in but Harvey! Harvey, with Claude right behind him. Harvey and Claude, laughing and bellowing, with their filthy great boots absolutely thick with mud—if that's what it was—and tracking whole squishy black chunks of *something* all over my nice clean kitchen floor. I could have wept. I just could have wept.

But I didn't. I screamed at them to get out of my kitchen, and of course old Claude was gone the moment I opened my mouth. Harvey was so drunk that he'd never have caught sight of Jack if the boy had only stayed still, but of course he was up on his feet and scurrying along the wall, dodging every which way like a good'un. Harvey let out a yell—"I'll get him! I got him!"—and he made this wild swipe, and Jack actually ran right between his legs, and I couldn't help it, I just wanted to cheer. I'd never tell anybody that but you, but I did! I really, *really* wanted to cheer.

Well, Harvey kept yelling, "I'll get him for you! I'll get him!" but he couldn't have pulled up his own mucky socks, the mess he was, clumping and stamping and scattering more dirt with every step. And that Jack, he could see how distracted I was, and quicker than *scat* he dived for the hole in the floor. Never mind cows, hens, harps, whatever, that boy was on his way home.

And he'd have made it, too, except Harvey somehow lunged and blocked him away, and what happened, Jack lost his balance and sort of skidded on the linoleum. He didn't *quite* fall down, but he was waving his arms, trying to keep his feet under him, and Harvey would have had him in another second. Another second, that's all it would have taken, even for Harvey.

Now I'm not going to swear that I did it out of spite...what I did. And I'm not even going to tell you that I did it a-purpose, because I don't know to this day. I *don't*. I'm just going to tell you what happened, which was that Harvey lunged again, and he...all *right*, he *somehow* tripped over my foot and went straight down through that hole. Harvey was always tripping over things.

It's a long way down, but we heard the crash. And we stood there, Jack and I—do you know, I never did get his last name?—we stood looking at each other for...minutes? Hours? I've no idea. The boy finally said, "Well. I guess I'll be going."

"And that's it?" says I. "That's *it*? You break into a lady's house, you call her a thief and a monster, you murder her husband, and now you guess you'll be off somewhere? I thought better of your manners than that, I don't know why. Go on, then, run along with you, by all means. I'm sure *I* don't care."

Jack looked flustered, as he never had when I was chasing him with my broom. "Well, ma'am," he says, "what would you like me to do? I'll surely do what I can to oblige you."

"You could stop for a cup of tea," I answered him straight out. "That's what *civilized* people do when they've killed somebody's husband."

So he stayed on for tea, sitting by the hole with his legs dangling down—a bit rude, I must say, and me too stricken by my loss to have much of an appetite—and we chatted some, and he apologized for saying I was a thief, since it wasn't me stole his cow, and I told him please to give my best regards to his lady mother, and he even helped me clean up a bit, best way he could. He said he'd get the whole village together to bury Harvey, and I asked him to say a few words about Harvey being such a good speller, and a *very* good social dancer, and he said he would. I mean, Harvey had his faults, no denying that, but fair's fair.

No, I haven't remarried, nor likely neither. I'm quite content as I am, thank you, and well enough occupied with my embroidery and my reading. And people *do* keep climbing my old beanstalk, no matter how poor Jack runs all over, warning them not to, so there's any amount of company, and I hardly ever have to eat out. It's princes, mostly—they don't taste any better than anyone else, no matter what you hear—and once there was this whole bunch of dwarves, the dearest little fat fellows. Perfect timing, that was, because my bridge circle was meeting over here that day. So I stay *interested*, that's what's important—being *interested*.

But I do miss Harvey sometimes, I'll admit it. He was always so good at getting the oven going on a cold morning.

THE RABBI'S HOBBY

I was never bar mitzvah (which, for those of you who are not Jewish or don't happen to know, is a specific religious coming-of-age ceremony for thirteen-year-old Jewish boys, and literally means "son of the commandments"). My brother was bar mitzvah, though—our parents left the choice up to us—as were most of my male childhood friends. So I'm more or less familiar with the ceremony, and I know something of my narrator's struggle with Hebrew and with his fearful attitude toward the whole ritual in general. I have also met more than one rabbi as wise and patient and sensitive as lucky Joseph's Rabbi Tuvim, and know the world is better for them. Beyond that, I can only say with certainty that like "The Rock in the Park," and several other favorite stories of mine, "The Rabbi's Hobby" was born out of my old neighborhood, and out of a time and a culture grown more intensely real and clear to me today than perhaps it was then. Back then I was mostly reading science fiction, and listening to baseball games on the Crosley radio in the kitchen...

✳

It took me a while to get to like Rabbi Tuvim. He was a big, slow-moving man with a heavy-boned face framed by a thick brown beard; and although he had spent much of his life in the Bronx, he had never quite lost the accent, nor the syntax, of his native Czechoslovakia. He seemed stony and forbidding to me at first, even though he had a warm, surprising laugh. He just didn't look like someone who would laugh a lot.

What gradually won me over was that Rabbi Tuvim collected odd, unlikely things. He was the only person I knew who collected, not baseball cards, the way all my friends and I did, but *boxers*. There was one gum company who put those out, complete with the fighters' records and a few lines about their lives, and the rabbi had all the heavyweights, going back to John L. Sullivan, and most of the lighter champions too. I learned everything I know about Stanley Ketchel, Jimmy McLarnin, Benny Leonard, Philadelphia Jack O'Brien, Tommy Loughran, Henry Armstrong and Tony Canzoneri—to name just those few—from Rabbi Tuvim's cards.

He kept boxes of paper matchbooks too, and those little bags of sugar that you get when you order coffee in restaurants. My favorites were a set from Europe that had tiny copies of paintings on them.

And then there were the keys. The rabbi had an old tin box, like my school lunch box, but bigger, and it was filled with dozens and dozens of keys of every shape and size you could imagine that a key might be. Some of them were *tiny*, smaller even than our mailbox key, but some were huge and heavy and rusty; they looked like the keys jailers or housekeepers always carried at their belts in movies about the Middle Ages. Rabbi Tuvim had no idea what locks they might have been for—he never locked up anything, anyway, no matter how people warned him—he just picked them up wherever he found them lying loose and plopped them into his key box. To which, by the way, he'd lost the key long ago.

When I finally got up the nerve to ask him why he collected something as completely useless as keys without locks, the rabbi didn't answer right away, but leaned on his elbow and thought about his answer. That was something else I liked about him, that he seemed to take everybody's questions seriously, even ones that were really, *really* stupid. He finally said, "Well, you know, Joseph, those keys aren't useless just because I don't have the locks they fit. Whenever I find a lock that's lost its key, I try a few of mine on it, on the chance that one of them might be the right one. God is like that for me—a lock none of my keys fit, and probably never will. But I keep at it, I keep picking up different keys and trying them out, because you never know. *Could* happen."

I asked, "Do you think God wants you to find the key?"

Rabbi Tuvim ruffled my hair. "*Leben uff der keppele.* Leave it to the children to ask the big ones. I would like to think he does, Yossele, but I don't know that either. That's what being Jewish is, going ahead without answers. Get out of here, already."

The rabbi had bookshelves stacked with old crumbly magazines, too, all kinds of them. Magazines I knew, like *Life* and *Look* and *Colliers* and *The Saturday Evening Post*; magazines I'd never heard of—like *Scribners,*

The Delineator, The Illustrated London News, and even one called *Pearson's Magazine,* from 1911, with Christy Mathewson on the cover. Mrs. Eisen, who cleaned for him every other week, wouldn't ever go into the room where he kept them, because she said those old dusty, flappy things aggravated her asthma. My father said that some of them were collector's items, and that people who liked that sort of stuff would pay a lot of money for them. But Rabbi Tuvim just liked having them, liked sitting and turning their yellow pages late at night, thinking about what people were thinking so long ago. "It's very peaceful," he told me. "So much worry about so much—so much certainty about how things were going to turn out—and here we are now, and it *didn't* turn out like that, after all. Don't ever be too sure of anything, Joseph."

I was at his house regularly that spring, because we were studying for my Bar Mitzvah. The negotiations had been extensive and complicated: I was willing to go along with local custom, tradition and my parents' social concerns, but I balked at going straight from my regular classes to the neighborhood Hebrew school. I called my unobservant family hypocrites, which they were; they called me lazy and ungrateful, which was also true. But both sides knew that I'd need extensive private tutoring to cope with the *haftarah* reading alone, never mind the inevitable speech. I'd picked up Yiddish early and easily, as had all my cousins, since our families spoke it when they didn't want the *kindelech* to understand what they were talking about. But Hebrew was another matter entirely. I knew this or that word, this or that phrase—even a few songs for Chanukah and Pesach—but the language itself sat like a stone on my tongue, guttural and harsh, and completely alien. I not only couldn't learn Hebrew, I truly didn't *like* Hebrew. And if a proper Jew was supposed to go on studying it even after the liberating Bar Mitzvah, I might just as well give up and turn Catholic, spending my Sunday mornings at Mass with the Geohegans down the block. Either way, I was clearly doomed.

Rabbi Tuvim took me on either as a challenge or as a penance, I was never quite sure which. He was inhumanly patient and inventive, constantly coming up with word games, sports references and any number of catchy mnemonics to help me remember this foreign, senseless, elusive, *boring* system of communication. But when even he wiped his forehead and said sadly, *"Ai, gornisht helfen,"* which means *nothing will help you,* I finally felt able to ask him whether he thought I would ever be a good Jew; and, if not, whether we should just cancel the Bar Mitzvah. I thought hopefully of the expense this would save my father, and felt positively virtuous for once.

The rabbi, looking at me, managed to sigh and half-smile at the same time, taking off his glasses and blinking at them. "Nobody in this entire congregation has the least notion of what Bar Mitzvah *is*," he said wearily. "It's not a graduation from anything, it is just an acknowledgment that at thirteen you're old enough to be called up in temple to read from the Torah. Which God help you if you actually are, but never mind. The point is that you are still Bar Mitzvah even if you never go through the preparation, the ritual." He smiled at me and put his glasses back on. "No way out of it, Joseph. If you never manage to memorize another word of Hebrew, you're still as good a Jew as anybody. Whatever the Orthodox think."

One Thursday afternoon I found the rabbi so engrossed in one of his old magazines that he didn't notice when I walked in, or even when I peered over his shoulder. It was an issue of a magazine called *Evening*, from 1921, which made it close to thirty years old. There were girls on the cover, posing on a beach, but they were a long way from the bathing beauties—we still called them that then—that I was accustomed to seeing in magazines and on calendars. These could have walked into my mother's PTA or Hadassah meetings: they showed no skin above the shin, wore bathing caps and little wraps over their shoulders, and in general appeared about as seductive as any of my mother's friends, only younger. Paradoxically, the severe costumes made them look much more youthful than they probably were, innocently graceful.

Rabbi Tuvim, suddenly aware of me, looked up, startled but not embarrassed. "This is what your mother would have been wearing to the beach back then," he said. "Mine, too. It looks so strange, doesn't it? Compared to Betty Grable, I mean."

He was teasing me, as though I were still going through my Betty Grable/ Alice Faye phase. As though I weren't twelve now, and on the edge of manhood; if not, why were we laboring over the utterly bewildering *haftarah* twice a week? As though Lauren Bacall, Lena Horne and Lizabeth Scott hadn't lately written their names all over my imagination, introducing me to the sorrows of adults? I drew myself up in visible—I hoped—indignation, but the rabbi said only, "Sit down, Joseph, look at this girl. The one in the left corner."

She was bareheaded, so that her whole face was visible.

Even I could tell that she couldn't possibly be over eighteen. She wasn't beautiful—the others were beautiful, and so what?—but there was a playfulness about her expression, a humor not far removed from wisdom. Looking at her, I felt that I could tell that face everything I was ashamed of, and that she would not only reassure me that I wasn't the vile mess I firmly believed I was, but that I might even be attractive one day to someone besides my family. Someone like her.

I looked sideways at Rabbi Tuvim, and saw him smiling. "Yes," he said. "She does have that effect, doesn't she?"

"Who is she?" I blurted out. "Is she a movie star or something?" Someone I should be expected to know, in other words. But I didn't think so, and I was right. Rabbi Tuvim shook his head.

"I have no idea. I just bought this magazine yesterday, at a collectors' shop downtown where I go sometimes, and I feel as though I have been staring at her ever since. I don't think she's anybody famous—probably just a model who happened to be around when they were shooting that cover. But I can't take my eyes off her, for some reason. It's a little embarrassing."

The rabbi's unmarried state was of particular concern in the neighborhood. Rabbis aren't priests: it's not only that they're allowed to marry, it's very nearly demanded of them by their congregations. Rabbi Tuvim wasn't a handsome man, but he had a strong face, and his eyes were kind. I said, "Maybe you could look her up, some way."

The rabbi blinked at me. "Joseph, I am curious. That's all."

"Sure," I said. "Me too."

"I would just like to know a little about her," the rabbi said.

"Me too," I said again. I was all for keeping the conversation going, to stall off my lesson as long as possible, but no luck. The rabbi just said, "There is something about her," and we plunged once more into the cold mysteries of Mishnaic Hebrew. Rabbi Tuvim didn't look at the *Evening* cover again, but I kept stealing side glances at that girl until he finally got up and put the magazine back on the bookshelf, without saying a word. I think I was an even worse student than usual that afternoon, to judge by his sigh when we finished.

Every Monday and Thursday, when I came for my lessons, the magazine would always be somewhere in sight—on a chair, perhaps, or down at the end of the table where we studied. We never exactly agreed, not in so many words, that the girl on the cover haunted us both, but we talked about her a lot. For me the attraction lay in the simple and absolute aliveness of her face, as present to me as that of any of my schoolmates, while the other figures in the photograph felt as antique as any of the Greek and Roman statues we were always being taken to see at museums. For Rabbi Tuvim...for the rabbi, perhaps, what fascinated him was the fact that he *was* fascinated: that a thirty-year-old image out of another time somehow had the power to distract him from his studies, his students, and his rabbinical duties. No other woman had ever done that to him. Twelve years old or not, I was sure of that.

The rabbi made inquiries. He told me about them—I don't think there was anyone else he *could* have told about such a strange obsession. *Evening* was long out of business by then, but his copy had credited the cover photograph only to "Winsor & Co., Ltd., Newark, New Jersey." Rabbi Tuvim—obviously figuring that if he could teach me even a few scraps of Hebrew he ought to be able to track down a fashion photographer's byline—found address and phone number, called, was told sourly that he was welcome to go through their files himself, but that employees had better things to do. Whereupon, he promptly took a day off and made a pilgrimage to Winsor & Co., Ltd., which was still in business, but plainly subsisting on industrial photography and the odd bowling-team picture. A clerk led him to the company archive, which was a room like a walk-in closet, walled around with oaken filing cabinets; he said it smelled of fixatives and moldering newsprint, and of cigars smoked very long ago. But he sat down and went to work, and in only three hours, or at most four, he had his man.

"His name is Abel Bagaybagayan," he told me when I came the next day. I giggled, and the rabbi cuffed the side of my head lightly. "Don't laugh at people's names, Joseph. How is that any stranger than Rosenwasser? Or Turteltaub, or Kockenfuss, or Tuvim, or your own name? It took me a long time to find that name, and I'm very proud that I did find it, and you can either stop laughing right now, or go home." He was really angry with me. I'd never before seen him angry. I stopped laughing.

"Abel Bagaybagayan," Rabbi Tuvim said again. "He was what's called a freelance—that means he wasn't on anyone's staff—but he did a lot of work for Winsor through the 1920s. Portraits, fashion spreads, architectural layouts, you name it. Then, after 1935 or so...nothing. Nothing at all. Most likely he died, but I couldn't find any information, one way or the other." The rabbi spread his hands and lifted his eyebrows. "I only met a couple of people who even remembered him vaguely, and nobody has anything like an address, a phone number—not so much as a cousin in Bensonhurst. Nothing. A dead end."

"So what are you going to do?" I asked. The old magazine lay between us, and I marveled once again at the way the mystery-girl's bright face made everyone else on the cover look like depthless paper-doll cutouts, with little square tabs holding their flat clothes on their flat bodies. The rabbi waggled a warning finger at me, and my heart sank. Without another word, I opened my Hebrew text.

When we were at last done for the day—approximately a hundred and twenty years later—Rabbi Tuvim went on as though I had just asked the question. "My father used to tell me that back in Lvov, his family had a saying: *A Tuvim never surrenders; he just says he does.* I'm going to find Abel Bagaybagayan's family."

"Maybe he married that girl on the cover," I said hopefully. "Maybe they had a family together."

"Very romantic," the rabbi said. "I like it. But then he'd probably have had mouths to feed, so if he didn't die, why did he quit working as a photographer? If he did quit, mind you—I don't know anything for sure."

"Well, maybe she was very rich. Then he wouldn't *have* to work." I didn't really think that was at all likely, but lately I'd come to enjoy teasing the rabbi the way he sometimes teased me. I said, "Maybe they moved to California, and she got into the movies. That could have happened."

"You know, that actually could," Rabbi Tuvim said slowly. "California, anyway, everybody's going to California. And Bagaybagayan's an Armenian name—much easier to look for. I have an Armenian friend in Fresno, and Armenians always know where there are other Armenians...thank you, Detective Yossele. I'll see you on Monday."

As I left, feeling absurdly pleased with myself, he was already reaching for the old *Evening,* sliding it toward him on the table.

In the following weeks, the rabbi grew steadily more involved with that face from 1921, and with the cold trail of Abel Bagaybagayan, who wasn't from Fresno. But there were plenty of people there with that name; and while none of them knew the man we were looking for, they had cousins in Visalia and Delano and Firebaugh who might. To my disappointment, Rabbi Tuvim remained very conscientious about keeping his obsession from getting in the way of his teaching; at that point, the Fresno phone book would have held more interest for me than *halakha* or the Babylonian Talmud. On the other hand, he had no hesitation about involving me in his dogged search for either photographer or model, or both of them. I was a great Sherlock Holmes fan back then, and I felt just like Doctor Watson, only smarter.

This was all before the Internet, mind you; all before personal computers, area codes, digital dialing...that time when places were further from each other, when phone calls went through operators, and a long-distance call was as much of an event as a telegram. Even so, it was I, assigned to the prairie states, who found Sheila Bagaybagayan, only child of Abel, in Grand Forks, North Dakota, where she was teaching library science at the university. I handed the phone to Rabbi Tuvim and went off into a corner to hug myself and jump up and down just a bit. I might not know the *Midrash Hashkern* from "Mairzy Doats" but, by God, I *was* Detective Yossele.

Watching the rabbi's face as he spoke to Sheila Bagaybagayan on the phone was more fun than a Saturday matinee at Loew's Tuxedo, with a double feature, a newsreel, eighteen cartoons, Coming Attractions and a *Nyoka the Jungle Girl* serial. He smiled—he laughed outright—he frowned in puzzlement—he spoke rapidly, raising a finger, as though making a point in a sermon—he scratched his beard—he looked suddenly sad enough to weep—he said, "Yes...yes...yes..." several times, and then "Of course—and *thank* you," and hung up. He stood motionless by the phone for a few minutes, absently rubbing his lower lip, until the phone started to buzz because he hadn't got it properly back on the hook. Then he turned to me and grinned, and said, "Well. That was our Sheila."

"Was she really the right one? Mr. Baba...uh, Abel's daughter?" The passing of weeks hadn't made me any more comfortable around the photographer's name.

Rabbi Tuvim nodded. "Yes, but her married name is Olsen. Her mother died when she was practically a baby, and Abel never remarried, but raised her alone. She says he stopped working as a photographer during the Depression, when she was in her teens, because he just couldn't make a living at it anymore. So he became a salesman for a camera-equipment company, and then he worked for Western Union, and he died just after the war." He smacked his fist into his palm. *"Rats!"*—which was his strongest expletive, at least around me. "We could have met him, we could have asked him...*Ach, rats!"* I used to giggle in *shul* sometimes, suddenly imagining him saying that at the fall of Solomon's Temple, or at the news that Sabbatai Zevi, the false Messiah, had turned Muslim.

"The girl," I asked. "Did she remember that girl?"

The rabbi shook his head. "Her father worked with so many models over the years. She's going to look through his records and call me back. One thing she did say, he preferred using amateurs when he could, and she knows that he sneaked a lot of them into the *Evening* assignments, even though they ordered him not to. She thinks he was likely to have kept closer track of the amateurs than the professionals, in case he got a chance to use them again, so who knows?" He shrugged slightly. "As the Arabs say, *inshallah*—if God wills it. Fair enough, I guess."

For quite some time I cherished a persistent hopeful vision of our cover girl turning out to be Sheila Olsen's long-gone mother. But Abel Bagaybagayan had never employed his wife professionally, Sheila told us; there were plenty of photographs around the Grand Forks house, but none of the young woman Rabbi Tuvim described. And no magazine covers. Abel Bagaybagayan never saved the covers.

All the same, Sheila Olsen plainly got drawn into the rabbi's fixation— or, as he always called it—his hobby. They spoke on the phone frequently, considering every possibility of identifying the *Evening* girl; and my romantic imagination started marrying them off, exactly like the movies. I knew that she had been divorced—which was not only rare in our neighborhood then, but somehow exotic—and I figured that she had to be Rabbi Tuvim's age, or even younger, so there we were. Their conversations, from my end, sounded less formal as time went on; and a twelve-year-old romantic who can't convert "less formal" into "affectionate" at short notice just isn't trying.

No, of course it never happened, not like that. She wasn't Jewish, for one thing, and she really *liked* living in North Dakota. But her curiosity, growing to enthusiasm, at last gave the rabbi someone besides me to discuss his hobby with, and fired up his intensity all over again. I wasn't jealous; on the contrary, I felt as though we were a secret alliance of superheroes, like the Justice Society of America, on the trail of Nazi spies, or some international warlord or other. The addition of Sheila Olsen, our Grand Forks operative, made it all that much more exciting.

I spoke to her a couple of times. The first occasion was when a call from old Mrs. Shimkus interrupted my Monday Hebrew lesson. I was always grateful when that happened, but especially so in this case, since we were doing vowels, and had gotten to *shva*. That is all you're going to hear from me about *shva*. Mrs. Shimkus was always calling, always dying, and always contributing large sums for the maintenance of the temple and scholarships for deserving high-school students. This entitled her, as the rabbi said with a touch of grimness, to her personal celestial attorney, on call at all times to file suit against the Angel of Death. "Answer the phone, if it rings. Go back to page twenty-nine, and start over from there. I'll be back sooner than you hope, so get to it."

I did try. *Shva* and all. But I also grabbed up the telephone on the first ring, saying importantly, "Rabbi Tuvim's residence, to whom am I speaking?"

The connection was stuttery and staticky, but I heard a woman's warm laughter clearly. "Oh, this has simply got to be Joseph. The rabbi's told me all about you. *Is* this Joseph?"

"All about me?" I was seriously alarmed at first; and then I asked, "Sheila? Olsen? Is this you?"

She laughed again. "Yes, I'm sure it is. Is Rabbi Tuvim available?"

"He's visiting Mrs. Shimkus right now," I said. "She's dying again. But he ought to be back pretty soon."

"Very efficient," Sheila Olsen said. "Well, just tell him I called back, so now it's his turn." She paused for a moment. "And Joseph?" I waited. "Tell him I've looked all through my father's files, all of them, and come up empty every time. I'm not giving up—there are a couple of other possibilities—but just tell him it doesn't look too good right now. Can you please do that?"

"As soon as he gets back," I said. "Of course I'll tell him." I hesitated myself, and then blurted, "And don't worry—I'm sure you'll find out about her. He just needs to find the lock she fits." I explained about the rabbi's key collection, and expected her to laugh for a third time, whether in amusement or disbelief. But instead she was silent long enough that I thought she might have hung up. Then she said quietly, "My dad would have liked your rabbi, I think."

Rabbi Tuvim, as he had predicted, returned sooner than I could have wished—Mrs. Shimkus having only wanted tea and sympathy—and I relayed Sheila Olsen's message promptly. I hoped he'd call her right away, but his sense of duty took us straight back to study; and at the end of our session we were both as pale, disheveled and sweating as Hebrew vowels always left us. Before I went home, he said to me, "You know, it's a funny thing, Joseph. Somehow I have connected that *Evening* model with you, in my head. I keep thinking that if I can actually teach you Hebrew, I will be allowed to find out who that girl was. Or maybe it's the other way around, I'm not sure. But I know there's a connection, one way or the other. There *is* a connection."

A week later the rabbi actually called me at home to tell me that Sheila Olsen had come across a second *Evening* with what—she was almost certain—must be the same model on the cover. "She's already sent it, airmail special delivery, so it ought to be here day after tomorrow." The rabbi was so excited that he was practically chattering like someone my age. "I'm sure it's her—I took a photo of my copy and sent it to her, and she clearly thinks it's the same girl." He slowed down, laughing in some embarrassment at his own enthusiasm. "Listen, when you come tomorrow, if you spot me hanging around the mailbox like Valentine's Day, just collar me and drag me inside. A rabbi should never be caught hanging around the mailbox."

The magazine did arrive two days later. I used my lucky nickel to call Rabbi Tuvim from school for the news. Then I ran all the way to his house, not even bothering to drop my books off at home. The rabbi was in his little kitchen, snatching an absent-minded meal of hot dogs and baked beans, which was his idea of a dish suitable for any occasion.

The *Evening* was on a chair, across from him. I grabbed it up and stared at the cover, which was an outdoor scene, showing well-dressed people dining under a striped awning on a summer evening. It was a particularly busy photograph—a lot of tables, a lot of diners, a lot of natty waiters coming and going—and you had to look closely and attentively to find the one person we were looking for. She was off to the right, near the edge of the awning, her bright face looking straight into the camera, her eyes somehow catching and holding the twilight, even as it faded. There were others seated at her table; but, just as with the first cover photo, her presence dimmed them, as though the shot had always been a single portrait of her, with everyone else added in afterward.

But it was just this that was, in a vague, indeterminate way, perturbing the rabbi, making him look far less triumphant and vindicated than I had expected. I was the one who kept saying, "That's her, that's her! We were right—we found her!"

"Right about what, Joseph?" Rabbi Tuvim said softly. "And what have we found?"

I stared at him. He said, "There's something very strange about all this. Think—Abel Bagaybagayan kept very precise records of every model he used, no matter if he only photographed him or her once. Sheila's told me. For each one, name, address, telephone number, and his own special filing system, listing the date, the magazine, the occasion, and a snapshot of that person, always. But not *this* one." He put his finger on the face we had sought for so long. "Not this one girl, out of all those photographs. Two magazine covers, but no record, no picture—*nothing*. Why is that, Detective Yossele? Why on earth would that be?"

His tone was as playful as when he asked me some Talmudic riddle, or invited me to work a noun suffix out for myself, but his face was serious, and his blue eyes looked heavy and sad. I really wanted to help him. I said, "She was special to him, some way. You can see that in the photos." Rabbi Tuvim nodded, though neither he nor I could ever have explained what we meant by *seeing*. "So maybe he wanted to keep her separate, you know? Sort of to keep her for himself, that could be it. I mean, he'd always know where she was, and what she looked like—he'd never have to go look her up in his files, right? That could be it, couldn't it?" I tried to read his face for a reaction to my reasoning. I said, "Kind of makes sense to me, anyway."

"Yes," the rabbi said slowly. "Yes, of course it makes sense, it's very good thinking, Joseph. But it is *human* thinking, it is *human* sense, and I'm just not sure..." His voice trailed away into a mumble as he leaned his chin into his fist. I reached to move the plate of baked beans out of range, but I was a little late.

"What?" I asked. "You mean she could be some kind of Martian, an alien in disguise?" I was joking, but these were the last days of the pulp science-fiction magazines (*and* the pulp Westerns, *and* romances, *and* detective stories), and I read them all, as the rabbi knew. He laughed then, which made me feel better.

"No, I didn't mean that." He sighed. "I don't know what I meant, forget it. Let's go into the living room and work on your speech."

"I came to see the magazine," I protested. "I wasn't coming for a lesson."

"Well, how lucky for you that I'm free just now," the rabbi said. "Get in there." And, trapped and outraged, I went.

So now we had two photographs featuring our mystery model, and were no closer than we'd ever been to identifying her. Sheila Olsen, as completely caught up in the quest as we two by now, contacted every one of her father's colleagues, employers, and old studio buddies that she could reach, and set them all to rummaging through their own files, on the off-chance that one or another of them might have worked with Abel Bagaybagayan's girl twenty or thirty years before. (We were all three calling her that by now, though more in our minds than aloud, I think: "Abel's girl.") Rabbi Tuvim didn't hold much hope for that course, though. "She didn't work with anyone else," he said. "Just him. I know this." And for all anyone could prove otherwise, she never had.

My birthday and my Bar Mitzvah were coming on together like a freight train in the old movies, where you see the smoke first, rising away around the bend, and then you hear the wheels and the whistle, and finally you see the train barreling along. Rabbi Tuvim and I were both tied to the track, and I don't know whether he had nightmares about it all, but I surely did. There was no rescue in sight, either, no cowboy hero racing the train on the great horse Silver or Trigger or Champion, leaping from the saddle to cut us free at the last split-second. My parents had shot the works on the hall, the catering, the invitations, the newspaper notice, and the party afterward (the music to be provided by Herbie Kaufman and his Bel-Air Combo). We'd already had the rehearsal—a complete disaster, but at least the photographs got taken—and there was no more chance even of postponing than there would have been of that train stopping on a dime. Remembering it now, my nightmares were always much more about the rabbi's embarrassment than my own. He had tried so hard to reconcile Hebrew and me to one another; it wasn't his fault that we loathed each other on sight. I felt terrible for him.

A week before the Bar Mitzvah, Sheila Olsen called. We were in full panic mode by now, with me coming to the rabbi's house every day after school, and he himself dropping most of his normal duties to concentrate less on teaching me the passage of Torah that I would read and comment on, but on keeping me from running away to sea and calling home from Pago Pago, where nobody gets Bar Mitzvahed. When the phone rang, Rabbi Tuvim picked it up, signed to me to keep working from the text, and walked away with it to the end of the cord. Entirely pointless, since the cord only went a few feet, it was still a request for privacy, and I tried to respect it. I did try.

"What?" the rabbi said loudly. "You found *what?* Slow down, Sheila, I'm having trouble.... When? You're coming...Sheila, slow *down!*... So how come you can't just tell me on the phone? Wait a minute, I'm not understanding— you're *sure?*" And after that he was silent for a long time, just listening. When he saw that that was all I was doing too, he waved me sternly back to my studies. I bent my head earnestly over the book, pretending to be working, while he tried to squeeze a few more inches out of that phone cord. Both of us failed.

Finally the rabbi said wearily, "I do not have a car, I can't pick you up. You'll have to...oh, okay, if you don't mind taking a cab. Okay, then, I will see you tomorrow.... What? Yes, yes, Joseph will be here...yes—goodbye, Sheila. Goodbye."

He hung up, looked at me, and said *"Oy."*

It was a profound *oy,* an *oy* of stature and dignity, an *oy* from the heart. I waited. Rabbi Tuvim said, "She's coming here tomorrow. Sheila Olsen."

"Wow," I said. *"Wow."* Then I said, "Why?"

"She's found another picture. Abel's girl. Only this one she says she can't send us—she can't even tell me about it. She just has to get on a plane and come straight here to show us." The rabbi sat down and sighed. "It's not exactly the best time."

I said, "Wow," for a third time. "That's *wonderful.*" Then I remembered I was Detective Yossele, and tried to act the part. I asked, "How did she sound?"

"It's hard to say. She was talking so fast." The rabbi thought for a while.

"As though she *wanted* to tell me what she had discovered, really wanted to— maybe to share it, maybe just to get rid of it, *I* don't know. But she couldn't do it. Every time she tried, the words seemed to stick in her throat, like Macbeth's *amen*." He read my blank expression and sighed again. "Maybe they'll have you reading Shakespeare next year. You'll like Shakespeare."

In spite of that freight train of a Bar Mitzvah bearing down on us, neither the rabbi nor I were worth much for the rest of the day. We never exactly quit on the Torah, but we kept drifting to a halt in the middle of work, speculating more or less silently on what could possibly set a woman we'd never met flying from Grand Forks, North Dakota, to tell us in person what she had learned about her father and his mysterious model. Rabbi Tuvim finally said, "Well, I don't know about you, but I'm going to have to drink a gallon of chamomile tea if I'm to get any sleep tonight. What do you do when you can't sleep, Joseph?"

He always asked me questions as though we were the same age. I said, "I guess I listen to the radio. Baseball games."

"Too exciting for me," the rabbi said. "I'll stick with the tea. Go home. She won't be here until your school lets out." I was at the door when he called after me, "And bring both of your notebooks, I made up a test for you." He never gave up, that man. Not on Abel Bagaybagayan, not on me.

Sheila Olsen and I arrived at Rabbi Tuvim's house almost together. I had just rung the doorbell when her cab pulled around the corner, and the rabbi opened the door as she was getting out. She was a pleasant-faced blonde woman, a little plump, running more to the Alice Faye side than Lauren Bacall, and I sighed inwardly to think that only a year before she would have been my ideal. The rabbi—dressed, I noticed, in his second-best suit, the one he wore for all other occasions than the High Holidays—opened the door and said, "Sheila Olsen, I presume?"

"Rabbi Sidney Tuvim," she answered as they shook hands. To me, standing awkwardly one step above her, she said, "And you could only be Joseph Makovsky." The rabbi stepped back to usher us in ahead of him.

Sheila—somehow, after our phone conversations, it was impossible to think of her as Mrs. Olsen—was carrying a large purse and a small overnight bag, which she set down near the kitchen door. "Don't panic, I'm not moving in. I've got a hotel reservation right at the airport, and I'll fly home day after tomorrow. But at the moment I require—no, I request—a glass of wine. Jews are like Armenians, bless them, they've always got wine in the house." She wrinkled her nose and added, "Unlike Lutherans."

The rabbi smiled. "You wouldn't like our wine. We just drink it on Shabbos. Once a week, believe me, that's enough. I can do better."

He went into the kitchen and I stared after him, vaguely jealous, never having seen him quite like this. Not flirtatious, I don't mean that; he wouldn't have known how to be flirtatious on purpose. But he wasn't my age now. Suddenly he was an adult, a grownup, with that elusive but familiar tone in his voice that marked grownups talking to other grownups in the presence of children. Sheila Olsen regarded me with a certain shrewd friendliness in her small, wide-set brown eyes.

"You're going to be thirteen in a week," she said. "The rabbi told me." I nodded stiffly. "You'll hate it, everybody does. Boy or girl, it doesn't make any difference—everybody hates thirteen. I remember."

"It's supposed to be like a borderline for us," I said. "Between being a kid and being a man. Or a woman, I guess."

"But that's just the time when you don't know *what* the hell you are, excuse my French," Sheila Olsen said harshly. "Or *who* you are, or even *if* you are. You couldn't pay me to be thirteen again, I'll tell you. You could not pay me."

She laughed then, and patted my hand. "I'm sorry, Joseph, don't listen to me. I just have...associations with thirteen." Rabbi Tuvim was coming back into the room, holding a small tray bearing three drinks in cocktail glasses I didn't know he had. Sheila Olsen raised her voice slightly. "I was just telling Joseph not to worry—once he makes it through thirteen, it's all downhill from there. Wasn't it that way for you?"

The rabbi raised his eyebrows. "I don't know. Sometimes I feel as though I never did get through thirteen myself." He handed her her drink, and gave me a glass of cocoa cream, which is a soft drink you can't get anymore. I was crazy about cocoa cream that year. I liked to mix it with milk.

The third glass, by its color, unmistakably contained Concord grape wine, and Sheila Olsen's eyebrows went up further than his. "I thought you couldn't stand Jewish wine."

"I can't," the rabbi answered gravely. *"L'chaim."*

Sheila Olsen lifted her glass and said something that must have been the Armenian counterpart of *"To life."* They both looked at me, and I blurted out the first toast that came into my head. *"Past the teeth, over the gums / Look out, gizzard—here she comes!"* My father always said that, late in the evening, with friends over.

We drank. Sheila Olsen said to the rabbi, clearly in some surprise, "You make a mean G&T."

"And you are stalling," Rabbi Tuvim said. "You come all this way from Grand Forks because you have found something connecting your father and that cover girl we're all obsessed with—and now you're here, you'll talk about anything but her." He smiled at her again, but this time it was like the way he smiled at me when I'd try in every way I knew to divert him from *haftarah* and get him talking about the Dodgers' chances of overtaking the St. Louis Cardinals. For just that moment, then, we were all the same age, motionless in time.

I wasn't any more perceptive than any average twelve-year-old, but I saw a kind of grudging sadness in Sheila Olsen's eyes that had nothing in common with the dryly cheerful voice on the phone from North Dakota. Sheila Olsen said, "You're perfectly right. Of course I'm stalling." She reached into her purse and took out a large manila envelope. It had a red string on the flap that you wound around a dime-sized red anchor to hold it closed. "Okay," she said. "Look what I found in my father's safety-deposit box yesterday."

It was a black-and-white photograph, clipped to a large rectangle of cardboard, like the kind that comes back from the laundry with your folded shirt. The photo had the sepia tint and scalloped edges that I knew meant that it was likely to be older than I was. And it was a picture of a dead baby.

I didn't know it was dead at first. I hadn't seen death then, ever, and I thought the baby was sleeping, dressed in a kind of nightgown with feet, like Swee'Pea, and tucked into a little bed that could almost have fitted into a dollhouse. I don't know how or when I realized the truth. Sheila Olsen said, "My sister."

Rabbi Tuvim had no more to say than I did. We just stared at her. Sheila Olsen went on, "I never knew about her until yesterday. She was stillborn."

I was the one who mumbled, "I'm sorry." The rabbi didn't bother with words, but came over to Sheila Olsen and put his arm around her. She didn't cry; if there is one sound I know to this day, it's the sound people make who are not going to cry, *not going to cry.* She put her head on the rabbi's shoulder and closed her eyes, but she didn't cry. I'm her witness.

When she could talk, she said in a different voice, "Turn it over."

There was a card clipped to the back of the mounting board, and there was very neat, dark handwriting on it that looked almost like printing. Rabbi Tuvim read it aloud.

> *"Eleanor Araxia Bagaybagayan.*
> *Born: 24 February 1907*
> *Died: 24 February 1907*
> *Length: 13½ inches*
> *Weight: 5 lbs, 9 oz.*
> *We planned to call her Anoush."*

Below that, there was a space, and then the precise writing gave way to a strange scrawl: clearly the same hand, but looking somehow shrunken and warped, as though the words had been left out in the rain. The rabbi squinted at it over his glasses, and went on reading:

> *"She has been dead for years—she never lived—*
> *how can she be invading my pictures? I take a*
> *shot of men coming to work at a factory—when*
> *I develop it, there she is, a little girl eating an*
> *apple, watching the men go by. I photograph a*
> *train—she has her nose against a window in the*
> *sleeping car. It is her, I know her, how could I not*
> *know her? When I take pictures of young women*
> *at outdoor dinner parties—"*

"That's your magazine cover!" I interrupted. My voice sounded so loud in the hushed room that I was suddenly embarrassed, and shrank back into the couch where I was sitting with Sheila Olsen. She patted my arm, and the rabbi said patiently, "Yes, Joseph." He continued:

> *"—I see her sitting among them, grown now,*

as she was never given the chance to be. Child
or adult, she always knows me, and she knows
that I know her, She is never the focal point of
the shot; she prefers to place herself at the edge,
in the background, to watch me at my work, to
be some small part of it, nothing more. She will
not speak to me, nor can I ever get close to her;
she fades when I try. I would think of her as a
hallucination, but since when can you photograph
a hallucination?"

The rabbi stopped reading again, and he and Sheila Olsen looked at each other without speaking. Then he looked at me and said, somewhat hesitantly, "This next part is a little terrible, Joseph. I don't know whether your parents would want you to hear it."

"If I'm old enough to be Bar Mitzvah," I said, "I'm old enough to hear about a baby who died. I'm staying."

Sheila Olsen chuckled hoarsely. "One for the kid, Rabbi." She gestured with her open hand. "Go on."

Rabbi Tuvim nodded. He took a deep breath.

"She was born with her eyes open. Such blue eyes,
almost lavender. I closed them before my wife
had a chance to see. But I saw her eyes. I would
know her eyes anywhere...is it her ghost haunting
my photographs? Can one be a ghost if one never
drew breath in this world? I do not know—but it
is her, it is her. Somehow, it is our Anoush."

Nobody said anything for a long time after he had finished reading. The rabbi blew his nose and polished his glasses, and Sheila Olsen opened her mouth and then closed it again. I had all kinds of things I wanted to say, but they all sounded so stupid in my head that I just let them go and stared at the photo of Sheila Olsen's stillborn baby sister. I thought about the word *still...* quiet, motionless, silent, tranquil, at rest. I hadn't known it meant *dead*.

Sheila Olsen asked at length, "What do Jews believe about ghosts? Do you even *have* ghosts?"

Rabbi Tuvim scratched his head. "Well, the Torah doesn't really talk about supernatural beings at all. The Talmud, yes—the Talmud is up to here in demons, but ghosts, as we would think of them...no, not so much." He leaned forward, resting his elbows on his knees and tenting his fingers, the way he did when he was coaxing me to think beyond my schooling. "We call them *spirits,* when we call them anything, and we imagine some of them to be malevolent, dangerous—demonic, if you like. But there are benign ones as well, and those are usually here for a specific reason. To help someone, to bring a message. To comfort."

"Comfort," Sheila Olsen said softly. Her face had gone very pale; but as she spoke color began to come back to it, too much color. "My dad needed that, for sure, and from Day One I couldn't give it to him. He never stopped missing my mother—this person I never even knew, and couldn't be—and now I find out that he missed someone else, too. My perfect, magical, *lost* baby sister, who didn't have to bother to get herself born to become legendary. Oh, Christ, it explains so much!" She had gone pale again. "And you're telling me she came back to comfort him? That's the message?"

"Well, I don't know that," the rabbi said reasonably. "But it would be nice, wouldn't it, if that turned out to be true? If there really were two worlds, and certain creatures—call them spirits, call them demons, angels, anything you like—could come and go between those worlds, and offer advice, and tell the rest of us not to be so scared of it all. I'd like that, wouldn't you?"

"But do you believe it? Do you believe my stillborn sister came back to tell my father that it wasn't his fault? Sneaking into his photographs just to wave to him, so he could see she was really okay somewhere? Because it sure didn't comfort him much, I'll tell you that."

"Didn't it?" the rabbi asked gently. "Are you sure?"

Sheila Olsen was fighting for control, doggedly refusing to let her voice escape into the place where it just as determinedly wanted to go. The effort made her sound as though she had something caught in her throat that she could neither swallow nor spit up. She said, "The earliest memory I have is of my father crying in the night. I don't know how old I was—three, three and a half. Not four. It's like a dream now—I get out of my bed, and I go to him, and

I pat him, pat his back, the way someone...someone used to do for me when I had a nightmare. He doesn't reject me, but he doesn't turn around to me, either. He just lies there and cries and cries." The voice almost got away from her there, but she caught it, and half-laughed. "Well, I guess that *is* rejection, actually."

"Excuse me, but that's nonsense," Rabbi Tuvim said sharply. "You were a baby, trying to ease an adult's pain. That only happens in movies. Give me your glass."

He went back into the kitchen, while Sheila Olsen and I sat staring at each other. She cleared her throat and finally said, "I guess you didn't exactly bargain for such a big dramatic scene, huh, Joseph?"

"It beats writing a speech in Hebrew," I answered from the heart. Sheila Olsen did laugh then, which emboldened me enough to say, "Do you think your father ever saw her again, your sister, after he stopped being a photographer?"

"Oh, he never stopped taking pictures," Sheila Olsen said. "He just quit trying to make a living at it." She was trying to fix her makeup, but her hands were shaking too much. She said, "He couldn't go through a day without taking a dozen shots of everything around him, and then he'd spend the evening in his closet darkroom, developing them all. But if he had any more photos of...*her,* I never saw them. There weren't any others in the safe-deposit box." She paused, and then added, more to herself than to me, "He was always taking pictures of me, I used to get annoyed sometimes. Had them up all over the place."

Rabbi Tuvim came back with a fresh drink for her. I was hoping for more cocoa cream soda, but I didn't get it. Sheila Olsen practically grabbed the gin-and-tonic, then looked embarrassed. "I'm not a drunk, really—I'm just a little shaky right now. So you honestly think that's her, my sister...my sister Anoush in those old photographs?"

"Don't you?" the rabbi asked quietly. "I'd say that's what matters most."

Sheila Olsen took half her drink in one swallow and looked him boldly in the face. "Oh, I do, but I haven't trusted my own opinion on anything for... oh, for years, since my husband walked out. And I'm very tired, and I know I'm halfway nutsy when it comes to anything to do with my father. He was kind and good, and he was a terrific photographer, and he lost his baby and his wife, one right after the other, so I'm not blaming him that there wasn't much left for me. I'm *not!*"—loudly and defiantly, though the rabbi had said nothing. "But I just wish...I just wish...."

And now, finally, she did begin to cry.

I didn't know what to do. I hadn't seen many adults crying in my life. I knew aunts and uncles undoubtedly *did* cry—my cousins told me so—but not ever in front of us children, except for Aunt Frieda, who smelled funny, and always cried late in the evening, whatever the occasion. My mother went into the bathroom to cry, my father into his basement office. I can't be sure he actually cried, but he did put his head down on his desk. He never made a sound, and neither did Sheila Olsen. She just sat there on the couch with the tears sliding down her face, and she kept on trying to talk, as though nothing were happening. But nothing came out—not words, not sobs; nothing but hoarse breathing that sounded terribly painful. I wanted to run away.

I didn't, but only because Rabbi Tuvim did know what to do. First he handed Sheila Olsen a box of tissues to wipe her eyes with, which she did, although the tears kept coming. Next, he went to his desk by the window and took from the lowest drawer the battered tin box which I knew contained his collection of lost keys. Then he went back to Sheila Olsen and crouched down in front of her, holding the tin box out. When she didn't respond, he opened the box and put it on her lap. He said, "Pick one."

Sheila Olsen sniffled, "What? Pick *what?*"

"A key," Rabbi Tuvim said. "Pick two, three, if you like. Just take your time, and be careful."

Sheila Olsen stared down into the box, so crowded with keys that by now Rabbi Tuvim couldn't close it so it clicked. Then she looked back at the rabbi, and she said, "You really *are* crazy. I was worried about that."

"Indulge me," the rabbi said. "Crazy people have to be indulged."

Sheila Olsen brushed her hand warily across the keys. "You mean, you want me to just *take* a couple? For keeps?" She sounded like a little girl.

"For keeps." The rabbi smiled at her. "Just remember, each of those keys represents a lock you can't find, a problem you can't solve. As you can see...." He gestured grandly toward the tin box without finishing the sentence.

I thought Sheila Olsen would grab any old key off the top layer, to humor him; but in fact she did take her time, sifting through a dozen or more, before she finally settled on a very small, silvery one, mailbox-key size. Then she looked straight at Rabbi Tuvim and said, "That's to represent *my* trouble. I know it's a little bitty sort of trouble, not worth talking about after a war where millions and millions of people died. Not even worth thinking about by myself—nothing but a middle-aged woman wishing her father could have loved her...could have *seen* her, the way he saw that strange girl who turned out to be my sister, for God's sake." Her voice came slowly and heavily now, and I realized how tired she must be. She said, "You know, Rabbi, sometimes when I was a child, I used to wish *I* were dead, just so my father would miss me, the way I knew he missed my mother. I did—I really used to wish that."

The rabbi called a taxi to take her to her airport hotel. He walked her to the cab—I noticed that she put the little key carefully into her bag—and I saw them talking earnestly until the driver started looking impatient, and she got in. Then he came back into the house, and, to my horrified amazement, promptly gave me the Torah test he'd written up for me. Nor could I divert him by getting him to talk about Sheila Olsen's photographs, and her father's notes, and the other things she had told us. To all of my efforts in that direction, he replied only by pointing to the test paper and leaning back in his chair with his eyes closed. I mumbled a theatrically evil Yiddish curse that I'd learned from my Uncle Shmul, who was both an authority and a specialist, and bent bitterly to my work. I did not do well.

I didn't imagine that I would ever see Sheila Olsen again. She had a job, a home and a life waiting for her, back in Grand Forks, North Dakota. But in fact I saw her that Saturday afternoon, in the audience gathered at the Reform synagogue to witness my Bar Mitzvah. Rabbi Tuvim's other students had all scheduled their individual ceremonies a year or more in advance, and I didn't know whether to be terrified at the notion of being the entire center of attention, or grateful that at least I wouldn't be shown up for the pathetic *schlemiel* I was by contrast with those three. We had a nearly full house in the main gathering room of the synagogue, my schoolmates drawn by the lure of the after-party, the adults either by family loyalty or my mother's blackmail, or some combination of both. My mother was the Seurat of blackmail: a dot here, a dot there....

The rabbi—coaching me under his breath to the very last minute—was helping me tie the *tefillin* around my head and my left arm when I messed up the whole process by pulling away to point out Sheila Olsen. He yanked me back, saying, "Yes, I know she's here. Stand still."

"I thought she went home," I said. "She said goodbye to me."

"Hold your head up," Rabbi Tuvim ordered. "She decided she wanted to stay for your Bar Mitzvah—said she'd never seen one. Now, remember, you stand there after your speech, while I sing. With, please God, your grandfather's *tallis* around your shoulders, *if* your mother remembers to bring it. If not, I guess you must use mine."

I had never seen him nervous before. I said, "When this is over, can I still come and look at your old magazines?"

The rabbi stopped fussing with the *tefillin* and looked at me for a long moment. Then he said very seriously, "Thank you, Detective Yossele. Thank you for putting things back into proportion for me. You have something of a gift that way. Yes, of course you can look at the magazines, you can visit for any reason you like, or for no reason at all. And don't worry—we will get through this thing today just fine." He gave the little leather phylactery a last tweak, and added, "Or we will leave town on the same cattle boat for Argentina. Oh, thank God, there's your mother. Stay right where you are."

He hurried off—I had never seen him hurry before, either—and I stayed where I was, turning in little circles to look at the guests, and at the hard candies ranged in bowls all around the room. These were there specifically for my friends and family to hurl at me by way of congratulations, the instant the ceremony was over. I don't know whether any other Jewish community in the world does this. I don't think so.

Sheila Olsen came up to me, almost shyly, once Rabbi Tuvim was gone. She gave me a quick hug, and then stepped back, asking anxiously, "Is that all right? I mean, are you not supposed to be touched or anything until it's over? I should have asked first, I'm sorry."

"It's all right," I said. "Really. I'm so scared right now..." and I stopped there, ashamed to admit my growing panic to a stranger. But Sheila Olsen seemed to understand, for she hugged me a second time, and it was notably comforting.

"Your rabbi will take care of you," she said. "He'll get you through it, I know he will. He's a good man." She hesitated then, looking away. "I'm a little embarrassed around both of you now, after yesterday. I didn't mean to carry on like that." I had no idea what to say. I just smiled stupidly. Sheila Olsen said, "I'll have to leave for the airport right after this is over, so I wanted to say goodbye now. I guess it was all foolishness, but I'm glad I came. I'm glad I met you, Joseph."

"Me, too," I said. We saw Rabbi Tuvim returning, waving to us over the heads of the milling guests. Sheila Olsen, shy again, patted my shoulder, whispered *"Courage,"* and began to slip away. The rabbi intercepted her deftly, however, and they talked for a few minutes, at the end of which Sheila Olsen nodded firmly, pointed to her big purse, and went to find a seat. Rabbi Tuvim joined me and went quietly over my Torah portion with me again. He seemed distinctly calmer, or possibly I mean resigned.

"All right, Joseph," the rabbi said at last. "All right, time to get this show on the road. Here we go."

I'm not going to talk about the Bar Mitzvah, not *as* a Bar Mitzvah, except to say that it wasn't nearly the catastrophe I'd been envisioning for months. It couldn't have been. I stumbled on the prayers, Lord knows how many times, but Rabbi Tuvim had his back to the onlookers, and he fed me the lines I'd forgotten, and we got through. Oddly enough, the speech itself—I had chosen to discuss a passage in Numbers 1–9, showing how the Israelites first consolidated themselves as a community at Sinai—flowed much more smoothly, and I found myself practically enjoying the taste of Hebrew in my mouth. If the rabbi could teach me nothing else, somehow I'd come to understand the sound. Not the words, not the grammar, and certainly not the true meaning...just the *sound.* Nearing the grand finale, I wasn't thinking at all about the gift table in the farthest corner of the room. I was already beginning to regret that the speech wasn't longer.

That was when I saw her.

Anoush.

Small and dark, olive-skinned, she was no magazine cover girl now, but a woman of Sheila Olsen's age. She stood near the back of the room, away on the margins, as always. Sheila Olsen didn't see her, but I did, and she saw that I did, and I believe she saw also that I knew who and *how* she was. She didn't react, except to move further into shadow—she cast none of her own—but I could still see her eyes. No one else seemed to notice her at all; yet now and then someone would bump into her, or step on her foot, and immediately say,

"Oh, sorry, excuse me," just as though she were living flesh. I tried to catch Sheila Olsen's eye, and then Rabbi Tuvim's, to indicate with my chin and my own eyes where they should look, but they never once turned their heads. It was very nearly as frustrating as learning Hebrew.

I finished the speech any old how, and when I was done, my mother came out and put her father's *tallis* on my shoulders, and everybody cheered except me. All I wanted to do was to draw Sheila Olsen's attention to the shy, ghostly presence of her sister, but I lost track of both of them when the hard round candies began showering down on me. It was going to make for an uncertain dance floor—Herbie Kaufman's Bel-Air Combo were busily setting up—but a number of my schoolmates were crowding onto it, followed by a few wary older couples. I was down from the little stage and weaving through the crush, *tallis* and all, pushing past congratulatory shoulder punches and butt slaps, not to mention the flash cameras—forbidden during the ceremony itself—going off in my face as I hunted for Sheila Olsen, frantic that she might already have left. She had a plane to catch, after all, and things to decide to remember or forget.

I was slowing down, beginning to give up, when I spotted her heading for the door, but slowed down by the press of bodies, so that she heard when I called her name. She turned, and I waved wildly, not at her, but toward the shadowless figure motionlessly watching her leave. And for the first time, Sheila Olsen and Eleanor Araxia Bagaybagayan saw each other.

Neither moved at first. Neither spoke—Sheila Olsen plainly didn't dare, and I don't think Anoush could. Then, very slowly, as though she were trying to slip up on some wild thing, Sheila Olsen began to ease toward her sister, holding out her open hands. She was facing me, and I saw her lips moving, but I couldn't hear the words.

But for every step Sheila Olsen took, Anoush took one step back from her, remaining as unreachable—*there, not there*—as her father Abel had found her, so many years before. Strangely, for me, since I had never seen her as beautiful on the magazine covers—only hypnotically *alive*—now, as a middle-aged woman, she almost stopped my newly-manly heart. There was gray in her hair, a heaviness to her face and midsection, and in the way she moved…but my heart wanted to stop, all the same.

I was afraid that Sheila Olsen might snap, out of too much wishing, and make some kind of dive or grab for Anoush, but she did something else. She stopped moving forward, and just stood very still for a moment, and then she reached into her purse and brought out the lacy little key that she had taken from Rabbi Tuvim's collection. She stared at it for a moment, and then she kissed it, very quickly, and she tossed it underhand toward Anoush. It spun so slowly, turning in the light like a butterfly, that I wouldn't have been surprised if it never came down.

Anoush caught it. Ghost or no ghost, ethereal or not, she picked Sheila Olsen's key out of the air as daintily as though she were selecting exactly the right apple on a tree, the perfect note on a musical instrument. She looked back at Sheila Olsen, and she smiled a little—I *know* she smiled, I *saw* her—and she touched the key to her lips...

...and I don't know what she did with it, or where she put it—maybe she *ate* it, for all I could ever tell. All I can say for certain is that Sheila Olsen's eyes got very big, and she touched her own mouth again, and then she turned and hurried out of the synagogue, never looking back, I was going to follow her, but Rabbi Tuvim came up and put his hand gently on my shoulder. He said, "She has a plane to catch. You have a special party. Each to his own."

"You saw," I said. "Did you see her?"

"It is more important that you saw her," the rabbi answered. "And that you made Sheila Olsen see her, you brought them together. That was the *mitzvah*—the rest is unimportant, a handful of candy." He patted my shoulder. "You did well."

Anoush was gone, of course, when we looked for her. So was the rabbi's key, though I actually got down on my knees to feel around where she had stood, half-afraid that it had simply fallen through her shade to the floor. But there was no sign of it; and the rabbi, watching, said quietly, "One lock opened. So many more." We went back to the party then.

Film took longer to develop in those days, unless you did it yourself. As I remember, it was more than a week before friends and family started bringing us shots taken at my Bar Mitzvah party. I hated almost all of them—somehow I always seemed to get caught with my mouth open and a goofy startled look on my face—but my mother cherished them all, and pored over them at the kitchen table for hours at a time. "There you are again, dancing with your cousin Marilyn, what was Sarah ever *thinking*, letting her wear that to a Bar

Mitzvah?" "There you are in your grandpa's *tallis,* looking so grownup, except I was so afraid your *yarmulke* was going to fall off." "Oh, there's that one I love, with you and your father, I *told* him not to wear that tie, and your friend what's-his-name, he should lose some weight. And there's Rabbi Tuvim, what's that in his beard, dandruff?" Actually, it was cream cheese. The rabbi loved cream cheese.

Then she turned over a photo she'd missed before, and said in a different tone, "Who's that woman? Joseph, do you know that woman?"

It was Anoush, off to one side beyond the dancers I'd been shoving my way through to reach Sheila Olsen. She had her arms folded across her breast, and she looked immensely alone as she watched the party; but she didn't look lonely at all, or even wistful—just alone. As long as it's been, I remember a certain mischievousness around her mouth and eyes, as though she had deliberately slipped into this photograph of my celebration, just as she had slipped comfortably into her father's work—yes, to wave to him, as Sheila Olsen had said mockingly then. To wave to her sister now...and maybe, a little, to me.

I practically snatched the picture our of my mother's hand—making up some cockamamie story about an old friend of Rabbi Tuvim's—and brought it to him immediately. We both looked at it in silence for a long while. Then the rabbi put it carefully into a sturdy envelope, and addressed it to Sheila Olsen in Grand Forks, North Dakota. I took it to the post office myself, and paid importantly, out of my allowance, to send it Airmail Special Delivery. The rabbi promised to tell me as soon as Sheila Olsen wrote back.

It took longer than I expected: a good two weeks, probably more. After the first week, I was badgering the rabbi almost every day; sometimes twice, because they still had two postal deliveries back then. How he kept from strangling me, or anyway hanging up in my ear, I have no idea—perhaps he sympathized with my impatience because he was anxious himself. At all events, when Sheila Olsen's letter did arrive, he called me immediately. He offered to read it to me over the phone, but I wanted to see it, so I ran over. Rabbi Tuvim gave me a glass of cocoa cream soda, insisted maddeningly on waiting until I could breathe and speak normally, and then showed me the letter.

It was short, and there was no salutation; it simply began:

"She sits on my bedside table, in a little silver
frame. I say goodnight and good morning to her
every day. I have tried several times to make
copies for you, but they never come out. I'm sorry.

Thank you for the key, Rabbi. And Joseph,
Joseph—thank you."

I still have the letter. The rabbi gave it to me. It sits in its own wooden frame, and people ask me about it, because it's smudged and grubby from many readings, and frayed along the folding, and it looks as though a three-year-old has been at it, which did happen, many years later. But I keep it close, because before that letter I had no understanding of beauty, and no idea of what love is, or what can be born out of love. And after it I knew enough at least to recognize these things when they came to me.

Oakland Dragon Blues

Once upon a time I tried to do a straight-up trade with Ursula K. Le Guin—my unicorns for the dragons from her Earthsea series—because Ursula's dragons are just that good. *Pretty much the definitive article, in fact, and there's an end on't.*

She declined to accept my offer, of course. Smart woman. I mean, I'm happy enough with my unicorns these days; but I'm convinced that dragons should have been put off-limits to fantasists after Earthsea.

So you can imagine my surprise a couple of years ago when I found myself writing an entire novel full of dragons, just because an idea came along that intrigued me too much to ignore. (That book, I'm Afraid You've Got Dragons, *will eventually be out in trade paperback from Tachyon, publisher of this very collection.) Then, as if stepping over the line once wasn't risky enough, in a moment of rash confidence I agreed to tackle a story for a dragon-themed original anthology. I started by consciously resolving to go for something as different as possible from anything of Ursula's. My chosen setting was the forests of rural northern California. My chosen time was right now. My invented gimmick: the notion that if dragons existed, then the illegal meth labs and marijuana farms that hide in those deep woods would certainly find them more useful than mere pit bulls or Dobermans...but the story I wrote, about the animal-control officers who have to handle such things, refused to come into sharp focus. A week before my deadline I knew I couldn't solve it in time and prepared to send my friendly, patient editor an apologetic admission of defeat.*

Then—as I'm always quoting Samuel Johnson's "When a man knows that he is to be hanged within a week, it concentrates his mind wonderfully"—I remembered that when I was twenty-two, and taking my first failed crack at what eventually became The Last Unicorn, *I'd included a particularly morose and colorful dragon in the opening chapter: a dragon that I had ruthlessly excised when I returned to work on the manuscript three years later.*

With that thought, this story was born.

✳

"I am happy to report," Officer Levinsky said to Officer Guerra, pointing to the dragon sprawled across the Telegraph and 51st Street intersection, "that this one is all yours. I've been off shift for exactly seven minutes, waiting for your ass to get here. Have a nice day."

Guerra stared, paling visibly under his brown skin. Traffic was backed up in all four directions: horns were honking as madly as car alarms, drivers were screaming hysterically—though none, he noticed, were getting out of their cars—and a five-man road crew, their drills, hoses, sawhorses and warning signs scattered by a single swing of the dragon's tail, were adding their bellows to the din. The dragon paid no attention to any of it, but regarded the two policemen out of half-closed eyes, resting its head on its long-clawed front feet, and every now and then burping feeble, dingy flames. It didn't look well.

"How long's it been here?" Guerra asked weakly.

Levinsky consulted his watch again. "Thirty-one minutes. Just plopped out of the sky—damn miracle it didn't crush somebody's car, flatten a pedestrian. Been lying there ever since, just like that."

"Well, you called it in, right?" Guerra wondered what the police code for a dragon in the intersection would be.

Levinsky looked at him as though he had suggested a fast game of one-on-one with an open manhole. "You *are* out of your mind—I always thought so. No, I didn't call it in, and if you have the sense of a chinch bug, you won't either. Just get rid of it, I'm out of here. Enjoy, Guerra."

Levinsky's patrol car was parked on the far side of the intersection. He skirted the dragon's tail cautiously, got in the car, slapped on his siren—for pure emotional relief, Guerra thought—and was gone, leaving Guerra scratching his buzz-cut head, facing both a growing traffic jam and a creature out of fairy tales, whose red eyes, streaked with pale yellow, like the eyes of very old men, were watching him almost sleepily, totally uninterested in whatever he chose to do. But watching, all the same.

The furious chaos of the horns being harder on Guerra's normally placid nerves than the existence of dragons, he walked over to the beast and said, from a respectful distance, "Sir, you're blocking traffic, and I'm going to have to ask you to move along. Otherwise you're looking at a major citation here."

When the dragon did not respond, he said it again in Spanish; then drew a deep breath and started over in Russian, having taken a course that winter in order to cope with a new influx of immigrants. The dragon interrupted him with a brief hiccup of oily, sulphurous flame halfway through. In a rusty, raspy voice with a faint accent that was none of the ones Guerra knew, it said, "Don't start."

Guerra rested his hand lightly on the butt of the pistol that he was immensely proud of never having fired during his eight years on the Oakland police force, except for his regular practice sessions and annual recertifications at the Davis Street Range. He said, "Sir, I am not trying to start anything with you—I'm having enough trouble just believing in you. But I've got to get you out of this intersection before somebody gets hurt. I mean, look at all those people, listen to those damn *horns*." The racket was already giving him a headache behind his eyes. "You think you could maybe step over here to the curb, we'll talk about it? That'd work out much better for both of us, don't you think?"

The dragon raised its head and favored him with a long, considering stare. "I don't know. I like this place about as well as I like any place in this world, which is not at all. Why should I make things easier for you? Nobody ever cares about making anything easier for *me*, let me tell you."

Guerra's greatest ambition in law enforcement was to become a hostage negotiator. He had been studying the technique on and off for most of his tenure on the force, both on site and through attending lectures and reading everything he could find on the subject. The lecturers and the books had a good deal to say concerning hostage-takers' tendency to self-pity. He said patiently to the dragon, "Well, I'm really trying to do exactly that. Let's get acquainted, huh? I'm Officer Guerra—Michael Guerra, but people mostly call me Mike-O, I don't know why. What's your name?" *Always get on a first-name basis, as early as possible. It makes you two human beings together—you'll be amazed at the difference it makes.* Now if only one of those books had ever covered the fine points of negotiating with a burping mythological predator.

"You couldn't pronounce it," the dragon replied. "And if you tried, you'd hurt yourself." But it rose to its feet with what seemed to Guerra an intense and even painful effort, and with some trepidation he led it away from the intersection to the side street where he had parked his blue-and-white patrol car. The traffic started up again before they were all the way across, and if people went on honking and cursing, still there were many who leaned out of their windows to applaud him. One driver shouted jovially, "Put the cuffs on him!" while another yelled, "Illegal parking—get the boot!" The dragon half-lumbered, half-slithered beside Guerra as sedately as though it were on a leash; but every so often it cocked a red eye sideways at him, like a wicked bird, and Guerra shivered with what felt like ancestral memory. *These guys used to hunt us like rabbits. I know they did.*

The phone at his waist made an irritable sound and rattled against his belt buckle. He nodded to the dragon, grunted "My boss, I better take this," and heard Lieutenant Kunkel's nasal drone demanding, "Guerra, you there? Guerra, what the fuck is going on up in Little Ethiopia?" Lieutenant Kunkel fully expected Eritrean rebels to stage shootouts in Oakland sometime within the week.

"Big, nasty traffic jam, Lieutenant," Guerra answered, consciously keeping his voice light and level, even with a dragon sniffing disdainfully at his patrol car. "All under control now, no problem."

"Yeah, well, we've been getting a bunch of calls about I don't know what, some sort of crazy dragon, UFO, whatever. You know anything about this shit?"

"Uh," Guerra said. "Uh, no, Lieutenant, it's just the time of day, you know? Rush hour, traffic gets tied up, people get a little crazy, they start seeing stuff. Mass hysteria, shared hallucinations, it's real common. They got books about it."

Lieutenant Kunkel's reaction to the concept of shared hallucinations was not at first audible. Then it became audible, but not comprehensible. Finally coherent, he drew on a vocabulary that impressed Guerra so powerfully for its range and expressiveness that at a certain point, phone gripped between his ear and his shoulder, he dug out his notebook and started writing down the choicest words and phrases he caught. If anything, Guerra was a great believer in self-improvement.

The lieutenant finally hung up, and Guerra put the book back in his pocket and said to the dragon, "Okay. He's cool. You just go on away now, go on home, back wherever you...well, wherever, and we'll say no more about it. And you have an extra-nice day, hear?"

The dragon did not answer, but leaned against his car, considering him out of its strange red-and-yellow eyes. Huge as the creature was—Guerra had nothing but military vehicles for comparison—he thought it must be a very old dragon, for the scales on its body were a dull greenish-black, and its front claws were worn and blunt, no sharper than a turtle's. The long low purple crest running along its back from ears to tail tip was torn in several places, and lay limp and prideless. The spikes at the end of its tail were all broken off short; and in spite of the occasional wheeze of fire, there was a rattle in the dragon's breath, as though it were rusty inside. He supposed the great purple wings worked: it was hard to see them clearly, folded back along the body as they were, but they too looked...*ratty,* for lack of a better word. Spontaneously, he blurted out, "You've had kind of a rough time, huh? I get that."

"Do you?" The dragon's black lips twitched, and for a moment Guerra thought absurdly that it was going to cry. "Do you indeed, Mike-O? Do you *get* that my back's killing me—that it aches all the time, right there, behind the hump, because of the beating it takes walking the black iron roads of this world? Do you *get* that the smell of your streets—even your streams, your rivers, your bay—is more than I can bear? That your people taste like clocks and coal oil, and your children are bitter as silver? The children used to be the best eating of all, better than antelope, better than wild geese, but now I just can't bring myself to touch another one of them. Oh, it's been dogs and cats and mangy little squirrels for months, *years*—and when you think how I used to dine off steamed knight, knight on the half shell, broiled in his own armor with all the natural juices, oh...excuse me, excuse me, I'm sorry..."

And, rather to Guerra's horror, the dragon did begin to cry. He wept very softly, with his eyes closed and his head lowered, his emerald-green tears smelling faintly like gunpowder. Guerra said, "Hey. Hey, listen, don't do that. Please. Don't cry, okay?"

The dragon sniffled, but it lifted its head again to regard him in some wonder. Surprisingly severe, it said, "You are a witness to the rarest sight in the world—a dragon in tears—and all you can say is *don't do that?* I don't *get* you people at all." But it did stop crying; it even made a sound like rustling ashes, which Guerra thought might be a chuckle. It said, "Or did I embarrass you, Mike-O?"

"Listen," Guerra said again. "Listen, you've got to get out of here. There's going to be rumors for days, but I'll cover with the lieutenant, whoever, whatever I have to say. Just *go*, okay?" He hesitated for a moment, and then added, "Please?"

The dragon licked forlornly at its own tears with its broad forked tongue. "I'm tired, Mike-O. You have no idea how tired I am. I have one task to complete in this desolate world of yours, and then I'm done with it forever. And since I'll never, never find my way back to my own world again, what difference does anything make? Afterward...*afterward*, you and your boss can shoot me, take me to prison, put me in a zoo...what wretched difference? I just don't care anymore."

"No," Guerra said. "Look, I'll tell you the truth, I do not want to be the guy who brings you in. For starters, it'll mean more reports, more damn *bookkeeping* than I've ever seen in my life. I *hate* writing reports. And besides that...yeah, I guess I'd be famous for a while—fifteen minutes, like they say. The cop who caught the dragon...newspapers, big TV shows, fine and dandy, maybe I'd even meet some girls that way. But once it all died down, that's all I'd ever be, the guy who had the thing on the street with the dragon. You think that's a résumé for somebody wants to be a hostage negotiator? I don't think so."

The dragon was listening to him attentively, though with a slightly puzzled air. Guerra said, "Anyway, what's this about finding your way back to your own world? How'd you get here in the first place?"

"How did I *get* here?" To Guerra's astonishment and alarm, the dragon rumbled croupily, deep in its chest, and the ragged crest stood up as best it could, while the head seemed to cock back on its neck like the hammer on a pistol. A brief burst of fire shot from the fang-studded mouth, making Guerra scramble aside.

"That's easy," it said, tapping its claws on the asphalt. "I got written here."

Guerra was not at all sure that he had heard correctly. "You got... *written*?"

"Written *and* written out," the dragon rasped bitterly. "The author put me in his book right at the beginning, and then he changed his mind. Went back, redid the whole book, and *phhffttt.*" More fire. Guerra ducked again, barely in time. "Gone, just like that. Not one line left—and I had some good ones, whole paragraphs. All gone."

"I'm having a very hard time with this," Guerra said. "So you're in a book—"

"*Was.* I *was* in a book—"

"—and now you're not. But you're real all the same, blocking traffic, breathing fire—"

"Art is a remarkable creative force," the dragon said. "I exist because a man made up a story." It mentioned the writer's name, which was not one Guerra knew. "I'm stranded here, loose and wandering in his world because he decided not to write about me after all." It bared double rows of worn but quite serviceable teeth in a highly unpleasant grin. "But I'm real, I'm here, and I'm looking for him. Followed him from one place to another for years—the man does move around—and finally tracked him to this Oakland. I don't know exactly where he lives, but I'll find him. And when I do he is going to be one crispy author, believe me." It snorted in anticipation, but Guerra had already taken refuge behind the patrol car. The dragon said, "I told you, after that I don't care what happens to me. I can't ever get home, so what does it matter?"

Its voice trembled a little on the last words, and Guerra worried that it might be about to start weeping again. He edged cautiously out from the shelter of the car and said, "Well, you sure as hell won't get back home if you fry up the one guy who maybe can help you. You ever think about that?"

The long neck swiveled, and the dragon stared at him, its eyes red and yellow, like hunters' moons. Guerra said, "He lives in Oakland, this writer? Okay, I'll find out the address—that's one thing cops are really good at, tracing people's addresses—"

"And you'll tell me?" The dragon's whole vast body was quivering with eagerness. "You would do that?"

"No," Guerra said flatly. "Not for a minute. Because you'd zip right off after him, and be picking your teeth by the time I got off my shift. So you're going to wait until I'm done here, and we'll find him together. Deal?" The dragon was clearly dubious. Guerra said, "Deal—or I won't give you his address, but I *will* tell him you're looking for him. And he'll move again, sure as hell—*I* would. Think about it."

The dragon thought. At last it sighed deeply, exhaling tear-damp ashes, and rumbled, "Very well. I'll wait for you on that sign." Guerra watched in fascination as the shabby purple wings unfolded. Worn claws scrabbling on the sidewalk, the beast took a few running steps before it lifted into the air. A moment later it landed neatly on the top frame of a billboard advertising a movie that apparently had a mermaid, a vampire and a giant octopus in the cast. The dragon posed there all during Guerra's shift, looking like part of the promotion, and if it moved even an inch he never saw it.

The road crew was back at work, and the intersection was in serious need of a patrolman. Both streets were torn up, the traffic lights were all off, and Guerra had his hands full beckoning cars forward and holding them up, keeping drivers away from closed-off lanes and guiding them around potholes. It kept his mind, as nothing else could have, almost completely off the dragon; although he did manage, during a comparative lull, to call in for the current address of the writer who had carelessly created the creature and then forgotten about it. *Like God, maybe,* Guerra thought, then decided he might not mention that notion to Father Fabros on Sunday.

His shift ended in twilight; the traffic had noticeably thinned by then, and he felt comfortable turning the intersection over to Officer Colasanto, who was barely in his second year. Walking to his car, Guerra gestured to the dragon, and it promptly took off from the billboard, climbing toward the night clouds with a speed and elegance he had never imagined from those ragged wings and age-tarnished body. Once again the bone-image came to him of such creatures stooping from the sky at speeds his ancestors could not have comprehended before it was too late. He shivered, and hurriedly got into the patrol car.

He checked in at the police station, joking amiably with friends about the morning's dragon alarm—neither Lieutenant Kunkel nor Officer Levinsky was present—changed into civilian clothes, and hurried back out, anxious lest the dragon should become anxious. But he saw no sign of it, and had to assume that it was following him beyond his sight, hungry enough for revenge that it was not likely to lose track of him. Not for the first time, Guerra wondered what had possessed him to take sides in this mess, and which side he was actually on.

The dragon's author lived in North Berkeley, past the chic restaurants of the Gourmet Ghetto, and on out into the classic older houses, "full of character," as the real-estate agents liked to put it, if a little short on reliable plumbing. Guerra found the house easily enough—it had two stories, a slightly threadbare lawn and a tentative garden—and pulled into the driveway, expecting the dragon, in its fury and fervency, to land beside him before he was out of the car. But he only glimpsed it once, far above him, circling with chilling patience between the clouds. A motion-detector floodlight came on as Guerra walked up the driveway and rang the bell.

The author answered with surprising quickness. He was a middle-sized, undistinguished-looking man: bearded, wearing glasses, and clad in jeans, an old sweatshirt, and sneakers that had clearly been through two or three major civil conflicts. He blinked at Guerra and said "Hi? What can I do for you?"

Guerra showed his badge. "Sir, I'm Officer Michael Guerra, Oakland Police, and I need to speak with you for a moment." He felt himself blushing absurdly, and was glad that the light was gone.

The author was sensibly wary, checking Guerra's badge carefully before answering. "I've paid that Jack London Square parking ticket."

Guerra had just started to say, "This isn't exactly a police matter," when, with a terrifyingly silent rush—the only sound was the soft whistle of wind through the folded wings—the dragon landed in the tentative garden and hissed, "Remember me, storyteller? Scribe, singer, sorcerer—*remember me?*"

The author froze where he stood in the doorway, neither able to come forward nor run back into his house. He whispered, "No. You can't be here... you can't *be*..." He did not seem able to close his mouth, and he was hugging himself, as though for protection.

The dragon sneered foul-smelling flames. "Come closer, you hairy hot pocket. I'd rather not singe your nice house when I incinerate you."

Guerra said, "Wait a minute now, just a minute. We didn't talk about any incineration. No incineration here."

The dragon looked at him for the first time since it had landed. It said, "Stop me."

Guerra's gun was in the car, but even if he could have reached it, it would have been no more practical use than a spitball. His mouth was dry, and his throat hurt.

Remarkably, the author stood his ground. He spoke directly to the dragon, saying, "I didn't write you out of the book. I dropped the damn book altogether—I didn't know how to write it, and I was making an unholy mess out of it. So I dropped a lot of people, not just you. How come you're the only one hunting me down and threatening my life? Why is this all about *you?*"

The dragon's head swooped low enough to be almost on a level with the writer's, and so close that a bit of his beard did get singed. But its voice was colder than Guerra had ever heard it when it said, "Because you wrote enough life into me that I deserved more. I deserved a *resolution*—even if you killed me off in the end, that would have been *something*—and when I didn't get it, I still had this leftover life, and no world to live it in. So of course, of course I have been trapped in your world ever since—miserable dungheap that it is, there is no other place for me to exist. And no other emotion, out of all I might have had...but revenge."

Its head and neck cocked back then, as Guerra had seen them do before, and he turned and sprinted for his car and the useless gun. But he tripped over a loose brick from the garden border, fell full length, and lay half-stunned, hearing—to his dazed surprise—the voice of the author saying commandingly, "Hold it, just hold the phone here, before you go sautéing people. You're angry because I didn't create a suitable world for you, is that it?"

The dragon did not answer immediately. Guerra struggled wearily to his feet, looking back and forth between the house and his car. A family across the street—a man in a bathrobe, his small Indian wife in a sari, and a young boy wearing Spider-Man pajamas—were standing barefoot on their own lawn, clearly staring at the dragon. The man called out, loudly but hesitantly, "Hey, you okay over there?"

Guerra was still trying to decide on his response, when he heard the dragon say in a different tone, "No, I'm angry because you did. You made up a fairy tale that I belonged in, and then you destroyed it and left me *outside*, in this terrible, terrible place that I can't escape. And I never *will* escape it, I know, except by dying, and we dragons live such a long time. But if I avenge myself now, as you deserve"—it swung its head briefly toward Guerra—"then policemen like *him* will in turn kill me, sooner or later. And it will be over."

"SWAT teams," Guerra said, trying to sound stern and ominous. "Whole patrols. Divisions. Bomb Squad, FBI, the Air Force—"

"Hold it!" The author was very nearly shouting. "That's it? That's your problem with me?" He held his hands up, palm out, looked at them, and began rubbing them together. "Give me five minutes—*three* minutes—I'll be right back, I'll just get something. Right back."

He turned and started toward the house, but a fireball neatly seared a stripe of lawn at his feet. The dragon said, "You stay. *He* goes."

The author looked down at the crumbling, crackling grass, then turned to Guerra. "Through the door—sharp left—turn right, straight through the other door. My office. Notebook beside the laptop, Betty Grable on the cover, you can't miss it. Grab that, grab a couple of pens, get back out here before he trashes the landscaping. You know how much it cost to put this lawn in?"

But Guerra was already at the door. He hurried through to the office as directed, snatched up notebook and pens, paused for a moment to marvel at the books and electronics, the boxes of paper and printer cartridges, the alphabetized manuscripts in their separate folders—*this is how they live, this is a real writer's workroom*—and raced back out to the lawn, where the author and his creation were eyeing each other in wary silence. Guerra was relieved to see that the dragon's head and neck were relaxed from the attack position, and horrified to realize that the neighboring family—with the addition of a smaller boy in Batman pajamas—were now standing at the edge of their lawn, while a girl coasting on in-line skates was gliding up the driveway, and a large man with a pipe in his mouth, who looked like a retired colonel in a movie, was striding across the street as though to direct the catapults. The larger of the two boys was telling his brother learnedly, "That's a *dragon*. I saw one on the Discovery Channel." *I could have switched shifts with Levinsky, like we were talking about the other day...*

"Thanks," the author said, taking the writing materials from Guerra's hands. Ignoring the growing assembly on his lawn and his driveway, and the cricketlike chirps of cell-phone cameras, he sat down cross-legged on his own doorstep and propped the open notebook on his knee. "I did this in Macy's window one time," he remarked conversationally. "For the ERA or the EPA, one of those." He rubbed his chin, muttered something inaudible, and began to write, reading aloud as he went.

Once upon a time, in a faraway place,

> *there lived a king whose daughter fell*
> *in love with a common gardener. The*
> *king was so outraged at this that he*
> *imprisoned the princess in a high tower*
> *and set a ferocious dragon to guard her.*

The dragon slithered closer and craned its neck, reading over his shoulder. The author continued.

> *But the dragon, fierce as it was, had a*
> *tender, sympathetic heart, greatly unlike*
> *the rest of its kind—*

"I don't like that," the dragon interrupted. "'The rest of its kind'—it sounds condescending, even a touch bigoted. Why not just say *family*, or 'the rest of its kinfolk'? Much better tone, *I* think."

"Everybody's a critic," the author mumbled. "All right, all right, *kinfolk*, then." He made the correction. The man who looked like a colonel was standing beside another man who looked like a hungover Santa Claus, and the Indian mother was gripping her sons' shoulders to hold both boys exactly where they were.

The author continued.

> *Now the dragon could not set the princess*
> *free against her father's orders, but it did*
> *what it could for her. It kept her company,*
> *engaging her in cheerful, intelligent*
> *conversation, comforting her when she*
> *was sad, and even singing to her in her*
> *most depressed moments, which would*
> *always make her laugh, since dragons are*
> *not very good singers.*

He hesitated, as though expecting some argument or annoyed comment from the dragon, but it only nodded in agreement. "True enough. We love music, but not one of us can sing a lick. Go on." Its voice was surprisingly slow and thoughtful, and—so it seemed to Guerra—almost dreamy.

> *But what the princess valued most, of all*
> *the dragon's kindnesses, was that when her*
> *gardener lover had managed to smuggle*
> *a letter to her, the dragon would at once*
> *fly up to her barred window and hover*
> *there, like any butterfly or hummingbird,*
> *to pass the letter to her and wait to carry*
> *her rapturous reply.*

He paused again and looked up at the dragon. "You won't mind if I make you a little bit smaller? Just for the sake of the hovering?"

With a graciousness that Guerra would never have expected, the dragon replied, "You're the artist—do as you think best." After a moment it added, a bit shyly, "If you wanted, you could do something with my crest. That would be all right."

"Easy. Might touch up your scales some, too—nobody's quite as young as they used to be." He worked on, still reading softly, as much to himself as to them. What struck Guerra most forcefully was that his was very nearly the only voice in the crowded darkness, except for one of the small boys—"Dragons *eat* people! He eat those men *up!*"—and the roller-skating girl sighing to a boy who had joined her, "This is *so* cool..." Guerra gestured at them all to move back, but no one appeared to notice. If anything, they seemed to be leaning in, somehow yearning toward the magnificently menacing figure that loomed over the man who still sat tailor-fashion, telling it a story about itself.

> *Now when the king came to visit his*
> *imprisoned child—which, to be as fair to*
> *him as possible, he did quite often—the*
> *dragon would always put on his most*
> *terrifying appearance and strut around*
> *the foot of the tower, to show the king*
> *how well he was fulfilling his charge...*

To Guerra's astonishment the dragon appeared not only somewhat smaller, but younger as well. Before his eyes, slowly but plainly, the faded greenish-black scales were regaining their original dark-green glitter, and the tattered crest and drab, frayed wings were springing back to proud fullness. The dragon rumbled experimentally, and the fire that lapped around its fangs—like the great claws, no longer worn dull—was the deep red, laced with rich yellow, that such fire should be. Guerra stared back and forth between this new glory and the ballpoint pen on the Betty Grable notebook, and no longer wished to have switched shifts with Officer Levinsky.

But beyond such wonders, the most marvelous change of all was that the dragon was beginning to fade, to lose definition around the edges and grow steadily more transparent until Guerra thought he could see his car through it, and the lights of houses across the street, and the rising moon. After a moment, though, he realized he was wrong. The lights were plainly coming from a number of low-roofed huts that clustered in the shadows at the base of a soap-bubble castle, and what he had taken for his car was in fact nothing but a rickety haywagon. The vision extended on all sides: whichever way he turned, there was only the reality of the huts and the castle and the deep woods beyond. And one of the castle towers had a single barred window, with a face glimmering behind it....

"Yes," said the dragon. For all its increasing dimness, its voice had grown as powerful and clear as a mountain waterfall. "Yes...yes...that was just how it was. *How it is...*"

The sense of one common breath being drawn and exhaled was abruptly broken by a soft wail, "Dragon gone!" and the little boy in the Batman pajamas suddenly shrugged free of his mother's grip and came racing across the street and the lawn. "*Dragon gone!*" Guerra made a dive for him, but missed, and was almost trampled by the boy's father. The whiskey-faced Santa Claus came charging after.

With the persistence and determination of a rabbit heading for his hole, the boy shot between several sets of legs straight for the splendid shadow that was fading so swiftly now. He tripped, skidded on his seat and looked up at the mighty head and neck, wings and crest, fading so swiftly against a sky of castles and stars. "Dragon gone?" It was a forlorn question now.

The head came slowly down, lowering over the boy, who sat unafraid as the dragon studied him lingeringly. Guerra remembered—shadow or no shadow—the dragon's comments on the heart-melting tastiness of children. But then the boy's father had him in his arms and was sweeping him off, darkly threatening to sue *somebody,* there had to be *someone.* And the dragon was indeed gone.

The castle was gone too; and so, in time, went most of the author's neighbors, hushed and wondering. But some stayed a while, for no reason they could have explained, coming closer to the house merely to stand where the dragon had been. Several of those spoke diffidently to the author; Guerra saw others surreptitiously pluck up grass blades, both burned and untouched, plainly as souvenirs.

When the last of that group had finally wandered off, the author closed the notebook, capped the pen, stood up, stretched elaborately and said, "Well. Coffee?"

Guerra rubbed his aching forehead, feeling the way he sometimes did when, falling asleep, he suddenly lunged awake out of a half-dream of stumbling down a step that wasn't there. He said feebly, "Where did he go?"

"Oh, into that story," the author answered lightly. "The story I was making up for him."

"But you didn't finish it," Guerra said.

"He will. It's his fairy tale world, after all—he knows it better than I do, really. I just showed him the way back." The author smiled with a certain aggravating compassion. "It's a bit hard to explain, if you don't—you know—*think* much about magic."

"Hey, I think about a lot of things," Guerra said harshly. "And what I'm thinking about right now is that that's wasn't a real story. It's not in any book— you were just spitballing, improvising, making it up as you went along. Hell, I'll bet you couldn't repeat it right now if you tried. Like a little kid telling a lie."

The author laughed outright, and then stopped quickly when he saw Guerra's expression. "I'm sorry, I'm not laughing at you. You're quite right, we're all little kids telling lies, writers are, hoping we can keep the lies straight and get away with them. And nobody lasts very long in this game who isn't prepared to lie his way out of trouble. Absolutely right." He regarded the ruined strip of lawn and winced visibly. "But you make the same mistake most people do, Officer Guerra. The magic's not in books, not in the publishing—it's in the telling, always. In the old, old telling."

He looked at his watch and yawned. "Actually, there might *be* a book in that one, I don't know. Have to think about it. What about that coffee?"

"I'm off duty," Guerra said. "You got any beer?"

"I'm off duty too," the author said. "Come on in."

THE BRIDGE PARTNER

I don't play bridge, and I don't know anything more about the game than I needed to know for this story, which is not a fantasy in any classic sense of the word. All I can really say about it is that I'd been reading a lot of Patricia Highsmith's work at the time, and Highsmith is one of those people who will sometimes stir depths you'd generally prefer not to have stirred. Since writing it, I've always seen "The Bridge Partner" in my head as a nouvelle vague movie by Truffaut or Resnais, or perhaps Claude Chabrol. Black-and-white, of course. Definitely black-and-white.

✻

I will kill you.

The words were not spoken aloud, but silently mouthed across the card table at Mattie Whalen by her new partner, whose last name she had not quite caught when they were introduced. Olivia *Korhanen* or *Korhonen*, it was, something like that. She was blonde and fortyish—Mattie was bad with ages, but the woman had to be somewhere near her own—and had joined the Moss Harbor Bridge Group only a few weeks earlier. The members had chosen at the very beginning to call themselves a group, rather than a Club. As Eileen Berry, one of the two founders, along with Suzanne Grimes, had said at the time, "There's an exclusivity thing about a club—a snobby, elitish sort of taste, if you know what I mean. A group just *feels* more democratic." Everyone had agreed with Eileen, as people generally did.

Which accounted, Mattie thought, for the brisk acceptance of the woman now sitting across from her, despite her odd name and unclassifiably foreign air. Mattie could detect only the faintest accent in her voice, and if her clothes plainly did not come from the discount outlet in the local mall, neither were they so aggressively chic as to offend or threaten. She had clear, pleasant blue eyes, excellent teeth, the delicately tanned skin of a tennis player—as opposed to a leathery beach bunny or an orange-hued tanning-bed veteran—and was pleasant to everyone in a gently impersonal manner. Her playing style showed not only skill, but grace, which Mattie noticed perhaps more poignantly than any other member of the Bridge Group, since the best that could have been said for Mattie was that she mostly managed to keep track of the trumps and the tricks. Still, she knew grace when she saw it.

I will kill you.

It made no possible sense—she must surely have misread both the somewhat long, quizzical lips and the intention in the bright eyes. No one else seemed to have heard or noticed anything at all unusual, and she really hadn't played the last hand as badly as all that. Granted, doubling Rosemarie's bid could be considered a mistake, but people make mistakes, and she *could* have pulled it off if Olivia Korhonen, or whoever, had held more than the one single miserable trump to back her up. You don't *kill* somebody for doubling, or even threaten to kill them. Mattie smiled earnestly at her partner, and studied her cards.

The rubber ended in total disaster, and Mattie apologized at some length to Olivia Korhonen afterward. "I'm not really a good player, I know that, but I'm not usually that awful, I promise. And now you'll probably never want to play with me ever again, and I wouldn't blame you." Mattie had had a deal of practice at apologizing, over the years.

To her pleasant surprise, Olivia Korhonen patted her arm reassuringly and shook her head. "I enjoyed the game greatly, even though we lost. I have not played in a long time, and you will have to make allowances until I start to catch up. We'll beat them next time, in spite of me."

She patted Mattie again and turned elegantly away. But as she did so, the side of her mouth repeated, clearly but inaudibly—Mattie could not have been mistaken this time—"*I will kill you.*" Then the woman was gone, and Mattie sat down in the nearest folding chair.

Her friend Virginia Schlossberg hurried over with a cup of tea, asking anxiously, "Are you all right? What is it? You look absolutely *ashen!*" She touched Mattie's cheek, and almost recoiled. "And you're *freezing!* Go home and get into bed, and call a doctor! I *mean* it—you go home right now!"

Virginia was a kind woman, but excitable. She had been the same when Mattie and she were in dancing school together.

"I'm all right," Mattie said. "I am, Ginny, honestly." But her voice was shaking as much as her hands, and she made her escape from the Group as soon as she could trust her legs to support her. She was grateful on two counts: first, that no one sat next to her on the bus; and, secondly, that Don would most likely not be home yet from the golf course. She did not look forward to Don just now.

Rather than taking to her bed, despite Virginia's advice, she made herself a healthy G&T and sat in the kitchen with the lights on, going over and over everything she knew of Olivia Korhonen. The woman was apparently single or widowed, like most of the members of the Moss Harbor Bridge Group, but judging by the reactions of the few men in the Group she gave no indication of being on the prowl. Seemingly unemployed, and rather young for retirement, still she lived in one of the pricey new condos just two blocks from the harbor. No Bridge Group member had yet seen her apartment except for Suzanne and Eileen, who reported back that it was smart and trendy, "without being too off-puttingly posh." Eileen thought the paintings were originals, but Suzanne had her doubts.

What else, *what else?* She had looked up "Korhonen" on the Internet, and found that it was a common Finnish name—not Jewish, as she had supposed. To her knowledge, she had never met a Finnish person in her life. Were they like Swedes? Danes, even? She had a couple of Danish acquaintances, a husband and wife named Olsen...no, they were nothing at all like the Korhonen woman; one could never imagine either Olsen saying *I will kill you* to so much as a cockroach, which, of course, they wouldn't ever have in the house. But then, who *would* say such a thing to a near-stranger? And over a silly card game? It made no sense, none of it made any sense. She mixed another G&T and was surprised to find herself wanting Don home.

Don's day, it turned out, had been a bad one. Trounced on the course, beaten more badly in the rematch he had immediately demanded, he had consoled himself liberally in the clubhouse; and, as a consequence, was clearly not in any sort of mood to hear about a mumbled threat at a bridge game. On the whole, after sixteen years of marriage, Mattie liked Don more than she disliked him, but such distinctions were essentially meaningless at this stage of things. She rather appreciated his presence when she felt especially lonely and frightened, but a large, furry dog would have done as well; indeed, a dog would have been at once more comforting and more concerned for her comfort. Dogs wanted their masters to be happy—Don simply preferred her uncomplaining.

When she told him about Olivia Korhonen's behavior at the Bridge Group, he seemed hardly to hear her. In his usual style of picking up in the middle of the intended sentence, he mumbled, "...take that damn game so damn seriously. Bud and I don't go yelling we're going to kill each other"— Bud Gorko was his steady golf partner—"and believe you me, I've got reason sometimes." He snatched a beer out of the refrigerator and wandered into the living room to watch TV.

Mattie followed him in, the second G&T strengthening a rare resolve to make him take her seriously. She said, "She did it twice. You didn't see her face." She raised her voice to carry over the yammering of a commercial. "She *meant* it, Don. I'm telling you, she *meant* it."

Don smiled muzzily and patted the sofa seat beside him. "Hear you, I'm right on it. Tell you what—she goes ahead and does that, I'm going to take a really dim view. A dim view." He liked the phrase. "Really dim view."

"You're dim enough already," Mattie said. Don did not respond. She stood watching him for a few minutes without speaking, because she knew it made him uncomfortable. When he got to the stage of demanding, "What? What?" she walked out of the room and into the guest bedroom, where she lay down. She had been sleeping there frequently enough in recent months that it felt increasingly like her own.

She had thought she would surely dream of Olivia Korhonen, but it was only in the sweet spot between consciousness and sleep that the woman's face came to her: the long mouth curling almost affectionately, almost seductively, as though for a kiss, caressing the words that Mattie could not hear. It was an oddly tranquil, even soothing vision, and Mattie fell asleep like a child, and did not dream at all.

The next morning she felt curiously young and hopeful, though she could not imagine why. Don had gone off to work at the real-estate office with his normal Monday hangover, pitifully savage; but Mattie indulged herself with a long hot shower, a second toasted English muffin and a long telephone chat with a much-relieved Virginia Schlossberg before she went to the grocery store. There would be an overdue hair appointment after that, then home in time for Oprah. A *good* day.

The sense of serenity lasted through the morning shopping, through her favorite tea-and-brioche snack at *La Place*, and on to her date with Mr. Philip at the salon. It ended abruptly while she was more than half-drowsing under the dryer, trying to focus on *Vanity Fair*, as well as on the buttery jazz on the P.A. system, when Olivia Korhonen's equally pleasant voice separated itself from the music, saying, "Mrs. Whalen—Mattie? How nice to see you here, partner." The last word flicked across Mattie's skin like a brand.

Olivia Korhonen was standing directly in front of her, smiling in her familiar guileless manner. She had clearly just finished her appointment: the glinting warmth and shine of her blonde hair made that plain, and made Mattie absurdly envious, her own mouse-brown curls' only distinction being their comb-snapping thickness. Olivia Korhonen said, "Shall we play next week? I look forward so."

"Yes," Mattie said faintly; and then, "I mean, I'm not sure—I have things. To do. Maybe." Her voice squeaked and slipped. She couldn't stop it, and in that moment she hated her voice more than she had ever hated anything in the world.

"Oh, but you must be there! I do not know anyone else to play with." Mattie noticed a small dimple to the left of Olivia Korhonen's mouth when she smiled in a certain way. "I mean, no one else who will put up with my bad playing, as you do. Please?"

Mattie found herself nodding, just to keep from having to speak again— and also, to some degree, because of the genuine urgency in Olivia Korhonen's voice. *Maybe I imagined the whole business...maybe it's me getting old and scared, the way people do.* She nodded a second time, with somewhat more enthusiasm.

Olivia Korhonen patted her knee through the protective salon apron, plainly relieved. "Oh, good. I already feel so much better." Then, without changing her expression in the least, she whispered, *"I will kill you."*

Mattie thought later that she must have fainted in some way; at all events, her next awareness was of Mr. Philip taking the curlers out of her hair and brushing her off. Olivia Korhonen was gone. Mr. Philip peered at her, asking,

"Who's been keeping *you* up at night, darling? You never fall asleep under these things." Then he saw her expression, and asked "Are you okay?"

"I'm fine," Mattie said. "I'm fine."

After that, it seemed to her that she saw Olivia Korhonen everywhere, every day. She was coming out of the drycleaners' as Mattie brought an armload of Don's pants in; she hurried across the street to direct Mattie as she was parking her car; she asked Mattie's advice buying produce at the farmers' market, or broke off a conversation with someone else to chat with Mattie on the street. And each time, before they parted, would come the silent words, more menacing for being inaudible, *"I will kill you."* The dimple beside the long smile always showed as she spoke.

Mattie had never felt so lonely in her life. Despite all the years she and Don had lived in Moss Harbor, there was no one in her local circle whom she could trust in any sort of intimate crisis, let alone with something like a death threat. Suzanne or Eileen? Out of the question—things like that simply did not happen to members of the Bridge Group. There was Virginia, of course... Virginia might very well believe her, if anyone did, but would be bound to fall apart under the burden of such knowledge. That left only going further afield and contacting Patricia.

Pat Gallagher lived directly across the Bay, in a tiny incorporated area called Witness Point. Mattie had known her very nearly as long as she had known Virginia, but the relationships could not have been more different. Pat was gay, for one thing; and while Mattie voted for every same-sex-marriage and hate-crimes proposition that came up on any ballot, she was honest enough to know that she was ill at ease with homosexuals. She could never explain this, and was truly ashamed of it, especially around someone as intelligent and thoughtful as Pat Gallagher. She found balance in distance, only seeing Pat two or three times a year, at most, and sometimes no more than once. They did e-mail a reasonable amount though, and they talked on the phone enough that Mattie still knew the number by heart. She called it now.

They arranged to meet at Pat's house for lunch on the weekend. She lived in a shingly, flowery, cluttery cottage, in company with a black woman named Babs, an administrator at the same hospital where Pat was a nurse. Mattie liked Babs immediately, and was therefore doubly nervous around her, and doubly shamed, especially when Babs offered in so many words to disappear graciously, so that she and Pat could talk in private. Mattie would have much preferred this, but the very suggestion made it impossible. "I'm sure there's nothing I have to say to Patricia that I couldn't say to you."

Babs laughed. "That you may come to regret, my dear." But she set out second glasses of Pinot Grigio, and second bowls of Pat's minestrone, and sat down with them. Her dark-brown skin and soft curly hair contrasted so perfectly with Pat's freckled Irish pinkness, and they seemed so much at ease with one another that Mattie felt a quick, startling stitch of what could only have been envy.

"Okay," Pat said. "Talk. What's got you scared this time?"

Babs chuckled. "Cuts straight to the chase, doesn't she?"

Mattie bridled feebly. "You make it sound as though I'm a big fraidy cat, always frightened about something. I'm not like that."

"Yes, you are." The affection in Pat's wide grin took some of the sting from the words. "You never call me unless something's really got you spooked, do you realize that? Might be a thing you saw on the news, a hooha with your husband, a pain somewhere there shouldn't be a pain. Maybe a lump you're worried about—maybe just a scary dream." She put her hand on Mattie's hand. "It's fine, it's you. Talk. Tell."

She and Babs remained absolutely silent while Mattie told them about the Bridge Group, and about Olivia Korhonen. She was aware that she was speaking faster as the account progressed, and that her voice was rising in pitch, but all she wanted was to get the words out as quickly as she could. The words seemed strangely reluctant to be spoken: more and more, they raked at her throat and palate as she struggled to rid herself of them. When she was done, the roof of her mouth felt almost burned, and she gratefully accepted a glass of cold apple juice from Babs.

"Well," Pat said finally. "I don't know what I expected to hear from you, but *that* was definitely not it. Not hardly."

Babs said grimly, "What you have there is a genuine, certified stalker. I'd call the cops on her in a hot minute."

"How can she do that?" Pat objected. "The woman hasn't *done* anything! No witnesses, not one other person who heard what she said—what she keeps on saying. They'd laugh in Mattie's face, if they didn't do worse."

"It does sound such a *silly* story," Mattie said wretchedly. "Like a paranoiac, somebody with a persecution complex. But it's true, I'm not making it up. That's just exactly the way it's been happening."

Pat nodded. "I believe you. And so would a jury, if it ever came to that. Anyone who spends ten minutes around you knows right away that you haven't the first clue about lying." She sighed, refilling Babs' glass and her own, but not Mattie's. "Not you—you have to drive. And we wouldn't want to frustrate little Ms. What's-her-face, now would we?"

"That's not funny," Babs interrupted sharply. "That's not a bit funny, Patricia."

Pat apologized promptly and profusely, but Mattie was absurdly delighted. "You call her Patricia, too! I thought *I* was the only one."

"Only way to get her attention sometimes." Babs continued to glower at an extremely penitent Pat. "But she's right about the one thing, anyway. Even if the cops happened to believe you, they couldn't do a damn thing about it. Couldn't slap a restraining order on the lady, couldn't order her to stay X-number of feet away from you. Not until..." She shrugged heavily, and did not finish the sentence.

"I know," Mattie said. "I wasn't expecting you two to...fix things. Be my bodyguards, or something. But I do feel a bit better, talking to you."

"Now, if you were in the hospital"—Babs grinned suddenly and wickedly—"we really *could* bodyguard you. Between old Patricia and me, nobody'd get near you, except for the surfers we'd be smuggling in to you at night. You ought to think about it, Mattie. Safe *and* fun, both."

Mattie was still giggling over this image, and a couple of others, when they walked her out to her car. As she buckled her seatbelt, Pat put a hand on her shoulder, saying quietly, "As long as this goes on every day, you call every day. Got that?"

"Yes, Mama," Mattie answered. "And I'll send my laundry home every week, I promise."

The hand on her shoulder tightened, and Pat shook her a little more than slightly. "I mean it. If we don't hear, we'll come down there."

"Big bad bulldykes on the rampage," Babs chimed in from behind Pat. "*Not* pretty."

It was true that she did feel better driving home: not at all drunk, just pleasantly askew, easier and more rested from the warmth of company than she had been in a long time. That lasted all the way to Moss Harbor, and almost to her front door. The *almost* part came when, parking the car at the curb, she heard a horn honk twice, and looked up in time to see an arm waving cheerfully back to her as Olivia Korhonen's bright little Prius rounded a corner. Mattie sat in her car for a long time before she turned off the engine and got out.

Is she watching my house? Was she waiting for me?

She did not call Pat and Babs that night, even though she lay awake until nearly morning. Then, with Don gone to work, she forced herself to eat breakfast, and called Suzanne for Olivia Korhonen's home telephone number. Once she had it in hand, she stalled over a third cup of coffee, and then a fourth, before she finally dialed the number and waited through several rings, consciously hoping to hear the answering machine click on. But nothing happened. She was about to break the connection, when she heard the receiver being picked up, and Ms. Korhonen's cool, unmistakable voice said, "Yes? Who is this, please?"

Mattie drew a breath. "It's Mattie Whalen. From the Bridge Group, you remember?"

If she has the gall to even hesitate, stalking me every single day... But the voice immediately lifted with delight. "Yes, Mattie, of course I remember, how not? How good to hear from you." There was nothing in words or tone to suggest anything but pleasure at the call.

"I was wondering," Mattie began—then hesitated, listening to Olivia Korhonen's breathing. She said, "I thought perhaps we might get together—maybe one day this week?"

"To practice our bridge game?" Somewhat to Mattie's surprise, Olivia Korhonen pounced on the suggestion. "Oh, yes. That would be an excellent idea. We could develop our own strategies—that is what the great players work on all the time, is it not? Excellent, excellent, Mattie!" They arranged to meet at noon, two days from that date, at Olivia Korhonen's condo apartment. She wanted to make cucumber sandwiches—"in the English style, I will cut the crusts off"—but Mattie talked her out of that, or thought she had. In her imagining of what she planned to say to Olivia Korhonen, there would be no room for food.

On the appointed day Mattie woke up in a cold sweat. She considered whether she might be providentially coming down with some sort of flu, but decided she wasn't; then made herself a hot toddy in case she was, ate Grape-Nuts and yogurt for breakfast, went back to bed in pursuit of another hour's nap, failed miserably, got up, showered, dressed, and watched Oprah until it was time to go. She made another hot toddy while she waited, on the off-chance that the flu might be waiting too.

The third-floor condo apartment turned out as tastefully dressy as Eileen and Suzanne had reported. Olivia Korhonen was at the door, smilingly eager to show her around. The rooms were high and airy, with indeed a good many paintings and prints, of which Mattie was no judge—they *looked* like originals—and a rather surprising paucity of furniture, as though Olivia Korhonen had not been planning for long-term residence. When Mattie commented on this, the blonde woman only twinkled at her, saying, "The motto of my family is that one should always sink deep roots wherever one lives. Because roots can always be sold, do you see?" Later on, considering this, Mattie was not entirely certain what bearing it had on her question; but it sounded both sensible and witty at the time, in Olivia Korhonen's musical voice.

Nevertheless, when Olivia Korhonen announced, "Now, strategy!" and brought out both the cards and the cucumber sandwiches, Mattie held firm. She said, "Olivia, I didn't come to talk about playing cards."

Olivia Korhonen was clearly on her guard in an instant, though her tone remained light. She set the tray of sandwiches down and said slowly, "Ah? Ulterior motives? Then you had probably better reveal them now, don't you think so?" She stood with her head tipped slightly sideways, like an inquisitive bird.

Mattie's heart was beating annoyingly fast, and she was very thirsty. She said, "You are stalking me, Olivia. I don't know why. You are following me everywhere...and that *thing* you say every single time we meet." Olivia Korhonen did not reply, nor change her expression. Mattie said, "Nobody else hears you, but I do. You whisper it—*I will kill you.* I hear you."

Sleepless, playing variations on the scene over and over in her head the night before, she had expected anything from outrage and accusation to utter bewilderment to tearful, fervent denial. What happened instead was nothing she could have conceived of: Olivia Korhonen clapped her hands and began to laugh.

Her laughter was like cold silver bells, chiming a fraction out of tune, their dainty discordance more jarring than any rusty clanking could have been. Olivia Korhonen said, "Oh, I did wonder if you would ever let yourself understand me. You are such a...such a *timorous* woman, you know, Mattie Whalen—frightened of so very much, it is a wonder that you can ever peep out of your house, your little hole in the baseboard. Eyes flicking everywhere, whiskers twitching so frantically..." She broke off into a bubbling fit of giggles, while Mattie stared and stared, remembering girls in school hallways who had snickered just so.

"Oh, yes," Olivia Korhonen said. "Yes, Mattie, I will kill you—be very sure of that. But not yet." She clasped her hands together at her breast and bowed her head slightly, smiling. "Not just yet."

"*Why?* Why do you want...what have I ever, *ever* done to you?"

The smile warmed and widened, but Olivia Korhonen was some time answering. When she did, the words came slowly, thoughtfully. "Mattie, where I come from we have a great many sheep, they are one of Finland's major products. And where you have sheep, of course, you must have dogs. Oh, we do have many wonderful dogs—you should see them handle and guide and work the sheep. You would be so fascinated, I know you would."

Her cheeks had actually turned a bit pink with what seemed like earnest enthusiasm. She said, "But Mattie, dear, it is a curious thing about sheep and dogs. Sometimes stray dogs break into a sheepfold, and then they begin to kill." She did not emphasize the word, but it struck Mattie like a physical blow under the heart. Olivia Korhonen went on. "They are not killing to eat, out of hunger—no, they are simply killing blindly, madly, they will wipe out a whole flock of sheep in a night, and then run on home to their masters and their dog biscuits. Do you understand me so far, Mattie?"

Mattie's body was so rigid that she could not even nod her head. Olivia's softly chiming voice continued, "It is as though these good family dogs have gone temporarily insane. Animal doctors, veterinarians, they think now that the pure *passivity*, the purebred *stupidity* of the sheep somehow triggers— is that the right word, Mattie? I mean it like *to set off*—somehow triggers something in the dog's brain, something very old. The sheep are blundering around in the pen, bleating in panic, too stupid to protect themselves, and it is all just too much for the dogs—even for sheepdogs sometimes. They simply go mad." She spread her hands now, leaning forward, graceful as ever. "Do you see now, Mattie? I do hope you begin to see."

"No." The one word was all Mattie could force out between freezing lips. "No."

"You are my sheep," Olivia Korhonen said. "And I am like the dogs. You are a born victim, like all sheep, and it is your mere presence that makes you irresistible to me. Of course, dogs are dogs—they cannot ever wait to kill. But I can. I like to wait."

Mattie could not move. Olivia Korhonen stepped back, looked at her wristwatch and made a light gesture toward the door, as though freeing Mattie from a spell. "Now you had better run along home, dear, for I have company coming. We will practice our strategy for the Bridge Group another time."

Mattie sat in her car for a long time, hands trembling, before she felt able even to turn the key in the ignition. She had no memory of driving home, except a vague awareness of impatient honking behind her when she lingered at intersections after the traffic light had changed. When she arrived home she sat by the telephone with her fingers on the keypad, trying to make herself dial Pat Gallagher's number. After a time, she began to cry.

She did call that evening, by which time a curious calm, unlike any other she had ever felt, had settled over her. This may have been because by then she was extremely drunk, having entered the stage of slow but very precise speech, and a certain deliberate, unhurried rationality that she never seemed able to attain sober. Both Pat and Babs immediately offered to come and stay with her, but Mattie declined with thanks. "Not much point to it. She said she'd wait...said she *liked* waiting." Her voice sounded strange in her own ears, and oddly new. "You can't bodyguard me forever. I guess *I* have to bodyguard me. I guess I just have to."

When she hung up—only after her friends had renewed their insistence that she call daily, on pain of home invasion—she did not drink any more, but sat motionless by the phone, waiting for Don's return. It was his weekly staff-meeting night, and she knew he would be late, but she felt like sitting just where she was. *If I never moved again, she'd have to come over here to kill me. And the neighbors would see.* The phone rang once, but she did not answer.

Don came home in, for him, a cheerful mood, having been informed that his supervisor at the agency, whom he loathed, was being transferred to another branch. He had every expectation of a swift promotion. Mattie—or someone in Mattie's body, shaping words with her still-cold lips—congratulated him, and even opened a celebratory bottle of champagne, though she drank none of her glass. Don began calling his friends to spread the news, and Mattie went into the kitchen to start a pot roast. The steamed-fish with greens and polenta revolution had passed Don quietly by.

The act of cooking soothed her nerves, as it had always done; but the coldness of her skin seemed to have spread to her mind—which was not, when considered, a bad thing at all. There was a peculiar clarity to her thoughts now: both her options and her fears seemed so sharply defined that she felt as though she were traveling on an airplane that had just broken out of clouds into sunlight. *I live in clouds. I always have.*

Fork in one of his hands, cordless in the other, Don devoured two helpings of the roast and praised it in between calls. Mattie, nibbling for appearances' sake, made no attempt to interrupt; but when he finally put the phone down for a moment she remarked, "That woman at the Bridge Group? The one who said she was going to kill me?"

Don looked up, the wariness in his eyes unmistakable. "Yeah?"

"She means it. She really means to kill me." Mattie had been saying the words over and over to herself all afternoon; by now they came out briskly, almost casually. She said, "We discussed it for some time."

Don uttered a cholesterol-saturated sigh. "Damn, ever since you started with that bridge club, feels like I'm running a daycare center. Look, this is middle-school bullshit, you know it and she knows it. Just tell her, enough with the bullshit, it's getting real old. Or find yourself another partner, probably the best thing." He had the cordless phone in his hand again.

The strange, distant Mattie said softly, "I'm just telling you."

"And I'm telling you, get another partner. Silly shit, she's not about to kill anybody." He wandered off into the living room, dialing.

Mattie stood in the kitchen doorway, looking after him. She said—clearly enough for him to have heard, if he hadn't already been talking on the phone—"No, she's not." She liked the sound of it, and said it again. "She's not." Then she went straight off to bed, read a bit of *Chicken Soup for the Soul*, and fell quickly asleep. She dreamed that Olivia Korhonen was leaning over her in bed, smiling widely and eagerly. There were little teeth on her tongue and small, triangular teeth fringing her lips.

Mattie got to the Bridge Group early the next afternoon, and waited, with impatience that surprised her, for Olivia Korhonen to arrive. The Group met in a community building within sight of the Moss Harbor wharf, its windows fronting directly on the parking lot. Mattie was already holding the door open when Olivia Korhonen crossed the lot.

Did she look even a little startled—the least bit taken aback by her prey's eager welcome? Mattie hoped so. She said brightly, "I was afraid you might not be coming today."

"And I thought that perhaps *you*..." Olivia Korhonen very deliberately let the sentence trail away. If she had been at all puzzled, she gathered herself as smoothly as a cat landing on its feet. "I am glad to see you, Mattie. I had some foolish idea that you might be, perhaps, ill?"

"Not a bit—not when we need to work on our strategy." Mattie touched her elbow, easing her toward the table where Jeannie Atkinson and old Joe Booker were both beckoning. "You know we need to do that." It was a physical effort to make herself smile into Olivia Korhonen's blue eyes, but she managed.

Playing worse than even she ever had, with foolish bids, rash declarations of trumps, scoring errors, and complete mismanagement of her partner's hand when Olivia Korhonen was dummy, she worked with desperate concentration—manifesting as lightheaded carelessness—on upsetting the woman's balance, her judgment of the situation. How well she succeeded, and to what end, she could not have said; but when Olivia Korhonen mouthed *I will kill you* once again at her as she was dealing a final rubber, she fought down the icepick stab of terror and gaily said, "*Ah-ah,* we mustn't signal each other—against the rules, bad, bad." Jeannie and Joe raised their eyebrows, and Olivia Korhonen, very briefly, *almost* looked embarrassed.

She left hurriedly, directly after the game. Mattie followed her out, blithely apologizing left and right, as always, for her poor play. At the car, Olivia Korhonen turned to say, evenly and without expression, "You are not spoiling the game for me. This is childish, all this that you are playing at. It means nothing."

Mattie felt her mouth drying, and her heart beginning to pound. But she said, keeping her voice as calm as she could, "Not everybody gets to know how and when they're going to die. If you're really going to kill me, you don't get to tell me how to behave." Olivia Korhonen did not reply, but got into her car and drove away, and Mattie walked back to the Bridge Group for tea and cookies.

"One for the sheep," Pat said on the phone that night. "You crossed her up—she figured you'd be running around in the pen, all crazy with fear, bleating and blatting and wetting yourself. The fun part. And instead you came right to her and practically spit in her eye. I'll bet she's thinking about that one right now."

On the extension, Babs said flatly, "Yes, she sure as hell is. And *I'm* thinking that she won't make that mistake again. She's regrouping, is what it is—she'll be coming from another place next time, another angle. Don't take her lightly, the way she took you. Nothing's changed."

"I know that." Mattie's voice, like her hands, was unsteady. "I wish I could say *I've* changed, but I haven't, not at all. I'm the same fraidy cat I always was, but maybe I'm covering it a little better, I don't know. All I know is I just want to hide under the bed and cover up my head."

Pat said slowly, "I was raised in the country. A sheep-killing dog doesn't go for it just once. This woman has killed before."

Babs said, "Get in close. You snuggle up to her, you tail her around like she's been tailing you. That's not part of the game, she won't like that at all. You keep *coming* at her."

Pat said, "And you keep calling us. Every day."

It took practice. All her instincts told her to turn and run the moment she recognized the elegant figure on the street corner ahead of her, or heard the too-friendly voice at her elbow. But gradually she learned not only to force herself to respond with equal affability, but to become the one accosting, waving, calling out—even issuing impromptu invitations to join her for tea or coffee. These were never accepted, and the act of proposing them always left her feeling dizzy and sick; but she continued doggedly to "snuggle up" to Olivia Korhonen at every opportunity. Frightened and alone, still she kept coming.

She had the first inkling that the change in her behavior might be having some effect when Eileen mentioned that Olivia Korhonen had diffidently sounded her out about being partnered with a more skilled player for the Group's upcoming tournament. Eileen had explained that the teams had already been registered, and that in any case none of them would have taken kindly to being broken up and reassigned. Olivia Korhonen hadn't raised the subject again, but Eileen had thought Mattie would want to know. Eileen always told people the things she thought they would want to know.

For her part, Mattie continued to make a point of chattering buoyantly at the bridge table as she misplayed one hand after another; then apologizing endlessly as she trampled through another rubber, leaving ruin in her wake. She announced, laughing, after one particularly disastrous no-trump contract, "I wouldn't blame Olivia if she wanted to strangle me right now. I'd have it coming!" Their opponents looked embarrassed, and Olivia Korhonen smiled and smoothed her hair.

But once, when they were in the ladies' room together, she met Mattie's eyes in the mirror and said, "I will still kill you. Could you hand me the tissues, please?" Mattie did so. Olivia Korhonen blotted her lipstick and went on, "You are not nearly so bad a player as you pretend, and you have not turned impudently fearless overnight. Little sheep, you are as just as much afraid of me as you ever were. Tell me this is not true."

She turned then, taking a single step toward Mattie, who recoiled in spite of her determination not to. Olivia Korhonen did not smile in triumph, but yawned daintily and deliberately, like a cat. "Never mind, dear Mattie. It is almost over." She started for the restroom door.

"You are not going to kill me," Mattie said, as she had said once before in her own kitchen. "You've killed before, but you are not going to kill me." Olivia Korhonen did not bother to look back or answer, and a sudden burst of white rage seared through Mattie like fever. She took hold of Olivia Korhonen's left arm and swung her around to face her, savoring the surprise and momentary confusion in the blue eyes. She said, "I will not let you kill me. Do you understand? I will not let you."

Olivia Korhonen did not move in her grip. Mattie finally let her go, actually stumbling back and having to catch herself. Olivia Korhonen said again, "It is almost over. Come, we will go and play that other game."

That night Mattie could not sleep. Even after midnight, she felt almost painfully wide awake, unable to imagine ever needing to sleep again. Don had been snoring for two hours when she dressed, went to her car, and drove to the condominium where Olivia Korhonen lived. A light was still on in the living-room window of her apartment, and Mattie, parked across the street, could clearly make out the figure of the blonde woman moving restlessly back and forth, as though she shared her observer's restlessness. The light went out presently, but Mattie did not drive home for some while.

She did the same thing the next night, and for several nights thereafter, establishing a pattern of leaving the house when Don was asleep and returning before he woke. On occasion it became a surprisingly close call, since whether the light stayed on late or was already out when she reached the condo, she often lost track of time for hours, staring at a dark, empty window. She continued to check in regularly with Pat and Babs in Witness Point; but she never told them about her new nighttime routine, though she could not have said why, anymore than she could have explained the compulsion itself. There was a mindless peacefulness in her vigil over her would-be murderer that made no sense, and comforted her.

From time to time, Olivia Korhonen came to stand at her window and look out at the dark street. Mattie, deliberately parking in the same space every night, fully expected to be recognized and challenged; but the latter, at least, never happened.

She took as well to following Olivia Korhonen through Moss Harbor traffic, whenever she happened to spot the gleaming Prius on the road. In an elusive, nebulous way, she was perfectly aware that she was putting herself as much at the service of an obsession as Olivia Korhonen, but this seemed to have no connection with her own life or behavior. She could not have cared less where the Prius might be headed—most often up or down the coast, plainly to larger towns—or whether or not she was visible in the rear-view mirror. The whole point, if there was such a thing, was to bait her bridge partner into doing something foolish, even coming to kill her before she was quite ready. Mattie had no idea what Olivia Korhonen's schedule or program in these matters might be, nor what she would do about it; only that whatever was moving in her would be present when the time came.

When it did come, on a moonless midnight, she was parked in her usual spot, directly across the street from the condominium. She was in the process of leaving a message on Pat and Babs' answering machine—"Just letting you know I'm fine, haven't seen her today, I'm about to go to bed"—when Olivia Korhonen came out of the building, strode across the street directly toward her, and pulled the unlocked car door open. She said, not raising her voice, "Walk with me, Mattie Whalen."

Mattie said into the cell phone, as quietly as she, "I'll call you tomorrow. Don't worry about me." She hung up then, and got out of the car. She said, "The people I was talking with heard your voice."

Olivia Korhonen did not answer. She took light but firm hold of Mattie's arm and they walked silently together toward the beach, beyond which lay the dark sparkle of the ocean. The sky was pale and clear as glass. Mattie saw no one on the sand, nor on the short street, except for a lone dog trotting self-importantly past them. Olivia Korhonen was humming to herself, at the farthest rim of Mattie's hearing.

Reaching the shore, they both took their shoes off and left them neatly side by side. The sand was cold and hard-packed under Mattie's feet, this far from the water, and she thought regretfully about how little time she had spent on the beach, for all the years of living half a mile away. Something splashed in the gentle surf, but all she saw was a small swirl of foam.

Olivia Korhonen said reflectively, as though talking to herself, "I must say, this is a pity—I will be a little sorry. You have been...entertaining."

"How nice of you to say so." Mattie's own odd calmness frightened her more than the woman who meant to kill her. She asked, "Weren't any of your other victims entertaining?"

"Not really, no. One can never expect that—human beings are not exactly sheep, after all, for all the similarities. Things become so *hasty* at the end, so hurried and awkward and tedious—it can be very dissatisfying, if you understand me." She was no longer holding Mattie's arm, but looking into her eyes with something in her own expression that might almost have been a plea.

"I think I do," Mattie said. "I wouldn't have once." They were walking unhurriedly toward the water, and she could see the small surges far out that meant the tide was beginning to turn. She said, "You're more or less human, although I've had a few nasty dreams about you." Olivia Korhonen chuckled very slightly. Mattie said, "You feed on the fear. No, that's not it, not the fear—the *knowledge*. Fear makes people run away, but *knowledge*—the sense that there's absolutely no escape, that you can come and *pick* them, like fruit, whenever you choose—that freezes them, isn't that it? The knowing? And you like that very much."

Olivia Korhonen stopped walking and regarded Mattie without speaking, her blue eyes wider and more intense than Mattie had ever noticed them. She said slowly, "You have changed. I changed you."

Mattie asked, "But what would you have done if I *had* run? That first time, at the Bridge Group, if I had taken you at your word and just packed a bag, jumped in my car and headed for the border? Would you have followed me?"

"It is a long way to the border, you know." The chuckle was deeper and clearer this time. "But it would all have been so messy, really. Ugly, unpleasant. Much better this way."

Mattie was standing very close to her, looking directly into her face. "And the killing? That would have been pleasant?" She found that she was holding her breath, waiting for the answer.

It did not come in words, but in the slow smile that spread from Olivia Korhonen's eyes to her mouth, instead of the other way around. It came in the slight parting of her lips, in the flick of her cat-pink tongue just behind the white, perfect teeth; most of all in the strange way in which her face seemed to change its shape, almost to fold in on itself: the cheekbones heightening, the forehead rounding, the round chin in turn becoming more pointed, as in Mattie's dreams.

...and Mattie, who had not struck another person since a recess fight in the third grade, hit Olivia Korhonen in the stomach as hard as she possibly could. The blonde woman coughed and doubled over, her eyes huge with surprise and a kind of reproach. Mattie hit her again—a glancing blow, distinctly weaker, to the neck—and jumped on her, clumsily and impulsively. They went down together, rolling in the sand, the grains raking their skins, clogging their nostrils, coating and filling their mouths. Olivia Korhonen got a near-stranglehold on a coughing, gasping Mattie and began dragging her toward the water's edge. Breathless and in pain, she was still the stronger of the two of them.

The cold water on her bare feet revived Mattie a moment before her head was forced under an incoming wave. Panic lent her strength, and she lunged upward, banging the back of her head into Olivia Korhonen's face, turning in the failing grip and pulling her down with both hands on the back of her neck. There was a moment when they were mouth to mouth, breathing one another's hoarse, choking breath, teeth banging teeth. Then she rolled on top in the surf, throwing all her weight into keeping the struggling woman's bloody face in the water. The little waves helped.

At some point Mattie finally realized that Olivia Korhonen had stopped fighting her; she had a feeling that she had been holding the woman under much longer than she needed to. She stood up, soaked and shivering with both cold and shock, swaying dizzily, looking down at the body that stirred in the light surf, bumping against her feet. There was a bit of seaweed caught in its hair.

In a while, in a vague sort of way, she recognized what it was. Something glinted at the edge of a pocket, and she bent down and withdrew a ring of keys. She walked away up the beach, stopping to slip on her shoes.

She did not go back to her car then, but went straight to the condo and walked up the stairs to the third floor, leaving a thinning trail of water behind her. Entry was easy: she had no difficulty finding the right key to open the doorknob lock, and Olivia Korhonen had been in too much of a hurry to throw the deadbolt. Mattie wiped her shoes carefully, nevertheless, before she went inside.

Walking slowly through the graciously-appointed apartment, she realized that it was larger than she recalled, and that there were rooms that Olivia Korhonen had not shown her. One took particular effort to open, for the door was heavy and somewhat out of alignment. Mattie put a bruised shoulder to it and forced it open.

The room seemed to be a catchall for odd gifts and odder souvenirs—"tourist *tchotchkes*," Virginia Schlossberg would have called them. There were no paintings on the walls, but countless candid snapshots, mostly of women, though they did include a handful of men. Their very number bewildered Mattie, making her eyes ache. She recognized no one at first, and then froze: a photo of herself held conspicuous pride of place on the wall facing her. It had obviously been taken by a cell phone. Below it, thumbtacked to the wall, was a gauzy red scarf that she had lost before Olivia Korhonen had even joined the Moss Harbor Bridge Group. Mattie pulled it free, along with the picture, and put them both in her pocket.

All of the photographs had mementos of some sort attached to them, ranging in size from a ticket stub to a pair of sunglasses or a paper plate with a telephone number scrawled on it in lipstick. None of the subjects appeared to be aware that their pictures were being taken; each had a tiny smiley-face drawn with a fine-tipped ballpoint pen in the lower right corner. An entire section of one wall was devoted to images of a single dark-eyed young woman, taken from closer and closer angles, as though from the viewpoint of a shark circling to strike. These prints were each framed, not in wood or metal, but by variously-colored hair ribbons, all held neatly in place by pushpins of matching hues. The central photo, the largest, was set facing the wall; there were two ribbons set around it, both blue. Mattie took this picture down, turned it around, and studied it for some while.

Hurt, still damp, bedraggled, she was no longer trembling; nor, somehow, was she in the least exhausted. Still cold, yes, but the coldness had come inside; while a curious fervor was warming her face and hands, as though the pictures on the walls were reaching out, welcoming her, knowing her, speaking her name. Still holding the shot of the dark-eyed girl she moved from one new image to the other, feeling with each a kind of fracturing, a growing separation from everything else, until the walls themselves had dimmed around her, and the photos were all mounted on the panelings of her mind. She was aware that there were somehow more there than she could see, more than she could yet take in.

The police will come. They will find the body and find this place. They'll call her the Smiley-Face Killer. The photographs were pressing in around her, each so anxious to be properly savored and understood. Mattie put the dark-eyed victim into her pocket next to her own picture, and reached out with both hands. She did not touch any of the pictures or the keepsakes, but let her fingers drift by them all, one after another, as in a kind of soul-Braille, and felt the myriad pinprick responses swarming her skin, as Olivia Korhonen's souvenirs and trophies joined her. It was not possession of any sort; she was always herself. Never for a moment did she fancy that she was the woman she had killed on the beach, nor did any of this room's hoarded memories overtake and evict her own. It was rather a fostering, a sheltering: a full awareness that there was more than enough room in her not for Olivia Korhonen's life, but for what had given that life its only true meaning. Aloud, alone in that room filled with triumph and pride, she said, "Yes, she's gone. Yes, I'm here. Yes."

She walked out of the room, leaving it open, and did the same with the apartment door rather than pull it shut behind her.

Outside the stars were thin, and there were lights on in some of the neighboring condos. Mattie got in her car, started the engine, and drove home.

As chilled as she still was, as battered and scratched, with her blouse ripped halfway off her shoulder, there was a lightness in her, a sense of invulnerability, that she had never felt in all her life. The car seemed to be flying. With the windows down her damp hair whipped around her face, and she sang all the way home.

Reaching her house, she ran up the steps like an exuberant child, opened the door, and stopped in the hallway. Don was facing her, his face flushed and contorted with a mixture of outrage and bewilderment. His pajama jacket was buttoned wrong, which made him look very young. He said, "Where the fuck? Damn it, where the *fuck?*"

Mattie smiled at him. She loved the feel of the smile; it was like slipping into a beautiful silk dress that she had never been able to afford until just now, this moment. Walking past him, she patted his cheek with more affection than she had felt in a long while. She whispered, hardly moving her lips, *"She killed me,"* and kept on to the bedroom.

DIRAE

In structure, language, and specific content this may be the strangest story I've ever written.

When Gardner Dozois and George R. R. Martin invited me to be part of their Warriors *anthology, it struck me that fantasy literature was rife with darkly swashbuckling epic heroes, noble-souled mercenaries, and miscellaneous military types—past, present, and future—busily taking on dragons, invading armies, Dark Lords of all degrees of wickedness, and probably entire Death Stars, for all I knew. That meant I couldn't even think of going that way: surely there had to be something different that could be done with such an anciently evocative and archetypal image.*

Well...different "Dirae" certainly is, especially in how it begins. Gardner and George urged their readers to take the early pages slowly, and with patience, because they aren't easy reading. Here I do the same. This particular warrior, and her evolving journey, aren't pre-read for you, so to speak; but I'm very proud of them both, and I do believe that they'll be worth the added effort.

*

Red.

    Wet red.

    My feet in the red.

    Look. Bending in the red. Shiny in his hand—other hand tears, shakes at something in the red.

    Moves.

    In the red, it moves.

    Doesn't want it to move. Kicks at it, lifts shiny again.

    Doesn't see me.

    In the red, it makes a sound.

Sound hurts me.

Doesn't want sound, either. Makes a sound, brings shiny down.

Stop him.

Why?

Don't know.

In my hand, his hand. Eyes wide. Pulls free, swings shiny at me.

Take it away.

Swing shiny across his face. Opens up, flower. Red teeth. Swing shiny again, other way.

Red. Red.

Another sound—high, hurting. Far away, but coming closer. Eyes white in red, red face. He turns, feet slipping in red. Could catch him.

Sound closer. At my feet, moves in red. Hurts me. Hurts me.

Sound too close.

Go away.

Darkness.

Darkness.

DARK.

I...

What? Which? Who?

Who *I?* Think.

What is *think?*

Loud. Hurting. Loud.

A fence. Boys. *Loud.* Hurts me.

One boy, curled on ground.

Other boys.

Feet. So many *feet.*

Hurts.

I walk to them. *I.*

A boy in each hand. I throw them away. *I.*

More boys, more feet. Pick them up, bang together. Throw away.

Like this. *I like this.*

Boys gone.

Curled-up boy. Clothes torn, face streaked red. This is blood. *I know.*

How do *I* know?

Boy stands up. Falls.

Face wet, not the blood. Water from his eyes. What?

Stands again. Speaks to me, words. Walks away. Almost falls, but not. Wipes face, walks on.

Turn, faces looking at me. *I* look back, they turn away. Alone here.

Here. Where?

Doors. Windows. Noise. People. In one dark window, a figure.

I move, it moves. *I* go close to see—it comes toward, reaching out.

Me?

Darkness. Darkness. DARK...

the one with the knife, just out of reach. Drops back, comes close, darts away again. Waiting, waiting, in the corner of my left eye. Old woman screams and screams. The one riding my back, forearm across my throat, laughing, grunting. I snap my head back, feel the nose go, kick between his legs as he falls away. Knife man moves in then, and I catch his wrist and break it, *yes.* Third one, with the gun, frightened, fires, *whong,* garbage can rolls on its edge, falls over. He drops the gun, runs, and I lose him in the alley.

The one I kicked, wriggling on his side toward the gun when I turn back. Stops when he sees me. The old woman gone at last, the knife man huddling against the warehouse wall. "Bitch, you broke my fucking wrist!" *Bitch,* over and over. Other words. I pick up knife and gun and walk away, find a place to drop them. The sky is brightening toward the river, pretty.

Dark...

and I am rolling on the ground, trying to take an automatic rifle away from a crying man. Hits out, bites, kicks, tries to club me with the gun. People crowding in everywhere—legs, shoes, too close, shopping bags, too close, someone steps on my hand. Bodies on the ground, some moving, most not. In my arms, he struggles and wails, wife who left him, job he lost, children taken from him, *voices, voices.* Gives up suddenly—eyes roll back, gone away, harmless. I fight off a raging man, little girl limp in his arms, wants the gun, *Give me that gun!* I am on my feet, standing over the gunman, surrounded, protecting *him* now. Police.

Revolving lights, red and blue and white, ringing us all in together, they yank the man to his feet and run him away, barely letting him touch the ground. Still weeping, head thrown back as though his neck were broken. Bodies lying everywhere, most of them dead. I know dead.

One policeman comes to me, thanks me for preventing more deaths. I give him the rifle, he takes out a little notebook. Wants my story—what happened, what I saw, what I did. Kind face, happy eyes. I begin to tell him.

...then the darkness.

Where do I go?

When the dark takes me—just after I am snatched up out of one war and whirled off into another—where am I? No time between, no memories except blurred battles, no name, no needs, no desires, no relation to anything but my reflection in a shop window or a puddle of rain...where do I live? Who am I when I am there?

Do I live?

No, I am not a *who*, cannot be. I am a *what*. A walking weapon, a tool, a force, employed by someone or something unknown to me, for reasons I don't understand.

But—

If I was made to be a weapon, consciously manufactured for one purpose alone, then why do I question? That poor madman's rifle had no such interest in its own identity, nor its master's, nor where it hung between uses. No, I am something more than a rifle: I must be something that...

wonders. Wonders even while I am taking a gas can away from a giggling young couple who are bending over the ragged woman blinking drowsily on the sidewalk, the man holding his cigarette lighter open, thumb on its wheel. I hit them with the can until they fall down and stay there; then pour the gasoline over them and throw the lighter into a sewer. The ragged woman sniffs, offended by the smell, gets up and mumbles away. She gives me a small nod as she passes by.

And for just an instant, before the darkness takes me, I stand in the empty street, staring after her: a weapon momentarily in no one's hands, aimed at no one, a weapon trying to imagine itself. Only that moment...

then dark again, *think about the darkness...*

and it is daylight this time, late afternoon. I can see her ahead of me, too far ahead, the calm, well-dressed woman placidly dropping the second child into the river that wanders back and forth through this city. I can see the head of the first one, already swept almost out of sight. The third is struggling now, crying in her arms as she picks it up and raises it over the rail. Other people are running, but I am weaving through, I am past them, I am *there*, hitting her as hard as I can, so that she is actually lifted off the ground, slamming into a sign I cannot read. But the child is already in the air, falling...

...and so am I, hitting the water only seconds behind her. That one is easy—I have her almost immediately, a little one, a girl, gasping and choking, but unharmed. I set her on the narrow bank—there are stairs ahead, someone will come down and get her—and head after the others, kicking my shoes off as I swim. *As I swim...*

How do I know how to swim? Is that part of being a weapon? I am cutting through the water effortlessly, moving faster than the people running along the roadway—how did I learn to use my legs and arms just so? The current is with me, but it is sweeping the children along in the same way. Ahead, one small face turned to the sky, still afloat, but not for long. I swim faster.

A boy, this one, older than the first. I tread water to scoop him up and hold him over my shoulder, while he spews what seems like half the river down my back. But he is trying to point ahead, downstream, even while he vomits, after the third child, the one I can't see anywhere. People are calling from above, but there's no time, no time. I tuck him into the crook of my left arm and set off again, paddling with the right, using my legs and back like one thing, keeping my head out of the water to stare ahead. Nothing. No sign.

Sensible boy, he wriggles around to hold onto my shoulders as I swim, so that the left arm is free again. But I can't find the other one—*I can't...*

...and then I can. Floating face down, drifting lifelessly, turning and turning. A second girl. I have her in another moment, but the river is fighting me for the two of them now, and getting them to the bank against the current is hard. But we manage it. We manage.

Hands and faces, taking the children from me. The boy and the little one will be all right—the older girl...I don't know. The police are here, and two of them are kneeling over her, while the other two are being wrapped in blankets. There is a blanket around my shoulders too, I had not noticed. People pressing close, praising me, their voices very far away. I need to see about the girl.

The police have the mother, a man on either side of her, holding her arms tightly, though she moves with them willingly. Her face is utterly tranquil, all expression smoothed away; she looks at the children with no sign of recognition. The boy looks back at her...I will not think about that look. If I am a weapon, I don't have to. I start toward the motionless girl.

One of the policemen trying to start her breath again looks up—then recognizes me, as I know him. He was the one who was asking me questions about the weeping man with the rifle, and who actually saw me go with the darkness. I back away, letting the blanket fall, ready to leap back into the river, soaked through and weary as I am. He points at me, begins to stand up...

...the darkness comes for me, and for once I am grateful. Except... except...

Except that now I will never know about that girl, whether she lived or died. I will never know what happened to the mother...

Once I would not—*could* not—have thought such thoughts. I would have had neither the words nor the place in me where the words should go. I would not have known to separate myself from the darkness—to remain *me*, even in the dark, waiting. Can a weapon do that? Can a weapon remember that small boy's face above the water, and the way he tried to help me save his sister?

Then that is not all I am, even as I wish it. *Who am I?*

If I am a person, I must have a name. Persons have names. What is my name?

What is my name?

Where do I live?

Could I be mad? Like that poor man with the gun?

I wake. That must mean that I sleep. Doesn't it? Then where do I...no, no distractions. What is sure is that I come suddenly awake—on the street, every time, somewhere in the city. Wide awake, instantly...dressed—neatly, practically and entirely unremarkably—and on my feet, *moving,* either already in the midst of trouble, or heading straight for it. And I will know what to do when I find it, because...because I will *know,* that's all. I always know.

No name, then...no home...nowhere to be, except when I am hurrying toward it. And even in daylight, darkness always near...silent, void, always lost before, but now this new place in the dark when I can feel that there *is* a *now,* and that *now* is different from *after-now.* If that's so, then I ought to be able to stand still in *after-now* and look back...

standing beneath a flickering street light, watching two young black girls walking together, arm in arm. They look no more than fifteen—thirteen, more likely—and they have just come from seeing a movie. *How do I know what a movie is?* This must have been a funny one, because they are giggling, quoting lines, acting out scenes for each other. But they walk rapidly, almost hurrying, and there is a strained pitch to their laughter that makes me think they know it is dangerous for them to be here. I parallel their progress on the other side of the street.

The five white boys materialize silently out of the shadows—three in front of the girls, two behind them, cutting off any chance of flight. The moment is perfectly soundless: everybody knows what everybody else is there for. The black girls look desperately around them; then back slowly against the wall of a building, holding hands like the children they are. One of the boys is already unbuckling his belt.

I am the first one to speak. I walk forward slowly, crossing the empty street, saying, "No. This is not to happen."

I speak strangely, I know that, though I can never hear what it is that I do wrong. The boys turn to look at me, giving the two girls an instant when they might well have made a successful dash for safety. But they are too frightened; neither of them could move a finger at this moment. I keep coming. I say, "I think everyone should go home."

The big one begins to smile. *The leader. Good.* He says loudly to the others, "Right, I'll take this one. Dark meat's bad for my diet." The rest of them laugh, turning back toward the black girls.

I walk straight up to him, never hesitating. The smile stays on his broad blond face, but there is puzzlement in the eyes now, because I am not supposed to be doing this. I say, "You should have listened," and kick straight up at his crotch.

But this one saw that coming, and simply turns his thigh to block me.

Huge, grinning—small teeth, kernels of white corn—he hurls himself at me, and we grapple on our feet for a moment before we fall together. His hand covers my entire face; he could smother me like that, easily, but I know better than to bite the heel and anchor myself to the consequences. Instead, I grab his free hand and start breaking fingers. He roars and pulls the hand away from my face, closing it into a fist that will snap my neck if it lands. It doesn't. I twist. Then my own hand, rigid fingers joined and extended, catches him under the heart—again, around the side, kidneys, once, twice—and he gasps and sags. I roll him off me fast and stand up.

The boys haven't noticed the fate of their leader; they are entirely occupied with the black girls, who are screaming now, crying to me for help. I take a throat in each hand and bang two heads together—really hard, there is blood. I drop them, grab another by the shirt, slam him against a parked car, hit him until he sits down in the street. When I turn from him, the last one is halfway down the block, looking back constantly as he runs. He is fat and slow, easily caught—but I had better see to the girls.

"This is not a good place," I say. "Come, I will walk you home."

They are paralyzed at first, almost unable to believe that they have not been raped and beaten, perhaps murdered. Then they are all questions, hysterical with questions I cannot answer. Who am I? What is my name? Where did I come from—do I live around here? How did I happen to be right there when they needed help?

I just saw, that's all, I tell them. Lucky.

"Where you ever learn all that martial arts shit?"

No martial arts, I tell them, no exotic fighting technique, I was just irritated—which makes them laugh shakily, and breaks the tension. Beyond that, I talk to them as little as I can, my voice still something unpracticed, oddly wrong. They do most of the talking, anyway, so glad merely to be alive.

I do walk them all the way to their apartment house—they are cousins, living with their grandmother—and they both hug me with all their strength when we say goodbye. The older girl says earnestly, "I'm going to pray for you every night," and I thank her. They both wave back to me as they run into the building.

I am glad the darkness did not snatch me away while I was with them:

my vanishing before their eyes would surely have terrified them, and they have been frightened enough for one night. And I am glad to have at least a moment to be a *who,* fumbling and confused, before I must once again be an invincible *what,* taken down from the wall and aimed at some new target.

This time, when the darkness takes me...this time my memory remains whole, clear, unhazy. Everything is still there: nothing tattered or smudged, gone. The two black girls stay with me. I *remember* them, even things they said to each other about the movie they had just seen, and their telling me that their grandmother worked in a school cafeteria. And from there I remember more, though I have no sure way of measuring when any of it happened. *The drunken old man stumbling in front of a bus...the two toddlers playing on a rusty, sagging fire-escape on a hot night...the children driving so slowly down a wide trash-strewn street, training a pistol through the passenger window on another child who has just come out of a liquor store...the woman looking behind her into a stir of shadows, walking a little faster...*

And each time—me. Rescuer. Savior. Wrath of God...somehow fortunately there at just the right moment; there, where I am necessary. But where is *there?*

I am beginning to know. It is a city—how big a city I cannot guess—and there is a river I almost remember swimming...yes, the children. (*What happened to the third one?*) There is a street or two that I have come to recognize. A handful of buildings that give me some kind of bearing as I hurry past on this or that night's mission. One particular row of crowded, crumbling houses has become almost familiar, as have a few shops, a few street corners, a few markets—even a face, now and then...

This city, then, is where I live.

No. This is where I *am.*

They live, but I am only *real.* There is a difference I cannot name...

outside an apartment door with bright brass numerals on it—4 and 2 and 9; for the first time they are more than shapes to me—my leg in mid-snap, heel of my foot slamming once, just under the lock, breaking cheap wood away from deadbolt and mortise to give me entry. And there they are, the pair of them, sitting together on a couch, his eyes all pupil, the skin of her arms covered with deep scratches. I have seen that before.

This time I could not care less about it. I am here for the baby.

Hallway, door on the right. Closed, but I can hear the whimpering, even though the man is on his feet, making outraged noises, and the woman—pretty, once—is telling him to call nine-one-one. I pay no heed to either of them, not yet. No time, no time.

I can smell the urine even before I have opened the door. He's soaked, and the mattress is soaked, and the blanket, but that's not what stops my breath. It's the little cry he gives when I pick him up: a cry that ought to be a scream, with those bruises, and the way his left arm is hanging—but he hasn't even got the strength to scream. I cannot even tell when I'm hurting him. I lift him, and look into his eyes. What I see there I have never seen before.

And I go completely insane.

Somewhere far away, the woman is tugging at me, shrieking something at me. The man is on the floor, not moving, his face bloody. Not bloody enough. I can fix that. I start toward him, but she keeps getting in my way, she keeps making that sound. What has she got to make noise about? Her arm's not broken, her body isn't one big bruise—she doesn't have those marks that had better not be cigarette burns. Pulling on the arm holding the baby, she will make me drop him. No, now she has stopped, now she is down there, quiet, like the man. Both in the red. Wet red. Good.

Still noise, so much noise. People shouting—the apartment is full of people, when did that happen? Police, lots of police—and one of them *that* one. He stares at me. Says, under all the racket, "What are you doing here? Who *are* you?"

"I am no one," I say. I hand the baby to him. He looks down at it, and his young face goes a terrible color. Before he can raise his head again, the darkness...

...but no. Different this time. I am back almost immediately, ordinary night, and I am on the street, outside an apartment house I have never seen, where two police cars stand blinking redly at the curb. It is a warm night, but I'm shaking, and cannot stop. Something on my face, I brush at it, impatient. I have been...crying.

No purpose here: I know this. I walk away down the street. Keep walking, maybe that will help. For the moment, no place I should be, no helpless, desperate appeal closing on me. No one to save, only escape, evasion. A little time to wonder...to ask myself questions—did I kill those two? I was trying, I really wanted to kill them.

Blood crusting on the knuckles of both hands—my blood as well as theirs. My back pains me where the man hit me with some sort of kitchen object before I threw him through the door. I never have time to notice or remember pain; this is new. Yet nothing tonight hurt me as much as the look in the eyes of that urine-soaked child with his little arm dangling so...that was when I started crying and trying to kill, not merely protect. I can cry, then; there's something else I know.

Perhaps learning to think was not a good idea. My head is crowded now, heaving and churning with faces, voices, moments...*the old man hammering an older one with a heavy paint can, swinging it by the handle...the wild-eyed homeless man ringed by jeering boys, who finally catches hold of the one constantly darting in to steal his possessions out of his shopping cart, and has him down, hands around his throat, as the others swarm over him...the man with the tire iron, and the bleeding, half-naked woman who attacked me so furiously when I was taking it away from him...*

But even so, even so, I can feel it coming closer, a fleeting space *between* strangers, between rescues, when *something* becomes almost clear, like the instant before dawn: the rush of paling sky, the first lights going on in windows, the earliest sounds of birds waking on rooftops. While in it I sense that there is a source of me, a *point* to me; a place, and a memory—and a name—and even my own dawn, where I belong...

wake not on the street but in a strange room, where I can see the sky—soft with early morning light, incomplete, the world heavy still with sleep—through tall narrow windows.

There are eight beds in this room, with bodies rounding the blankets in three of them, but no sound, except for the soft buzz and wheeze of machinery. A hospital. The woman in the nearest bed lies on her back, but twisted toward the right; if the tube plugged into a hole in her throat and a monitor beyond were not preventing it, she would be curled up on her side. Her breath is short and soundless, and too fast, and she smells like mildew. She is a big woman, but lying so makes her look shrunken, and older than she probably is. The chart at the foot of the bed is labeled JANE DOE. I sit down in a chair close to her.

She is very ugly. Her arms are thick, heavy, with tiny hands, the fingers all more or less the same size; you can hardly tell the thumb from the rest. Her black hair is lank and tangled, and her face is so pale that the blotches and faded pockmarks stand out like whip scars. Something once broke her nose and the bones of her face, badly. They are not right and clearly never will be. But her expression is utterly peaceful, serenely empty.

I know her.

The red. In the red, moving. Wants it not to move. Sound hurts me.

I say it out loud: "I know you." *You moved in the red. He kicked you. Shiny. I took it away.*

Why am I here?

Jane Doe does not answer me. I never expected that she would. But the young nurse does, a moment later, when she comes storming into the room, demanding to know who I am. I could tell her that I am constantly asking myself the same question, but instead I say that I am Jane Doe's friend. She promptly reaches for the telephone, saying that "Jane Doe" is the name they use for people whose real name no one knows—as I obviously do not. I could tear the phone out of her hand, out of the wall, but instead I sit and wait. She turns away to speak into the phone for a few moments, looking more and more puzzled and annoyed; then hangs it up and turns back to glare at me.

"How the hell did you get in here? Security says no one looking like you has been through at all." She is black, tall and slender, with a small, delicate head, a naturally somber face. Quite pretty, but the confusion is making her really angry.

I say, "There was no one at the door. I just walked in."

"Somebody dies for this," she mumbles. She looks at her watch, makes a note on a pad of paper. "Oh, heads will *roll,* I swear." Calming herself: "Go away, please, or I'll have to have Security up. You don't belong here."

I look back at Jane Doe. "What is the matter with her?"

The nurse shakes her head. "I don't think that's any of your business."

I stand up. I say, "Tell me."

The nurse looks at me for a long moment. I wonder what she sees. "I do that, you'll leave without making any trouble?"

"Yes."

"She was mugged. Ten, eleven months ago. Attacked on the street and beaten really badly—she almost died. They never caught the guy who did it. When she fell, she must have hit her head against something, a building. There was brain damage, bleeding. She's been in a vegetative state ever since." She gestures around her at the other silent beds. "Like the others here."

"And you don't know who she is."

"Nobody does. Do you? Is there something you're not telling me?"

Oh yes. Yes.

"Will she always be like this?"

The nurse—the name on her blue and white breast pin says FELICIA— frowns and backs slowly toward the door. "On second thought, maybe you better stay right there. I'm going to go get someone who can answer your questions."

She will come back with guards.

I sit down. I stare down into the big, blind, ugly face from my very first memory, trying to understand why the darkness brought me here. I watch the blinking monitors and wonder about so many things I do not even have *thoughts* for, let alone words. But it is more than I can grasp, and I have understood nothing when once more I lose the world.

Her name! Her name is...

another strange, dim street, and I am carrying a weeping, forlornly struggling girl out of a storefront that advertises ASIAN MAS AGE in its grimy window. She appears to be thirteen or fourteen years old. I cannot understand what she is saying to me.

But she is looking past me, over my shoulder; and when I turn, I see the group massing behind me. A hardfaced middle-aged couple, two younger men—squat, but burly in a top-heavy way—and a boy likely not very much older than the girl in my arms. He is the one holding the broken bottle.

I set the girl down on her feet, still holding her by the shoulders. She has a round, sweet face, but her eyes are mad with terror. I point at the sidewalk and say loudly, *"Stay here!"* several times, until it seems to get through, and she nods meekly. I cannot begin to guess how many times she must have made just that same gesture of bewildered submission in the face of power. I try to pat her shoulder, but she cringes away from me. I let her go, and turn back to face my new batch of enemies.

They are all shouting furious threats at me, but the boy seems to be the only one who speaks English. He eases toward me, waving the half bottle as menacingly as he can, saying, "You give her, get away. My sister."

"She is no more your sister than I am," I answer him. "She is a child, and I am taking her out of here." Neighbors, fellow entrepreneurs and curious nightwalkers are already gathering around the scene, silent, unfriendly. I say, "Tell the rest of them if they get in my way, that bottle goes up your nose, for a start, and I will beat those two fat boys to death with you. Tell them I am in a very bad mood."

In truth, I am anxious for the police to show up before things get worse than they are. My mood is actually a kind of detached anger, nothing like the madness that took me over so completely when I saw that baby's broken arm. Something changed then, surely. Even if it is what I am for—all I am for—I have no desire to fight anyone just at the moment. I want to go somewhere by myself and think. I want to go back to the hospital, and sit by Jane Doe's bed, and look at her, and think.

But the two burly men are moving slowly out to left and right, trying to flank me, and that stupid boy is getting closer, in little dancy jump-steps. The girl is standing where I left her, wide-eyed, a finger in her mouth. There is a woman just behind her, middle-aged, with a heavy face and kind eyes. I ask her with my own eyes to keep the girl safe while I deal with her former employers, and she nods slightly.

The boy, seeing my attention apparently distracted, chooses this moment to lunge, his arm fully extended, his notion of a war cry carrying and echoing off the low storefronts. I spin, trip him up—the half bottle crashes in the gutter—and hurl him by his shirtfront into the path of the bravo on my left. They go down together, and I turn on the other one, catching him under the nose with the heel of my right hand, between belly and breath with the balled left. He clutches hard at me as he falls, but he does fall.

There are women spilling out of the massage parlor now, all very young, all wearing cut-off shorts and T-shirts that show their flat, childish stomachs. Most simply stare; a few run back into the storefront; two or three slip away down a half-hidden alley. The boy struggles to his feet and here he comes again, jabbing the air with a single jagged splinter of the broken bottle, cutting his own hand where he holds it. I am trying not to hurt him more than necessary, but he is not making it easy. I kick the glass shard out of his grasp, so he won't fall on it when I side-kick his feet out from under him on my way toward the older couple. They back away fast—maybe from me, more likely from the lights and sirens coming up the street. I back off myself, and sigh with relief.

The girl is still where I left her, with the older woman's hand resting lightly on her trembling shoulder. I catch the woman's eye, nod my thanks, gesture toward the patrol car, and start to drift slowly away from there, eyes lowered.

One of the two policemen, Asian himself, is interrogating the massage parlor owners in their own language. But the other, much younger, sees me... looks past me...then looks again and heads straight for me. Through the shouting and the street noise, I hear his voice, "You! You hold it right there!"

I could still follow the escaping girls down the alley, but I stand where I am. He plants himself a foot in front of me, forefinger aimed at my chest. Surprisingly, he is smiling, but it is a tense, determined smile, not at all pleasant. He says, "We're going to stop meeting like this, right now. Who the hell *are* you?"

"I don't know."

"Yeah, right. And I'll bet you aren't carrying any ID, either." He is too agitated to wait for me to answer. He charges on: "Goddammit, first I see you at that mall shooting, but you just *disappear* on me, I don't know how. Then it was that crazy woman dropping her kids into the river—you dived in, went after them like some TV superhero—"

I interrupt him to ask, "The girl, the older one. Is she...will she be all right?"

His face changes; he stops pointing at me. He says nothing for a while, and his voice is lower when he speaks again. "We tried everything. If you'd bothered to stick around, you'd have known. But no—it's another disappearing act, like a damn special effect. Then that couple with the baby, those two meth-heads." It is a different smile this time. "Okay, they had it coming, but *you're* coming downtown with us on that one, and lucky it's not a murder charge. Both of them still in the hospital, you know that?"

I wonder whether they are in the same hospital as Jane Doe. I wonder where the baby is, and I am about to ask him, when he continues, "Now *this*. What, you think you're Batman, the Lone Ranger, rousting massage parlors, beating the crap out of rapists? You're really starting to leave a trail, lady, and we need to have a conversation. You can't *do* this shit."

He reaches for the handcuffs at his belt. My hands raise automatically and he steps back, reaching for his holstered gun instead. I begin to explain why I cannot let him arrest me...

but then it is bright afternoon, and I am standing on a street across from a schoolyard in time to see a boy push a smaller boy down hard and run off, laughing. The little one is whimpering dazedly over ripped new blue jeans or a scraped knee, and doesn't see the car coming. Other children and passersby do, but they're too far away, and their warning screams are drowned by the shriek of brakes. No one can possibly reach him in time.

But of course I am there. It is what I do, being there.

Not even a spare second to scoop him up—I crash into him from the side, and the two of us roll away into the gutter as the car slews by, skidding in a half circle, so that it comes to rest on the far side of the street, facing us. The boy ends up in my arms, his eyes wide and frantic, but not crying at all now, because he cannot get his breath. Children are running toward us, adults are coming out of the school; the driver is already down on his knees beside us, easily as hysterical as the boy. But it's all right. It is over. I was there.

My left shoulder hurts where I hit the asphalt, and I have banged my head on something, maybe the curb. Like Jane Doe. I stand up carefully and, as always, ease myself slowly away from the rejoicing and the praise. The boy has started to cry fully now, which is a relief to me.

Jane Doe doesn't cry. She hasn't cried for a very long time.

It is confusing to be suddenly thinking about her. She is somehow there with me, an intrusion, surplus from the darkness, only being felt now because there is no one I must save. Why? I am a ghost myself, always vanishing. How can I be haunted?

Her name is...

Oh. I—

I know her name.

I walk until I come to a bridge over that milky river which divides and defines this city. I sit on the stone guardrail to wait for the darkness. I feel a weariness in me more frightening than any boy with a broken bottle. I am real enough to break a jaw or a rib defending a child prostitute; not real enough ever to understand that child's life, her terror, her pain. I can go as mad with rage as any human over a beaten, half-dead infant, and do my very best to murder its abusers—and feel dreadfully *satisfied* to have done so—but now I think...now I think it is not my outrage and terrible pity I am satisfying; it is all, all of it, happening in that hospital room, behind those closed eyes whose color I do not know.

I gaze down from the bridge, watching a couple of barges sliding silently by, just below me. *If I were to leap down to them, right now, would I be killed? Can a dream commit suicide?*

Darkness...

that policeman is actively looking for me. We have not met again, but I have seen him from a distance once or twice, during one rescue—one *being there*—or another.

My ever-faithful darkness keeps returning for me, carrying me off to do battle with other exploiters, other abusers, other muggers, rapists, molesters, gang thugs, drive-by assassins. See me: lithe, swift, fearless, always barehanded, always alone, always conquering...and never in control, not of anything, not of the smallest choice I make. She is. I am certain of that now.

My missions—*her* missions—have always favored children, but lately they seem to feature them constantly, exclusively. More and more I wake to other massage parlors—endless, those—and trucks crammed full of ten-year-old immigrant laborers packed into shipping crates. Garment sweatshops in basement factories. Kitchens in alley diners. Lettuce fields outside the city. At the airport I intercept two girls arriving for hand-delivery to an old man from their home village. In a basement I break a man's arm and leg, then free his pregnant daughter and pregnant granddaughters from the two rooms he has kept them locked in for years. I have grown sharper, more peremptorily violent. I rarely speak now. There is no time. We have work to do, Jane Doe and I, and it is growing so late.

The blind force in the darkness grows fiercer, angrier, more *hurried*.

Sometimes I am not even finished when I am snatched up once again—by the back of my neck, really, like a kitten—and plopped straight into another crisis, another horror, another rescue. And I do what I do, what I am for, what Jane Doe birthed me to be: guardian, defender, invincible fighter for the weak and the injured. But it is all wearing thin; so thin that often I can see the next mission through the fabric of this one, the dawn through an increasingly transparent darkness. *Wearing thin...*

it happens while I am occupied in rescuing a convenience-store manager and his wife from three large men in ski masks. They are all drunk, they are all armed, and the manager has just made the mistake of hauling out the shotgun from behind the counter. All very noisy and lively; but so far no one is dead, and I have the old couple stashed safely out of the way. But the sirens are coming.

The bandits hear the sirens too, and the two who can still walk actually push past me to get out of the store. I hardly notice them, because I am starting to feel a vague, sickly unease—a psychic nausea surging up and over me in a wave of dislocation and abandonment. Outside, I double over against a wall, gasping, struggling for breath, unable to stand straight, with the patrol cars sounding in the next street over. Somehow I stumble to safety, out of sight behind a couple of huge garbage trucks, and lean there until the spasm passes. No—until it eases a bit. Whatever it is, it is not passing.

The sun is just clear of the horizon. I can feel the dark clutching blindly and feebly at me, but it hasn't the strength to carry me away. I am on my own. I look around to get my bearings; then push myself away from the garbage trucks and start wobbling off.

A car horn close beside me, almost in my ear. I sense who it is before I turn my head and see the blue-and-white police car. He is alone, glaring at me as he pulls to the curb. "Get in, superhero," he calls. "Don't make me chase you."

I am too weak, too weary for flight. I open the front passenger door and sit down beside him. He raises his eyebrows. "Usually we keep the escape artists in the back, with no door handles. What the hell." He does not start up again, but eyes me curiously, fingertips lightly drumming on the steering wheel. He says, "You look terrible. You look really sick." I do not answer. "You going to throw up in my car?"

I mumble, "No. I don't know. I don't think so."

"Because we've had nothing but pukers for the last week—I mean, *nothing* but pukers. So I'd really appreciate it, you know..." He does not finish the sentence, but keeps eyeing me warily. "Boy, you look bad. You think you ate a bad clam or something?" Abruptly he makes up his mind. "Look, before we go anywhere, I'm taking you to the hospital. Put your seat belt on."

I leave the belt catch not quite clicked, but as he pulls away into traffic an alarm goes off. He reaches over, snaps the catch into place. I am too slow to prevent him. The alarm stops. With a quick glance my way he says, "You don't *look* crazy or anything—you look like a nice, normal girl. How'd you get into the hero business?"

I am actually dizzy and sweating, as though I *were* going to throw up. I say again, "I don't know. I try to help, that is all."

"Uh-huh. Real commendable. I mean, pulling whole families out of the river and all, the mayor gives you medals for that stuff. Rescuing abused children, taking down mall shooters—that's *our* job, you're kind of making us look bad." He slaps the steering wheel, trying to look sterner than his nature. "But beating up the bad guys, *that's* a no-no. Doesn't matter how bad they are, you get into some really deep shit doing that. They sue. And somebody like me has to go and arrest you...not to mention explaining about sixteen million times to my boss, and *his* boss, why I didn't do it already, you being right there on the scene and all. All the damn time."

My head is swimming so badly I have trouble making sense of his words. Something very bad is happening; whether to me or to Jane Doe I cannot tell. *Could this hospital he is taking me to be her hospital?* The policeman is speaking again, his face and voice serious, even anxious. He says, far away, "That vanishing act of yours, now that worries me. Because if you're not crazy, then either you really *are* some kind of superhero, or *I'm* crazy. And I just don't want to be crazy, you know?"

In the midst of my faintness, I feel strangely sorry for him. I manage to reply, "Perhaps there is another choice...another possibility..." *Even if it is the right hospital, if the darkness does not come again, I will never reach Jane Doe's silent room—not in handcuffs, which are surely coming, and with his hand tight on my shoulder. What must I do?*

"Another possibility?" His eyebrows shoot up again. "Well, now you've got me trying to figure what the hell that could be."

I do not answer him.

He parks the patrol car in front of a squat gray-white building. I can see other cars coming and going: people on crutches, people being pushed in wheelchairs—an ambulance out front, another in the parking lot. He cuts the engine, turns to look straight at me. "Look, doesn't matter whether I *want* to bust you on a filing cabinet full of assault charges or not. I *got* to do that. But what I'd way rather do is just talk to you, first, because that other possibility... that other possibility is I've got reality wrong, flat wrong. All of it. And I don't think I'm ready to know that, you understand?"

It *is* Jane Doe's hospital. I can feel her there. This close, the pull of the darkness is still erratic but convulsively stronger. I know she is reaching for me.

With one hand I reach for the door handle, very slowly, holding his glance. With the other I start to unbuckle the seat belt.

"Don't—"

I start to say, "I never had your choice." But I don't finish, any more than I get a chance to throw the door open and bolt into the hospital. Between one word and the next the darkness takes hold of me, neck and heels, and I am gone...

once again in Jane Doe's room, standing at the foot of her bed.

And Felicia has seen me appear.

Her silence is part of the silence of the room; her breath comes as roughly as her patients' through the tubes in their throats; the speechless fear in her wide dark eyes renders me just as mute. All I can do for her is to move aside, leaving a clear path to the door. I croak her name as she stumbles through, but the only response is the soft click as she closes the door and locks it from outside. I think I hear her crying, but I could be wrong.

There is a little bathroom, just to the right of the door, with a toilet and sink for visitors. I walk in and wash my face—still dirty and bruised from my convenience store battle—for the first time. Then I take a moment to study the mask that Jane Doe made for me. The woman in the mirror has black hair, like hers, but longer—almost to the shoulders—and fuller. The eyes looking back at me are dark gray. The skin around them is a smooth light-olive. It is blankly calm, this face, the features regular yet somehow uninteresting: easily ignored, passed over, missed in a crowd. And why not, since that so clearly suited Jane Doe's purpose? Whatever terrified instinct first clothed me in flesh chose well.

It is a good face. A *useful* face. I wonder if I will ever see it again.

I walk back to Jane Doe's bed. The strange near-nausea has not left me—if anything, it seems to rise and fall with Jane Doe's breathing, which is labored now. She moves jerkily beneath the cover of her sheets, eyes still closed, her face sweaty and white. Some of the noises coming from the machines attached to her are strong and regular, but others chirp with staccato alarm: whether she is conscious or not, the machines say her body is in pain. And in the same way I know so many things now, I know why. The gift unleashed by the damage she suffered—the talent to give me life from nothingness, to sense danger, fear, cruelty from afar and send her own unlikely angel flying to help—has become too great for the form containing it.

I sit down by her, taking her heavy, limp hand between my own, and the darkness touches me.

There are too many.

My lips feel too cold to move, so I do not even try to speak. All I can do is look.

There are too many, and she cannot do enough.

Images comes to me, falling through my mind like leaves.

Red.

Wet red.

My feet in the red.

She made me up to save her, but I was too late. So we saved others, she and I. We saved so many others.

I look at the door. With every small sound I expect clamor and warning—gunshots, even, or barking dogs. I wonder whether Felicia will be back with the nice young policeman. I wish I could have explained to him.

There is warmth in the darkness. I feel it in my head, I feel it on my skin. It is pain...but something beyond pain, too.

On the wall next to the telephone there is a white board with words written on it, and a capped marker. Writing is new to me—I have never had to do it before—so it does not go as quickly or as well as I would like, but I manage. In a child's block letters I write down the name I found in the darkness, and three more words: WE THANK YOU.

Then I go back to her bed.

Voices in the hall now—Felicia, and another woman, and two or three men. I cannot tell whether the young policeman is one of them. No sound yet of Felicia's key in the lock; are they afraid of a woman who comes and goes by magic arts?

I think I would have liked to have a name of my own, but no matter. I lean forward and remove the cables, then the tubes. So many of them. Some of the machines go silent, but others howl.

Fumbling at the lock...now the sound of the key. It is so easy to close my hands around her throat, and I feel her breath between my fingers.

VANISHING

With any luck, this is as close as I'll ever come to passing a kidney stone.

The first seeds of "Vanishing" appeared in a story I wrote about ninety-seven times back in the very early '60s and never managed to sell. Called "The Vanishing Germans," it was an attempt at topical political satire that had all the subtlety of a Demolition Derby. One morning American Lieutenant Ethan Frome, guarding a checkpoint on the Berlin Wall, notices that all of West Germany has been replaced by a vast empty hole in the ground. His Russian counterpart, Captain Boris Godunov, confirms that the very same thing has happened to East Germany as well, leaving the Wall itself (and both of them) floating magically in space above an immeasurably deep chasm. The rest of the story contained no explanation for this event, but plenty of speculations; Kennedy and Kruschev both made appearances; and every remaining country in the world wanted the H-Bomb, just in case. Ultimately peace broke out as a direct result of Germany's disappearance, but I couldn't leave well enough alone and slapped on a quasi-science-fictional O. Henry ending that made even less sense than all the words preceding it.

The story was a mess. I wasn't surprised that it didn't sell, even back then, and after I buried the carbons in my filing cabinet I managed to forget they had ever existed.

Forty years later Connor Cochran discovered "The Vanishing Germans" in my files and started bugging me about it. The central visual of the story had seized him and would not let go; so he seized my metaphorical lapels and every now and then he'd shake them. Consider that image, he'd say. The floating Wall. What if you took it seriously?

"Vanishing" went through at least eleven drafts and any number of dodged deadlines, and remains further out of my normal range and comfort zone than any other story in this collection, including "Dirae." It's a ghost story, yes, but it's a lot of other things as well, and I suspect that I'll be rediscovering and relearning it for a long time to come. In the end I'm happy with how it came out, but I'd be almost as happy never to spend another hour of my life studying photographs of Checkpoint Charlie, pouring over architectural diagrams of East German guard towers, or cross-comparing Berlin street maps from 1964 and 2009.

*

Jansen knew perfectly well that when Arl asked him to drive her to the clinic for her regular prenatal checkup, it meant that every single one of his daughter's usual rides was unavailable. She had already told him that it wouldn't be necessary for him to wait; that Elly, her mother, would be off work by the time the examination was done, and could bring her home. They drove down to Klamath Falls in silence, except for his stiffly-phrased questions about the health of the child she was carrying, and the state of her preparations for its arrival. Once he asked when she expected her husband back, but her reply was such a vague mumble that he missed the sense of it completely. Now and then he glanced sideways at her, but when she met his eyes with her own fierce, stubborn brown ones, he looked away.

When they parked at the clinic, he said, "I'll come in with you."

"You don't have to," Arl said. "I told you."

"Yeah, I know what you told me. But it's my grandson in there"—he pointed at her heavily rounded belly—"and I'm entitled to know how he's getting on. Let's go."

Arl did not move. "Dad, I really don't want you in there."

Jansen consciously kept his voice low and casual. "Tell you what, I don't care." He got out of the car, walked around to the passenger side, and opened the door. Arl sat where she was for a moment, giving him the *I just dare you* face he'd known since her childhood; but then she sighed abruptly and pushed herself to her feet, ignoring his offered hand, and plodded ahead of him to the clinic. Jansen followed closely, afraid that she might fall, the walkway being wet with recently melted snow. He would have taken her arm, but he knew better.

This one would rather die than forgive me. Gracie almost has, Elly might— someday—but Arl? Not ever.

In the clinic they sat one chair apart after she signed in. Jansen pretended to be browsing through *Sports Illustrated* until Arl disappeared with the OB/ GYN nurse. He lowered the magazine to his lap then, and simply stared straight ahead at the gray world beyond the window. A sticky-faced child, running by, kicked his ankle and kept going, leaving its pursuing mother to apologize; a young couple sitting next to him argued in savagely controlled whispers over the exact responsibility for a sexually-transmitted disease. Jansen froze it all out and asked himself for the hundredth useless time why he shouldn't sell the shop—or just close it and leave, the way people were walking away from their own homes these days. Walk away and put some daylight between himself and trouble. Hanging around sure as hell wasn't doing him any good, and alimony checks didn't care whether you mailed them from Dallas or down the block. Neither did Elly and the girls, not so you'd notice. At least in Dallas he could be warm while he was lonely. He let his eyelids drift shut as he tried to imagine being somewhere else, being *someone* else, and failed miserably in the attempt. Eyes closed, all the screwups and disappointments just seemed to press in closer than ever.

Shit, he thought. *All of it, all of it.* And then, *At least the little rugrat quit zooming around. That's something.*

The magazine slid from his relaxed fingers, but he didn't hear it hit the floor, and when he opened his eyes to reach down and pick it up he saw that he wasn't in the waiting room anymore.

He wasn't in Klamath Falls anymore, either. It was night, and he was on the Axel-Springer-Strasse. Instantly alert, he knew where he was, and never thought for a second that he was dreaming. Despite shock, beyond the uncertainties and anxieties of age, he knew that after more than forty-five years he was back at the Wall. The Wall that didn't exist anymore.

Kreuzberg district, West Berlin, between Checkpoint Charlie and the checkpoint at Heinrich-Heine-Strasse, just past where the Zimmerstrasse runs out and the barbed wire and barriers start zigzagging west...

There it was, directly before him, just *there*, lit by streetlamps—not the graffiti-covered reinforced concrete of the *Grenzmauer 75* that had been hammered to bits by the joyously triumphant "woodpeckers," East and West, when Germany was reunited, and the pieces sold off for souvenirs, but the crude first version he had patrolled in 1963, a gross lump haphazardly thrown together from iron supports, tangles of barbed wire, and dirty gray cement building blocks the East German workers had pasted in place with slaps of mortar no one bothered to smooth. Jansen said softly, "No." He put his fingers to his mouth, like a child, shaking his head hard enough that his neck hurt, hoping desperately to make the clinic waiting-room materialize around him; but the Wall stayed where it was, and so did he.

He was sitting, he realized, in the doorway of a building he did not want to think about; had, in fact, refused to think about for many years. The old ironwork of the entrance was hard and cold against his shoulders as he pushed away from it and struggled to his feet.

Everything around him was familiar, his memory somehow fresher for so rarely having been examined. To his right the Wall angled sharply, blocking the road and continuing along the Kommandantenstrasse, while across from him he could see, just barely, the top of the eastern guard tower that looked down on the Death Strip, that deadly emptiness between the eastern inner fence and the Wall, where the VoPos and Russians would fire on anyone trying to make it across to West Berlin.

Jansen turned from the Wall and took a few hesitant paces along the street. Most of it had actually belonged to East Germany—the Wall had been built several meters inside the formal demarcation line between East and West, so in some places any West Berliner who stepped too close was in danger of being arrested by East German guards; but elsewhere, in the West Berlin suburbs and beyond, there had been small family gardens growing literally in the shadow of the Wall, and even a little fishing going on. Jansen had always admired the Germans' make-do adaptiveness.

Here in the city's urban heart, however, the buildings and shops and little businesses displayed a jumble of conditions, some still unrepaired nearly twenty years after the Allies had bombed and blasted their way into Berlin. Aside from the pooling glow of the streetlamps, Jansen could see no slightest sign of life. All the windows were dark, no smoke rose from any chimneys, and there was no one else in the street. The world was as hushed as though it had stopped between breaths. Beneath the unnaturally starless, cloudless black of the night sky there was not so much as a pigeon searching for crumbs, or a stray dog trotting freely.

Jansen moved on in the silence, confused and wary.

A few buildings past the Zimmerstrasse he couldn't take it any more. Feeling overwhelmed in the empty quiet, he knocked at the next door he came to, and waited, struggling to bring back what little German he had ever had. *Sprechen Sie Englische?* of course. He'd used that one a lot, and found enough Germans who did to get by. But there was also *Wo bin ich?*—

"Where am I?"—and *Was ist los?*—"What is happening?"—and *Bitte, ich bin verloren*—"Please, I'm lost." They all seemed entirely appropriate to his situation.

When no one responded, he knocked again, harder; then tried the next door, with the same result, and then the three doors after that, each one in turn. Nothing. Yet he had no sense of the city being abandoned, evacuated; even the front window of the little shop where he and Harding had taken turns buying sausages and cheese for lunch was still crowded with its mysterious, wondrous wares. He saw his dark reflection in the shop window, and recognized his daily grizzled self: lean-faced and thin-mouthed, with deep-set, distant eyes...*no change there*, he thought: an old man caught, somehow, in this younger Jansen's place.

He might have graduated from knocking to shouting, except for what he discovered at the next intersection.

Ernie Hamblin—one of the traffic section MPs quartered with Jansen in the Andrews Barracks—had gotten a big laugh out of Jansen getting turned around and lost, twice, in his first week on duty, all because the two streets that met here had four different names, one for each direction of the compass. Jansen looked to the right, up the Kochstrasse, and saw nothing unusual when compared with his memory. Straight ahead—as Axel-Springer-Strasse became the Lindenstrasse—looked wrong, but in the darkness he couldn't quite make out why. To the left though, down the Oranienstrasse, there was nothing.

Literally nothing. No street, no houses, no streetlamps...only the same endless black as the sky, extending both outward and downward without the slightest hint of change. He walked as close to the road's sharp edge as he dared, trying to make sense of what he wasn't seeing, but could not. It wasn't a cliff face or a pit: it was simply emptiness, darkness vast and implacable, an utter end to the world, as if God had shrugged, shaken His head and walked away in the middle of the Third Day. The ground that should have been there was gone. The city that should have been built on it was gone and worse than gone, carved away with absolute, unhuman precision. Looking out and away at that edge, where it floated rootless in the black sky, Jansen could see buildings that had been neatly sliced in half, as though by some cosmic guillotine, their truncated interiors looking pitifully like opened dollhouses.

After a while Jansen realized that the edge had a shape; and that it matched, block for receding block, the cartoon lightning jag that was the corresponding section of the Wall. In the face of that understanding, rational thought was impossible. He turned and ran, and didn't notice anything at all until he stopped, out of breath and shaking, in front of the same doorway where he'd come back to this place.

It was open.

Jansen stood for a long time at the foot of the narrow stair, looking up into the shadows and becoming more aware with every passing moment that the last thing he wanted to do was go even one step further, because that would commit himself irrevocably to whatever reality lay in wait at the top. When he did finally begin to climb, his body felt like the body of someone heavier than he, someone older, and even more weary.

The second floor stairs creaked on the sixth and eleventh steps, exactly as he remembered. All the interior doors were closed, blocking out the light from the street, so by the time he reached the fourth landing he was feeling his way, palms and fingers rasping over the rough burned wood and ragged wallpaper. The Berlin Brigade may have sworn by spotless uniforms and occupied fancy officers' quarters, but they took their OPs—their observation posts—largely as they found them. Jansen counted right-hand doorframes, stopping when he got to the third. His hand found the familiar shape of the brass doorknob, turned it, and eased the door open, grateful to see light again, even if it wasn't very strong this high above the streetlamps.

The first thing his eyes registered was the neatly folded khaki sweater on the one old armchair in the room. *Just where I left it...transferred to Stuttgart on half an hour's notice, never did get back here.* Then he saw the folding chair placed carefully on its handmade wooden riser, in front of the open window, and the crude signatures and battalion numbers and obscenities scratched into the walls, including six-inch high letters that said T HE "40" HIRED GUNS. Next to that was a blocky '50s-vintage German wall telephone, its cord dangling above a beaten-up oil heater. On the cheap metal table in the corner were a couple of paperbacks—Mickey Spillane, Erle Stanley Gardner—and some torn candy bar wrappers. *Harding,* he thought. *Three crap mysteries from the PX every week, like clockwork, along with half their*

Baby Ruths and Mounds. Good as gold or cigarettes when it came to bartering with the street kids.

Jansen picked up the Spillane book, opened it, and realized that it was completely blank inside its lurid cover. He frowned, then dropped the empty book and lifted the wall telephone's absurdly light-blue handset. He held it to his ear, and the result was exactly what he expected: no dial tone, no static sputter—nothing but the dark silence of a long-dead line. He jiggled the hook, which was pointless but irresistible, and then hung up, a little harder than he perhaps needed to do.

After that he moved to the window, easing gently down into the folding chair positioned before it, because the dream-prop wooden riser under its legs was obviously just as flimsy as the one he'd teetered on so many times back in the real West Berlin. All he needed were his old binoculars and some wet-eared short-time 1st Lieutenant bitching at him and it would be like he'd never left. Except, of course, that there had been a couple of Germanys then, and as he looked out across the street he could see that the world was just as gone on the GDR side of the Wall as on this one. Ahead of him lay the Death Strip he had looked down upon every day for almost two years, the pale gravel raked over the flat ground between the crude outer Wall, topped with Y-shaped iron trees supporting a cloud of barbed wire, and the even cruder inner wall on the other side of the ramshackle watchtower. But the VoPo barracks he knew from before, the decaying and abandoned pre-War buildings that should have been there, were not; and as he looked from right to left, as far as he could see, sharp-edged blackness traced a line that paralleled the Wall itself. Spotting one or two of the old Russian T-62 tanks would have been a strange but distinct comfort right now, but of course there weren't any.

The telephone rang.

Jansen spun in his chair and the riser gave way beneath his shifting weight with a sharp crack, spilling him heavily to the ground. His back twisted, muscles on the lower left side spasming, and his right knee flared red with pain. *Fuck. Real enough to hurt like a son of a bitch!*

The phone rang a second time, then a third ring, a fourth. It took him that long to struggle back to his feet and hitch straight-legged over to it, his right knee still not trustworthy.

He put his hand on the receiver. It seemed to buzz like a rattlesnake in his fingers, and he held onto it for a second before he could make himself pick it up and put it to his ear.

He said, "Who is this?"

An instant of silence; then a sudden burst of surprised laughter. "So who should it be, *bulvan?*" The accent was Russian, as was the gruff timbre of the voice. Even the laughter was Russian. "Come to the window, so I can see you again. I am wondering if you are the Rawhide or the Two-Gun Kid."

Jansen said, "For God's sake, who are you? *Where* are you?"

"Come look. I will turn on light."

Jansen moved stiffly back to the window, the receiver cord just long enough to stretch. Stepping over the fallen chair, he put his free hand on the windowsill and leaned down to look out. A hundred yards away, toward the far side of the Death Strip, the lights inside the East German guard tower were blinking on and off. As he watched, the pattern stopped and the lights stayed on, allowing him to see a bundled-up figure pointing one forefinger at him, sighting along it like a pistol.

Into the handset, Jansen said, "You?"

"*Garazhi,* Rawhide. Me. So good to see you again." The distant figure executed a clumsy bow.

"Why are you calling me that?" Jansen's mouth was so dry it pained him.

The chuckle came through the receiver again. "The glorious Soviet Army was not nearly as efficient as your leaders liked to believe. Knew only the names of your officers, no one else. But from first day we looked across at each other, I had to call you *something.* I was learning English from comic books—very big on black market, you see, the Westerns with horses and guns and silly hats, so I called you *Rawhide Kid* and that short man—"

"Roscoe Harding."

"Really? For us he was *Two-Gun Kid,* and your mostly night fellows, *Kid Colt* and *Tex Hopalong.* Very satisfying, very shoot-'em-up. We had many such jokes."

"You don't want to know what we called you."

Another laugh. "Possibly not. But what name should I give you now, Rawhide? We are both older, I see, and it does not suit."

"My name's Jansen. Henry Jansen. Listen, you, whatever your name is—"

"Leonid," said the voice in his ear. "Leonid Leonidovich Nikolai Gavrilenko."

"That's a mouthful."

"True. But we are such old acquaintances, you must call me *Lyonya*. Or not, as you prefer. I do not presume." He paused, then said, "Welcome back to the Wall, my friend Jansen. Henry."

"Look behind you." Jansen kept his voice deliberately flat, but he could feel himself struggling not to panic. "This place isn't real."

"*Da, temnyi.* The darkness. I have seen."

Jansen said, "What the hell is going on? I can't be here. I was in a clinic waiting room with my daughter. She's seven months pregnant, and her husband's run off somewhere. She'll need me." Even as he spoke the words, he tasted their untruth in the back of his mouth. Arl had never had a chance to need him, and wouldn't know how to begin now, even if he wasn't who he was. But the Russian was impressed, or sounded so.

"Lucky man, Henry. I congratulate you, to have someone needing you. A good life, then? Since we saw each other last?"

"No," Jansen said. "Not so good. But I have to get back to it right now. Arl—my daughter—she won't know where I am. Hell, *I* don't know where I am."

"That is, I think, what we should be finding out. We put our thinking caps on, you and I." A certain growling bemusement had entered the Russian's voice. "Do Americans still say that? It cannot be accident, this place. Something is happening to us, *something* has brought us here. Have looked, but seen no one but you. So I think now, yes, after all, we must meet in person, do you not agree? At last, meet. With thinking caps."

As absolutely as Jansen wanted to leave the room, the deep suspicion that had been born in him here—never to abate fully—had its own hold. "I'm not sure that's a good idea, *tovarich*."

"No one is using that word anymore." Gavrilenko's voice was flat, without rancor or any sort of nostalgia. "Except the comedians. A comedy word now. Listen, Jansen, we don't give it up so fast! It is not good to be in this place alone, surely, whatever it is. That is why I called you. Old place, old face from old place, old time—this cannot be coincidence."

Jansen frowned. "Maybe, maybe not. But that's another thing. How did you know this number? Nobody was supposed to have it but the commander and the NCOIC. They didn't even give it to us! Some kraut spy sneak it out to you? Was that another one of the *jokes?*"

"You are not thinking, Henry."

"Fuck you, Gavrilenko. Why should I trust a single goddamn thing you say? I want to go home!"

There was a long silence.

He threw the receiver down, grabbed the empty window frame with both hands and stuck his head out into the night. "Do you hear me, you fucking Russian asshole? I want to go home! *I have to go home!*"

He saw the woman then, entering the Death Strip from somewhere just beyond and to the right of the watchtower. She walked quickly, looking from side to side, shoulders tense, head forward. She wore a faded light-brown coat, a transparent kerchief over her hair, and flat, rundown shoes. In one hand she carried what looked like a small duffel bag.

Oh God, oh no, Jansen thought. *Not this, not this, not again.*

The Russian had seen her too. Even at this distance Jansen clearly heard him shouting in Russian, and then in German. But she kept coming on, and suddenly Jansen understood that she was a ghost. He had never seen one before, but there was no doubt in his mind.

As the woman came even with Gavrilenko's tower she began to run, racing toward the Wall. Halfway there a battery of searchlights came on, so bright they were blinding to Jansen's dark-adjusted eyes. *Automatic, self-activated, never did figure where the trip must be. Maybe they moved it around, be just like them...*

And then the firing started.

He couldn't tell where it was coming from: there were no snipers shooting from jeeps or gun-trucks, and in the guard tower there was only the Russian—yelling and screaming, yes, but without any weapon in his hands. Yet real bullets were somehow crackling and spitting all around the woman's churning legs, kicking up little spouts in the neatly-raked gravel like pettish children scuffling their feet. It wasn't happening exactly as it had happened, though. Back then there had been alarms, VoPos and

West Berliners shouting—Harding too, right in Jansen's ear—dogs barking, engines revving, the mixed sounds of panic and hope and adrenaline-spiked fear. Here, after Gavrilenko stopped shouting, there was only the spattering echo of gunfire as the woman dodged left and right between the concrete obstacles. *I couldn't have done anything.*

I couldn't!

The two paired hooks of a ship's ladder sailed over the Wall between two of the iron Ys, under the barbed wire, catching among the irregular concrete blocks and mortar. On the other side, out of his sight, the ghost pulled the ladder taut—Jansen could see the hooks shift, almost coming loose before catching. The woman climbed rapidly: in another moment her head topped the Wall, and she pulled a pair of clippers from her waistband and swiftly opened a gap in the barbed wire barrier. Then she braced herself with her hands and looked directly into Jansen's eyes.

She was twenty-three, or so he'd been told, though at the time he had thought she looked older. Now she seemed incredibly young to him, younger than Arl, even, but her plain little face was as gray as the Wall, and her eyes were an inexpressive pale-blue. They were not in the least accusatory or reproachful, but once they had hold of Jansen, he could not look away. He wanted to speak, to explain, to apologize, but that was impossible. The nameless dead woman held him with eyes that neither glittered nor burned, nor even judged him, but would not let go. Jansen stood as motionless as she, squeezing the window frame so hard that he lost feeling in his fingers.

Then a single shot cracked his heart and the woman was suddenly slammed forward, her body twisting so that she fell across the top of the Wall, her left foot kicking one of the ladder hooks loose. She rolled partway onto her side, lifting her head for a moment, and again he saw her eyes. When they finally closed and freed him, he began to cry silently.

How long he stood weeping, he couldn't say. Gavrilenko did not call out to him across the gap, and there were no other sounds anywhere in the world. Jansen was still staring at the body on the Wall when—exactly as though a movie were being run in reverse—the dead woman sat up, crawled backwards to the ladder, reattached the dangling hook, and began descending as she had come. This time she did not look at him at all, and as her head dropped almost out of view the barbed wire knitted itself together.

He watched for a time, but she did not reappear.

The receiver felt as heavy as a barbell when he finally lifted the telephone. He could hear Gavrilenko breathing hoarsely on the line, waiting for him. "The Friedrichstrasse," Jansen said. "Checkpoint Charlie. I'll meet you there."

It had never taken Specialist 4 Henry Jansen—twenty years old, of the 385th Military Police Battalion, specially attached to the 287th Military Police Company—more than eight minutes to cover the four and a half blocks from the Axel-Springer-Strasse observation post to Checkpoint Charlie. The sixty-six-year-old Jansen, kidnapped by the past and all but completely disoriented, took longer, partly because of his knee, but mostly due to mounting fear and bewilderment. The guillotine dark was constantly visible over the Wall that flanked him on his right, and to his left it waited at the end of every side street. Passing the T-intersections he couldn't help but stop and stare.

He consciously attempted to hold his shoulders as straight and swaggering as those of that young MP from Wurtsboro, but despite the effort his head kept lowering between his shoulders, like a bull trying to catch up with the dancing *banderilleros,* jabbing their maddening darts into him from all sides. The further he went into this unreal slice of an empty Berlin, the deeper the *banderillas* seemed to drive into his weary spirit.

I couldn't have helped her. I couldn't have helped, I couldn't... She lay there two hours, she bled to death right in front of me, and there wasn't anything I could do. Harding wouldn't let me go to her, anyway, and he outranked me.

But that thought didn't ease him, no more than it ever had. Why should he expect it to help now, in this false place and timeless time, this cage of memories?

By the time he reached Checkpoint Charlie he was sweating coldly, though not from exertion.

The checkpoint was a long, low shack set in the middle of the Friedrichstrasse, with a barrier of stacked sandbags arrayed facing the "Worker and Farmer Paradise" gate on the East German side. Just past the shack he could see the *imbiss* stand where he and his buddies had grabbed coffee, sodas, and sandwiches while on duty, and also the familiar hulk of a massive apartment building, abandoned and empty both then and now.

Someone was standing at the checkpoint, thoughtfully studying the guard shack, but it was not Gavrilenko. Jansen could tell that even from a distance. This stranger was a tall man with thinning blonde hair—probably American, to judge by his neat but casual dress—who looked to be in his middle to late forties. When the man turned and caught sight of Jansen he looked first utterly astonished, and then profoundly grateful to see another human being. He hurried forward, actually laughing with relief. "Well, thank *God*. I'd just about come to believe I was the only living creature in Berlin! Glad to see there's two of us."

He had the faintest of German accents, hiding shyly under the broad, flat vowels of the Midwest. When he got to Jansen he put out a hand, which Jansen took somewhat cautiously.

"Hi," the tall man said. "My name's Ben. Ben Richter."

"I'm Henry Jansen." He let go of Richter's hand. "This isn't Berlin, though. It's not anywhere."

"No," the stranger agreed. "But it's not a dream, either. I know it's not a dream." He peered closely and anxiously into Jansen's face. "Do you have *any* idea what's happened to us?"

"Don't fall asleep in a Planned Parenthood clinic, I'll tell you that much," Jansen said. "That's where I was."

"I was trying *not* to fall asleep," Richter answered. "I was driving home from a business meeting, and my eyelids kept dropping shut. Just a few seconds at a time, but it's terrifying, the way your head suddenly snaps awake, and you *know* you're just about to crash into someone. Couldn't figure it out. I wasn't tired when I started out, got plenty of rest the night before. Weird." He seemed suddenly alarmed. "Do you think my car just went on, with no driver?"

Jansen felt his face grow cold, almost numb. "Couldn't tell you." After a pause, he added, "Ben, was it?"

"Actually, it's Bernd, but everyone's always called me Ben, since I started school. Kids just decide, don't they?"

Jansen said, "I knew somebody named Richter when I was in junior high. You got any relatives in Wurtsboro, New York?"

The tall man laughed slightly. "I don't know if I've got any relatives *anywhere.* Not in the States, for sure."

"Forget it. Guess I'm just looking for connections."

Richter grinned. "Not exactly surprising, given the circumstances."

"We're not alone," Jansen told him. "There's at least one more of us, anyway, a Russian. Name's Gavrilenko. We spotted each other across the Wall. He was supposed to meet me here—I don't know what's keeping him." After a moment, he added, "Don't know how *he* got here; I mean, if he was asleep or not."

Richter asked hesitantly, "Did you and your friend—uh, the Russian— did you have any luck figuring this out?"

Jansen thought of the running dead woman, and the barbed wire mending itself. Even now some things were too crazy for him to say straight out.

"It has to be something to do with the Wall. Right? Has to. I mean, it's what's *here.*" He watched for a reaction, but saw none. "And Gavrilenko and me, we were both on the Wall a couple of years after it went up. Nineteen sixty-three, sixty-four—kids, both of us. He was a guard over there, I was an MP over here. Never got above Specialist 4, so I did some of everything. Pulled patrol, hauling drunk GIs out of bars, clubs, like that. A little checkpoint duty right here"—he gestured around him—"but mostly I was in an observation post over on the Axel-Springer-Strasse. That's how we knew each other back then, two strangers waving across the Wall in the mornings." He realized that he was now talking much too fast, and consciously slowed his speech. "Long ago, all that crap. You wouldn't be interested—you weren't even born then."

"Yes, I was," Richter said quietly. He said nothing more for a few moments, studying Jansen out of chestnut-brown eyes set in an angular, thoughtful face. "There's a Marriott there now, you know, at that corner. In the real world, I mean. Right where the Wall was."

"How do you know that?"

"I've stayed there. My wife's German, so we visit. And I've got a little business going." He looked around slowly, then shrugged. "Weird. Only seen it like this in pictures. Maybe you can tell me about it?"

Jansen blinked. "Tell you about *what?*"

"Berlin in those days. When you were a kid MP—probably a couple of years out of high school, right?" He did not wait for Jansen's answering nod. "See, I was born in Berlin, but I wasn't raised here. Didn't come back until the Wall fell in '89—just felt I had to, somehow—and that's how I met Annaliese." The smile was simultaneously proud and tender. "We live in St. Paul. Three boys, a girl, and an Irish setter. I mean, how bourgeois American can you get?"

"Wouldn't know," Jansen said. "Wish I knew what's keeping Gavrilenko."

"Listen, let's sit down somewhere, okay? While we wait for your Russian friend."

Richter walked around the guard shack and hoisted himself up onto the top row of sandbags. Jansen followed him, and he and Richter sat with their legs dangling, looking straight ahead, both of them unconsciously kicking their heels against the sandbags' brown canvas. The tall man was the first to speak. "Hard to believe these were for real. Not exactly a lot of protection."

"Better than nothing," Jansen said. "I wasn't in the Army then, but in October of '61, a few months after the Wall went up, there was an all-day standoff right here between our guys—40th Armor, 6th Infantry—and about thirty Russian tanks. See, we were set to show them that we could still drive anywhere we wanted in the GDR, and they were going to show *us* that those days were *over*. And you better believe there were dogfaces crouching behind these same sandbags, locked and loaded and ready to start World War Three, just say the word. I saw the pictures in the Wurtsboro paper."

Richter shrugged. "I've read about the standoff. Seems a little ridiculous, frankly. Awful lot of chestbeating for something that didn't even last a day."

"True. But it *could* have been worse. Ask me, the Russkies came out on top, any way you slice it—from that point on they handed out a lot of shit here, every crossing, and it may have been small shit, but we couldn't give it back since we had orders to play nice. Well...not all of them. That's not fair. Mainly it was the generals who were trouble, the big ones who gave the orders and made asses of themselves when they'd come into West Berlin. The men were okay. Russkies, Krauts, they were okay. Even some of the VoPos."

"Ah. The *Volkspolizei*."

"Just like us MPs, only with more training and a *lot* more firepower." Jansen chuckled in his throat. "We had a big snowball fight with a bunch of VoPos one time." He paused, reflecting. "Couldn't make a decent snowball for shit, most of them. Always wondered about that."

Richter cocked his head slightly to the side, considering Jansen meditatively. "So you actually had fun, too. It wasn't all confrontations with tanks and going into bars after drunken soldiers."

"Trick was to keep from staying *in* the bars *with* the drunken soldiers," Jansen told him. "The city was booming with bars, with clubs, a couple new ones opening every week. Some you'd go to for the beer, some for the great music—one time I heard Nat King Cole and Les Paul and Mary Ford on the same night. Two-buck tickets! Some places, you'd take a young lady, some others you'd go to *find* a young lady. Yeah, we had a lot of fun in Berlin. Nineteen-, twenty-year-old kids with guns and money, never been away from home before, never drunk anything stronger than Pabst? We had fun."

Jansen studied Richter. The man's expression was an odd mixture of wistfulness and something deeper, something impatient beyond his interest in Jansen's surfacing memories. For his part, Jansen had not talked this much to anyone in a very long while, and he'd never shared these stories, not even with Elly or the kids. Sharing would have meant deliberately remembering everything, which even the drinking couldn't deal with. Here, though, that self-imposed restriction was as pointless as the rest of it.

"There was a game we used to play," he said. "Worked best in the winter too, only we didn't need snow for this one, we needed ice." He pointed ahead of them, toward a broad white line painted on the ground. "That's the border, near as anybody could figure. Ground got good and icy, you'd take a run and throw yourself down, and *slide*, like you're sliding into a base, only you're sliding right into the GDR." He laughed outright at the memory. "Then you'd get up and run right back across the line, safe in the good old American Sector. The Krauts used to watch us and just laugh themselves silly."

Richter said musingly, almost to himself, "All those good times...and all the things going on just under the surface." Jansen frowned, not understanding. Richter went on. "More than a hundred thousand people tried to escape into West Berlin from East Germany in the twenty-eight years the Wall sealed it off. Did you know that, Henry?"

"Knew it was a lot," Jansen said. "Didn't know it was that many—thought the big rush was all before the Wall."

"It was. But another hundred thousand, afterward. Most went to jail.

Maybe five thousand made it through. And a lot died. But you were here. You know that."

Her dark hair, her pale-blue eyes, the little sound she made at the last, dying...

"Yeah. I do."

Richter had turned away, looking toward the point where the blackness slashed down forever on the East German apartment buildings. But his voice was clear and precise as he said, "Different organizations have different estimates. When the Wall fell, when Germany was reunited, the East German state wasn't in any hurry to release records that made them look like the killers they were. We've had to build up a database one case at a time, literally. One escape attempt at a time. One body at a time. Counting the heart attacks, the wounds that turned fatal on the other side of the Wall, the ones who just disappeared forever, the babies smothered trying to keep them quiet. Officially—you check the encyclopedia articles, the tourist handouts—only 136 people died. But we're figuring twelve hundred, minimum. Not that we'll ever be able to prove half of them." His voice was calm and almost expressionless, utterly dispassionate.

"We," Jansen said. "Who's *we?"*

Richter laughed suddenly, warmly, with a touch of embarrassment as faint as his accent. "I'm sorry. I forget not everyone is as obsessed with this as I am. *We* is the August 13 Society—I do fundraising for them in the States, and volunteer work for them when I'm here...I mean, *there.* Real Berlin. We're actually trying to document every case where people died trying to cross, not just the Wall, but the entire East-West border—to memorialize them, make them real for everybody. So they won't be forgotten again."

Jansen nodded, but did not respond.

Richter said presently, "What I can't figure out is the connection between all three of us—you and me and our absent Russian. Before you showed up I thought I'd driven into a rail, that maybe I was dead and this was Hell; or else maybe I'd stroked out and was in a coma somewhere while my imagination played really bad games with me. But those two possibilities would exclude you, so cross them off the whiteboard...which leaves nothing. I've never before met either one of you, and you were both long gone from Berlin by the time I came back. So what's the link?"

"What's if it's just...I don't know, random. Coincidence."

"I don't buy that. I'm a mathematician, Henry. Anyway I *was* a mathematician, before I put together my little software company. This place may be impossible, but the odds against a common pattern when two of the three of us have an obvious connection? Maybe not totally impossible...let's just say *highly* unlikely."

Jansen said, "We sort of have the Wall in common. But it isn't the same. You obviously know a lot about it, what with this Society thing you do. But it's not like you ever served here. You didn't live with it every day, like us. You weren't ever *on* the Wall—"

"No," Richter agreed. "I wasn't."

To Jansen's eye, Richter seemed suddenly tense and hesitant, like someone trying to avoid making up his mind.

"Well," Jansen spoke up. "What is it? You going to shoot that bird or let it fly?"

The tall man nodded. "Interesting choice of words."

"My stupid mouth is half the reason I'm divorced. What'd I say this time?"

Richter hopped off the sandbags and walked a few steps before answering. When he did, his voice was dry and tight. "My mother was a Berliner."

"Yeah, you said you were born here. So?"

"*East* Berlin, Henry. She died on the Wall."

Jansen wanted to run again, like before, but his legs wouldn't get him down off the barrier. If he couldn't run, maybe he could scream?

Not your hell, maybe, you poor bastard. Definitely mine.

When he finally found words, they surprised him. "You don't sound like you're sure."

Richter turned and looked at him oddly. Jansen wondered if something unheard in his voice had given him away. He was about to speak again when the tall man finally answered.

"The records are all scrambled—when there are records at all—and they mostly don't have names in them, just scraps of facts and description. An address here, an occupation there, a set of initials, shorthand reports of a thousand disconnected, meaningless conversations...it's a jigsaw puzzle with most of the pieces missing. I've been digging through the archives for a long time, learning how to read what's there *and* what's been omitted." His mouth tightened. "She died on the Wall, all right. The pieces of the picture are there."

"But you aren't certain."

"If you're asking me whether I have the *Stasi*-stamped file folder to prove it, no." Bitterness colored Richter's voice, and something Jansen couldn't begin to put a name to. He watched as the tall man stared fiercely at the ragged fringe of East German buildings that were visible from here.

"I never knew her," Richter continued. "My step-parents were friends with my mother, and they brought me with them when they got out of East Germany in 1960. It was her idea. She wasn't well—pregnancy and childbirth had been rough—and anyway she knew it would be easier for them, because they'd had a baby who died and they still had the right papers. The idea was that my mother would make it out on her own when she got better, and we'd all be in America together." His faint smile was small and young. "Only they built the Wall, and things didn't work out. She never showed up. One letter made it: nothing else. The Bruckners raised me on their own, in Wisconsin. They were good people. I can't complain."

"What about your father? Where the hell was he?" Unsummoned, there was a vision of Arl in Jansen's head, crying into Elly's arms because Larry had left without so much as a note two days after the little pink dot on the dipstick changed everything.

"Apparently I'm the by-product of a little too much Pilsner at a college party. She never told anyone his name, not even the Bruckners, not even with all the pressure of being nineteen and pregnant in a police state where social pressure favored abortion. All I know about *der fehlende vater* is that he must have been tall and blonde, because according to my step-parents nobody in my mother's family was. It had to come from somewhere."

The woman at the Wall. Got to be his mother. Goddamit, goddamit, tell him what you saw, you stupid fucking coward...but maybe I don't have to. Maybe, maybe if I just shut up he'll talk about something else.

Where the hell's Gavrilenko?

At the same moment, Richter said "Enough with my sob story. I seriously don't think your Russian's coming. Let's go find him." He started off without looking back.

"Hold up," Jansen said, easing down off the sandbags. His knee had stiffened while he was sitting. "Old guy, here. Anyway, maybe we shouldn't be in such a hurry."

Richter stopped and looked at him quizzically. "Why not?"

Tell him you saw his mother. Tell him you saw her die. Twice.

"No reason." Jansen stared into Richter's eyes. How could he have missed how much they looked like hers? "It's just...what if we take a different route than he does, coming here, and we miss each other?"

"Then we'll come back. Anyway, there's not a whole lot of *there* over there. Come on," Richter said, and this time his grin was a young boy's. "It's not icy, but I bet we can imagine we're sliding across the line."

The Wall on this side ran behind houses that looked like an abandoned stage or movie set: if the west side looked as though every inhabitant had suddenly left town, but might return at any second, here the air of a forced and permanent evacuation was glaringly inescapable. Doors and windows were not merely boarded over, but bricked up as well; many buildings had been demolished, and the rubble—often topped with barbed wire—left in place, to block any passage to the Wall. There were warnings, genuine or not, of minefields—Richter translated the signs for Jansen—and the whole effect was of desertion and neglect. The two men walked close together, automatically speaking in low voices and moving at a pace tailored to accommodate Jansen's slower steps.

Chickenshit. You could walk faster. You're just afraid of getting there.

Jansen asked presently, "You got into it, this August thing, because of your mom?" But Richter shook his head.

"Not exactly, not the way you mean. My step-parents wanted me to grow up to be a good American, so I was assimilated as hell. They told me about my mom—her name was Zinzi, by the way—but not much else, not until I was older. I definitely had the American habit of not thinking about the past very much, and certainly not some faraway European past that might as well have been in an old library book, as far as I was concerned. My head was all forward, all the time. I went to a good college, studied math and computer programming, got naturalized, taught for a while. I was an assistant professor of Mathematics at the University of Wisconsin when I came to Berlin to drink dark beer and knock down my own piece of the Wall and wound up meeting Annaliese instead. Hah. Hey, I never asked—you married?"

"Already told you I was divorced. Twice, actually."

"Oh. Sorry."

"Don't be. Just the ways things are." Jansen felt his heart thudding harder in his chest. "My first ex used to say I was a coconut in a world of bananas. I can hurt people just bumping into them."

"Colorful. Any kids?"

"Two daughters. They hate my guts too, but the pregnant one hates me worse. So there's a bright spot."

Richter stopped walking and turned to face Jansen. "Even if things righteously suck with your kids, I'm sure you remember when they were little. So maybe you'll get this. When Jacob—my son—when Jacob turned six months old, the same age I was when I was brought to America...I remember, I looked down at him in my arms, burping bubbles and trying to eat my shirt buttons, and I tried to imagine what Zinzi Richter would have said if she could have seen him, her first grandchild. And I thought how lucky I was to be able to tell him everything my step-parents had told me about her, even if it wasn't all that much. Then I started thinking about all the people who wouldn't ever know what happened to their grandparents or their parents, and I'd read about the August 13 Society, and one thing led to another. I'd started up my company by then—we do case-management software for big legal firms—and our code was pretty useful for what the Society does, so I had an in. And here I am." He smiled crookedly, spreading his hands.

"Makes sense," Jansen said.

"You should tell Jacob that. He thinks I'm crazy. My mother really is just a page in a scrapbook to him. He's going to be fifteen next June, and what *he* likes about coming over here is that he's tall enough now to get away with telling the local girls he's really seventeen."

They started on again, both of them unconsciously keeping to the right side of the road, away from the darkness they could see on the other side of the decayed and empty buildings. To Jansen it definitely seemed closer here, which bothered him. He thought of the suddenly open door back on the Axel-Springer-Strasse, and the words *herding us* passed through his mind.

Richter said, "You can tell I'm nervous, because I'm talking too much."

That surprised Jansen. "You don't *act* nervous."

"Quaking in my Nikes. Not the slightest sign of danger since I showed up here, but this place is really starting to creep me out. Hence the talking."

"So talk," Jansen said firmly. "Tell me more about your kids."

"I'd rather listen. Tell me what you do."

Jansen grunted, waved the question away.

"No, seriously."

"Nothing important. I remodel stuff. Kitchens and bathrooms, mostly. One-man gang, hire extra help when I have to. Been doing it more or less since I left the Army."

"That's good work," Richter said. "You do your job, and then when you're finished, when you look at what you've done, you get to see that you've made something better, made it work, made it beautiful. There's pride in that. You're a lucky man."

"Gavrilenko called me that too," Jansen said slowly. "I don't think I'm so fucking lucky." Richter regarded him curiously. Jansen said, "I'm good with my hands, with wood and tile and plastic piping, but that's it. Sinks and toilets, cabinets and countertops? Sure. People? Forget it. My exes, my kids, they're all right about me. Since I got back from Germany, I can't think of one damn thing that's gone right, except work. Not one damn thing in forty years."

Richter said, "It's the Wall." Jansen looked up in surprise. "People I work with—former refugees, their families—they tell a story that one guy who didn't make it over put a curse on the Wall with his dying breath. He made it so even if you escape, even with the Wall down and gone, there's still a curse that follows you in your life. Because you got out and he didn't."

Jansen thought *nobody ever gets out*. But what he said was, "No offense, but that's bullshit. Anyway, I didn't have anything to escape from. I did my time, got rotated to Stuttgart and then stateside. Period."

They walked a little way further in silence before Richter continued. "Maybe. But people tell stories like that because they mean something. And you said yourself that your troubles started here. It wasn't all snowball fights, Henry."

"Crap. I was a kid."

"Which makes it better how?" Richter's tone had shifted, the hint of impatience becoming more pronounced. "Jesus Christ, man, you *know* I've been through the East German records fifty-seven times. I'm the guy with the damn database. So why are you dancing with me like this? Even on the official record there are at least three or four deaths that correlate with the time you must have been here. Fechter, he's the most famous, but there were others. And at least twenty, thirty more the Society is researching. Are you telling me none of that ever touched you, that you never saw anything? If not, then why the hell are you here? *What's our connection?*"

Jansen was shaking his head before Richter was halfway finished. "That's not it! It *can't* be it."

"*What* can't be it?"

Jansen started to turn away, but Richter squared off on him. The tall man's hands came down on Jansen's shoulders, and they were bigger hands than Jansen had noticed. He said nothing. He only waited.

Oh, God.

Jansen said tonelessly, "You can't put this on me."

"I didn't," Richter answered. "But you can take it off."

"Shit!" For just a moment Jansen couldn't breathe.

Richter's eyes were hot behind a face suddenly flattened into an unyielding mask. "I'm not an idiot. You've been wanting to tell me something since we were back at the sandbags. Spill."

"I—I don't know who it was. Just some girl, some woman...I never knew her name." Jansen heard the sirens and shouting, the gunfire; only by Richter's lack of reaction did he understand that the blaring cacophony was all in his head. "But I'll never forget what happened. Fuck, I still dream it."

Richter nodded him on.

"It was 1963. I was almost out, just screwing around on duty in the observation post, joking with Harding about making a midnight run to clip a little barbed wire off as a souvenir, something to take home with me. Then his eyes went all spooky and he said 'Fuck me, Lord,' just like that, quiet as if we were in a library...and I saw what he was seeing. This woman—"

"Wait a sec. That was the Axel-Springer-Strasse OP?"

Jansen nodded.

Richter bored in. "July or November?"

"July. I wasn't here in November."

"Tell me what she looked like."

Jansen felt himself snapping. "Don't make me do this!"

"*Tell* me."

"You have to hear me say it? It was your mother! Of *course* it was your mother. She had your goddamn eyes, you bastard, and she came out of nowhere on the far side of the Death Strip, and maybe she would have made it if she were a little faster, or maybe she wouldn't, I don't know, I only know it was like they were *playing* with her, like they could have cut her down at any time, but they waited until she was halfway over the top. Then somebody took her out with a single shot and she lay there on top of the wall for two hours, *two fucking hours,* bleeding out, never making a sound until the end, and the whole time I...the whole time..."

He turned his head, unable to bear looking into Richter's face.

"I wanted to go to her. Harding wouldn't let me. I did call the NCOIC and scream for a doctor, for help, for somebody, but nobody came. Nobody came. It was just me and Harding, and he wouldn't look. But for the whole two hours I did. I saw her die."

Richter's hands closed once, briefly. They seemed to sink past flesh and muscle to leave their fingerprints in his bones; yet, strangely, Jansen felt no pain at all. When Richter let go and lifted them away, something iron went with them that Jansen never tried to name.

"Yes," Richter said without expression. "I thought that might have been the one." He turned away.

"That's not all," Jansen said to the tall man's stiffened back.

Richter slowed down, but didn't stop.

"Here's the thing." Jansen had to raise his voice as the other man moved away. "You fell asleep in your car, and you woke up here in this theater set, but you didn't get to see the play. Me, I had to watch it all over again. So did Gavrilenko, from his guard tower. The run, the bullets, her death on top of the Wall. Everything. Do you hear me? *I saw your mother die all over again...* and when it was over I saw her climb back down, just like she was getting ready for another show. *That's* why Gavrilenko and I were supposed to meet. I don't know why I'm here, I swear to God I don't, but whatever I've done wrong in my life I can't possibly deserve having to see that again—and you don't want to see it either. Trust me on that!"

Richter stood still and said nothing for what felt to Jansen like a very long time, but which was certainly only seconds. Then he heard Zinzi Richter's son say, simply, "Huh," and had to hurry to catch up with the tall man as he walked, with quickening strides, toward the darkness.

The guard tower had looked considerably more impressive and ominous from a dingy room in a crumbling apartment house across from the Wall than it did at close range. At once splintery-new and yet already rickety, it had far more of an agricultural air than a military one, looking somewhere between a flattened silo and a hayloft. Jansen felt that there should have been a weathervane on its squared-off roof.

Richter stopped in his tracks so suddenly that Jansen bumped into his back before he could halt himself. At the foot of the tower stairs stood the ghost of Zinzi Richter.

Ashen, slender, with dark auburn hair limp against her skull, as though with sweat, she paid absolutely no attention either to Jansen or to her staring son. All her concentration was directed up the single flight of rusted metal steps to the doorway where a big old man stood hugging himself as he rocked erratically against the doorframe. Zinzi Richter made no attempt to go up to him, but simply stood waiting at the foot of the stair.

"That's her," Richter whispered. "The Bruckners had one photo. Oh my God."

As though she had put on her Sunday best for the occasion, the ghost looked as clear and solid as any human being whose heart still jumped in the cage of her ribs, still ordered blood out to her fingertips and back through her throat and her thighs. Richter took a step toward her, but this time it was Jansen's hand clamping hard on his arm. Jansen said softly, "Wait. She's here for *him*."

Through binoculars—the closest acquaintance he had ever had with Leonid Leonidovich Gavrilenko over the Wall—Jansen had always seen the Russian as bull-featured and powerfully built, with an undomesticated mass of heavy black hair that stood up crazily on either side of his broad, high-boned face when he pulled off his knit woolen cap. The man he saw now had none of that force, nothing of that implicit swagger: he only slumped against the door frame, his lips moving as though in prayer. Jansen thought, *He's old;*

and then, *No, I'm old, and I don't look like that. What's happened to him?*

"That's why he didn't come to the checkpoint. He can't come down," Jansen said to Richter. "*She's* there, and he's afraid of her."

Richter ignored him. He pulled away from Jansen's grip and approached the ghost of Zinzi Richter, plainly trying not to run to her. He said, "Mother, it's me, I'm your son. I'm Bernd." He tried to take her hands in his, but she did not move, or look at him, or respond in any way. She stayed where she was, looking up the stair at Gavrilenko.

Jansen said, "Ben." A strange calmness was upon him, as though for the first time in his life he actually knew what to do. He said, "Ben, we have to go up there."

Richter turned to him, so determinedly *not* crying that Jansen felt tears starting in his own eyes. "I can touch her—I didn't know you could touch ghosts. But she doesn't see me, she doesn't even know I'm here. I don't understand."

"She's waiting for Gavrilenko," Jansen said. "She'll wait forever, if she has to. You want to find out what all this is about, we have to bring him to her. Now."

The last word snapped out in a tone that surprised him; he hardly recognized his own voice. But it seemed to help Ben, who managed to get hold of himself and follow Jansen as the older man started up the guard tower stairs. *Well, I did make it to corporal before it was all over. Might have made sergeant if I'd stayed in. Things I could have been.* Jansen looked back once at the ghost. She had not stirred at all from her position, nor changed the direction of her gaze. *Holy shit, the Russian's treed, is what it is. She's got him treed.* He could not control a swift shiver.

Near the top of the stair he looked away from the tower and saw the darkness closing in, pitilessly paring away everything that was not itself.

The guardroom door was open. Gavrilenko backed away as Jansen and Richter came in, still seemingly holding himself together with both arms. In a rough, throaty grumble, a ghost itself of the striding peasant vigor Jansen had heard over the phone, the Russian said, "Unavoidably detained, Rawhide. Trouble on the range, I am afraid."

"You have to come down to her, Gavrilenko," Jansen said. "It's time."

"Is time, is time." Something of the jovial telephone derision flickered in the Russian's gruff voice. "Now you are sounding like a priest come to walk me to firing squad. No, Rawhide, I do not go with you. I stay here until she goes away. I can stay here." He rose shakily to his full height, arms firmly folded across his chest.

"Leonid," Jansen said. "That woman down there—the man with me is her son. Talk to him."

Gavrilenko turned to face Richter. His still-powerful face had gone grayish-white, making the beard stubble stand out starkly, like the last stalks of a gleaned-over wheat field.

"Her son..." Gavrilenko did not move, nor take his eyes from Richter's face for a long moment; then, to Jansen's astonishment, he began to smile. His teeth were remarkably white, unusual for an East European of his generation. He drew a short breath and recited, in the classic half-chanting Russian style, "*After the first death, there is no other.* Mr. Dylan Thomas, English poet."

When there was no response, Gavrilenko repeated, "*He* understood. Shakespeare, Pushkin, they did not understand so well as Mr. Dylan Thomas." He seemed unable to take his eyes from Richter. He said suddenly, "Your mother—I knew her." The smile drew his lips flat against the good white teeth. "This one—" he jerked a thumb at Jansen—"he only sees her dying, no more. But I...*I* saw her living—she was good at living, Zinzi. Only a short time, we had, but we made of it what we can. *Could*—what we *could*. You see, I forget my English so soon." The wide smile still clung to his lips, fading only slowly, like the shape of a cloud.

Richter's face was also taut, but his eyes remained steady and composed. He said quietly, "You were not my father."

Gavrilenko sighed. It was a long, slow sigh, almost theatrically Russian, and its wordless tone carried the suggestion of sorrow at once too deep to be born, and too hopeless to be worth bothering with. "No, I am not your father—that was some student, she told me, gone off to the West before she even knew she was pregnant. But I could have been. For three weeks, I could have been."

It was not said boastingly or mockingly, but was somehow part of the sigh. Jansen thought about Arl's vanished husband and had to shake free of a sudden spasm of pure rage. "You helped her plan that run, didn't you? Had to be someone who knew the triggers, the timing."

"I do more, Rawhide. I show her the weak places, I show where the big searchlights are, where the VoPos hide—everything I know, she knows." His voice had taken on the same singsong quality as when he quoted the Thomas line. "She had a little money, not so much. I spread it among the VoPos, everybody getting something—so when she runs we are all turning into very bad shots, you understand? No big deal, everybody getting something." He clasped his big hands at the waist, like a child set to recite at school. To Richter he said, "I do all that for Zinzi Richter, for your mother. Because she was funny, and I liked her, you know? Also, I was young."

"Because you were screwing her and taking her money," Richter said harshly. "You used her."

"So? She is using me too." Gavrilenko appeared genuinely indignant. "You think she sleeps with me out of love? *Chort*—she knows what she does, and so did I. She comes to me, straight to bed, down payment, right? Was a bargain, and both kept our word." He laughed abruptly. "Like I said, young."

Jansen said, "Something obviously went wrong."

Gavrilenko was silent for a long time. He did not turn away from them, but he ceased to look directly at Richter, and his glances at Jansen had become defiantly despairing. He said finally, "The Stasi, Stasi, KGB—eyes everywhere, even when you know they have eyes. The day she makes her run...suddenly, no VoPos I recognize, no VoPos I pay money to, whole new crowd. Stasi agents, every one—I know this. What to do? I want to warn her, but I am on duty, they have made sure I have no chance. You understand?" He was glaring at them both now, looking more like an old bull than ever. "You understand? I had no chance!"

After a moment he shrugged, long and deliberately. "Also no choice." Now he clearly forced himself to meet Richter's eyes, and the physical effort was visible on his face. He repeated doggedly, "No choice."

Richter's silence was more than Jansen could bear. He had to speak. "So you shot her. She trusted you, and you killed her."

"*They were watching me!*" It sounded as though Gavrilenko's throat was tearing from the words. "All of them, firing wide, missing and missing, *watching*, looking like this—" he mimicked someone stealing covert side-glances—"waiting for *me* to shoot and miss, so they know I am traitor. Her or me, and what would *you* do, brave Rawhide?" He was breathing like a runner whose strength has ended before his race. "Sweet, funny little Zinzi, nice girl—you tell me what you would do, eh? I wait."

Neither Jansen nor Richter responded, nor did they look at each other. For his part, the constant image in Jansen's mind of Zinzi Richter's doomed attempt to reach her baby kept being replaced by one of his own daughters. Outside the guardroom door, the edged darkness was slicing in closer, while through the window, in a strangely dizzying sweep, he could see back across the Death Strip and the Wall to the apartment where he had spent much of two years staring at this very room.

"I wait," Gavrilenko repeated, and this time it was not a mocking challenge. This time it was soft and urgent, almost plaintive, as though he really did want an answer, was in desperate need of any reply at all. For a third time he said, "I wait to be told what I should have done. Speak, wise Americanski friends."

"That's a comedy word," Jansen said. "Nobody uses that anymore."

Then Richter answered him at last, his words falling like the muffled strokes of an old clock. He said, "Mr. Gavrilenko, I have to thank you. If your guilt were not so great, if you had just been an agent, a VoPo, who shot my mother and went off to lunch, it would never have dragged you here to see her again. It would never have called to Henry's guilt, or to my own guilt for being born, and causing her death...her stupid, stupid, needless death." For those few words there was a sound in his voice like claws on stone, and his hands kept opening and closing at his sides.

"You can't think that," Jansen said. "She could have died the exact same way, even if you hadn't been born. Believe me, you do *not* want to spend your life thinking—"

Richter cut him off. "What I think is not important. We're here, and this has got to be why we're here. What we *do* now is what matters. We go down to my mother, to look into her face. All three of us. This is not a request."

He looked sharply at Jansen, who nodded. But Gavrilenko backed away, shaking his head, saying, "No, *no,* I cannot, will not, *no,* never possible." He wailed and struggled frantically when Jansen and Richter caught hold of his flailing arms and literally dragged him out of the guard room. Old and

ill, half-mad or not—his eyes were rolling as wildly as those of a terrified
stallion—he was still stronger than either of them alone, and their cramped
passage down the guard tower's stairway was a battle. Jansen had a bloody
nose by the time they had the Russian near ground-level, and Richter's shirt
was splitting down the back seam. Through it all, Gavrilenko wailed and
cursed in an absurd and piteous mix of Russian, German, and English, going
utterly limp at the last, which meant hauling him the final few steps like a
side of beef or bale of hay, until they were finally able to dump him at Zinzi
Richter's feet and step back, breathless and exhausted.

The ghost saw them.

On her plain, unremarkable little face the joy of Richter's presence, his
existence—the *fact* of him—leaped up like a flame in dry grass. Seeing this
recognition, the tall man took her hands between his, bowed over them,
and began to cry, almost soundlessly. She drew her hands free and held him
close; but over his shoulder her eyes met Jansen's, and he actually staggered
back a pace, shaken by the depth of the sorrow and sympathy—sorrow
specifically for him—that he read there. He heard himself saying aloud, in
absurd embarrassment, "Hey, it hasn't been as bad as all that. Really." But it
had been, it had been, and she knew.

Then she gently released her son, and knelt down beside Gavrilenko,
where he lay on his face, hands covering his eyes. With her own hands on
his upper arms, she silently coaxed him to face her. Gavrilenko screamed
once—not loudly, but in a tone of pure terror, and of resignation to terror as
well, like a rabbit unresisting in the clutches of a horned owl. He scrambled
to a sitting position, his hands now flat on the ground beside him, face dazed
and alien. The ghost commanded his eyes as she had Jansen's—how long
ago?—holding them in thrall to her own, seeing through them and past
them, down into uttermost Gavrilenko, his body shaking with the need to
hide his eyes again but unable to do so. He whimpered now and then; and
still clung to himself.

By and by he began to speak. "After first death, really is no other. You and
me, Henry—you remember us? Two tired, lonely, nervous boys in uniform,
pretending to be men, doing job..." He rose slowly to his feet. "I kill so many
people since then—you know? Easy, really. *Easy.* Killings, I am telling you
honestly, but no *deaths*...not after her." He did meet Zinzi Richter's quiet eyes

then, though again Jansen saw the physical shock spread through his body. He said, "Different, you understand?"

Jansen asked, "You stayed in the army? No...what, you were KGB?"

"Oh, please, no KGB anymore," Gavrilenko reproved him. "In new democratic Russia, FSB—execute you with new democratic pistol. No, Henry, I did my time in private enterprise. Big capitalist, all American values, even before it was common. You would be proud."

"The Mafia." Richter's voice was tight and thick, for all its evenness. "You worked for the Russian Mafia. You killed people for them."

Gavrilenko grinned at him like a skull. "Kill for the Mafia, kill for Mother Russia—what difference? I was an independent contractor, just like American plumber." He nodded toward Jansen. "I went here, I went there, fix the sink, the toilet, go home, rest tired feet, watch the TV." He spoke directly to Zinzi Richter now, to no one else in the world. He said, "This is your blessing. You made me so."

Something he couldn't guess at made Jansen look away, and he fancied that he could actually see the darkness moving in around them if he watched it closely enough. From where they stood, nothing was visible now but the tower, the Wall in one direction, and the dark wall itself in the other...and after studying it, when he looked again on Gavrilenko he saw something that he could not have been expected to recognize, yet felt he should have seen from the moment he and Richter had entered the guardroom. With a sudden surge of wonder and pity, he whispered, "Leonid. You're like her..." He was trembling, and it was hard to get words out, or to remember what words were.

Gavrilenko shook his head slowly, heavily. "Not like her. She is long dead, forever young, forever innocent. While Leonid Leonidovich Nikolai Gavrilenko lies in Petersburg hospital, Walther PPK bullet in coward's brain." He grimaced in bitter disgust. "So many heads, so many bullets, one to a customer...only Gavrilenko, pig-drunk, old, sick, shaking with fear, cannot even kill himself decently...coward, coward, pathetic..." There were a few more words, all Russian.

The ghost of Zinzi Richter spoke then, without making a sound. Picking up her blue duffel bag, she looked at the three of them and mouthed a single word, rounding it out with great care and precision. Jansen could not read her lips, but Richter nodded. His mother gestured broadly, intensely with her free arm: pointing first toward the crouching, stalking darkness, then toward the Wall, unmistakably inviting them all to run with her while there was still time. She mouthed the silent word a second time.

Jansen and Richter both sensed Gavrilenko's decision before he even turned. They clutched at his arms, but he broke free with a frantic, wordless cry and dashed away from them, lunging and stumbling back toward the East Germany of their memories. Richter, quicker off the mark than Jansen, almost caught him at the inner wall; astonishingly, the old Russian hurled himself at it like a gymnast, leaping to catch the top, and was up and over it and straight into the darkness without hesitating. He vanished instantly, like a match-flame blown out, leaving no sound or glance behind him.

Richter stopped, staring at the edge.

Jansen joined him, and they stood together in silence for some minutes. The darkness, if it did not retreat, at least advanced no further. Jansen said finally, "You really think it was him that brought us here? It wasn't your mother?"

"I have no idea," Richter said, turning away from the void. "Maybe we all did it."

Jansen looked at the ghost of Zinzi Richter, waiting for them by the guard tower, forming for a third time the word he could not understand. "What *is* that?" he demanded of Richter. "What's that she's saying?"

Richter smiled. "*Freiheit*. German for *freedom*."

Abruptly Zinzi Richter turned and began to run, heading once again for the Death Strip, and Richter ran after her, his face as bright and determined as the face of any small boy racing with his mother. Jansen came panting in the rear, no better conditioned than the average sixty-six-year-old kitchen remodeler, but resolved not to be left behind in this place, to find his way back to a maternity clinic in Klamath Falls, Oregon. *Arl...Arl...I'll be right there...*

The spotlights came on, and the gunfire began.

Crossing the Death Strip, Jansen placed his feet exactly in Zinzi Richter's tracks, as her son was doing, and hunched down as low as he could, even as the rifle shots kicked up gravel close enough to sting his face and twitch at his shirt. He tried to shut the awareness out of his consciousness. *Real bullets? Memories of bullets? Ghost bullets, fired by ghosts back in 1963—God!* And then, despite a sudden blossoming fear of dying where he didn't belong, a single thought consumed him. *It's not enough to follow. I've got to get there first.*

Just as Gavrilenko's old legs and big old hands had taken him over the inner wall without assistance, so Jansen's legs, when called upon, somehow responded with speed that did not belong to him, and never had. He passed up a surprised Richter and forcefully crowded past Zinzi Richter as she set her ladder's hooks, stopping only long enough to pull the wire cutters from her duffel before starting to climb. Up the shaking rungs, atop the Wall, he worked faster than she could have, snapping wires real enough to tear his face and hands in half a dozen places. Then they were there with him, the mother and the son, and he swept them before him through the gap he had created, holding their hands as they eased themselves over the other side. He turned his back on the gunfire, covering both his charges with the width of his own torso, breath pulled deep into his lungs as if he could somehow expand to shield not just these two, but everything in the world. He felt their fingers slip away from his and he smiled.

The rifle fire kept up, but Jansen didn't move, thinking *shit, if the Krauts didn't fire in damn platoons, they'd never hit anybody.*

He heard the one sharp crack they say you never hear, and closed his eyes.

Arl, hugely pregnant and wheezing with the effort, was trying to keep him from falling out of bed in what must be the clinic's emergency ward. There were half a dozen beds around him, most empty, a couple with curtains drawn around them and nurses coming and going. Jansen caught himself, scrambled crabwise back onto the bed, said, "What the Christ?" and tried to sit up. Arl pushed him back down, hard.

"No, you don't—you stay *put*, old man." There was relief in her voice—he caught that, having looked long for such things—but also the same dull rancor and plain dislike that colored their every conversation, even the most casual. "You're staying right here until Dr. Chaudhry comes."

"What happened? The baby?"

"The baby's all right. I'm all right too, thanks." That wasn't just him, he knew; everybody asked about the baby first, and it was starting to piss her off as she neared her term. She said, "They found you on the floor in the waiting room. They thought it might be a stroke."

"Oh, Jesus. I just fell asleep, that's all. Been staying up too late watching old movies. I'm fine, shit's sake." He looked at his hands and wrists, saw no barbed-wire wounds, and started to get up, but she pushed him down again, and he could feel the real fury in her hands.

"You *stay* there, damn it. A lot of people think they're just fine after a stroke, and they get on their feet, take a few steps, and *bang,* gone for good this time." Her face was sweaty with effort and anger; but he saw fear there as well, and heard it in her voice. "On good days I can just about stand you, and on the bad ones...God, do you have any *idea?*"

"Yes," Jansen said. "Matter of fact."

Arl drew a long breath. "But when I saw you..." Her voice caught, and she started again. "I realized right there, I am not ready to have you gone, I'm *not.* Not you too, it's too damn *much,* do you understand me? Don't you dare die on me, not now. Not fucking *now.*"

Jansen found her hand on the bed, and put his hand over it. She did not respond, but she did not pull the hand away. "You look like me," he said. "Gracie's all Elly, but you've got my chin, and my nose, and my cheekbones. Must have really hated that, huh?"

The smile was thin and elusive, but it was a smile. "I hated my whole face. Most girls do, but I had reasons." She looked down at their hands together. "I even hated my hands, because they're too much like yours. I'm okay with them now, though, more or less."

Jansen said, "You're like me. That's what you hate." Her eyes widened in outrage, and she jerked away, but he held tightly to her hand. "What I mean, you're like the *good* me. The best of me. The me I was supposed to be, before things...just happened. You understand what I'm saying?"

Arl was beginning to frown in an odd way, staring at him. "You sure you haven't had a stroke? I wish the doctor'd get here. You talked while you were out, I couldn't make anything out of it, except it was really weird. Like you were having a weird dream."

"Not a stroke," Jansen said. "Not a dream." He did not try to sit up again, but kept his eyes fixed on her. He said, "Just someplace I needed to be. Don't ask me about it right now, and I won't ask you about stuff you don't want to tell me, okay?" She did not reply, but her hand turned slightly under his, and a couple of fingers more or less intertwined. "And I promise I won't die until you're finished yelling at me. Fair?"

Arl nodded. "But this doesn't mean I actually like you. Just so you know that."

"Fair," Jansen said again. He did withdraw his hand from hers now.

Dr. Chaudhry came in, a brisk young Bengali with a smile that was not brisk, but thoughtful, almost dreamy. He sat down on the opposite side of the bed from Arl and said, "Well, I hear that you have been frightening your good daughter quite badly. Not very considerate, Mr. Jansen."

"I'm not a very considerate person," Jansen said. "My family could tell you."

"This is something you must change right away," Dr. Chaudhry said, trying to look severe and not succeeding. "You are going to be a grandfather, you know. You will have responsibilities."

"Yeah," Jansen said. He looked up at the lights on the ceiling then, and let Dr. Chaudhry count his pulse.

THE WOMAN WHO MARRIED
THE MAN IN THE MOON

The title "The Woman Who Married the Man in the Moon," with its natural waltz rhythm, came unbidden into my head a good many years ago. I tried developing something from it a few times, both as story and song lyric, got absolutely nowhere, and set it aside. I was almost to the point of forgetting it forever, until I needed to recreate Schmendrick the Magician as he was before he ever encountered a certain unicorn, or found dubious employment with the Midnight Carnival.

This is one of three stories that I actually know about Schmendrick's early life. I'm sure there are others, and perhaps someday I'll stumble across them.

✳

Findros had just begun to sniffle, and Mourra was still impatiently denying her own rising fear, when the tall man with the ragged cloak and the funny, pointy hat fell out of a tree in front of them. The children both yelped and recoiled, but only for a moment: there is simply nothing alarming or impressive about a man, whatever his size, wearing a hat that looks like a cross between a dunce cap and a crown. Raised not to stare rudely at strangers, Findros and Mourra nonetheless gaped shamelessly as the man stumbled to his knees, then quickly found his feet. He was certainly the tallest person either of them had ever seen, yet not *big*, not in a menacing way, like a giant or an ogre. Politely, he was slender, lean; less politely, gangleshanked; rudely, skinny, meager, gaunted-down. His thinness made his hands and feet look bigger than they really were, like those of a puppy yet expected to grow into his floppy paws, while his generous, flaring nose definitely belonged on an older, fiercer face. And if the green eyes were at once deep and distant, his voice was light and warm, a voice that tried not to call attention to itself. The man asked, "Children, are you in trouble? Are you lost?"

It was the word *lost* that did it—that, and the genuine concern in the tall man's tone. Findros promptly burst into tears, and Mourra swung a hard little fist at him, hissing, "*Stop* it, you baby! Don't you cry!" She herself would have died a silent martyr before ever admitting to any sort of fear or pain; though where that streak in her came from neither her mother Sairey, nor anyone else in the family, could ever have said. Mourra herself had long ago decided that it was a special gift from the father she could barely recall—he had died when she was not quite four—and treasured it accordingly. Findros had no such tradition to keep up.

"No," she said loudly to the stranger. "We're *not* lost, we're just going home a different way. I keep *telling* him."

The tall man rubbed the back of his neck, shaking his head. He said, "Boy, I've mislaid the road myself, all my life. Believe me, it's not the end of the world." But Findros howled as loud as ever, pointing a dirty forefinger at his sister. The man raised heavy eyebrows without speaking.

"He keeps saying I got us lost," Mourra told him wearily. "But I didn't, I never did. We went to the picnic, and then on the way home *he* was the one who just *had* to pick blackberries, and then we got turned around a little bit, but I *still* knew right where we were, and then—" her voice faltered for the first time—"then we *had* to go round through Craighley Wood, because old Mr. Willaby's turned his bull into the north field, and so then we..."

"Then you losted us!" Findros seized on her hesitancy, triumphant in terror. "You losted us, and you don't know the way home, and it's getting *dark*—"

"I do so know how to get home, you liar!" The presence of the strange tall man made Mourra feel much younger than her eleven years, which in turn made her angry. "But I'm not going to move an inch until you stop your baby bawling! Look, I'm sitting down right now, you little *baby!*" She promptly plopped herself down by the roadside, in a patch of dry grass, folding her arms and grinning mockingly at Findros. "And if you don't stop that crying, I'll just sit here until it's *really* dark, and the nightfliers will come and eat you, and they won't leave a thing except your anklebones and your nasty dirty toes—"

"Enough." The tall man raised his hands, gesturing them both to silence.

He sighed in the unmistakable way of a tired, exasperated grownup. He said, "Well, I had other plans, but never mind. I will see you home."

Findros stared, and went back to just sniffling. He eyed the tall man suspiciously. "You don't live here. You don't know where we live. You don't know *anything*."

From another adult, stranger or no, Mourra would have expected anger at such insolence, even braced herself to defend Findros from swift and merited chastisement. But the stranger only smiled. He said, "That is perfectly true. I come from very far away, and I have never been in this country before in my life. But I will still take you home, because I am a magician, and magicians can do things like that. Come."

Without another word, he turned and began walking away from them down the narrow little road, still muddy from the rain of two days before. To Mourra's amazement, Findros—from birth as wary as any wild animal of anyone he didn't know—ran after him, taking hold of his left hand, exactly as he did with their mother when the three of them went out walking together. Mourra wavered briefly between fascination and distinct annoyance that her brother should have admitted an outsider to the kind of confidence he almost never granted her; then got to her feet and hurried after them, placing herself firmly on the stranger's right, though without so much as looking at the inviting free hand, easily available. She decided on the spot that she was far too old to need such childish reassurances of protection, and she made the vow stick all the rest of that day.

"Why were you up in the tree?" she heard Findros questioning the stranger. "Were you doing a trick? Gicians do tricks."

"Do they so?" The tall man looked mildly surprised, as though he had never heard of such a thing. "Well, would this count, do you suppose?" In rapid succession, lightly ruffling Findros' hair, he produced a handful of cowrie shells, along with a turtle egg, a few old coins and a tiny bell, all of which he handed to the boy.

Findros closed his hand over his new treasures, but his mouth remained slackly open in wonder. Mourra said scornfully, "*You* put all those things in his hair. You had them in your hand, up your sleeve. I saw."

The green eyes considered her, and the tall man nodded slowly. "You're quite right. It was just a trick, nothing more. That's what I do, tricks." His voice sounded to Mourra as though he were biting down on something hard. "But then again, I know your names—Findros and Mourra, children of Sairey. There's a good trick, surely?"

Both children stared—Findros in wide-eyed fascination, Mourra in sudden alarm. No one outside family was ever supposed to know a person's birth name: you could never tell what might be done with it by the ill-meaning. The stranger said, "*My* name is Schmendrick."

Findros shook his head. "That's a funny name."

The stranger agreed cheerfully. "It is, indeed, but I'm used to it. Now that's a fine, strong name you have—Findros! I'd much rather have a name like that."

"I'm just Findros for right now." The boy made a gesture with two fingers, as though he was flicking something away into the grass. "When I grow up, I'm going to tell people my name's Joris, because that was my father's name. *Our* father's name," he added, in a quick concession to his scowling sister. "He's dead." The stranger nodded sympathetically, but said nothing.

A low-hanging twig brushed Mourra's hair, and a small spider dropped onto her arm. She screamed involuntarily, shaking the creature to the ground, lifting her foot to crush it. Schmendrick said quickly, "Ah, don't do that," and although he neither raised his voice nor reached to interfere, she moved away without stamping on the spider. This made her even more annoyed with the tall man, for reasons she could not explain. She kicked a stone, and followed sullenly on.

The magician said, "I knew a woman once who collected spiders." Mourra shuddered in revulsion, and though she made no sound, Schmendrick turned his head to regard her out of his green eyes. "She treated them so kindly," he went on, "and they became so fond of her, that in time the spiders wove all her clothes, every last garment she wore. What do you think of that, Mourra?"

How did he know our names? Mourra's own voice was thin, but steady and clear, as she answered, "I'd never ever touch a dirty old spiderweb. I hate spiders."

"Mmm." The stranger nodded thoughtfully. "Oh, but you should have seen my friend in those gowns and capes and dresses that the spiders made for her. I promise you, Mourra, when she walked out in the moonlight, when she spun on her heels with her arms straight out, the same way you spin and dance when no one is watching—" Mourra flushed angrily—"oh, then you would have thought that she carried the moon inside her, so that it shone right through her. That is just the way those spider-clothes made her look, and that is *one* reason why you should always be good to spiders, among many others." He reached for her hand, but she sidled a step away, and he did not press the issue. He said, "You should always be good to anyone—any *thing*—that can create such beauty. Do you understand me, Mourra?"

"No," she said, and nothing more. He walked on, matching his stride to Findros' short legs; even slowing down a little to accommodate Mourra's sulkily dragging pace. It seemed to her that he was beginning to look a trifle anxiously from side to side; now and then he made an odd, twisting gesture with his free right hand, or mumbled something under his breath that she could not catch. By and by he said, "I am very sorry your father died. How did it happen?"

Findros looked at Mourra, for once waiting for her to speak. She muttered, "The dragon."

"Dragon?" Schmendrick wrinkled his forehead. "This is not dragon country. Far too low and wet. Dragons hate wet."

"It was lost, too," Mourra said. "It didn't belong here." She bit back the impulse to say, *like you,* and only continued, "It was going to eat us, but Papa fought with it. Papa killed it."

"A rogue dragon," the magician murmured, as though to himself. "I suppose that could be."

He had not questioned the story, but Mourra bristled as though he had. "I was there! I was little, but I was there! Papa killed it, all by himself, but it killed him too. I remember!"

"Me too," Findros said to no one in particular. "Me too, I member."

Mourra turned on him scornfully. "You do not! You were a baby, you were in your cradle—you never even *saw* the dragon!" Seeing his eyes grow large with tears, she yet could not keep herself from adding, "You don't even remember *Papa!*"

A sound came out of Findros that might have started out to be *you take that back,* but had dissolved into a wordless screech of outrage by the second word. Schmendrick caught him round the waist in midair as he lunged at his sister. Studying her over the boy's struggling body, he said, mildly enough,

"That was a cruel thing to say."

Mourra had known that before the words were out of her mouth, but she would have dared Willaby's bull before apologizing to Findros in this man's presence. The magician set Findros on his feet with some caution, saying, "Come, we must walk faster if I am to have you home before dark." Findros took his hand again without question.

Brooding behind them as they walked, Mourra heard the boy announcing, "*You* could have killed the dragon. Gicians can kill dragons, can't they?"

"Some of us can," the tall man answered absently. "Myself, I usually try to talk to them. You learn more that way." He was silent for a moment, and then asked, "What sort of a dragon was it?"

Findros looked confused for only a moment. "It was black. All black and normous, and with big orange eyes. And horns, and things all over it. Bumples."

Mourra said tonelessly, "It was gray. A kind of purply-gray, like a storm cloud. Like thunder. And its eyes were silver, and it didn't have any horns or anything—it just had fire. Fire and teeth and claws."

The magician said, "Your father must have been a very brave man. I never knew even a knight or a soldier dared face a dragon alone."

He was not looking at Mourra now, but she felt his eyes on her even so. She said, "He was the bravest man in the world." When Schmendrick did not reply, she continued fiercely, "There's going to be a statue of him in the town, on the green. Him fighting the dragon. It'll be finished soon."

"And I wish I could be here to see it properly dedicated," the magician responded heartily. "But I must deliver you to your mother and be on my way, for I've a long journey yet to go. Yes..." The last word was uttered in a different, softer tone, almost a whisper, as though he had not meant to say it, or for the children to hear. Mourra still did not take hold of his hand, but she moved slightly closer.

Findros said stubbornly, "It was a *black* dragon. I was there." Mourra did not answer him. Findros peered cautiously into his closed left fist. "I like turtle eggs. You can bounce them."

Schmendrick halted, no longer attempting to conceal the fretful, mysterious movements of his long hands, nor to disguise the fact that he was looking apprehensively in every direction. Mourra said, "You're lost." It was not a question.

The magician looked embarrassed. After a moment, he said, "Yes. I have taken you even further out of your way than you were, and I haven't the slightest notion of how to bring you home. I am very sorry."

Mourra had expected her brother to burst into frightened tears a second time—the horizon was definitely growing transparent with approaching sunset—but Findros only said confidently, "But you're a gician. You can do a trick." He leaned against Schmendrick's leg.

Schmendrick said, as though to himself, "I thought I had that much magic in me. At least...that much. I was wrong."

Findros looked up at him, and began to sniffle again. Mourra said, "Maybe if we go left, just up there, maybe..." But her voice trailed away, and she could do no more than point diffidently to a path further ahead. The magician shook his head.

"There is one more...*trick* I can try, but I will need your help. I cannot do it without you." He held his hands out, reaching silently for theirs. Surprisingly, it was Mourra who—after a long moment—took firm hold of his left hand, while Findros hesitated until his sister nudged him sharply. The boy's grip on Schmendrick's hand was more than tentative, barely making contact with all five fingertips. But the tall man smiled at him, saying, "Very good, thank you. Now close your eyes, and repeat everything—*everything*—I say. We will get home together."

He closed his own eyes and began to chant softly and musically. The syllables meant nothing to the children, but their sound was curiously comforting, though Mourra could not imagine why that should be. She kept her eyes tightly shut and repeated the words as clearly as she could, half-singing them as the magician did. *When I open my eyes again, I'll be home. I'll be home with Mama.*

But when her eyes did open, they saw nothing at all different. The countryside around them was as unchanged as the stones under her feet and the pale-gold clouds over the distant red-oak hills. Schmendrick had let go of her hand and her brother's, and his face was so despairing that Mourra would have felt sorry for him if she had not been so concerned to forestall a second tearful panic on Findros' part. She said, "I think we ought to turn around. There's a cowpath we always take, we must have missed it." The magician neither answered nor looked at her.

They had started to turn back—Schmendrick offering neither leadership nor resistance—when they saw a farm wagon emerging from the narrow path Mourra had pointed out earlier and swinging toward them. The driver recognized them, as did the horse; it stopped before he had even touched the reins. He was a big man with a white hair topping an amiable red face, set in its turn above broad shoulders and a cheerfully aggressive belly. He grumbled, "Sairey's lot—I know you. Whatever be you doing, so far from home at dinnertime?"

Mourra answered him quickly, saying, "We were coming back from the picnic, and we got lost." She nodded toward Schmendrick. "This is our friend. He was helping us."

The farmer eyed Schmendrick up and down, turned his head and spat to the side. "H'ant done much of a job, got to say. Get y'selves up behind me." He considered Schmendrick again, at some length, before he nodded. "Him, too."

Mourra yanked her brother away from feeding handfuls of grass to the old horse, and the children scrambled into the wagon. Schmendrick hesitated, looking as though he would have preferred to walk, and not necessarily in the same direction. But after a moment he sighed briefly, then shrugged and climbed up beside them, doubling his long legs like a grasshopper to leave room. The driver grunted a single word, and the wagon started on.

They had indeed, following Schmendrick, wandered far enough from their road home that it was full twilight by the time the horse halted of its own accord and the farmer pointed down a wildflower slope toward a small, tidy house tucked into a ripple of hillsides. A woman stood in the doorway, shading her eyes, beckoning uncertainly.

Findros was out of the cart and running before the farmer had had a chance to growl, "Figure *he'll* likely get you the rest of the way," jerking his chin at Schmendrick. "Best to your ma."

The woman was hurrying toward them now, picking up her skirts, as the farm wagon rumbled off. The magician said quietly, "Not much use for finding your way home, are they? Tricks."

Mourra stood still, peering up into the magician's green eyes, suddenly so far above her. She said, "We got home. Maybe the wagon...maybe *that* was the magic. That could be."

Schmendrick stared at her without replying. She looked away, looked back at him, stood on one foot, scuffling the other in the soft earth, and finally asked, "I know you had all those things in your sleeve—I *know* that—but... but is there anything in *my* hair? Like with Findros?"

The magician went on regarding her for a long moment before putting his hand lightly on her head. "Mmm...well, definitely no eggs of any sort... no money, more's the pity...no pretty shells...hello, hello—now what on earth have we *here?*"

Mourra found herself holding her breath. Something smooth and cool moved in her hair—*don't let it be a snake, I'll scream if it's a snake*—and the magician grunted with effort, as though he were hauling an anchor up from the depths of the sea. Then the coolness was fresh dew on her cheek, the smoothness a velvet petal. The magician was holding up a single flower as pale scarlet as the approaching sunset, as golden as a bee. There was nothing else in his hand.

Mourra took the flower from him slowly, without speaking. Sairey was nearing them, her expression a mixture of anger and immense relief, her right arm occupied by a clinging Findros, the left reaching out for her daughter. Mourra put the flower into her hand, saying, "I found this for you. It's a magic flower." She closed her eyes then and leaned into her mother.

Sairey was a small, dark, sturdily-made woman, with a quick eye and a disturbingly level glance. She considered the magician briefly, bent her head in acknowledgment, but immediately turned to Mourra and Findros, demanding, "Why are you so late? Where have you been?"

"She got us losted, I *told* you," Findros mumbled against her shoulder. "The Gician saved us. His name's Schmoondrake."

Mourra was too tired to contradict him. She said only, "I'm sorry. I thought I knew the way home from the picnic."

Sairey swept her into her free arm before Mourra had finished speaking. "I kept *looking* for you under the willow." The magician could hear that her voice was shaking. She waved her hand toward the huge old tree in front of their cottage. "I kept thinking that you might be having a tea party under there, and forgot it was getting dark. The way you do sometimes."

A child on either hip, she looked up at the magician, smiling slightly. "I thank you for bringing my pair of disasters home to me. Though perhaps you'll be thanking me now for taking them off your hands."

Schmendrick bowed more formally than she had done. "A man with a cart's more to be thanked than I, who only led them more astray than they already were, being lost myself. As I am still."

"I don't understand," she said slowly; and then, "But where are my manners? Will you not come in and sit to dinner with us? It's the least I can offer you, surely." She eyed him more critically than she had at first meeting, and could not forbear adding, "And a good meal or two would do you no harm, I'll say that much."

The magician hesitated—seemed about to decline the offer—then abruptly smiled and nodded. "My thanks. I do sometimes forget that I am hungry."

"I, never," she said; then, quickly, laughing, "As you see, they never let me," for Mourra and Findros were already tugging her toward the little house. "And getting food ready for them always makes me want to eat something myself, and will end by making me as big as a barn, I know this." She shooed the children ahead of her, telling them briskly, "There's lentil soup, and if you don't wash your hands *and* your faces, nobody gets any." They whooped and ran off, and she led the magician into the house, calling after them, "And, Findros, the turtle egg is *not* coming to dinner."

There was a vegetable stew as well as the soup, and cold, sweet well water. Dinner was—according to Sairey—a quieter affair than usual, the children both being too weary to squabble. Findros actually fell asleep at the table, but Mourra lingered, fishing sleepily but stubbornly for reasons not to go up to bed. She still avoided sitting close to the magician, nor did she meet his glance often. But the flower that he had taken from her hair reposed precariously in a lopsided clay drinking mug next to her own, and now and then she brushed it against her closed eyes, as though to feel its colors through the lids.

A dog howled, somewhere nearby, and Sairey half-rose from her chair, apologizing as she sat back. "I don't know why that one always startles me. There's no harm in him—he's only an old sheepdog baying at the moon."

"He sleeps all day," Mourra muttered scornfully. "The sheep make fun of him."

Schmendrick asked, "Do you know why dogs do that?" Both mother and daughter stared at him. "Because the moon used to be part of the Earth, and that is the part that all the dogs come from. But the moon wanted to be free, and it struggled and struggled until one night it broke loose from the Earth and sailed right off into the sky, the way it is now. Only all the dogs had their families there, all their mothers and fathers, and their children, their houses and all their buried bones, and their books—"

Mourra giggled. "Not *books*. Dogs don't read *books*—"

"Of course not, because they're all gone up in the sky, you see. And every night the moon comes out and all the dogs in the world see it, and they cry for their families. That is why they always sound so terribly sad."

Sairey refilled his cup from the sweating pitcher of well water. She said, "I don't believe I ever heard that story."

"It is well-known where I come from." The magician's expression was entirely serious.

"And that would be...where?" He was savoring the cold water, and did not appear to have heard her. Sairey said, "Daughter. You are about to fall asleep in your stew. Go to bed."

Mourra did not protest. Drowsily finding her way to her feet, she asked, "Can I take my flower with me? Just tonight?"

"I thought it was *my* flower," her mother teased her. "Very well, I will lend it to you for the night." She rose herself to give the girl a quick, warm hug; then prodded her gently toward the stair. "But you must not be upset when it dies, in a day or two. Flowers die."

Trudging up to the loft she shared with her brother, Mourra heard Schmendrick's reply, "Perhaps not this one." She looked over her shoulder to observe Sairey's wordless surprise, and to hear the magician continue, "It did not come from the earth, after all, but from her hair—from her head. The flowers in our heads...those survive."

Her mother did not respond, not until Mourra had put on her nightdress and crawled under her blanket with the blue and green birds on it that Sairey had woven especially for her. She brought her flower with her, pressing the fragrant stem against her cheek. Then, distant but clear, Sairey's quiet, even voice, "Who are you?"

Mourra fell asleep before she heard the magician's answer, but the full moon rose into her open window, and she woke to see it burning itself free of the willow branches that she could almost have touched. *Like a firefly in a spiderweb,* she thought, remembering the story of the woman whose clothes were made for her by spiders. She sat up and leaned her elbows on the windowsill to see her mother and Schmendrick standing near the old tree. The earliest stars were waking in the deep sky, one by one, and the magician was telling a story.

"No, they used to stick straight up, just as though the tree were reaching for the sky. That is a fact—any willow will tell you that. Listen now. The rain god's daughter fell in love with a mortal, a human, and they ran away together, for fear of his anger. He could never catch them, because they fled so fast, but they could never rest, either, for he would always find them, no matter where in the world they hid themselves. Because all the trees of the world were afraid of the rain god, and none would give them shelter. Only the willow."

Sairey laughed softly. "Yes, of course. It would be the willow."

"The willow felt sorry for them and said it would take them in, which obviously wasn't much help, not with its branches as wide-apart as they were. So the willow tried and tried—slowly, painfully, so painfully, all night long—"

Like that time I got my finger bent back, playing ball with Findros...

"—but at last it managed to get all its branches turned down, all the way to the ground, touching the ground, and so they hid the rain god's daughter and her husband, and the rain god never could find them. So then they were safe."

"The rain god must have been very angry. Gods don't take that sort of thing well. As I know."

"Oh, naturally he was furious! So he commanded the willow to stay like that forever, with its branches drooping down, as a warning to all the other trees." Mourra heard the magician chuckle himself. "And he still makes certain to send rain, constant rain, wherever the willow trees are. But he forgot that the willow *likes* rain—indeed, *loves* rain—so he is content in his vengeance, his daughter is happy with her husband, the willow's deep roots are always damp and happy—"

"And my children have a place for their tea parties. Thank you." They passed into the moon-traced shadow of the tree, and Mourra lost sight of them for a moment, but she heard her mother say, "I like that story. I will tell it to them."

Schmendrick said something in response that Mourra could not catch entirely, ending with "...sad story they told *me*. About the dragon."

"Dragon?" Sairey's shadow stood still, turning to face the magician's shadow. "What dragon?"

"The one who killed their father. I am very sorry."

Another puzzled silence in the willow-shadow. "They told you—a *dragon...?*" There was a sound under the words that could have been laughter, and was not.

"It was either black, with horns and things all over it, or it was the color of a thunderstorm, and had silver eyes. Depending on whom you talk to." The magician's voice was as quiet as the small night breeze in the willow branches. "Was that not so?"

Sairey sighed. "My husband's name was Joris. He was killed plowing a field, when a sinkhole opened under his feet without warning and swallowed him up. One of the rocks in the hole broke his skull." There was a laugh in her voice now, but it hurt Mourra to hear. "That was all there was to his death, and little more to his life as well. No wonder the children made up a brave ending for him."

No. No, that isn't how it happened. There was *a dragon—there was!* Mourra fought back the urge to shut the window and clap her hands over her ears, She leaned against the frame, head bowed, hugging herself, rocking back and forth.

Schmendrick's voice remained expressionless. "Death is death—loss is loss. Grief is grief. What difference?"

"None, except to children—children nourished on the fairy tales their father so loved to tell them. Findros was too young, but Mourra...Mourra knows."

I didn't make it up! Mourra ground her knuckles painfully into her eyes, warning them against tears. The magician said, somewhere far away, "Have you ever faced her with the truth? I rarely recommend it, but sometimes..."

"Once. Not again."

"Ah. Quite wise." Her mother made a sound that Mourra could not translate. *Grownup talk, grownup noises.* They were clear of the willow shadow now, and Sairey had seated herself in the wooden chair that the children's father had made for her shortly before his death. Mourra knew from her own experience that Joris had not been a particularly good carpenter: the chair was ruthlessly uncomfortable, however one shifted position; there was no natural headrest; and there were always previously-unnoticed splinters to be dealt with. She could never imagine how her mother could possibly find any ease on the rough planks, but from time to time she would stubbornly sit there herself, as long as she could bear it.

Sairey was saying, "I'm sorry, I have no other chair."

"As well. I have far to go, and if I sat down it might be a long time before I rose again. Thank you for your kindness. I will not forget."

Her mother's answer came slowly. "The pathway back to the main road is elusive at night. You may lose your way."

"I have no *way*, as you mean it, and my road is elusive by any light. As I told you, when I encountered your children, they were a little bit lost, yes, but I was much more so. Lost and very weary, and out of stories to tell myself, out of all the games I know to persuade myself that I am what I pretend to be. The children's company...helped."

She wants him to stay, I know she does. My mother wants him to stay.

"Well, you're a storyteller, no doubt of that." Sairey was leaning back in the old wooden chair, considering him with her arms folded across her breast. "And you may ask my children if you need reassurance about being a magician. Findros would have taken that silly turtle egg to bed with him if I'd permitted it, the same way you saw Mourra asking to have her flower. *They* recognize you, those two."

"As a trickster, nothing more. What I did to amuse them—to distract them from their fear—any half-competent parlor entertainer could have done. In truth, I am amazed that I managed those common little flummeries as well as I did. It is not always so."

In the moonlight Mourra could see her mother lightly touch Schmendrick's arm, then draw her hand back quickly. "But they tell me you knew their names without being told—and mine as well. True?"

"Mmm. Yes, well. A very small charm, much less difficult than people imagine. A beginner's practice spell, really—I get it right perhaps half the time. Perhaps a little less."

"So? But Mourra's flower?" When he did not reply she pressed further. "Mourra's flower that you said would never fade. Surely, anyone who could manage such a thing..." She left the words hanging in the air.

"Ah," the magician said. "Mourra. Yes." He chuckled dryly. "Well, if that bloody flower does die, I won't know about it, will I?"

"Oh, I think you will," Mourra's mother said. "And I think that flower may very well survive."

"Then it will be her doing, the magic of that child's will, and none of mine." Schmendrick's voice had risen sharply. "No, I didn't put it in her hair... but I didn't find it in her head, either. Or perhaps I did, and never knew. I never know why any attempt at enchantment succeeds or dissolves in my hands. I search for patterns, for signs, guideposts, masters, for anything to tell me who I am—*what* I am, wizard or carnival cardsharp, either one. I could live if I knew!"

At the window Mourra clutched her flower, understanding nothing of his words but the sorrow and loneliness under them. The magician chuckled suddenly, mimicking himself. "'I could live...' Now, *that's* funny. That *is* funny." He turned and bowed to her mother, not at all mockingly, but with a kind of slow, formal courtesy. "Well. Thank you for that excellent dinner, and for...for the loan of your children. Good night."

He had been turning the funny many-pointed hat in his hands all the while they spoke. Now he set it on his head, bowed a second time, more briskly, and turned away. Even from her window, even in the dimness, Mourra could see him straighten his thin shoulders under the ragged cloak, as though settling a peddler's pack. Then he set off, and the moon-shadows swallowed him quickly.

Sairey said after him, "I will tell *you* a story." Her voice was soft but very clear in the still night.

Mourra could only tell that he had halted and turned by the angle of the funny hat. Her mother said, "You are a magician who cannot believe in his own gift. I am a widow with two children. I do not imagine that I will ever marry again, since I have no intention of ever giving another hostage to a sky that can snatch love away from me so randomly, so absurdly, so completely. So I believe in nothing—*nothing*—except looking at my sleeping Mourra, my Findros who always curls up into such a tight little ball, twice and three times during the night." Sairey's voice was now as tight and thin as her lips became when she was truly angry. Mourra put her fingers to her own mouth and bit down hard on them.

Schmendrick did not respond. Sairey said, "So I tell myself stories, just as you do, to comfort myself, to endure—simply to get through to another morning. And there is one story in particular that has always meant something to me. Different things at different times, perhaps, but something always. Sit down where you are, magician, in the soft grass, and listen."

The night had grown so dark that Mourra could not even be certain whether Schmendrick was still there, until, after a moment, she saw the pointy hat slowly lower itself. Sairey began, "There was a woman once who fell in love with the Man in the Moon—yes, a moon story of my own. This woman loved the face she imagined she saw—everyone sees something different in the moon, you know—and she let it be known that if that man should ever choose to walk on this earth, she would marry him instantly. As to whether or not he would have her, she never questioned that, no matter that she had always been a plain woman, even rather drab and dowdy. She knew beyond any doubt that the Man in the Moon would come for her in time."

"And so he did." The tall man's voice was almost without inflection.

"Well, *somebody* did. Because one evening a strange man came to her door."

The pointy hat nodded. "And naturally told her that he was the Man in the Moon."

"That was not necessary. She merely looked at him and *knew*, as happens sometimes. To anyone with any doubts, she pointed out that there was no longer a man visible up there—which was true, because, for whatever reason, there had come a season of clouds and mist hiding the surface of the moon, and there was nothing at all to be seen but a few dark craters. It was plain for anyone to see that the Man in the Moon had at last come down to claim her."

"Which, of course, he had not done at all—merely taken advantage of a lonely woman's foolish fantasy. I told you and your children better tales."

"Perhaps because we were not forever interrupting you, ordering the story this way and that. Listen to me now, pay for your dinner. Like herself, this lady's lover was no great beauty, at least on earth, being rather short and decidedly gray-complected, with no grace that any of her friends ever noticed. Nevertheless, by all accounts he was kind to her, and she appeared to be blissful in his company. She listened enraptured to his own stories of his palace in the moon, and sighed in wonder as he described the beauty of shooting stars, comets and constellations seen from the far side no human ever sees. Who knows anything about anyone else's happiness, after all?"

"Go on, then," the magician said when she fell silent. "What became of them?"

"He only came to her by night, of course, just as the moon would, and she thought it perfectly proper that there were always one or two nights in the month when he did not come at all. And it must be said that his attentions made a wonderful difference in her appearance, for her hair and her skin and her manner alike all took on a certain shimmer very like that of the moon itself, and as time passed people began to say that she walked in moonlight, such was the radiance of her joy. It can happen so, even with foolish fantasies."

Resting her chin on her folded arms in the window, Mourra thought, *yes, that was how she looked when Papa was here—shimmery. I remember. I do.*

As though she had heard her, Sairey went on, "Her man suited this woman very well, in the moon or out of it, and so she lived contentedly for quite a long time. And the world jogged along serviceably with no Man in the Moon—especially since many folk see no Man there at all, but a Woman, or even a Fox. And they went on together as well, those two."

Schmendrick said, "I can see sorrow coming. I can smell it on the wind. This story is going to end badly."

"Stories never end. *We* end. If we could but live long enough, we would see how all tales go on and on past the telling. Now there came a night when the woman could tell that her lover was not falling restfully asleep in her arms, as he had always done, nights without number, even though he left her before each dawn. So she said to him, 'Beloved, what troubles you? Tell me, and I will help if I can.' For loving had made her sensible of others' griefs and fears—which also happens, as I am sure you know."

"I have been...told so. Go on."

"And the Man in the Moon—if that indeed is what he was—answered her, 'My dearest Earthwoman, one love of my endless lunar life, the time has come for me to return to my lonely home. It is home to me no longer—*this,* our bed, this is my true home—but the moon is my fate, the moon is where

I am ordained to be. If I stay away even one day further, it will fall from the sky, likely causing the world's end. Tonight must be our last together, for the very planet's sake.'"

"What nonsense!" The magician was surprisingly indignant. "The scoundrel was just seeking to be rid of that poor woman!"

"Was he, then?" Sairey's voice was as slow, and even tentative, as though she were telling the story for the first time. "Yet when she said to him, 'May I not go with you, as I have been ready to go from the night we met?' he replied, 'I had not dared to ask you. I do not ask it now. You will be lonely for the Earth, and there will be no returning. I cannot take such advantage of you.'"

Schmendrick snorted contemptuously. "One of the oldest ruses in the world to discard a woman. Your Mourra would never be taken in so easily."

"Perhaps not. She is a very perceptive child. But this woman answered, 'I was lonely for the Earth until you came. You may be from the moon, but you are my planet—*you* are my Earth. I know this as an animal knows its home, if it knows nothing else of the universe. Take me with you.'

"'My palace is a little cold,' said her lover. 'Bright, but cold. I should warn you of this.'

"'Then we will warm it together,' answered the woman. 'Where did I leave my good shoes?'"

"And in what town, what miserable inn, what hovel, did he finally abandon her?" Schmendrick was on his feet now. "Or did they find her body in some river? On some dungheap?" He was shaking his head, half in anger, half in amusement. "Go ahead—tell me the wretched rest of it."

"All I can tell you," came the quiet answer, "is that on that same night there came a total eclipse of the moon, and when it passed, both the woman and the man were gone, and were never seen again. Nor was any trace of them ever found."

As the magician drew breath to respond, she added, "I am sorry if my story displeases you. I told it for a reason."

"Of course you did. To make the point that, whether or not her lover was actually the Man in the Moon, the real magic was in her belief—it was belief that kept her blissful and *shimmering*, and what else matters, after all? Understood, but my fairy tale is a little different, and I have already known too many who flourished on the belief of others. Thank you once more for the meal and the delightful children. And so good night and farewell, mistress."

He turned, tugging the old cloak closer around himself. Mourra could not see her mother's face clearly, but she heard her begin to speak—then stop herself—then finally say "You are a fool."

Over his shoulder, the magician answered her, "Oh, I know that."

Sairey said, "I did not tell you that tale in praise of blind belief. I meant you to understand that it was her faith in herself—not in *him*, not for a moment—that made whatever magic there was. I've no least idea whether or not she ever credited a word that man told her, but what I am sure of is that she knew—not believed, she *knew*, always—that she was a woman for whom the Man in the Moon would certainly come down to Earth." Her voice sounded strangely breathless to Mourra's ears, as though she had been running. She said, "Magic is not what you think it is, magician."

She had also risen to her feet, and was standing with her back fiercely straight and her hands on her hips. Schmendrick had stopped walking, but had not turned again. "All I know," he said, "all I have ever known, is that there is just enough magic in me to do me no good." He drew a deep breath and held himself as erect as she. "Your children found me in a tree, where I was looking for a certain branch, one strong enough to take my weight. I thought I had at last found the right one, but it broke and I fell at their feet. Do you understand me now?"

Mourra heard a strange sound in her mother's throat: a muffled click, as of a soft lock closing. The magician said, "I had been searching for some while. It is not as simple a matter as one might suppose. Not just any tree or branch will do for a man with my...blessings."

From her window, Mourra saw her mother's lips move, but no sound came out. Schmendrick continued, "But then, of course, I was obliged to see your Findros and Mourra safely home—which I accomplished no more skillfully than I had that other. Not my finest showing, all in all."

Sairey whispered *"Why?"* more clearly this time, and Mourra's face was suddenly so cold that she did not even notice that she was crushing her flower against it. She was terribly thirsty, but she could not move from the window, even for a moment, to reach the pitcher of water near Findros's bed. Sairey said, *"Why?"* again.

"Your son said it—magicians do tricks. I was weary of tricks before he was born." His laugh sounded as painful as though his throat and his mouth were full of glass. "Before *you* were born."

Sairey's voice softened, as it had when she spoke of watching her children sleep. "Listen. Listen. You don't know. That branch breaking when you...what if that were the magic, protecting itself and you? That farm cart coming when you were lost with the children, when you called for help together..."

"Mourra said that." The magician might have been talking to himself. "But the child was being kind."

Sairey said, "The woman in my story never thought about whether what she was doing was magic or not. She was no magician at all, she simply opened herself to whatever there might be within her. You must do just the same as she to allow yourself what you wish for."

Schmendrick stubbornly kept his back to her. "Wishing will not make it so. Believe me, I would know."

Mourra heard her mother's breath catch briefly once more before she spoke again. "So would I."

The magician finally turned. He said nothing for the longest while, his face shadowed, his shoulders pale with the moon. "I expect to go on being a fool. I feel you should know this."

"You're alive. It's much the same thing."

"No more searching for the perfect branch, you think? Mind, I can't promise." He walked slowly toward her as he spoke.

"Oh, you'll do as you must. People do."

"But you will hope."

She nodded thoughtfully. "Yes."

"So, then." He leaned down, holding his open hands to either side of her own, where they rested in her lap. "Another gift. Palms out, please."

From the window Mourra saw her mother raise her hands slowly, almost shyly. She wished she could see her face.

The magician laid his own palms gently against Sairey's, his large, smooth hands completely hiding her small rough ones from view. He stood still for a very long time, murmuring, his head bowed and his hat near tumbling off, before he finally stepped back and said, simply, "There."

Sairey spread her fingers. "I don't see anything."

"No, neither do I. But I don't think I'm supposed to." His tone, which might have been expected to be sad or frustrated once more, was in fact curiously pleased. "You might ask Findros in the morning, or Mourra."

Ask me what? Mourra thought sleepily.

"You are a very strange man...and always welcome. Farewell, friend. Come to us again."

To Mourra, eyes closing, chin now on her window ledge, it seemed that she heard the magician's faint answer, "I will," though later she thought that she might have dreamed that part. He never once looked back; her last glimpse of him was of a silly hat bobbing with determined jauntiness against the rising moon. As young as she was, and no matter what adults told her, she had never convinced herself to see more than a profile of some sort on the moon: now it seemed that she could make out almost the entire figure of a man leaning forward over something that might have been a fishing line. And behind him, over his shoulder...

Maybe that's Papa. Maybe that's Papa in the moon.

Sairey looked after the magician for a long time, before she finally patted the arm of the old chair. "Well, you were always *my* Earth," she said aloud into the soft night air. "And I would have gone to the moon with you, or anywhere else. Except for the children, I would have gone."

But Mourra missed the last words, and only noticed the new flower lying next to hers on the window ledge—white as the stars, except for its wine-red center—when the sun turned her pillow golden, and she awoke.

Act 27 Infinity 1, Premonition

Pretty Guardian *Sailor Moon*

CONTENTS

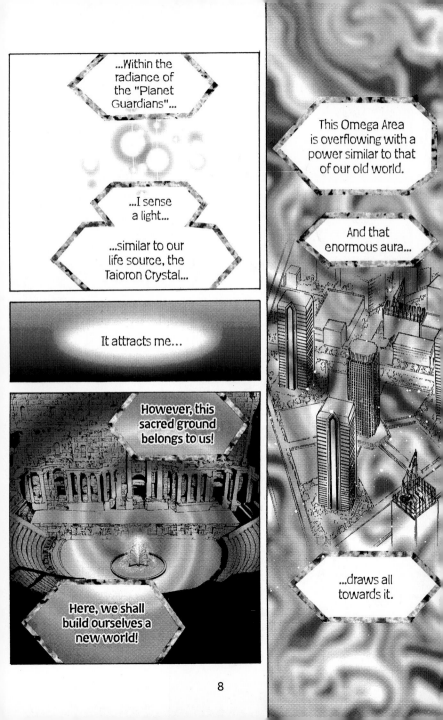

...Within the radiance of the "Planet Guardians"...

...I sense a light...

...similar to our life source, the Taioron Crystal...

It attracts me...

However, this sacred ground belongs to us!

Here, we shall build ourselves a new world!

This Omega Area is overflowing with a power similar to that of our old world.

And that enormous aura...

...draws all towards it.

8

9

10

11

...where an unidentified monster appeared and attacked students from the private Mugen Academy...

A bizarre incident took place yesterday at S Park in Minato Ward...

Witnesses claim it was a fellow female student of said Mugen Academy, who suddenly transformed into this monster...

...and authorities state that this may be a type of atavism...

So atavism means reverting back to that form.

You know, mankind's ancestors looked a lot like gorillas.

Kenji-Papa, what's "atavism?"

Be careful out there! ♡

Kenji-Papa! I'm heading to school! ♡

...Humans devolving into monsters...

"Monster." If that's true, it's scary!

15

16

...And everything around me...

But now that awful battle seems like an old dream.

...Black Moon attacked the Earth.

See you later! ♡

...GLOM...

...returned to day after day of peace...

...Awaken!

...LET THE DESTRUCTION BEGIN!

Um...

...It's nothing.

...
Mamo-chan?

...I think we'll be happy, right away...

...a wave of anxiety washes over me.

Every time...

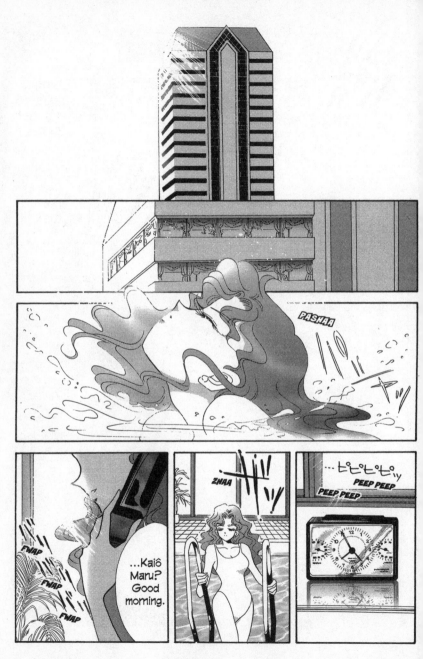

PASHAA

FWAP
FWAP
FWAP

ZHAA

...Kaiô Maru? Good morning.

ピピピピッ
PEEP PEEP
PEEP PEEP

23

28

29

33

Are you jealous?

You and that girl got quite friendly.

That Dumpling-head...

She was cute.

...still seems very much like a child.

He was even wearing a Mugen Academy uniform!

Hey, Usagi! That really hot guy is famous! I know I've seen that face before! ♡

...That Tokyo Bay land reclamation project that's now a top commercial district.

GWIMM

It's a new private school located in the Mugen District [Infinity District] of Sankakusu [the Delta]...

It is I, Gurio Umino! ♡

Oh, no! You don't know about it?

Mugen Academy?

35

Mugen Academy has gotten quite famous, even getting the nickname "Genius Academy!"

It's full of amazing people, like actors, Olympic athletes and musicians!

Right! Right!

CLOSE UP
Japanese winner!

give as as an a very you looking i year of t

Haruka the cool guy

It says he's a race car driver! Haruka Ten'ô!

That's him!

Timothy Collings may as about for men big ego in 1000 fished for his 1000 filled for Ad for your

See, look! I *knew* I'd seen him somewhere before!

...and just transferred to Mugen Academy!

He went from the prefectural Jûban High...

Really?! He's an actual racer?

No wonder he was so good!

cow ant ing on pisto five statio me on

Maybe we'll see him again! ♡

I wonder if he comes to Jûban Shopping District often? ♡

Haruka the cool !!

37

42

43

...The "Legendary Silver Crystal" reacted...?

...my brooch...

...Just as that girl was transforming into the monster...

Mina?

....No- body's there?! Was it my imagin- ation?!

CHATTER

CHATTER

Luna?

...Ata- vism...

So this strange creature was possessing that girl, huh.

CROWN GAME CENTER

44

You saw this morning's news, didn't you?

The piece about atavism, of a person who transformed into a monster and attacked others.

And I believe that was a Mugen Academy student too.

...An enemy?!

It looks like we need to investigate Mugen Academy.

Mugen Academy and atavism?

This smells real fishy.

STOP!?

That much-talked about new amusement park, Mugen C Park, is located on *that* delta.

Yup, the same one as Mugen Academy.

TOKYO AREA MAP

Usa?

WAHHH WAAHHH

I'll make sure you can reach me on the communicator, so that I can run right over if anything happens.

The amusement park is right next to the school.

Mugenzu.
[Infinity sandbank]

They make up a full-fledged city. Family housing and office buildings all lined up.

It is so named because three of the reclamation grounds, called Ten'ôzu, Kaiôzu, and Meiôzu, are arranged in such a way that they form a triangle.

PEEP PEEP

The center of the Tokyo Bay Land Reclamation Project.

...The delta...

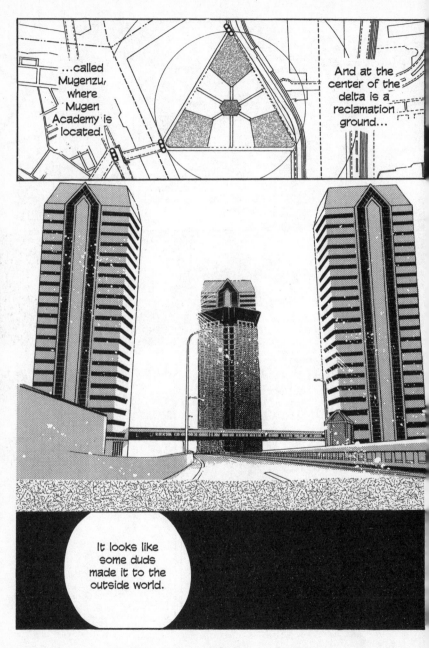

...called Mugenzu, where Mugen Academy is located.

And at the center of the delta is a reclamation ground...

It looks like some duds made it to the outside world.

...that gives the right to contact our Master, Pharaoh 90, directly...

...and receive the blessing of the Taioron Crystal.

And to the one who raises their level and survives through to the end...

...I shall grant the same status of Magus that I have...

...Magus!

The status that is permitted contact with Master, and to receive the blessing of our life source, the Taioron Crystal...!

And...

...you will gather...

..."Vessels" and "Hostes"...

...so that we may continue on!

51

...I feel a storm coming.

These are no ordinary sky-scraper breezes.

The wind is agitated.

HYUUU

I feel some-body's eyes on us!

...Again!

Mina?

53

KANG KANG KANG KANG KANG

ゴゴガガガ

YAAAAY!

Chibi-Usa and Momo sure like roller coasters! They're going around a second time!

Sorry, Asanuma, for usurping your after-school period.

You should go ride with them, Mamoru-sempai.

KYAAA

...Nah, I'm not really into that sort of stuff...

ZLURP

I'll get you more juice. Wait here.

Yes!

Are you all Chibi-Usa's classmates?

FWAA

KYAA AH HA HA

Ah!

KANG

Go have fun with everybody!

I saw where it landed, so I'll be fine!

Ehhh?! Then I'll go too!

Momo-chan, I'm gonna go get my hat!

I'll be right back!

Mamo-chan! That's the thing...

Huh? Momo-chan? Where's Chibi-Usa?

∞ 無限学園
MUGEN ACADEMY

MUGEN ACADEMY

Wooow! Amazing! ☆

That's a private school for you! ☆

I can't believe the school takes up this entire 60-floor building! ☆ How posh! ☆

Information

26F–30F	FACULTY OFFICES	57F–
22F–25F	POST-GRADUATE DIVISION	56F
18F–21F	UNDERGRADUATE DIVISION	48F–
14F–17F	HIGH SCHOOL DIVISION	44F–
10F–13F	MIDDLE SCHOOL DIVISION	
6F–9F	GRADE SCHO⟋ DIVISIO⟋	
3F–5F	KINDERGA⟋ DIVISIO⟋	
1F–2F	LABORATORI⟋	

CHATTER

59

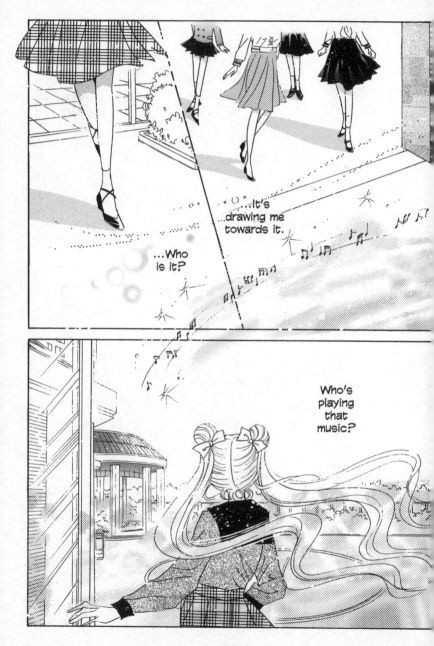

61

HAHN
はあ

HAHN
はあ

For an instant...

Stop right there!

Oh, no!

DASH

That girl's eyes went so cold and dark, I felt they could pierce right through me!

.....It sent shivers all through my body!

Could she be...an enemy?!

I've got to get back to the others!

This is the back of the building?!

HAHN
はあっ

TMP

Usagi?!

Chibi-Usa?!

WHOOSH

!!

...

I lost the hat that Ikuko-Mama bought me...and then this person... She looks like she's in pain, see?

Do you think she's okay?

It's dangerous!

What are you doing here, all by yourself?!

She's wearing a Mugen Academy uniform...

...GRRR

69

70

72

Act 28
Infinity 2, Ripples

77

79

83

84

Hotaru?

KACHAK
カチャ

KNOK
コーン
KNOK
コーン

Just give it a little time. It's all right.

HYAA
ひやっ

...but it's not working.

NAHN
はぁ
NAHN
はぁ

...I did, but...

Papa...!

What's wrong? The sick spell's not going away?

Have you taken your medicine?

SST
すっ

It's an amulet that's been handed down for generations in our family. Your late Mama wore it as well.

It will help you to sleep soundly.

Hotaru, let me give this to you.

...A Sailor Guardian and Tuxedo Mask ?!

CROWN GAME CENTER

I don't believe it!

It's no mistake!

I'm not kidding!

...They looked just like...

No doubt about it! Those two...

...flew through the sky like it was nothing...!

Could they be new Guardians?!

It's dangerous to draw conclusions based on observations made from a distance!

Wait!

...That's true.

For them to vanish like they were running away from us...

Why don't they come and meet us?!

Yeah! If they were Sailor Guardians, why did they disappear like that?!

...So they might be enemies, huh?

90

...If they'll show up again.

...I won-der...

Whether they're friend or foe...

...I bet they'll show up again!

...The eyes I've felt on us ever since we started getting involved with the atavistic monsters and Mugen Academy... as if someone was watching us...

Could they have belonged to that Sailor Guardian and Tuxedo Mask...?!

There are also other individuals we should watch out for, everyone!

I know.

Be extra careful!

No... there's no way he's an enemy...

Either of them...

...B-BMP
...ドキン

...They couldn't be... Could they?

...ドキン
...B-BMP

CRO 👑 WN

Take care!

Bye-bye!

See you!

しゅん
GLOOM

From now on, don't give away our identities to anyone unless there's a really good reason to.

Say, Chibi-Usa?

Like you did back there. ☆

...Maybe that girl and I could become friends.

But, it seemed like...

...I'm sorry.

Since we don't know what our enemies look like.

She's so pretty, isn't she?

Hotaru-chan had that white skin, like you could almost see through it!

She seemed so grown-up.

...And what was that power of hers that healed Chibi-Usa's wound...?

It's a pretty stone that's so white, it looks like it could be a clump of snow.

"Alabas-ter?"

...They call that "alabaster skin."

カチャ
カチャ
KLIK
KLIK

CROWN GAME CENT

PEEP
ヒ°ッ

Souichi Tomoe. ...Mugenzu, Tomoe Research Lab and Mugen Academy...?

■ SOUICHI TOMOE
(Professor of Genetic Engineering)
Mugenzu Corporation
Tomoe Research
Laboratory Inc.
Educational Corporation,
Mugen Academy
Corporate Representative
As of 199X,
currently living in Tokyo

A man named Souichi Tomoe.

Mamo-chan...

...the same person owns both Mugenzu and Mugen Academy.

■ SOUICHI TOMOE
(Professor of Genetic Engineering)
Mugenzu Corporation
Tomoe Research
Laboratory Inc.
Educational Corporation
Mugen Academy
Corporate Representa
As of 199X,
...tly living in Tok

94

ZHAA

ZHAA

...but that defective Daimon that escaped from the lab...

I was thinking it was odd...

Hm...

If I can get my hands on that power, I'm sure the Master would be pleased...!

...No, it's even stronger... what amazing power...!

Could this be the power of the light that is similar to the Taioron Crystal...

...that my Master, Pharaoh 90, had mentioned?

It was crushed by the Sailor Guardians right in front of that little girl's, Hotaru's, eyes.

PASH

95

96

...Assemble!

...the three talismans...

And the light that
shall guide them...

...Let the destruction begin...!

AH!

...but just as
I was about
to, someone
interfered?!

Three lights...?
I feel like I
was real close
to gleaning
more...

....ZAAN

ZHAA

!!

CHEEP
CHEEP

...That dream again...?

SNOORE

Somebody was telling somebody else...

...to "Awaken!"...

...in my dream...

Three Talismans?

...Are we being told *not* to obtain them...

...because they bring about destruction?

...or...

Three Talismans?

De-struc-tion?

Are we being told to gather them?

MUGEN ACADEMY
Elementary School,
Middle School
High School, Univ

Representative:
Souichi Tomoe
Professor of Genetic Engine
in the Medical Sciences Se
Private Mugen Academy
University.

**LATEST EQUIPME
ELITE INSTRUCT**

...Pro-
fessor
Tomoe,
hm?

本
BOOKS

SCHOOL GUIDE
TO FAMOUS PRIVATE
SCHOOLS
Middle Schools, High Schools
at You Need for Your Exams

Are you
looking
up Mugen
Academy?

The
owner of
the school,
Professor
Tomoe, is a
renowned
instructor.

はっ
AH!

...He was
ousted from
academic
circles quite
a long time
ago.

Al-
though
...

TEE—
HEE
くす,

Perhaps because it's an assembly of multi-talented people.

...A training school for sorcerers. Did you know that?

Or maybe it's...

You know, there are some who call Mugen Academy...

Ousted?!

....くすっ
...TEE HEE

Um...

I'm a huge fan! I'd love an autograph! ♡

KYAA ♡

Yes.

Are you the violinist Michiru Kaiô-san?

I'll give you tickets.

That's right! I have a concert coming up. Please attend.

...So you're...

...A multi-talented sorceress, too?

The violinist, Michiru Kaiô...?

...That
girl...

ドキン
B-BMP

...Isn't
that...

...Mamo-
chan?

..doing
toge-
ther?

...ドキン
B-BMP

B-BMP

...ドキン

...What
are
those
two...

...ドキン
B-BMP

...What
could
you be
discussing,
Mamo-
chan?

We were
just saying
that
she was
someone to
watch out
for...

B-BMP
...ドキン

103

Huh?

What's that?

"Sailor Guardian?"

HEH

TAK

ZLIMM

...Sailor Guardian?

You guys play war games or something?

You...

...and your friends...

Like "Guardians"...

...and "Battles?"

...So you like that sort of thing?

Ahhh! I'm such an idiot! Usagi the dummy! Of course he isn't! He's male!

HUMPH

...Geez! Have it your way.

Ah...

You stay away from Usagi!

War games?! They're not...

105

... ドキン
...B-BMP

ドキン
B-BMP

That's right! ♡

So you're class president of your new homeroom class, Chibi-Usa-chan...?

Wow...

PARLOR CROWN

CROWN FRUITS

She can use her shameless and bratty sides to full advantage!

I think I can understand that.

World's coming to an end.

Chibi-Usa, class president, huh.

And "cute"...?

The incoming students are so cute! ♡

And I got to attend the school entrance ceremony as class rep, too! ♡

106

Kaolinite!

...I pledge to thoroughly coach the students on the school's rules and regulations...

...and offer up both Vessels and Hostes to our Master in the process!

As Yûko Arimura... in charge of Etiquette and the Philosophy class at Mugen Academy...

Please allow me, Eudial of Witches 5, to carry out this mission!

GATHER...

...THE THREE TALISMANS...!

...The three
talismans...?
Are they the true
identities of the light
that shall lead us
into destruction...?!

...The
three
talismans
?!

KAK

PLASSH

Is this the key phrase that will help us destroy our next enemy?!

The three talismans?

...What do you mean, "destruction?" Is something about to begin?!

Where are they?!

The three talismans! We must find and destroy them...!!

Rei-chaaan!

Rei-chan, do you always train at places like this?!

It's the very top of a mountain!

I thought I was gonna die!

PANT PANT
はあ
はあ

WHEEZE WHEEZE

What are you all doing here?!

All you guys?!

Ah! It's Rei-chan!

PANT PANT
はーっ
はーっ

WHEEZE WHEEZE
ぜーっ
ぜーっ

Finally, we're here!

GAK
ギクッ

...

PHEW
はーあっ

M-Mako-chan?!

111

CHEEEEERS

Rei-chan! Happy fifteenth birthday!

Use them with your grandfather, Rei-chan! ♡

Of course if you get a boyfriend, you should use them with him! = ♡♡ =

I decided to go with Laura Ashley! ♡

Mind your own business, Usagi!

I got you a set of his-and-her cups! ♡

I brought you flowers! ♡ They're your favorite! Casa-Blanca Lillies! ♡

I baked the cake! ♡ I really wanted to throw a party with everybody! ♡

After all, we're in the third year of middle school now, so let's study hard together! ♡

Just 'cuz you go to an integrated girls' school doesn't mean you should take exams lightly.

SMIILE

See?

HIGHEST LEVEL WORKBOOK

You know what I got you, Rei-chan? ♡

A *must-have* problem book!

...that you knew?

...Don't tell me, Rei-chan...

Don't worry, I got one for each of us!♡ Let's hold a study session! ♡

...Ami-chan...

SNIFF SNIFF

I don't want to see such things deep in the mountains!

112

To tell the truth, part of the reason I came here was because of that.

...is taking place here, at a lodge on Mount M.

Mugen Academy's retreat for incoming students...

...You could say that.

...Because I had...

...a bad feeling about it.

How could you come alone?

Why didn't you say anything to the rest of us?!

...Yeah.

...without involving Usagi.

Things we can prevent, we must stop ahead of time, before they happen...

...do our best to protect Usagi.

...We have to...

That was my thinking.

113

115

116

117

I was just talking to some kids who are here on another school's retreat.

Oh, nothing.

I see.

Mm?

...もぞっ
SHFFL

...ポラッ
POHH

Can you believe they're holding an assembly this late at night?

Sh!

Rei-chan?

ZHAAA

Look! ...They're purifying themselves in the waterfall.

GWOO
OOO

Now we shall begin new-student orientation.

To ensure that you have the best academic life possible, let us study Mugen Academy's credo together.

First, you shall love the Academy, and devote yourselves to it.

Next, you must never defy the leaders of the Academy! ...And lastly...

...There, among the flames... ...The shape of a black star ...?!

GWOOGH

Now give my Master, Pharaoh 90...

...Your bodies and minds!

The Academy's founder!

...My master, Pharaoh 90, is the one to whom you must offer your body and mind!

POHH

...You shall temper and forge yourselves daily to become exceptional Vessels!

...And for our continued existence...

For our master...

And little by little...

121

Pretty Guardian ★ Sailor Moon

Act 29
Infinity 3, Two New Soldiers

129

130

SHAAA

Sailor
Moon
!!

ZHAA

...Could
that
person
possibly
be...

...a Sailor
Guardian?!

Did she
say her
name?
...What
is it?!

And?!

You made
contact
with a Sailor
Guardian?!

CROWN

133

...And nail down their true identities.

Not until we catch her and any others...

Haruka-san!

16-YEAR-OLD GENIUS RACER HARUKA TEN'Ō

...Haruka Ten'ō...

TSUKINO

"Dumpling!"

"Yo, Dumpling!"

Eh?

...suu...

...They look a lot alike.

"Dumpling-chan."

EVENING WITH A VIOLIN

It's her!

Wow! ☆
So she's a professional violinist!

MICHIRU KAIô RECITAL

EVENING WITH A VIOLIN

Michiru Kaiô?!

MICHIRU KAIô RECITAL

EVENING WITH A VIOLIN

Oh, no! I just can't meet his eyes...

B-BMP
B-BMP ドキドキ

Are you... thinking about Michiru-san?

Mamo-chan...

A make-up test for English.

I'm going to make an appearance at the Physics Club.

ENTROPY

Go to the game center without us.

Just me?

Strangely, I don't have any make-up tests or cleaning detail, so I got done early.

DINNG DONNG
キンコーン...

カンコーン...
DINNG DONNG

It's been a while. I'll go play a game and de-stress.

CROWN GAME CENTER

...Ah...

...B...BMP
...ドキ...ン

...Your friends told me to stay away, too...

...So I wasn't going to ever come here again.

But then I suddenly wanted to see you.

...ドキン

...B...BMP

...Why is my heart pounding like this?

...ドキン

...B...BMP

It must be because I had that dream.

...ドキン

...B...BMP

140

SHAA

...Haruka Ten'ô...

...She seems just like...

...the wind.

The Tokyo Bay Reclamation Project is experiencing a construction boom centering around Mugenzu."

"A hotel and condominium complex next to Mugen Academy is also slated for completion.

"Built on Mugen Academy grounds, the Mugen Memorial Dome has finally been completed."

It is Japan's largest multi-purpose grand hall."

BUILT ON MUGEN ACADEMY GROUNDS THE MUGEN MEMORIAL DOME HAS FINALLY BEEN COMPLETE

CROWN GAME CENTER

143

CHATTER CHATTER ゆい ゆい

Welcome, Usagi-chan!

Ah! Usagi, you're finally here! ♡

Sorry I'm late!

ワイー VEEEN

MICHIRU KAIÔ
RECITAL

EVENIN
WITI
VIO

MIMI HANYÛ

A CONCERT FOR MUGEN ACADEMY STUDENTS ONLY.

MIMI HAN

A CONCERT FOR MI STUDENTS ONLY.

It's a Mimi Hanyû concert just for Mugen Academy students!

ゆい
CHATTER
ゆい
CHATTER

Only Mugen Academy students can attend?! That's unfair! I wanna go too!

The opening act of the just-completed Mugen Academy Memorial Dome is going to be a Mimi Hanyû concert!

This Sunday!

Mimi Hanyû?

Usagi!!

What's up, Mina-chan?

I think that's your only option!

Dam it, I guess I'll have to transfer to Mugen Academy so I can go to the concert!

I wanna go!

144

What's wrong with that? If I can sneak into the concert, I can also snoop around! Two birds with one stone!

You really love idol stars, don't you, Mina!

Sheesh! You aren't a groupie!

Oh, geez! ☆ Mimi Hanyû is the top-selling idol star right now, appearing in tons of drama series and commercials!

She has an amazingly cute voice! ♡

This is a must-see concert. I wanna go so bad! ☆

But Mina... the snooping around is secondary, isn't it. ☆

I guess that's true...

Look at the next poster over. The violinist, Michiru Kaiô, is also holding a concert.

VEEEN

'MIMI HANYÛ
CELEBRATING THE OPENING OF THE MUGEN ACADEMY MEMORIAL DOME

CELEBRATING THE OPENING OF THE MUGEN ACADEMY MEMORIAL DOME
MICHIRU KAIÔ
RECITAL

EVENING WITH A VIOLIN

MUMBLE

...May-be I should go...

...To the con-cert.

So Michiru-san's concert is also in the Mugen Academy Memorial Dome?

Yeah. I sort of got them as a present. I have enough for everybody.

You have tickets?

To the Michiru Kaiô concert.

Ehh?! You're going to the Mimi Hanyû concert?

Let's all go and check the place out together.

Will it be safe?

I just love Michiru-san's violin-playing!

And both of them are in the Mugen Academy Memorial Hall...?

The Michiru Kaiô concert and Mimi Hanyû concert are on the same day. Hmm...

—SCRATCH SCRATCH
...ポリポリ

It won't be scary if we all go together!

MICHIRU KAIÔ

"I'll give you two tickets. Take someone with you."

Both of them are suspicious! I think you should check out Mimi Hanyû's concert, too.

Me too! My thoughts exactly! Diana-chan, you're so smart!

Mimete
Level 40

Eudial
Level 78

Viluy Level 202

Tellu
Level 404

Cyprine
Level 999

ZHAA

ZHAA

For you to defeat Eudial of the Witches 5 so easily... ...Your power is formidable.

WAVRR

...Sailor Guardians...

A power close to that of the Taioron Crystal's...

.....I want it!

The frightening power of that light...

147

Kao-linite!

WAVRR

I must procure them as soon as possible and destroy them!

...of the Witches 5.

SUU

Just leave that to me, Mimete...

You must make up for Eudial's failure!

I'll use my angelic singing voice...

...to gather Hostes for our Master, Pharaoh 90.

As the idol singer Mimi Hanyû, with her own fan club...

...and head of the Performing Arts class at Mugen Academy...

But first, before anything else, I must discern...

...the identity of the three talismans that shall lead to destruction...

...that appeared in my water mirror's oracle...

...Vessel transformation is complete!

Remember, I shall tolerate no failure until our Master, Pharaoh 90's...

...I was thinking of using this internationally renowned violinist to draw more people to Mugen Academy.

In order to exponentially increase the number of sacrifices gathered for us Death Busters...

WAVRR

And what's this?

Hm...

And perhaps even convert this violinist into a Vessel afterwards...

The Sailor Guardians will definitely try to interfere again! Prepare yourself!

...into a second Tau Star System, no matter what it takes!

We must make this Omega Area...

However, do not rush the plan...

...or overdo it. That leads to failure.

149

A new hand-kerchief.

I think it was behind the amusement park?

TOMOE RESEARCH LABORATORY

Hotaru-chan may not even be home from school yet...

I guess there's no guarantee I'll get to see her if I just drop by out of the blue.

The gate is shut... is nobody home?

!

Hotaru-chan!

Ah!

151

154

Hotaru-chan?

GRIMP

PACHINK

I'll help *you* this time.

Close your eyes...

...your amulet?

...So is that...

The pain stopped...

It's so warm...

It's what they call charms that protect you through some wondrous power.

Amulet?

I feel strength welling up...

...don't think I ever learned your name.

...You know, I...

...you too, Hotaru-chan, not just me. But its power can protect...

.....Yeah! This is my most precious charm!

But everybody calls me Chibi-Usa.

Although I'm not ♡ that little.

I'm Usagi Tsukino.

...And there's something I should...

...apologize for.

That monster that attacked you before... I think it's a test animal that escaped from Papa's laboratory.

...nor about the fact that you're Sailor Chibi Moon...

Not about your amulet...

...Chibi-Usa-chan, I won't tell a soul about this.

She may not know us...

...but we know her... very well!

You're pretty close to Hotaru-chan, aren't you, Chibi-Usagi-chan?

FWAP FWAP FWAP

This is so cool! I've never ridden in a helicopter before!

We talked about amulets.

Amulets?

It's a secret!

FWAP FWAP

What did you two talk about?

How about you two? Do you have charms?

I've got an amulet and so does Hotaru-chan!

That's what they call charms that protect you through some wondrous power!

160

FWAP FWAP FWAP FWAP FWAP

Really!

Really?

I only told them about Hotaru-chan.

...What did you talk about?

163

What in the world...?!

...Those two...?!

MICHIRU KAIŌ
RECITAL

EVENING WITH A VIOLIN

A CONCERT FOR MUGGEN ACADEMY STUDENTS ONLY.
MIMI HANYŪ

MICHIRU KAIŌ
RECITAL

EVENING WITH A VIOLIN

She's a violinist?

That's one of the girls who gave me the ride in the helicopter! I'm sure of it!

CHATTER
CHATTER

MICHIRU KAIŌ
RECITAL

EVENING WITH A VIOLIN

CHATTER

MICHIRU KAIŌ
RECITAL

EVENING WITH A VIOLIN

CHATTER

...I'm at the bottom of the sea...

...It's like...

...Waves rolling in and then ebbing...

...It's like a swirling ocean current...

What's she doing all the way in the corner?

...Haruka-san!

That Stradivarius she's playing, the "Marine Cathedral" or "Temple of the Sea," supposedly costs close to 500 million yen!

Michiru Kaio's performance is magnificent!

500,000,000 yen ≈ about $5,000,000

I guess I'm going to have to follow Usagi's example and use a dirty trick to sneak in!

CHATTER CHATTER

Moon Power!

My compact from my V-chan years! ♡

SHF

Change me into a male student from Mugen Academy! ♡

Heh heh heh! Success! Success! ♡

♪

Thank you!

To be able to sing for all of you from my precious Academy today...

Mmm! ♡ I'm so glad I came!

...sooo happy! Mimi is...

わあああ
YAAAAAAY

167

169

174

175

176

Act 30 Infinity 4,
Sailor Uranus, Haruka Ten'ô,
Sailor Neptune, Michiru Kaiô

Talisman?!

Sailor Neptune is the Michiru-san who gave me a ride on the helicopter ?!

We meet again, Chibi-Usagi-chan.

...That hand mirror is a talisman, Chibi-Usa?!

...telling us to gather talismans, would you...? What in the world is their significance...?

Dreams?

...Right.

So you've been feeling it, too, huh? A premonition of misfortune and the threat of destruction....

That hand mirror is a talisman?!

...You wouldn't happen to be the ones who sent us those ominous dreams...

191

...There were still more Guardians other than just Pluto ...?!

They are guardians who ought to be in a far-off place, that you wouldn't ever encounter...

...They may be Sailor Guardians just like you, but their role and jurisdictions are different.

... Just like Pluto ...

I wonder if we're n a time of crisis ...

And to appear before us.

...let alone be reborn in the here and now.

I never imagined that they actually existed...

...Who are said to have been protecting Silver Millennium from the far reaches...

They are legendary Guardians shrouded in mystery...

But even so, to attack us...

Or is there something else...?!

You mean the invasion of the Death Busters?

"A time of crisis"...

192

193

...be after ...?!

But what in the world could those two...

...A tsunami?!

What happened here?!

...What's this...?!

194

...A dream?!

GRIMP

AH!
は、

AH!
は、

What was that dream...?

...The god of destruction...?

Did we just have the same dream?

Mamo-chan...

But there are three talismans that will bring about destruction...

...so where could the other two be?

...One talisman is Sailor Neptune's mirror...!

GWOO

196

201

...Whenever danger threatened, a wondrous power would well up from the grail...

She's talking about the sacred chalice that Neo Queen Serenity was said to have possessed when she was young.

...grant strength to Neo Serenity...

...and save the populace.

It was covered in jewels and all sparkly, and I've been wanting something like it for a really long time!

You see, I once saw a painting of it in Mama's room!

And all I know is the little that Luna and Artemis told me.

I'm actually not supposed to go into Mama's room, so I never asked anybody about it...

I don't know.

Did she use it as a weapon or something?

When you say, "Mama," you mean it's something Sailor Moon had?

203

Is coffee okay?

Yeah.

Mamo-chan might be home by now, so I'm gonna go check his place.

SHAAA

HU~~~~~!USH

Hey...

Um... Mamo-chan!

But...but there was nothing I could do! I mean, Haruka-san is Sailor Uranus...

Is he mad?

AH HA HA HA

...I wonder what Mamo-chan thought when he saw me with Haruka-san back there.

205

207

Where'd you get the idea for such a complicated...

The Holy Grail?!

"Legendary Holy Grail?"

I'd decided to make the "Legendary Holy Grail!"

Okay...

So what were you trying to make with the clay?

The Holy Grail!

The Holy Grail!

What's this Holy Grail?

What does it do?

...That little... Can't say no.

The Holy Grail!

GLEEM GLEEM

TWINKLE

TWINKLE

Make me the Holy Grail!

Please, Mamo-chan!

...to purify one's body or grant one strength.

It's a special cup that one would put wine or holy water into during sacred ceremonies...

It's a sacred chalice whose tale has been passed down from ancient times.

208

I shouldn't have been with Haruka-san like that...

I'm sorry!

...Mamo-chan...

I trust you, Usagi.

...I was so jealous!

...when I saw you with Michiru-san...

But Mamo-chan...

I'm an idiot to react to such a little thing, aren't I?

...Me too.

211

...of that guy.

I've been jealous a lot, too...

But deep down, I know there's a reason.

It's true. ...Back there, it was because I subconsciously sensed Haruka-san's pain and distress...

...that those tears came to my eyes.

I'm sure you're right, Mamo-chan.

Yeah.

I think there's some really painful circumstance surrounding the two of them.

That guy always looks like he wants to tell you something.

212

APTITUDE TEST RANKING CHART

	2	1
	YURIKA SATÔ	AMI MIZUNO
9	487	500

Whoa! Ami Mizuno got a perfect score and took first place again!

Oh, right.

Of course there are lots of tests! We *are* exam candidates!

It really is depressing, with mid-terms, aptitude tests, finals, tests, tests and more tests!

SNIFF SNIFF

It rains so much, it's a depressing time of year.

GLOOM

Ami-chan, you're the last one in the world who needs it!

You just *like* studying, don't you?!

Say, do you want to come with me to this new prep school?

I guess so.

HIGHEST LEVEL WORK BOOK
MUGEN PREPARATORY SCHOOL EDITION

Ami-chan, you always make sure to take their tests, don't you?

...Mugen Preparatory School?

You can't mean...

214

Yui Bidô, who attends Mugen Academy.

I want to meet her.

There's one prep school student that always takes first place.

I just can't seem to pass her, no matter how hard I try.

NATIONWIDE OPEN MOCK EXAM

1 Yui BIDÔ
2 Ami MIZUNO
3 Ema TAMAKI
4 Naoki TACHIB...
5 Keiichi OGAW...
Ryo YANA...
Katsu...

SKRTCH SKRTCH SKRTCH

It's an honor that she wants to attend our prep school.

I was wondering who got perfect marks on the placement exam. It's the girl genius, Ami Mizuno-san.

If your test score is among the top 20, you get admitted to Mugen Academy tuition-free, so everyone's desperate.

What a charged atmosphere!

SHAAA

MUGEN PREPARATORY SCHOOL

Mugen Preparatory School is a fine institution...

...but nothing beats the Academy's system.

SHAAA

I am Yui Bidô.

I suppose you could say I'm the girl genius of this prep school.

SST

Nice to meet you, Ami Mizuno-san.

215

CROWN GAME CENTER

That's an enemy trap!

A trial enrollment at Mugen Academy?!

Mizuno-san, won't you come for...

...a trial enrollment at my school?

Say, Mizuno-san! Won't you join me at the Academy?

You can elect to take as many classes in your weak subjects as you want, so you can focus on and conquer them.

No other school can match our curriculum...

...or perfected academic environment.

...All right.

...Okay?

And I'll contact you if anything happens...

Ami-chan!

I'll pick up where Usagi left off and finish snooping around.

Don't worry, I won't be that easy to catch.

RUMBLE RUMBLE
...ゴロゴロ

...I don't like these rain clouds.

It's almost like they're billowing out of that building.

The middle-school division is on the 13th floor.

Please proceed to the third-year science class.

You're Ami Mizuno-san, here on a trial enrollment, correct?

4—1
CHINGG

KLATTER
ガラッ

3RD YEAR
SCIENCE CLASS

B-BMP
ドキッ

217

...top students, such as myself, can be named section teachers and coach students on Mugen Academy credo.

...And aside from each subject matter's instructors...

At our Academy, each class year is split into five sub-classes: Philosophy, Performing Arts, Science, Athletics and Pre-Professional...

...For a brief instant, I thought I would be sucked in...

Tau Star System...

I've never heard of it.

...I wonder if this is a hologram.

キンコーン
DINNG DONNG

Would you please wait for me?

I must attend the next lecture.

Excuse me.

...This power is...

I feel an unusual power emanating from the water's surface...

ユラリ!!
WAVRR

219

...A.K.A. Viluy, to take her on.

Please allow me, head of the Science Class, Yui Bidō...

Did she come all alone?

She couldn't be...a Planet Protector...

...a Sailor Guardian ?!

...And Eudial Level 78, it was clear they would lose even before they fought.

Since Mimete was Level 40...

Kao-linite!

KLIK
KLIK
KLIK

I'm sure Master will be pleased!

...shall obtain the Hoste of a Sailor Guardian for you.

With my system, I, Level 202 Viluy...

KLIK

?!

WAVRR

A Sailor Guardian's Hoste...must almost certainly have immense energy.

VWA ASH

220

221

222

VMATCH

!!

THWAKK

SPLOOSH

VWAA

VWAA

Don't let them escape! After them!!

Capture all of the Sailor Guardians, at any cost!

Yes, Ma'am!

I will not permit any precious Vessels to escape!

What is this uproar?!

Ms. President!

Where are they?! Find the Sailor Guardians!

I don't think we can attend the Academy anymore.

Seems so.

225

DOM

HYUUM

Mosaic Buster!!

Something's happening to my body?!

?!

VZZT VZZT VZZT

Nooo...!

My body... I can't move...!

Now offer up your strong and beautiful...

...Sailor Guardian Hoste to my Master! Ah ha ha ha!

Invisible nano machines extracted from one of my programs are working their way into your body and trying to take it apart!

Ho ho ho, does it hurt?

All that'll be left is your beautiful soul, your Hoste!

227

...Mer- cury!

Dai- mons!

GRAAA

Go!

Lend your power to my Heart Moon Rod!!

Neo Queen Serenity!

SST

228

Uranus! Neptune!

...They came to our rescue...?!

Wait!

K O UNIVERS

SCIENCE DEPARTMENT

Reika-san, we're thinking of going out for a drink...

Are you a lab assistant?

Oh, somebody's finally going to be using that run-down lab next to ours.

がっくし
SLUMP

はは、ははは
HA HA

Oh, okay.

Sorry, Furuhata-kun! I've got Mineralogy Club today.

I'm a 2nd-year student. Reika Nishimura. Nice to meet you!

We hold Mineralogy Club meetings next door every so often.

I'm in the science department, too.

They're just letting me help out with this lab.

No, I'm a student in the science department.

Setsuna Meiô. Nice to meet you!

I'm a first-year science department student, majoring in theoretical physics within the fundamental physics section.

● *to be continued* ●

Translation Notes

Japanese is a tricky language for most Westerners, and translation is often more art than science. For your edification and reading pleasure, here are notes on some of the places where we could have gone in a different direction with our translation of the work, or where a Japanese cultural reference is used.

Page 15, Mugen
Mugen is a Japanese word meaning "infinity."

Witnesses claim it was a fellow female student of said Mugen Academy that suddenly transformed into this monster...

...where an unidentified monster appeared and attacked students from the private Mugen Academy...

A bizarre incident took place yesterday at S Park in Minato Ward...

Page 26, Kaiô Maru & Ten'ô Maru
When the Japanese name their boats, they often put the *kanji* for *maru* (meaning "circle") at the end of the name. There are all sorts of theories about why boats are named *maru*, including the perfection of a circle, a prayer for the boat's safe return to its port of origin, and simply because a thousand years ago it was a naming convention used with people, swords and even pet dogs.

They're going to go to school in a chopper, huh?

...And Kaiô Maru, the favorite ride of Haruka's girlfriend.

There's Haruka's favorite ride, the Ten'ô Maru...

♪ Wow.

FWAP FWAP FWAP

Page 50 Ten'ôzu, Kaiôzu, Meiôzu

In the notes for Volume 5, it mentions that this series was influenced by the time that Takeuchi-sensei spent in the Tennozu district. It is an island of reclaimed land a little to the southeast of Azabu Jûban, and it developed into a shopping destination for fashionable Tokyo. Takeuchi-sensei has taken this idea a bit farther by adding more islands to the setting. Ten'ôzu (Sky King Island), Kaiôzu (Sea King Island), and Meiôzu (Underworld King Island) follow the same pattern of Uranus, Neptune and Pluto, which in Roman mythology were Gods of the heavens, sea and underworld respectively.

Page 51, Hoste

In Japanese, the word is accompanied by *kanji* which mean "sacred body," and come along with the pronunciation guide "osuti." Checking on both the meaning and the pronunciation, I found that the wafer of leavened bread that represents the body of Christ in Catholic mass, the "host," was taken from the old French word "hoste." The word comes from a Latin word meaning "enemy" or "stranger" because of an ancient pagan practice of the victors in war offering up the bodies of one's enemies to their Gods. Somehow, the sound, the *kanji* meaning and the story of the word's origin seemed to fit with the story.

Page 54, Juice

In Japan, the English word, "juice" (pronounced jûsu) is used to mean nearly any sweet bottled or canned drink. Juice is commonly considered a drink for children, though adults make up a large portion of the market.

Page 107, Third Year of Middle School

Being in the third and final year of middle school in Japan isn't quite as stressful as being in the third and final year of high school, but both have their stresses. Like entrance exams for college, there are also entrance exams for high school, and the better the high school, the harder the entrance exam. Also, although most middle schools in Japan are general education, high schools tend to have specialties such as college prep, agriculture, engineering, etc. So it is in one's final year of middle school where one begins to make decisions on what kind of work one expects to go into as an adult.

Page 214, Rainy Season

The rainy season usually comes in June in Japan, when the weather pattern changes and it starts a month-long period where it rains nearly every day. Because of the lack of sun and general dampness, it's known to bring on the blues.

Page 232, KO University

One of the top two private universities in Japan is Keio University (pronounced K.O.) in the Minato Ward of Tokyo, just east of Azabu Jûban. Students from this university are considered elite, and are almost guaranteed good jobs with the government or top private employers after graduation.

Preview of *Sailor Moon 7*

We're pleased to present you a preview from
Pretty Guardian Sailor Moon 7. Please check
our website (www.kodanshacomics.com) to
see when this volume will be available.

Ohh...

The light of the Taioron Crystal, the origin of life, it grows weaker and weaker.

We must gather more and more of those muddy, human Hoste! I don't have nearly enough!

SHHH

Accept my deepest apologies, Master Pharaoh 90! With our next mission, I guarantee a huge load of Hoste to offer to you!

But so far, abnormalities have been interfering.

We are attempting to implant the eggs into human Vessels after their Hoste has been removed.

...Presently in this world, this is our only option.

I expect you are progressing in making Vessels?

The Pretty Guardians are back!

Kodansha Comics is proud to present *Sailor Moon* with all new translations.

A Kodansha Trade Paperback Original.

Pretty Guardian Sailor Moon volume 6 copyright © 2004 Naoko Takeuchi
English Translation copyright © 2012 Naoko Takeuchi

Published in the United States by Kodansha Comics, an imprint
of Kodansha USA Publishing, LLC, New York.

Publication rights for this English edition arranged through
Kodansha Ltd., Tokyo.

First published in Japan in 2004 by Kodansha Ltd., Tokyo, as
Bishoujosenshi Sailor Moon Shinsoban, volume 6.

ISBN 978-1-61262-002-2

Printed in Canada.

www.kodanshacomics.com

9 8 7 6

Translator/Adapter: William Flanagan
Lettering: Aaron Alexovich

TOMARE!
STOP

You're going the wrong way!

Manga is a completely different type of reading experience.

To start at the beginning, Go to the end!

hat's right! Authentic manga is read the traditional Japanese way—
om right to left, exactly the opposite of how American books are
ad. It's easy to follow: Just go to the other end of the book and read
ach page—and each panel—from right side to left side, starting at
e top right. Now you're experiencing manga as it was meant to be!